MUSSOLINI'S ISLAND

SARAH DAY

MUSSOLINI'S ISLAND

First published in Great Britain in 2017 by Tinder Press
An imprint of HEADLINE PUBLISHING GROUP

1

Cataloguing in Publication Data is available from the British Library

Hardback ISBN 978 1 4722 3819 1
Trade Paperback ISBN 978 1 4722 4696 7

Typeset in Sabon LT Std by Jouve (UK), Milton Keynes

Printed and bound in Great Britain by Clays Ltd, St Ives plc

Headline's policy is to use papers that are natural, renewable and recyclable products and made from wood grown in well-managed forests and other controlled sources. The logging and manufacturing processes are expected to conform to the environmental regulations of the country of origin.

HEADLINE PUBLISHING GROUP
An Hachette UK Company
Carmelite House
50 Victoria Embankment
London EC4Y 0DZ

www.tinderpress.co.uk
www.headline.co.uk
www.hachette.co.uk

For my parents

Go, and be happy
but remember (you know
well) whom you leave shackled by love

Sappho

PART ONE

Fascism is now clearly defined not only as a regime but as a doctrine. This means that fascism, exercising its critical faculties on itself and on others, has studied from its own special standpoint and judged by its own standards all the problems affecting the material and intellectual interests now causing such grave anxiety to the nations of the world, and is ready to deal with them by its own policies.

Benito Mussolini, 'The Doctrine of Fascism', 1932

20 January 1939

From: Alfonso Molina, Chief of Police, Catania
To: His Excellency the President of the Provincial Commission for the Assignment of Confino, Catania
Subject: Proposal for the confinement of . . . (name to be inserted)

The plague of pederasty in this province's capital is worsening and spreading because youths so far unsuspected are now so taken by this form of sexual degeneracy, both passive and active, that they often develop venereal diseases. In the past, one rarely saw a pederast frequenting cafés and dance halls, or wandering around in crowded streets; even more rarely was he publicly accompanied by young lovers or clients. Before, pederasts and their admirers preferred lonely streets where they could avoid salacious jokes and comments, which were generally despised not only by the most timid homosexuals, but also by those more bold and unscrupulous, but who in the end were of sound morality.

Nowadays, we can see that a lot of spontaneous and natural disgust has been overcome, and we must admit sadly that some cafés, dance halls, seaside and mountain resorts, according to the seasons, welcome these sick people, and that young people from all social classes publicly seek their company, preferring their love, and thus become enfeebled and brutish.

The spread of degeneration in this city has attracted the attention of the local police, who have intervened to suppress or, at least, to stem this serious sexual aberration that offends morality and is fatal to the health and improvement of our race. Unfortunately, the means used so far have proven insufficient. Indeed, pederasts have become more cautious to avoid our vigilance.

I therefore think it is essential, in the interests of morality and the health of our race, to intervene with more drastic measures, so that the breeding ground of this disease can be attacked and cauterised. In the absence of a particular law, we must resort, in the case of the most obstinate offenders, to the use of *confino*.

One

Catania, February 1939

He knows, before he hears them knocking. Something about the sudden silence of the street outside, the hush, as though all the many eyes of the city have been trained towards him. Then the sound of feet marching on cobbles, doors banging, and then his own. Three heavy, slow knocks. He imagines the raised gloved fist on the other side.

His mother, standing in the kitchen, looks up. She is wearing a white silk dressing gown, her dark hair uncombed across her shoulders. He notices, for the first time, how it is beginning to lighten with streaks of grey. Her face is thin and tired.

He has sewn and resewn the dressing gown for her many times since they came to Catania. He has been promising to buy her a new one for months. Soon. In time. A few more weeks at the restaurant will be enough.

The knocking starts again.

'Francesco Caruso. Does Francesco live here?'

She looks at him. There is nothing in her face to say she knows. She doesn't know. What will he tell her? He has stolen something. Bribery, perhaps, or fraud. Anything that isn't violent, or the truth. She opens her mouth to speak.

'Caruso?' the voice says again. 'Francesco Caruso. You will answer. We are coming inside either way.'

He wipes a hand across his eyes as a sound escapes her, a stifled, wordless sound. He can't look at her now. His hands begin to shake. She has always had such pride in him, in his goodness. Despite all the times he has been in trouble, she has believed in him. He thinks of his father, the last time they were all together, thirteen years ago in that terrible rented room in

Naples. 'They will come for us now,' she had whispered, her face pale with fear, and Francesco's father had smiled. Shaken his head.

'You've got him,' he had said, gesturing towards Francesco, ten years old, standing in the doorway. 'He'll grow up strong.' He had turned to Francesco then, holding out his hands. 'You will grow up to be a man, Francesco. You will fight like a man.' And Francesco had nodded, without considering for a second what that meant. 'What must you remember?'

He had buried his face in his father's soft woollen jumper, curling his fists around it, breathing him in, not wanting to be a man. Not wanting to be anything but a child, willing his father to stay. 'Never strike first,' his father had whispered, rubbing Francesco's back, rocking him softly. 'And do not give up.'

Non mollare. Never give up.

The knocking starts again, harder now. His mother moves towards the door and Francesco puts a hand out to stop her. He remembers the promise he made that night they left Naples. Not to leave her. Just the two of them, alone in a new city. He would never leave her. He would be a real man, the kind of man his father would be proud of.

He stands up slowly. Takes a deep breath. Clenches his fists. Unlocks the door with slow, steady fingers.

But when he sees them on the other side, their pressed uniforms, the shadows of guns in their belts, so many of them when he is just one man, his instincts react. It is no surprise, perhaps. They call him Femminella at the dance hall. Feeble woman. He hears Emilio's voice, loud in his ear. *Run. It doesn't matter where, Cesco. Just run. Now.*

Now.

And he is running, past his mother, through the kitchen, through the door to the courtyard; he is vaulting over the wall and out through a narrow back alley into the street, and running hard, in no particular direction, just away.

Catania is quiet. Usually, as the evening pales into night, there is a steady hum of voices, footsteps, radios playing through open doorways. Women shouting across balconies, calling their children in. Men walking in groups towards the castle square, fights breaking out in narrow alleys, the last street vendors carting home what's left unsold.

Tonight, the streets are empty. As though they know it is a night for hiding, for keeping silent. All Francesco can hear is the slow sighing of the sea beyond the railway arches, and the shouts of the men who are following him.

He pauses, breathing hard. He knows this city better than any of them. He has been living a second life in its shadows for long enough to know every side street, every hidden alleyway and dark recess. There is nowhere he cannot hide.

He looks east, towards the arches. Remembers the nights he hid there with Emilio, holding their breath to keep from making a sound. They will look there first. North, towards San Antonio and the dance hall; they will know he is not stupid enough to go there, but they might send one of the men, just to be sure. Or down towards the Duomo, the wider, lit-up streets, where the city's fashionable residents will be dining in the open air, women walking arm in arm with their husbands, elegant bands playing in the squares. It is not his Catania, those streets. He would be mad to try there.

They will never think to look.

He runs through a series of dark side streets, making sure to cross back on himself, to take an illogical way. After a few turns, he reaches the castle, still standing intact amidst a sea of lava cooled centuries ago. He pauses for a second to catch his breath. Then downhill, hurtling along the Via Garibaldi, in full view but moving fast.

The open space, after so many narrow streets, is shocking. A few men are still lingering in the Duomo square, sitting around the fountains, dealing cards and sipping from flasks. There is no sound but the murmur of the fountains, the *flick,*

flick of the cards and, from somewhere far behind him, a shrill whistle.

He pauses to look up. His father used to teach him to do this, whenever he felt afraid. *If you can see the sky, you know there is a way out. You are still free.* The sky is dark but clear above the cathedral dome. Against it, the blank, hard-eyed faces of saints are leaning over him, hooded in white stone.

It is still warm, though the sun has long since set. Francesco feels like a stranger in the square. His city is one of narrow darkness, of hiding and whispering, just two turns of a street away. He doesn't know this square, its open, lit-up spaces. He longs for the shadows of the railway arches by the sea, or the thick, hot air of the dance hall, the *arrusi* pressed together in a space hardly larger than the living room of his flat, arms wound around his waist, breath hot on his neck, a voice in his ear. Emilio, whispering to him: *Femminella, Francesca, stavo cercando, I was looking for you . . .*

He straightens, and keeps running.

He stops on the Via Etnea. At the end of the street, shadowed against the darkening sky, the volcano rises high above the city, dark clouds rolling from its slopes. A familiar threat. Francesco can see its snow-tipped crater from his window at home. It is quiet now, but it is always watching. When Francesco was thirteen, it had woken and buried a nearby village in fire. Then retreated in silence as quickly.

Once, when he was a boy, his father had taken him to climb it. They were holidaying in Sicily, back when his life had been one of holidays, trains and boats and expensive dinners. Francesco had not known then that he would one day live in the volcano's shadow. That everything of that life would vanish, faster than the red glow of lava as it cooled. He had not known what the mountain could do, but close to the summit, the two of them gasping and laughing together at the effort of it, he had seen whispers of steam emerging from between rocks, and put his hand down to touch them, reeling back at the burning air on his skin. His father had poured out the contents of his water bottle across Francesco's palm, then hoisted him up onto his shoulders and carried him the rest of the way, not quite to the summit but as high as they could go. He remembered the feeling of his father's hands on his ankles, holding him steady. The strange, undulating rhythm of the climb, his hands gripping his father's wiry hair, the two of them pressed so closely together that Francesco forgot the pain in his hand, forgot how far they still had left to go.

He has still never climbed to the summit. On days when the restaurant is quiet, he and Gio sometimes leave the city and walk together through the hills, but on foot they don't get very far. The volcano is a distant, unreachable presence, a background solidity, like a painted piece of set dressing. In Francesco's dreams, it is where his father has gone. He is somewhere on the slopes of Etna, waiting for Francesco to catch up with him, holding out a hand as he climbs on up towards the summit, hot steam rising from the rocks around him.

He hears a shout, and ducks into a side street. It is still wider than the streets around the castle, trees planted along its length, street lights flickering at its corners. He can hear laughter from behind a fogged window, glasses clinking. Further in, the road narrows into shadows. Francesco heads towards the darkness, hands in his pockets, trying to walk slowly, casually, without looking back.

He knows now he can never go home. He will not see his mother again, Emilio, Gio, the Via Calcera, the castle or even the volcano. He will keep running. Somehow he will find his father and they will run together.

For a moment, he has forgotten where he is. What he is. He has forgotten that on an island, men like him can't run forever. In Naples, his mother tells him, he was another person, loud and conversational, happy to talk to strangers when they came to the house. Since Catania, he has learned to be quiet, to guard what he says and who he talks to. It is what drew him to the *arrusi* in the first place, perhaps, that acquired art of silence. He knows now that it has not been enough. He will always be caught, whichever direction he takes, however guarded his silence. When he hears the whistle again, closer now, then the shouting of the police behind him, he remembers.

Something hard meets the back of his skull and he feels himself falling. A boot shoves his face into the narrow seam of dirt running through the gutter at the side of the street.

'*Arrusu!*' he hears one of them spitting over him. 'Fucking whore.'

He tries to grip the paving stones with his fingers, finding no purchase on the smooth black lava stone. He tries to breathe, and his mouth fills with earth. He thinks of Emilio, the two of them running together from the dance hall, laughing, towards the sea. He tries to turn his head, to look up at the sky, to feel free, but he is pinned beneath a heavy weight. He feels a cold circle of metal against the back of his neck. He can hear Emilio's voice in his ear again, see his dark eyes widen with fear. *Run.*

This is my curse, Francesco thinks, as arms reach around him, hauling him up, his hands pinned behind him. Someone spits in his face and he closes his eyes. Not standing still, but running at all the wrong moments.

Two

San Domino, June 1939

The first prisoners had arrived in the spring. It was the wrong kind of spring that year. Still winter, really. In San Domino, everyone was waiting for the sun to break, but something held it back behind the clouds. The tomatoes refused to swell on their stalks.

Of the fifty or so inhabitants of the island, Elena Pirelli always claimed she had been the first to see them arrive. She saw a boat from the pantry window, she said, a shadow in the corner of her eye. To get a better view, she had pulled a stool against the wall and climbed up until she could raise her eyes to the glass, her fingers gripping the sill. The boat was large, approaching from the neighbouring island of San Nicola. It was not unusual for boats to pass between the two islands, but they were usually small; rowing boats or fishing trawlers. She had never seen a boat so large approach San Domino.

Behind her, her mother was beating dough roughly against the table. It shook beneath the force of her fists.

'What is that boat?' Elena turned from the window.

'Boat?'

'There is a boat coming in. From San Nicola. Look.'

Her mother shook her head, as if that were an answer, and pounded the bread even harder. Elena looked back. There was no sign of a boat now. It must have passed beneath the shadow of the cliffs surrounding the beach. She wondered if she had imagined it. Perhaps it had only been a group of birds, gathered for shelter against the wind and the salt spray, or the shadows of spruces on the horizon.

There was no reason, after all, to come here. No one came

to San Domino. Rarely, pleasure seekers might stop to sun themselves on the thin strip of sand by the port, or explore the sea caves in their tiny boats, but they didn't stay long, and they hardly ever came back.

It was different on San Nicola. A steady stream of boats had been passing between it and the mainland for as long as Elena could remember, bringing with them men to be kept shut up within the island's towering walls of rock. Though it was the smaller island, San Nicola in the last few months had been swelling with anti-fascists and agitators, men the state wished to hide away. The island swarmed with officers of the carabinieri – she could see them sometimes from San Domino, black specks against the fortress walls. The prisoners, in their pale uniforms, were harder to see, but sometimes she could make them out between the barracks where they were housed, pacing the yard or standing together in groups. Shut up tight like mice in a trap, her mother said, whenever she looked towards San Nicola. They will not trouble us here, *furetto*. San Domino, with its crumbling cliffs and dense thickets of pine trees, would be left alone.

But later, standing with her ear pressed against the pantry door, Elena had heard her parents talking in the room beyond.

'Twenty, in that boat,' her mother spat.

'I know.' Her father sounded tired.

'You know what they are saying. And more to come still!'

'Perhaps more.'

'You said they were politicals.'

'I did. They are.'

'Then why can't they stay there? And why do I hear these things about them? That you are to be a keeper of animals?'

'Work is work,' her father said dully. His new job, whatever it was, had come suddenly, after weeks of travelling to the mainland, then returning and sitting silently indoors, staring at the floor. Then had come a trip to San Nicola, and everything since had been brighter. Her father had a uniform now. A gun.

'They are a contagion,' her mother continued. 'They spread disease.'

Elena drew back from the door.

A few days later, she had walked the length of the island, tracing the paths through the dense pine woods to the south, back through the village at its centre to the north side, where the land fell away sharply to the sea. She walked for hours in the still, heavy silence. Towards the Cala Tramontana to the west, she saw several figures dressed in white standing amongst the trees. Men, clustered together in groups. She darted quickly behind a tree before they could see her.

When she reached the cliffs, she looked down at the beach that was San Domino's only port. There was no large boat there now. Only a small row of fishing boats tied up tight against the rocks. She looked across the water to the steep, pale cliffs of San Nicola, which seemed to mould themselves into the walls of the fortress as though it had grown from the island in place of trees. She thought of the boat she had seen crossing the water that had brought those men with it. There was no sign of it now.

A contagion. She tasted the word. *A keeper of animals.*

In June, the second boat came. This time, Elena was climbing the pines that grew in clusters on the cliffs above the port, high enough to gain a view across the water towards the mainland. The boat, as large as the other, was just leaving San Nicola, turning not towards the mainland, but to San Domino.

The sun had found San Domino at last, fruit finally fattening and bursting from trees, landing in soft puddles of juice on the dry ground. Elena had felt her own body change with it, as though the sun were drawing her out for the first time. The narrow hips and bony shoulders the children on San Nicola had once teased her for were giving way to softer, rounder skin. The dresses her mother had sewn for her years before suddenly needed letting out and adjusting. She noticed it, too, in the way the men looked at her when she walked across the island. Once, she would have gone barefoot and careless, unnoticed by the few people she passed in the fields. For the first time that summer, she found herself drawing her arms across her chest and hunching her shoulders, keeping her eyes to the ground.

It had come late, her mother said. She had long been expecting it, and there was a kind of eagerness to her fingers as she tore the seams of Elena's clothing to add new folds of cloth. She had been a child for too long already. Elena knew what it meant. She saw the way her mother eyed up boys on San Nicola, boys who seemed hardly more than children. She knew the life her mother had planned for her: endless island summers, endless children, endless work. Never to leave. To live as all the other island women lived, with no chance to see anything beyond San Domino's narrow horizons. Not even this new Italy that everyone spoke of.

As if to pull something back, as if growing up were a kind of battle to be fought, territory to be defended, Elena was resisting as hard as she could. She only needed a few more months to plan her escape. Some way to the mainland, perhaps, or further.

She watched the boat coming closer. Far on the horizon, others were making their way along the dark shadow of Italy's coastline, no more than inky spots against the sky. To them, her island must look just as small, she thought. A speck of dust above the water.

Whenever she watched the boats, which never turned towards her island, Elena tried to imagine the world they came from, the palaces and ballrooms and crowded, wide streets of a mainland she had never seen. She imagined herself, draped in expensive cloth, walking along even, neatly paved streets. Strangers parting to let her through. A table, a white pressed cloth, plates of strange, expensive food. The mainland was all she thought about when she wasn't helping her mother at home, or reciting lessons in housekeeping on San Nicola. Sometimes she imagined a boat from the mainland pulling up on the narrow beach, left unattended long enough for her to hide herself away before it turned back, stowing away like boys did in story books, then climbing out on the other side into a new, brighter world.

She turned back to watch the boat approaching from San Nicola. As it came closer, she could see the faces of the men standing at its stern. They were carabinieri officers, and a number of other official-looking men. As the boat drew up against the beach, they jumped down and began dragging it along the sand, shouting orders. Elena shrank back amongst the branches, suddenly wanting to hide herself away.

As the officers shouted, more men began to emerge from the cabin. Around twenty of them, all wearing the same pale clothing she had seen weeks before on the men standing amongst the trees. They were blinking and shielding their eyes with their hands, as if they had not seen daylight in a long time. They stepped down from the boat and gathered together on the beach, as the police officers conferred with other men at the port. Papers were exchanged. She watched the passengers standing together in a tight group, staring up with bewildered faces at the cliffs that rose above them. There was a flicker of light as one of them lit a cigarette. Then a shout, as one of the carabinieri officers knocked it from his hand. Afterwards, the man stood still, his hand raised to his lips as though he expected the cigarette to still be between his fingers.

The sun was sinking now behind her, the last of it slanting across the sand in seams of gold. Between her knees, the tree bark was pressing roughly into her skin. As she watched, the police officers organised the men on the beach into two long lines. Then, as they gave a shout, the men began to march. Elena paused for a moment in her tree, watching as they spread out along the beach towards her. *A contagion.* She whispered it out loud.

She slid down, pine needles scratching at her ankles, and ran to catch up with them on the road.

Elena knew how to hide on San Domino. She knew every road and dirt track, every tree, every secluded clearing and hidden pathway. Apart from weekly trips to San Nicola for the Fascist Saturday, she had never left her island. She had seen pictures of the mainland in books and the newspapers that were brought by boat every two weeks, and which her father allowed her to look at when he was finished with them. It was a place where people lived packed together like sardines in a tin. Where you could spend a whole day walking across a city and not see even half of what was there. Elena could cross San Domino in just over an hour. Less if she was running.

She had seen a picture of a volcano in one of the books, towering above the city that clung to its slopes, ochre and white houses like barnacles sticking to a rock. One day, her father had told her, the volcano would wake up and the city would be buried in fire. He had shown her pictures of people, too: Il Duce standing on a balcony wearing a black suit, rows and rows of men holding guns, looking up at him with serious faces. This was not so unfamiliar. She saw something like it on Saturdays, when they went to the square in San Nicola and the Director made his speeches.

She heard the men before she saw them; feet marching on the paved street that took them up the steep climb from the beach. She moved closer to the road, emerging from amongst the trees in time to see them rounding the corner and marching towards her, two carabinieri officers leading them.

They were chained. Twenty, perhaps twenty-four of them, each joined to his partner at the wrist. What had, from a distance, looked like military precision was irregular; they moved at different speeds, one of them tripping, his partner raising their chained hands as if to catch him. Elena stood watching at the side of the road, close enough to make eye contact with any of them, had they not all been staring at the ground.

Except one. One of them was staring up at the sky. His eyes were blue. He looked much like the rest of them, skin tanned despite the too-long winter, his hair untidy about his shoulders, which stooped as though with resignation. His hand, the hand not chained to the man beside him, was gripping a bag, and all the time, while the others watched their feet in the dust, he was looking up intently, as though he could see something worth watching in the clouds. Elena looked up too, and saw nothing but the branches of pine trees knitted against the sky. When she looked back, the man was staring at her, turning his head as they passed. He was young. Twenty, perhaps, or a few years more. She hardly knew any men that age. Only her brothers, Andrea and Marco, and Nicolo, a boy from San Nicola whose parents owned the grocery store her father had once worked in. She saw him every week at the Fascist Saturday, where her mother would encourage her to talk to him while he wiped his nose on his sleeve and stared at her dumbly.

She felt again that new awkwardness, and drew her hands instinctively across her chest. She remembered how her dress was frayed at the edges, felt the curves of it clinging awkwardly to her own, noticed that her feet were bare in the dust. As the man walked on, his eyes still on her, she felt a pooling of warmth in her stomach. His lips curled slightly at the corners, the beginnings of a smile. Elena smiled back, feeling the thud of her heart, heavy in her chest. His face grew more beautiful as she looked at it, like the paintings she had seen in pictures in her father's books. Pale, glowing skin on church walls.

She heard a shout then. The suddenness of it made her close her eyes, and when she opened them, the column of men had stopped. The man with the beautiful face had been whipped to the ground by one of the carabinieri. He lay in the dust, clutching his stomach. The officer raised his hand, which held a strip of leather, and brought it down again, hard. The man howled.

Elena stared, trying not to call out. As she did so, the officer turned his head. The realisation came to her more slowly than it should have done. The uniform had changed him, the hat low over his eyes, but as he looked in her direction she recognised her father.

She ducked down quickly in the bushes, watching through the leaves as he brought the whip down once more. The man screamed as her father struck him again. And again, and again, until he stopped making a sound.

She stared at her father's fist, the leather strap wrapped so tight it was cutting into the skin. A few hours ago he had cupped her chin with that hand, kissed the crown of her head, patted Andrea's shoulder. She wanted to scream. To run forward and catch the whip in her hands.

His wasn't even a real carabinieri uniform, she realised as she watched him. It was black like the other man's, but the shiny buttons were missing, and there were no tassels or colourful stitches at his shoulders. He was only playing at being one of them. She felt a hollowed-out feeling in her stomach as the man on the ground gave a low, heavy moan.

Her father bent down and hauled him upright. He swayed for a moment on the spot, supported by the prisoner he was chained to, before they marched on.

As they walked, the man turned his head again, as though looking for her. Elena kept herself hidden, her eyes fixed on him until he had disappeared over the rise of the hill, her mind filled with the image of her father's face, red with an anger she had never seen before.

Three

'You will not listen to radios.'

Francesco stared at his feet. One of his boots had worn itself a hole towards the tip. He could feel the cold floorboards through it. His back stung with the memory of the carabiniere's whip.

'If we find one, it will be taken, and you will be punished. You will not gather in public places, nor attend public meetings or entertainments.'

He could still feel the movement of the boat sliding over the waves, some memory of its unsteady rhythm preserved beneath his skin. The dormitory was dark, after the blinding light outside. On the march from the beach, he had tipped his head back and felt the sun on his face. The *arrusi* had lived in prisons, by then, for four months. First the prison in Catania, then in Foggia, then the filthy dormitories of San Nicola. To feel so much sun, all at once, was like drinking cold water after a drought.

As the darkness resolved around him, he looked at the men standing with him, lined up in the centre of the dormitory. Around twenty of them had been marched from the beach. They had passed through a grove of pine trees, the air heavy with their scent, then taken a right turn along a dirt road towards the sea, pausing at two long, low dormitories, half hidden amongst foliage. Ten of them had been marched into each.

He studied the faces of the men beside him. Most were known to him, and at the same time unfamiliar. He imagined his own face was similar. Wide-eyed and afraid. Streaked with dirt from the prisons, exhausted from their long journey north. They seemed out of place, standing together in a neat line, all wearing the same pale, plain uniforms.

They were all boys of the *arvulu rossu*. The name was for the tree the younger *arrusi* sometimes met beneath on the corner of a street by the docks in Catania, where the authorities had usually left them alone. Francesco knew each man by name; their true names, and the names they had given themselves. Luca the Lioness, for his golden hair. Mattheo the Seamstress, his fingers light and quick with a needle. Gio the Amazon, a joke because he was so slight. Francesco was Femminella. Feeble woman. They said it with affection, for his beautiful face, and because others used the term so differently. It did not hurt so much to hear it spat at him in the street after it had been whispered softly in his ear.

Gio was standing beside him. His eyes were shut tight, and Francesco could sense his shaking, a slight tremor in his shoulders. He tried to keep his own back straight, his chin raised to the carabinieri officer who addressed them in a quiet, disinterested voice.

'You will not discuss politics, or disseminate political views.'

The officer was younger than the two who had brought them from the beach, but it was clear that, despite this, his was the superior rank. All three wore identical uniforms, but his seemed smarter, a better fit, perhaps. Its dark felt rendered him barely visible in the shadows of the dormitory. Only the glint of polished silver buttons marked him out as he paced the line of prisoners. Francesco eyed the dark shape of a pistol in his hand.

The two carabinieri who had brought them from the beach were standing further back, eyeing the scene nervously, sharing an occasional whisper. The man who had whipped Francesco on the road seemed, in the presence of his superior, to have lost all of his strength and assurance. He was much older than the other two. His uniform was clearly too large for him, sagging at the knees, and Francesco saw now that it was not a true carabinieri uniform, only a close imitation. Borrowed perhaps from another man, who had left for something better on the mainland. He was still holding the whip, winding it nervously around his fist. Beneath the cap they all wore, his hair was white, his face lined with age.

Slowly, the darkness of the dormitory began to resolve itself to shapes, and Francesco saw that it was already occupied. More men were lying on bunks, others sitting at a long, low table. The third carabiniere, a middle-aged, moustached man with drooping eyes, went to the far side of the room and pushed open a door, beyond which Francesco could see a large, dusty yard, ringed with a wire fence. The sun was falling behind the trees, shadows stretching across the floor towards him. In the half-light, he looked around at the faces of the other men, and realised they were familiar too. In Catania, the two groups of *arrusi* had largely kept themselves separate, but Francesco knew their faces anyway. The *primogeniti.* That was what they had called themselves – the firstborn, the older *arrusi.* They had been the first to disappear, back in January, a month before the *arvulu rossu* boys were taken. So this was where they had been brought. Francesco searched frantically among their faces for Emilio's.

In Catania, the *primogeniti* met in one another's houses, or in the more expensive salons. The *arvulu rossu* boys, young men in their twenties without the luxury of their own homes, or the means for salons, met in the shadows of the city, in dance halls and cinemas and forgotten back streets. Francesco doubted there had ever been so many *arrusi* together in one place before.

'You will not hold weapons.'

He studied the young carabinieri officer's face. In the light from outside, he seemed suddenly less sure of himself. There was a hesitation in his eyes as he addressed them, as though he was uncertain of what they might do now that their chains had been removed. His dark features were those of a classical sculpture, perfectly symmetrical: long-lashed oval eyes, a wide forehead and defined cheekbones. How they would have pursued him in Catania. Francesco wondered if the others were thinking it too. The hearts he might have broken.

'If you have implements for labouring, you will surrender them to us at the end of each day.' He spoke slowly, enunciating the words, as though they were idiots. 'You will be given four lire each day for food and necessities. The rest, if you want it, you earn yourselves.'

Francesco thought of the days in the restaurant in the castle square with Gio, washing dishes in the tiny back kitchen while Gio carried plates to tables. What would they do now? How many dishes were there in a place such as this? How many willing to pay an *arrusu* to wash them?

'I am Officer Salvatore Santoro. I am in charge. For you, this island is the whole world. You will carry your identities with you at all times.'

Francesco looked down at the small square of paper in his hand, on which was written his name, birth date and occupation. *Francesco Caruso. 15.06.15. Dishwasher.* The invented surname was still unfamiliar, even after fourteen years of pretence. Would they look into his records carefully enough to know? Was there anything left for them to find? Next to his details, a box for his parents' names. The words were printed in stark capitals. *MADRE: MARGHERITA CARUSO. PADRE: NON CONOSCIUTO.* Unknown.

'You will be here at eight, when the doors are locked. If you are not, you are too late. In the morning, you will be punished.'

There was a blurred photograph, too, on the card. It had been taken the morning after his arrest, at the police station he had been marched to. He was wearing a woollen jumper, covered in holes, the shirt beneath it torn and streaked with stains. In the photograph, he could see some of his attempts to mend the shirt: the neat rows of stitching along its collar, the places where a stitch had been too large, or he had missed his target with the needle; their flat in Catania was badly lit and he had done the mending in the evenings after work, straining his eyes to the light of a couple of candles. In the past few years, as the taxes had risen, they had both become so thin, he had begun to learn to take in clothing, narrowing waistlines and tightening collars.

His mother hardly sewed any more. Because they wanted her to, she said. Because they said it was what she was born for. She wouldn't give them the satisfaction. Francesco didn't mind. He enjoyed it, although he knew it was not what he was born for. It was not work for real men.

The house in Naples where he was born and lived the first ten years of his life must have had electric lights, because he always remembered it as brightly lit, no shadows in the corners of the rooms, the ceilings high, the windows wide. His mother sewing late into the night, a pair of lace gloves folded on the table beside her. Dinners that lasted for hours, the sound of the guests' laughter, the soft ringing of glasses rising through the house to the room where Francesco slept. His father. His father, lifting Francesco onto his shoulders. His father, bent over pages in the library. The library's rich, heavy curtains. The earthen smell of books and dust, and the pamphlets piled on the polished table, their bold heading repeated over and over. *Non mollare.* Never give up. The memory of it all baffled him. It felt like someone else's life.

'It is a mistake.'

Everyone's heads turned at once.

'A mistake?' Santoro repeated.

'Yes.' Elio spoke quietly and firmly. He held his face high, the curve of his neck dark against the pale shirts they all wore. They called Elio Duchessa. His father was something high up in the authorities, and in Catania he had walked and spoken with the air of a duchess. It hadn't saved him. 'My father will write and tell you. I should not have been brought here.' Francesco saw a few of the *primogeniti* smile. 'He is a member of the Fascist Party. Venucci. Mario Venucci. He will tell you. I should not be here. I am not . . . perverted.'

Santoro regarded Elio with his head tilted slightly to one side, then reached slowly for his gun. There was a silence. Then a sickening crack as he brought the gun down on Elio's forehead. Francesco closed his eyes. When he opened them, Elio lay curled on the floor, clutching his forehead, blood pooling between his fingers.

'You are permitted to trade,' Santoro continued, smiling at them all now, sensing the growing atmosphere of fear. 'But you are not permitted to sell your clothing, or any other government-owned property.'

Francesco looked down at Elio. None of the *arrusi* had moved. They had left him there, curled up at their feet.

'In the morning, we will open the dormitories and you will be dressed, ready to be counted. You will be counted again at midday, and again in the afternoon. If you are not present, you will be punished.'

As the carabiniere spoke, Francesco looked down again at his identity card, trying to recognise some hint of his father's face in his photograph. Trying to find some clue there to what he should do. What his father would think of him now.

His mother had told him so many times how he was growing up to resemble his father. In the picture, Francesco looked afraid. He couldn't imagine his father feeling afraid. He remembered other emotions too, after they had taken him to the police station. Not defiance, though he had tried to feel that. He remembered anger. Not at the men who had held him roughly by the wrists as the photograph was taken, but at himself, because he had been told, weeks before, that this would happen. Emilio had told him. *Run. It doesn't matter where, just run.* And Francesco had not listened to him. Perhaps it was better that Emilio was not here, to see how foolish Francesco had been, left on his own.

'Most importantly,' Santoro's voice grew louder, 'you will not talk to the islanders. You will not approach them. You have been brought here to be kept separate from Italy's people.

They do not want you here, any more than you wish to be here yourselves. You will keep away from them, or you will be punished.'

There was a moan from somewhere far away, and Francesco looked down at Elio. The blood on his fingers was drying. He hesitated. Then, emboldened by the thought of his father, he knelt down, pressing a hand against Elio's damp forehead.

'It's all right,' he whispered. 'Stay quiet.'

Elio stared up at him with wide, wild eyes. Francesco looked around him. There was nothing he could use for a bandage. He considered tearing his own shirt, but even as the thought crossed his mind, he felt hands on his arms, pushing him down, rough floorboards against his cheek, the warm touch of saliva as he was pressed against the floor. He was back in Catania, hands on his arms, a voice in his ear. *Arrusu. Fucking whore.*

He closed his eyes. Tried to think of his father. How safe he had felt with his father's hands holding tight to his ankles as they climbed the slopes of Etna. How safe he had felt, even on the night they had run from the flames of their house in Naples, hoisted again on his father's shoulders, his mother screaming behind them. His father's voice in his ear as he shook with fear afterwards in a bed that was not his own, his face still streaked with smoke and ashes. *They can't hurt you, Francesco. Guns don't make them powerful. Never think they are stronger than you because they have guns and fire. They are nothing.* And the words he had said most often, that Francesco had repeated to himself over and over as he was marched between prisons, as he was spat on and laughed at, trying to recall the sound of his father's voice. The words he had only disobeyed once in his life. *Never strike first.*

'Who will help him?' Santoro demanded. Inwardly Francesco cursed himself. He knew what Emilio would say. It is a mistake to try to help anyone but yourself. It singles you out.

No one moved. He felt himself being lifted onto his knees, his arms pulled behind his back.

'Who will help him now?'

Still nobody moved. Francesco's knees ached against the rough floorboards. He could feel the breath of the man who held him on the back of his neck.

Santoro's face was close to his own. 'Open your mouth.'

Francesco hesitated.

'Open your mouth, *recchione*! Do what you're good for.'

As he opened it, he felt something cold and hard slide between his lips.

Francesco knew nothing of guns. His father had always forbidden him from holding one. Until forced to learn how to use one during drills on the Fascist Saturday, he had only seen them from a distance, held by soldiers marching through the streets. He wondered if there was a way to tell if a gun was loaded just by looking at it. The barrel glistened in the last of the sun from the yard, casting splinters of light into his eyes.

He heard himself gag, and felt bile rising in his throat. At the point where it threatened to escape, Santoro laughed, and took the gun away.

After the police had gone, he lay on the floor, keeping his eyes closed, shutting out the sound of doors slamming heavily behind them. After a few minutes, he felt a hand on his arm, lifting him up.

'I saved you a bunk.' Gio smiled, nodding to the rows of beds, holding Francesco's hand tightly in both of his.

As he sat down on the thin mattress, Francesco looked around the room, searching again for Emilio. He had not seen Emilio since that night of the first arrests in January, when the *primogeniti* had been taken. In Catania, Emilio had not associated with either group. His age was somewhere between the two, not young enough for the *arvulu rossu* boys, not quite old enough for the *primogeniti*. He had kept himself apart, lived alone, attended some of the dances, gone to the salons sometimes, but he had no particular favourites among the *arrusi*. It had fascinated them all, how Emilio kept his distance. Where were his family? Who did he go with? They took bets, sometimes. Who could seduce him first. Who would win him. No one had ever succeeded. If he were here, Emilio would already be thinking of ways to escape.

'There are three ways to leave the island.' Francesco looked up quickly, but it was Arturo who had spoken. He was addressing a small group of the new arrivals, gathered around him at one end of the table.

Arturo had worked with Emilio in the mechanics' yard. He was not built like most of the *arrusi*. He was broad, imposing, his height hidden by his slouching stance. He was like a bull, Francesco always thought, his upper body disproportionately large, his nostrils wide. When Arturo was angry, if a customer refused to pay or a machine to cooperate, his face turned a deep, violent purple, a shade none of the other *arrusi* could have achieved even with rouge. It was as though his blood was always close to the surface.

Arturo marked the three ways on his fingers as he spoke them. 'Illness takes you to the infirmary on San Nicola. If it is very bad, to Foggia. Piss them off badly enough, and after a few beatings they'll take you to the prison in Manfredonia. Or it is possible to be granted leave to go home for a few days if a relative is sick. But they'll give you hell if it turns out not to be true.'

Arturo had disappeared with the *primogeniti* in the first arrests in January. The same night Emilio had been taken. Afterwards, they had all wondered why. They had not thought he was one of them. No one had ever seen him in the salons or at dances. He had had a girl, even, although that need not be proof of anything; many of them had had girls. He had fought like a tiger, they said, when he was taken. He had bitten one of the guards until he drew blood.

'You are not planning an escape?' Mattheo said, wide-eyed beside him.

Arturo smiled and spread out his hands. 'I am telling you the situation. That's all. You do with it what you decide to do with it.'

'There is another way,' Elio said from where he sat with a cloth pressed to his forehead. Arturo looked at him sharply. Elio swallowed before continuing. 'My father is writing a petition to the governor. He has many friends in the Ministry of the Interior. He is an important member of the regime. Very high-ranking.'

Some of the men around him smiled. They were used to Elio's tales of his father.

'It may have some effect,' Elio said indignantly, holding the bloodstained cloth out to examine before pressing it to the wound again. 'I am his only son. It is an injustice, to send me here. I am a loyal fascist, and they send me here!'

Arturo stood and moved over to him, placing a hand on Elio's shoulder. Francesco watched his fingers whiten as his grip strengthened, until Elio yelped with pain. Arturo laughed, and patted his cheek. 'You believe it, Duchessa, if it brings you comfort.' Then he put his face close to Elio's ear and spoke slowly, deliberately. 'We are all writing petitions, little one. And our families. Hundreds, I should imagine. We are all loyal fascists in those letters.' He laughed, gesturing to one of the *primogeniti*, sitting alone at the table. 'Marcello there fought in the war!'

Marcello looked up. Francesco found it hard to imagine him as a soldier. He had been a lawyer, long since retired, in Catania. Francesco had been to his flat once, seen the walls lined with books. Marcello's eyes narrowed as Arturo's voice grew hard, angry. 'Marcello fought for our country, for our way of life. He fought at Caporetto! Do you think they give a damn about that when they read it in his letters? Do you think that will get him out of here?'

'Caporetto!' Elio laughed. 'How could that save him? They were all cowards at Caporetto. They lost us the war.' Elio waved a dismissive hand towards Marcello, and pushed open the door to the yard. Sunlight flooded the dormitory for a few seconds, before the door swung shut behind him.

There was a silence after he had gone. Everyone was watching Marcello, but he did not get up. Francesco looked at him, stooped over the table, the skin around his eyes creased with age, and tried to picture him, twenty years ago, in the mud of Caporetto. He had heard the battle referenced a hundred times back home. How hundreds of thousands of Italian soldiers had been taken prisoner, while others had run from the fight. How his country had fallen to degeneracy, to cowardice. How the next generation must prove themselves to be stronger. There was no room any more for pacifists, for weak, feminised men.

'That's it?' Luca said at last. 'There are no other ways out?'

Again they fell silent. Outside, the wind had risen, mingling with the sound of the sea. The floor of the dormitory, thin slats of wood, creaked as men shifted and settled in their beds, or paced the narrow space at the centre of the room. Francesco felt for a moment that they were on a ship, surrounded by the whispers of waves rising slowly into a storm.

'There is over the cliffs,' Arturo said, shrugging and taking his seat again. 'If any of you prefer it that way.'

Four

After she had watched the chained men pass, Elena began to walk homewards after them, but found her feet were taking her in the other direction, north towards the steep cliffs at the edge of the island. The image of her father, a whip in his hand, shifted in front of her eyes. The man crouched in the dust as her father brought the whip down on his back. His eyes, a deep blue, staring at her as he passed. Was he smiling? Had he noticed her at all? And who *were* those men, kept chained, and whipped for looking at the sky?

She walked the paths through the pine trees, breathing in the heavy scented air. The cliff edge was hardly visible until she passed beyond the trees, where the land fell away suddenly to the clear water below. Reaching into the pocket of her dress, she pulled out one of her paper birds. These were another part of her childhood she refused to shake off; she had been making them for years, with scraps of paper or sheets of newspaper, folded into stiff approximations of wings and narrow, pointed beaks. She wanted them to fly, but they never did. This one she held above her head and threw in a straight line. It twisted in the air, then fell meanderingly onto the rocks below, skipping along the shore and settling on the crest of a wave, before sinking out of sight.

She did not start for home until the sun had fallen low behind the trees. She moved quickly, taking short cuts and narrow paths, only now remembering that her mother had insisted she be home for the evening meal. They were receiving an important guest, she had said. Elena could not think who she meant. The few families who lived on San Domino often gathered together for meals, especially during the colder months, but none of them would be a visit worthy of her mother's mention.

The house Elena had been born in stood in a patch of treeless land to the south, a single storey of roughly cut stone. To reach it, she passed first through the new village, a small square at the confluence of three straight roads. Twelve houses were spaced out along the roads. They were identical: red walls, tiled roofs and freshly painted doors with a small yard in front of each.

The islanders still called the village new, though it had been constructed two or three years earlier, when men had come to build on what had been a patch of unused scrubland. They had talked of new families moving to San Domino, a growing population, Italy's strength extending even here. Elena had thrilled at the thought of more people to talk to. People who had seen the mainland, even. People who could take her back there with them. She had imagined the parties and dinners they would have, in a fine house in one of the sardine cities, the clamour of noise and heat and life beyond their windows.

She had waited, getting up each morning with the excitement that this might be the day they came, these new islanders, the day her horizons widened just a little. But in the end, no one had come to live in the village. Most of the houses had remained empty, standing silently at the side of empty paved streets, doors occasionally banging in the breeze, vines crawling across roughly plastered walls. No one had come to San Domino. No one ever did.

She reached home as dusk began to fall. A light shone from the kitchen window, flickering through the trees as she quickened her pace towards it.

Her father had spoken often of extending the house, but as the work on San Nicola had begun to dwindle, he had done nothing but sit for long hours in the yard, while her mother continued to work the small patch of land where they grew vegetables and grazed a goat, whose milk was drying up as fast as her father's work.

'You could at least help with this, Felice,' her mother would sigh, as she scratched at the earth with a spade and he sat watching her.

'I should be managing the store by now,' he would mutter, flicking away flies. He had worked for years in the grocer's on San Nicola. When the fascists began to take over more of the island for prisoners, they had brought their own workers. He had returned to San Domino one morning with a letter in his hand, his face pale, and since then had hardly lifted a finger as the house, the land, crumbled around him. The new job had given him back some of his old pride. Elena could see it in the way he walked, the way he held his head high, leaving the house in his black clothing each morning, polishing his gun at the kitchen table. She thought again of the whip, and flinched as though it were for her.

Though she had been out far longer than she was allowed, Elena didn't try to slip unnoticed into the house. The more she walked, the more her anger at the chains, the sight of her father with the whip, had grown in her.

'Who were those men?' she said loudly as she entered.

The house was quiet. That should have been a warning. Usually her brothers would be arguing, or her mother would be banging pots on the stove. Standing in the hallway, she could hear voices from the kitchen.

Before entering, she took a few moments to brush herself down in case a hint of the outdoors had remained on her skin, or some leaves had caught on her dress, then rubbed the bottom of her bare feet with an apron. She said it again, loudly, as she entered the kitchen – 'Who were those men?' – before looking up. The Director was sitting at the table, glass to his lips, staring at her parents over it. Her father was still wearing his imitation of a uniform. She stood by the door and stared at his hands, thinking of the whip wound tightly around his fist. Now, the same hands held a chunk of bread. She watched as he tore it slowly into pieces.

Her brothers were sitting together at the table, wearing their best suits, their hair neatly brushed. They turned as Elena entered. Andrea smirked. He knew the trouble she would be in.

The table was covered in a white cloth; she remembered her mother that morning scrubbing hard at it, rubbing the cutlery against it, trying to breathe shine into the mismatched blunt knives. The remains of a meal were scattered across it. The Director's hat was on the cloth beside his plate, felt the colour of mud, gold brocade stitched roughly to the hem.

He stood up, tall and oddly straight. She kept her eyes lowered and searched his uniform for creases, a game she always played with police and soldiers. It took away her fear, and gave her eyes something to focus on.

'And this must be . . .'

'Elena.' She stuck out a hand. She tried not to meet her parents' eyes beyond it, already feeling the heat of their anger in the room.

Until now, she had only ever seen the Director from a distance, standing on the steps of the square in San Nicola on the Fascist Saturday as they lined up to hear him speak. All she knew about him was that his name was Coviello, and he was in charge of the prisons on the islands. She felt his eyes travelling over her, lingering in places, a half-smile on his lips. His hand was cold.

'I have been working with your father,' he said at last.

'I know.'

'A pleasure to meet you, Elena Pirelli.' He turned back to her parents, speaking as though she had not interrupted them. 'So, it is understood?'

They both nodded. The Director smiled, taking his seat again. He took a sheaf of papers from a leather folder and laid them on the table, sliding one across towards Elena's father. It was a poster: words in large capitals printed above a photograph of a man in uniform. A policeman. Beneath the photograph, more words were printed in smaller type. Elena studied the image. The man looked young; much younger than her father or the Director. It was full length; his gloved hand was holding the barrel of a gun, resting against the floor. It was almost as tall as his waist. She wondered what the words around him said.

'This is his picture,' the Director said. 'He was one of Molina's men in Catania. These prisoners were . . . his particular project.' He looked nervously back at Elena before continuing. 'They found him beneath the railway tracks. His head was . . .' He paused. 'It was . . . savage. In the dark, he would have had no warning if they came up behind him. He was young. His whole career waiting.'

Elena's father pursed his lips and made a tutting sound with his tongue.

'Cowards, to murder a man like that in the dark.' The Director looked up from the poster. 'I want you to determine which of them it was.'

'Which of . . .'

'The prisoners. Animals – it must have been one of them.'

'But they are . . .'

'Feminine, yes.' He smiled. 'I know what you're thinking. Hard to believe they could do such a thing. Barely men at all. But they have fight in them. They are like cats if you corner them. It was done on the night the first of them were taken, in January. It must have been one of them.'

Her father looked hesitant. 'I am not police,' he said slowly. 'I have no—'

'They are a poison,' the Director said. 'You agree?'

Felice Pirelli nodded slowly.

'They have been removed from their environment so that they can do no further harm, but one of them, it is clear, is doubly a criminal. We must find a separate way to deal with him. You understand?'

'I . . .'

Elena saw the Director's hands clench, a barely perceptible tension ripple through his body. 'Yes?'

'It's just . . . I cannot see how they could do it. Any of them. Surely there are others, in Catania, we could—'

'Do you need this job, Pirelli?' Coviello spoke quietly, conversationally, but there was an edge to his voice. Her father nodded again. The Director's voice lowered as he leaned forward. 'Do you think it is regular, to employ an untrained man in this way? It is an indulgence to allow it. Necessity has driven me to it, but there are others I could have asked. So many who would not find it difficult to follow orders. Who would find out what I want to know in a matter of days, if they really had to. If they had no other choice, I mean.'

Slowly Elena's father looked down at the poster. Elena looked too. They stared together at the policeman's dark, hollow eyes. His skin was pale, his face thin and angular. She felt he was staring back at her, hard, from the page. She studied his head, trying to imagine what had been done to it. A vision came to her of blood dripping from his forehead and into his eyes, and she looked away quickly. Her father took a deep, resolute breath.

'Of course.' He shook the Director's hand. 'I will get the truth from them. You have my word on that.' Elena looked at her mother. Her face was a mask of politeness, but she recognised the tight-lipped smile.

'The truth.' Coviello smiled. 'It is not so easy to know what that is, is it? What I am asking for, Pirelli, is an answer. One that will satisfy everyone involved. Whether it is the truth or not is a different question. You understand?'

Her father nodded. He was twisting his hands together, his fingers white with tension.

'You should think yourself lucky,' Coviello said. 'You might be guarding those animals on San Nicola. They are the real danger.'

'The subversives?'

'They have families. Money, some of them. Supporters back on the mainland – I am ashamed to admit it is true. It is all I can do to keep them there where they can do no harm. Your pederasts, they are nothing. They have no one to help them.'

Elena thought of the men she had seen lined up on San Nicola. The anti-fascists. *They have money. Supporters back on the mainland.* She saw again herself stowed into the hull of a boat, as one of the prisoners made a single-handed, daring attempt at escape. Taking her with him back to a great house on the mainland, where she would be hailed with him as a hero. She smiled at the thought, and saw the Director looking strangely at her.

'Still, they won't be here forever,' he said slowly, still staring at her. 'You should take the work while you can get it. Later, especially if there is war, we may have to find a different solution for all of them.' His casual smile made Elena feel cold all over.

'So,' her father said, in a tone that tried to be conversational, 'you think there will be war?'

Elena saw her brothers exchange a look. The Director smiled. 'It is all I am asked about now, when I visit you people. Will there be war?' He leaned back in his chair. 'Do you think so?'

Her father smiled, and dipped his head as though to say it would be an embarrassment to share his own opinion with the Director. Elena knew those words would have stung him. She could see him trying to hide it in his blank, polite smile. *You people.* 'If it is God's will,' he mumbled.

'For now, I want you to know that your work here will not be interrupted. It is part of the fight, what we are doing here. Keeping those men away from the rest of the population. They spread degeneracy.' He stood up. 'And now I must go.'

Elena watched her father bend slightly as the Director moved to the door. She hated to see him do that. As her parents followed him out, the Director paused in the doorway and looked back at her, his eyes surveying her body again, less guardedly now. She found she was stepping back from the light, trying to hide herself away. It felt different to when the man on the road had stared at her. Under his gaze, she had only felt flushed and embarrassed. Now, she wanted to disappear.

She looked back at the table. The posters still lay there, the man's dark eyes staring at her. She turned away.

'For God's sake keep your children away from them,' the Director said as he closed the door behind him.

She listened for the sounds of the front door opening and closing. When she heard her parents returning, she stood still, waiting for the blow to come. But they were already arguing with each other.

'Animals!' her mother spat. 'More and more of them. We are overrun.'

'Shh . . .' Her father put his hands on her shoulders, pausing as though afraid the Director was still outside the door, listening. 'It is nothing. They are just prisoners. They will not be here long.'

'You should not be in contact. They spread disease!'

'I won't touch them.'

Elena thought of the whip, the blows that had landed on the man's back as he lay in the dust.

'And what does that matter?' He drew himself up, and smiled at his wife. 'When has Coviello ever come to us for a meal? It has brought us standing.'

'It will bring us trouble. You heard what he said. One of them has done this terrible thing. Has . . .' She paused, turning to Elena and her brothers, and shut her mouth tightly.

'Where are they going to stay?' Elena said.

Her father smiled faintly, in a way that she knew meant questions were over.

'Far away from us, *furetto*. Far away from us.' He frowned. 'Have you been outside, *furetto*?'

'No.'

'She has.' Her mother pulled a twig from Elena's hair, and held it up. 'If you weren't all day with those *recchioni*, you would know that.'

'You mustn't,' he said, putting a hand on her arm awkwardly. Once, he would have drawn her to him, sat her on his lap and reached his arms around her. 'You know you mustn't, after dark. It isn't safe.'

'You let Andrea and Marco go out.' She eyed their mud-caked boots by the door.

'That's different.'

'Why? Why is it different?'

'Elena, there are rocks. Cliffs! Do you want to fall and break your neck? You are better here.' His grip tightened on her arm. 'And you will not go looking for those prisoners, either. They are there to be kept away from us.' Her parents exchanged a look. 'The Director is right. They are a contagion.'

Five

'This is nothing, Dante *sorcio*!' Elio shouted, as Francesco led a shaking Dante to an empty bunk. The boys of the *arvulu rossu* had called Dante Mouse in Catania. He worked with his father as a shoemaker near the Via Calcera. So much work in a dim outhouse had made him stooped, his eyes peering. He looked always as though he were flinching, about to run from a fight. 'You wait until they take us out to a firing squad!'

'Be quiet!' Francesco shouted back. 'Let him be.'

Elio laughed, throwing his bundle down on a bunk, still holding a cloth to his wounded forehead. Francesco glared across the dormitory at him, but he understood why Elio did it. It was hard to acknowledge fear. After the guards had gone, the *arrusi* had greeted each other loudly, shaken hands, exchanged news. The *primogeniti* had asked after their families back home, the *arvulu rossu* boys told stories of their journey, joked about the guards. Far easier than to acknowledge their real feelings. Better to forget the cloud of fear that hung about them, to mock those who showed it openly. It was a strategy that all the *arrusi* had devised silently, unspoken, over years. Only when they were alone, or in smaller groups, did anyone admit to being afraid.

'Why are we here?' Dante whispered as he sat on the bunk and pulled off his shoes. 'What is it for?'

'I don't know.' Francesco shook his head. Did anyone know? In Catania, they had spoken of cleaning up the city, of ridding it of a contagion. They had spoken of venereal diseases, of a plague that would spread to the most impressionable youths, rid Italy of its soldiers. Yet when the *primogeniti* had been arrested in January, there was not a word of it in the papers. Emilio, Marcello, Arturo, the rest of them, had disappeared as silently as a shadow in sunlight. The second arrests, his own included, had no doubt been the same. What had they told his mother? What did she know? He shook the thought away.

'And why only us?' Dante continued. 'Why only Catania?'

'Perhaps there are others, somewhere else,' Gio said, sitting beside them.

'I don't know,' Francesco said. 'There are only so many islands.'

'But here, we are alone.' Dante looked up, as though recalling the march across the island. The sound of their footsteps ringing out on the humid, pine-scented air.

'Not alone,' Francesco said. 'I saw a girl on the way. A woman. You must have seen her. Standing by the road as we passed?'

He remembered her bare feet, her muddy yellow dress torn at the hem, her face streaked with dirt. She had smiled at him as though she could not see the chains, the police, the guns. And he had felt himself begin to smile back, seen her cheeks redden, and then the whip had fallen. He shivered at the memory.

Dante and Gio shook their heads. 'You are the only girls here, *arrusi*!' Arturo said, looking over at them from where he sat at the table. '*Arrusi!*' He spat at the ground. His voice was loud, addressing the whole room. 'You are all girls.'

'How long, for you?' Dante said. He was twisting his hands in his lap, his fingers knotted tightly together.

'Five years,' Gio replied.

Dante nodded. 'Five years. And me. Five years for all of us, I think.' He leaned forward, resting his forehead on his knees, and gave a quiet, low moan. Francesco put a hand on the back of his head. Dante's hair was soft. He could feel the warmth of his neck beneath it.

Five years. It was too long a stretch of time to imagine properly. Five years ago, Francesco had barely been older than that girl on the road. His father had been more than a dim memory.

Gio shook his head. 'You think they will let us out then? The world might have changed entirely in five years.'

'It might change in six months,' Francesco said, thinking of the slogans he had seen on posters in Catania, the sound of feet marching rhythmically through the streets. The gun at the back of his neck. 'We won't even know.'

'It will change,' Arturo shouted from across the room. 'Your kind will be wiped out.'

'Our kind?' Gio turned around.

'Yes, your kind.' Arturo stood up. 'I am not one of you. I am not perverted. I am a real man, a true Italian. There are a dozen women waiting for me back home!'

'Then why are you here?'

Arturo shrugged. 'I spent too long with the wrong kind. I didn't know, did I? I didn't know I was hanging around with *recchioni*. I didn't know such a crime was even possible.'

Gio laughed. 'Of course,' he said, 'it is all a mistake for you. They'll realise when you tell them, and let you go home.'

'I will tell you something, *arrusu*. They will send me home long before any of you. Except one, maybe.' His lips curled in a smile.

'What do you mean?'

'Haven't you ever wondered?' Arturo said, addressing the room again. 'Haven't any of you wondered how they knew where to find us all so easily? They came to our houses, to the salons. They knew our names. How did they know that?'

The room was silent.

'I will tell you how,' Arturo said quietly. 'One of you has talked. One of you has sold his friends.'

Everyone was listening now. They looked at each other, eyes wide in the darkness. Eventually Elio said, 'What about Antonio?'

'What about him?' Marcello said, looking up quickly.

'Well, the authorities let him out. Doesn't that mean . . .'

'It doesn't matter what that means,' Arturo said dismissively. 'He was dead, wasn't he? Long before the arrests.'

Francesco tried to push away the memory of Antonio's blood soaking into the flagstones in the square. It felt so long ago now. Another life.

'And anyway,' Arturo went on, 'he wasn't the only one they released, was he?' He stared at Gio. 'You know what I think, Amazon.'

'Leave him alone.' Francesco moved to stand beside Gio. But it was true, what Arturo said. Gio had been taken, that night at the dance hall. A year ago. The same night he had met Emilio. Francesco had been so sure Gio would not come back, and then there he was a few days later, smiling outside the restaurant. As though nothing had happened.

'You should not trust him, Femminella. He will betray you in the end, your Amazon. He has done it before.'

Francesco shook his head, but when he felt Gio looking at him, he could not meet his eyes.

'Fran?' Gio gripped his hand as Arturo turned away. 'I wouldn't . . .'

'I know.' He squeezed Gio's hand tightly.

'Fran, do you ever wonder . . . Emilio is not here.'

'No.' He gave Gio a sharp look. 'I don't. Nor should you.'

Francesco had never slept in a room with so many others before. Not even in San Nicola, where the dormitories had been larger. He found he could not shut out the sound of breathing, all around him, some of it slow and shallow, some quicker; quiet crying, or just tiny moments of panic, breaking out across the room in ripples, then quickly dying away.

He heard a muted whispering, before the light had completely died. Looking in its direction, he saw Dante kneeling beside his bed, his hands pressed together, his eyes shut tightly, whispering frantic prayers. A photograph lay on the bunk before him. Francesco could not see the face from where he lay, but he knew it was Antonio's. Elio was sitting up beside a basin of water, dipping the cloth into it and dabbing at his forehead, sucking in pained breaths as it touched his skin. The water rang out on the bowl as he twisted the cloth again. Behind it all, the rise and fall of the sea, so close it seemed about to break through the walls of the dormitory.

Francesco lay in the dark, thinking of the city, his mother, police marching through the streets, life in Catania continuing as though none of the *arrusi* had ever been there, as though they had drifted so far into the shadows they had dissolved entirely. Had it been a choice, to be what they were? Could they have avoided any of it?

It is a pathology, the doctors had said to him in the hospital where the *arrusi* were taken after their arrest. They called him a whore. Everyone called him that. 'I have a job,' he had said, but quietly, under his breath, like a coward. They probably didn't even hear him. He was always so compliant, so easy to cow. Emilio had reminded him often enough.

After their tests, their examinations – he tried now not to think of them in detail, just the blank, nondescript names of what was done to him – they told him he was more dangerous to society than he knew, because in him, the pathology was not overt. He did not dress in women's clothing or cover his face with paint. *You have ingratiated yourself*, they said slowly, as to a child or an idiot. *You cannot even see it, the threat that you pose.*

'I am Francesco,' he had said back to them, his chin raised. 'The dangerous thief of bicycle tail lights. I know what I am.' It had sounded defiant in his head, but out loud he could hear the tremor in his voice, even before they had laughed. He wanted to tell them who he really was. Who his father was. He wanted to speak his father's name, his own true name. Then they would be afraid of him. They would know then that he was a real man, a true Italian, whatever else they thought about him. He had felt his fists clenching, and tried to hold on to his father's voice. *Never strike first*. Emilio would have done it. Emilio would have spat in their eyes.

But by then, Emilio had already been taken. Later, Francesco heard that he had thrown a whole plate of rations in one of the guards' faces.

And where was Emilio now? On the edge of sleep, Francesco thought of Arturo's words. The knowing smile on his face as he said it. *They knew where to find us all so easily.*

He closed his eyes and tried to dream himself back to Catania, lying on his bed, the sounds of the city seeping through the windows. He had thought he hated the city, after Naples, but now he longed for it. Catania, where everything was done in shadows, where he knew every street and alleyway, every dark corner, every hiding place.

As with all cities, he supposed, there had been two Catanias, and he had known them both. The first was a city of wide, interlocking streets, bustling with crowds and street traders, thick with citizens on festival days, adorned with flowers for Ferragosto in the summer. The cathedral's creamy facade rising above the central square, the gardens a flurry of colour between streets of dark volcanic rock.

The second Catania, the Catania of the *arrusi*, overlapped the first in places. It touched the gardens, the square and the fountain. It spread across the courtyards and past the cathedral, but it travelled by different streets, avoiding the wide piazzas and the public areas, taking the dark back streets, the dusty, hidden spaces under the railway arches, following the shadows towards the sea, cut up by the brickworks of the docks, down towards the water's edge. It was never still, shifting and changing as the police delved further, seeking out new places to hide.

Francesco had found this second Catania by accident. One evening when he was fourteen, working late in the kitchens of the restaurant, one of the waiters had turned out the lights, not realising he was still there scrubbing dishes. He had shouted out, 'Hey!' and heard only the man's breathing in response. He had lifted his hands out of the lukewarm water, then felt the man approach him. Footsteps, slow and steady. Hands on his waist. They had stood in the dark, listening to each other's breathing. Francesco had turned slowly, felt the man's heat edging closer to him, arms reach around his shoulders, pulling him in. Lips pressing wetly against his. A hand fumbling with the buttons of his shirt, unlooping his belt. The next day, in the light, he did not know which of the waiters it had been.

After that, it was easy. He learned quickly that he had only to sit outside a bar, draped at a table with a beer or a coffee, and men would pass, meet his eyes, then pass again. On the third, maybe fourth pass, they would stop for a few moments, whisper times and places in his ear, and then they were gone.

Why had he given in to it? Loneliness, perhaps, but there was something else, something about the ease of it, the way they had drawn him in, the *arrusi*, like a noose slipped gently around his neck. It had been so simple. He had allowed himself to forget everything else, what his mother would say, what the authorities would think of him. It hadn't seemed to matter. He was so used to hiding by then, four years after Naples. It was just another part to play. Sometimes he didn't move from those seats outsides cafés and bars, sitting in a pool of sun, enjoying the possibility more than the act, knowing it was waiting for him, knowing he would not go. Sometimes he swallowed the beer, the coffee, the last few mouthfuls of food, and got up slowly, languidly, and followed them into the dark.

He never took money, though he knew that some did. He never even knew their names, most of the time. He knew the shapes of them, the curve of their noses, their gait as they strolled through the emptier streets, trying not to look back to see who was following them; then later, the way they held him, the weight of their hands, their grip, the heat of their mouths. Often, it was not even others like him. It might be men who, during the day, were respected, influential figures in the city. Men with families, wives and children, jobs behind wide desks. At night, they sought out men like Francesco. *Arrusi.* That was what the Catanians called them. Sometimes just 'the girls'.

And then, one evening when they were both barely fifteen, it was Gio.

He hadn't realised at first. Neither of them had. Francesco was sitting on the kerb, watching boys pass him, weighing them up in his mind, until one paused opposite him and gestured with that unmistakable incline of his head. Francesco had stared through the dark at him, deciding. Each of them seeing the other as nothing more than a target. As the boy moved away, he stood up slowly, hands in his pockets, looking about him, trying to appear indecisive, and followed him into a narrow alleyway.

The boy stopped beside a doorway and looked back. When he saw Francesco following him, he began to move faster. Francesco, decided now, sped up too. Only when he was a few steps away did he recognise the shape of Gio's head, his hair, those blue eyes. They stood opposite each other, both of them too shocked to move. For a moment, Francesco couldn't alter the image he had of his friend, the boy he had known for five years, who had taught him the pattern of the streets in Catania, walked home with him after church, helped him to build shelves, his mother to cook. They stared at each other without speaking.

Gio moved first. He put out a hand, drew Francesco into the doorway with him. They stood still, breathing hard, their eyes locked together, then Francesco grasped Gio's shoulders and pulled him close, kissed him fiercely, felt Gio's arms reach for his belt, his fingers working their way between the rough hemp of his trousers and his skin, and gasped as Gio's hand curled around him.

It hadn't felt strange, not then. He had been surprised by the ease of it, how quickly they had adjusted to a new closeness, how simple it was to hide it from everyone they knew. After that, Francesco had disappeared further into the second, shadowy Catania. There had been dances, meetings in the quieter squares. The *arvulu rossu* boys, gathered beneath a gnarled tree on a street corner by the sea's edge, swapping stories of the men they had been with, following each other into the shadows, even as the police followed them. And always, Gio had been with him. Was it love? Was love even possible for an *arrusu*? Francesco didn't know. And if it was love, why could he not stop thinking about Emilio?

He closed his eyes in the dark, listening to the waves outside the dormitory. The sea had been as loud as this on his first night in the prison in Catania, four months ago. The police station was cold and damp, its cells little more than airless holes. There had been nothing except a blanket, which he had laid out on the floor, feeling every crack and indentation of the rough stone beneath it. He hadn't slept at all that first night. He had lain in the dark thinking of his mother at home, what she would think of him when they told her. What the rest of the city would think of her. What she would do now, without him. He had promised his father he would stay with her. He had promised him they would both be all right if his father didn't come back. Now he had abandoned her too.

In the dormitory, he gripped his pillow tightly, stifling a sob against it. *Men don't cry like this.* He wondered, as he had then, if the guards were watching him in secret. Listening in, recording his weakness as more evidence against him. *Femminella.*

So why couldn't he stop? He cried for his mother, who was alone now. He cried for Emilio, because he must have gone through these nights too, and whatever came afterwards. He would be all right, wherever he was. Emilio was always all right. Not the cleverest or the most patient of them, that was true, but he was always practical. He knew how to look after himself, so long as he didn't fly into a rage and do something stupid. The thought made Francesco feel stronger. The smell of engine grease, Emilio's fingers stroking his guitar strings, his arms around Francesco's waist as they danced together. His voice in Francesco's ear. *My little idiot.*

Six

In the morning, as the sun began to slant across the dormitory through cracks in the roof, Francesco heard the bolts being drawn back. It was a new carabiniere today, younger even than Santoro. He entered the room with a look of faint disgust on his face, which he quickly attempted to hide behind a cautious, apologetic smile. With him was the older man without a proper uniform, hastily smoothing his hair and brushing the dust from his sleeves.

The two policemen stood regarding them for a moment in silence. The young carabiniere's hair was a startlingly white blond, a shade Francesco had never seen before. It stood out starkly against his dark uniform. His face was round, smiling more broadly now, as though facing a room of children.

'Line up.' His voice was soft.

Most of the *primogeniti* were already up, had been sitting at the table in semi-darkness. The younger men were still lying in their bunks. They moved quickly, the memory of Elio lying bleeding, of Francesco kneeling with a gun in his mouth, still fresh in their minds, but the carabiniere stood patiently as they arranged themselves in front of him.

'I am responsible for you from the morning count until midday,' he said as they stood, heads bowed. 'And again in the evenings. You are permitted to leave the yard, but I would not recommend it. There is nowhere to go, and if you are found talking to an islander, you will be punished.' He smiled, more apology in his eyes. He looked no older than they were. 'My name is Benito,' he added. 'Officer Favero. This is Pirelli.' He nodded to the man beside him, who was studiously avoiding their eyes. Francesco eyed the whip still curled around his fist.

*

They carried out the count quickly. Afterwards, Favero wrote it down in a notebook, then looked over at Pirelli, still standing in the background.

'You have something to say, I think.'

The older man nodded. Francesco thought he saw a brief hint of nervousness pass across his face, before he covered it with a frown. Stepping forward, he reached into his pocket and took out a piece of paper, holding it up to face them. A picture of a policeman was printed on it. Above it, words in bold capitals, some smaller writing beneath.

There was silence in the dormitory as they all studied the poster. The man in the picture was young. He stood stiffly in his uniform, a gun the height of his hip balanced beside him. His narrowed eyes stared out at the photographer from a thin, angular face.

None of the *arrusi* moved. Looking sideways at them, Francesco could see fear in some of their eyes. Gio had cast his to the ground. Dante's were squeezed shut. The print was grainy, but they all recognised the man's face. They had run from him enough times to know.

'You know who he is, I think.' Francesco could hear how Pirelli was trying to make his voice stern, threatening, the way Santoro had spoken on the previous night, but there was a tremor in it he was struggling to disguise. 'You know, I think, what happened to him.' He stood still, waiting for one of them to speak.

There was something like agreement in their silence. They would not speak, even if they knew something. They would not give each other away. That had always been their unspoken pact, and they kept it now, though it had been broken in the past.

Pirelli split the silence by bringing his whip down, hard, on the floor. Several of them jumped at the sound. Francesco felt the sting on his shoulders again, the taste of dirt in his mouth. He saw Favero look up, a hint of alarm in his face.

'Personally,' Pirelli said quietly, pacing in front of them, 'I have my doubts. I cannot imagine any of you capable of such an act.' He paused in front of Arturo. 'What does the Doctrine say? *Man is man only by virtue of the spiritual process to which he contributes as a member of the family.* So. You are hardly men at all, are you?' He stared into Arturo's hard, unblinking eyes. A flicker of a smile crossed his face. 'Perhaps I am wrong. Perhaps. Others,' he said, moving along and putting his face close to Dante's, 'if it is an act, it is a good one.' Without warning, he put out a hand and pulled Dante forward, pushing him to the ground. Dante gasped, and reached out, pulling a chair down with him. Favero moved quickly to put a hand on Pirelli's arm.

'This is not the way to—'

He fell silent as Pirelli turned and raised the whip. The two officers stared at each other for a moment, before Favero shook his head and stepped back.

'Any of you with information will be treated with leniency,' Pirelli said, winding the whip back around his fingers. Then, in a different, quieter voice, 'You will speak. You will tell me everything. Five years is a long time to stay silent.' He turned and pinned the poster to the door.

The *arrusi* stood in silence after the guards had gone, all of them staring at the words printed in capitals above the photograph of the policeman. *DIEGO RAPETTI.* And then, in bold, *REWARD.*

Francesco walked out into the yard, where men were lying on benches, stretched out beneath the sun, or pacing the dusty ground without direction. He could see Officer Pirelli walking the wire perimeter fence, the whip wound tight around his fist. Francesco's back still ached from it; he stretched himself out and winced at the shiver of pain running across his spine, out to each shoulder blade. Two other guards were at the fence too, leaning on it and exchanging conversation. The occasional burst of laughter carried on the air towards him.

They were all holding guns. He wondered how quickly they would react if he made a run for the sea. He thought of Pirelli's bargain. *Any of you with information will be treated with leniency.*

In the yard, there were more greetings, as men from the second hut met those from his. Some of them had started up a game of football with a rounded stone, chasing each other across the yard and kicking up flurries of dust as they slid for it.

Francesco walked out among them, ignoring their shouts as he interrupted the game, and took in the emptiness surrounding them. It was quiet, the sound of the sea already so familiar he no longer heard it. Behind him, the whitewashed walls of the dormitory were lit up by the sun. The land beyond it, towards the sea, had been laid out in small squares of freshly turned earth. Already the men had begun to talk of how they might occupy themselves with the growing of food. Beyond the village he had seen fields of wheat clustered amongst houses, burnished a brilliant gold. He felt in his pocket for the four lire he had been given by the guards. He would have to find some way of supplementing it.

Gio came and stood beside him.

'Not so bad, this,' he said, pushing his hands into his pockets. Francesco stared at him. Gio looked brighter in the morning light. The pallor of fear was gone; his cheeks had colour again. His shirt was unevenly buttoned, a small triangle of pale skin visible where one half of it was pulled up unevenly. He shrugged. 'I mean, we have food. Somewhere to sleep. I mean . . .' He looked down at his feet, shuffled them in the dust. 'I just mean . . . it could be worse, Fran.'

Francesco shook his head. But as he turned away, he wondered if Gio was right. Were they lucky to be here? If war did break out, they would be luckier still, unless they were sent back to face it. But something told him they would not want an *arrusu* in war. Perhaps the police had been right. Perhaps there was no place for *arrusi* in the fight. It might even have been too dangerous to stay, war or no war. In which case, San Domino might be the best they could hope for. He had tried so hard, for so long, to stay hidden. Now that he was exposed, what was the point of going home?

He knew what his father would say to that. *Never give up.*

He looked at Gio, standing calmly beside him. Was it safer for Gio here, with Arturo's rumours spreading so fast? Francesco knew what the *arrusi* could do to traitors, proven or not. He had seen men beaten for informing on other men. He shivered.

'You don't believe him, do you? Arturo. What he said . . .' Gio stopped, looking at where Arturo was pacing at the far end of the yard. His eyes swept over the rest of the men. 'They don't think I did it, do they? Gave them away?'

Francesco shook his head, hoping he looked more certain than he felt. 'No. Of course not.'

Gio smiled at him. For a second, the smile brought back the old days. Gio as a child, kicking a stone across the street, smiling widely at a stranger. Years later, their first encounter, both of them so tentative, so inept, clumsily pulling at buttons and shirts, laughing despite the fear in the back of their minds. He felt Gio's fingers brush against his, as they had when their wrists were chained together. 'Fran,' Gio whispered, and moved closer to him, taking his hand. Francesco breathed in the scent of him, allowing him to close the space between them. Why not, he thought, when they no longer needed to hide? He was thrilled by the thought that he could stand here in the sunlight, in front of the guards, and take Gio's hand, even kiss him, and there would be no consequences. In Catania, they had waited until they were somewhere dark – an alleyway, an empty street, the dance hall – and still they had never felt safe. What could happen to them now? He leaned his face closer to Gio's.

'*Ragazze!*' The shout came from behind them. Out of instinct, Francesco flinched, and searched for a shadowy corner to hide in. '*Recchioni!*' Gio stepped back, suddenly pale. Arturo was walking quickly towards them.

'This is why you're no good to your country,' Arturo said, grabbing Francesco's collar. 'You spend all your time fucking your allies, when you should be fighting.'

He spat. Francesco felt it land on his cheek and stood still, hoping it would seem like defiance. *Never strike first.* From the corner of his eye, he saw Gio shrink away from them.

'Go on,' Arturo said, pushing Francesco back against the dormitory wall. 'Hit me. Pretend you are a man. It doesn't look like your Amazon will protect you anyway. Why should he, if he is the reason you are here?'

He pushed harder. Francesco could feel the rough stone pressing into his back.

'Not going to fight, *arrusu*? Perhaps it is because you have no father. It makes you weak.'

Francesco's forced smile vanished. 'Fuck off, Arturo.'

'If you ever had one, he must have been more of a *ragazza* than you, *arrusu*.'

'Stop it.'

'Why? Everyone knows you never fight back!' Arturo laughed. 'How did he ever fuck your mother, if he was half the girl you are?'

Francesco seized Arturo by the collar. The speed of it took them both by surprise. He spun Arturo round and slammed him against the wall. He felt the anger flame in him, after being contained for so long. 'You know nothing about my father. Nothing! You understand?' He raised a fist. Arturo met it in a tight grip, then moved his feet and threw Francesco to the ground. He could hear men cheering, feel the ground vibrate as they ran to get a closer view. In Catania, men had paid good money to watch Arturo fight.

Francesco tried to stand, and felt Arturo's boot press his chest to the ground. He coughed, and braced himself for the blow. But just as he closed his eyes, he felt something collide with Arturo, hard, and the weight lifted.

'You come near him again,' he heard a voice saying quietly, 'I'll kill you.'

The circle of men around them was still for a moment. The laughter, the cheering had stopped. Everyone was watching the two men in the centre, wondering who would strike first.

It was only the tiniest movement. Hardly perceptible, but it was enough to break the tension. Arturo took a small step back, and the breath of all the men around him was released.

The other man nodded slowly, and relaxed his fists. As he walked away, Francesco got to his feet and followed him, watching as he took a cigarette from behind his ear and sat down against the dormitory wall, leaning his head back and closing his eyes. He was hardly recognisable, after so long. His hair had grown longer, his body thinner, but Francesco knew his voice. The shape of his profile. His hair, a mass of dark curls. The beginnings of a beard on his chin. Francesco's breath quickened. They had spent a whole night in the same room, lying in the same darkness, and he had not even known it.

He could feel Gio watching them. Francesco remembered a night, eight months ago. Gio and Emilio standing on either side of him, each of them shouting his name. It was always that way, the two of them pulling at Francesco until he felt he would break apart between them. He had stood still as they called out to him, watching a thin river of blood snaking its way across the dark paving stones towards him. Wondering, through a daze, what the blood would feel like through the newly worn hole in his shoe. Would it still be warm? Emilio's voice, shouting at him to run. Gio, pulling on his arm. He had chosen wrongly, perhaps, that night. If he had chosen differently, would they still have been here? Or perhaps it had begun even earlier. If he had never met Emilio, that night in the courtyard a year ago, could all this somehow have been avoided?

'You're blocking the sun.' Emilio didn't look up as he

spoke. His head was bowed in the shadow Francesco was casting over him.

'I know.'

'And what did I say about the kid? He'll get you into trouble.' Gio was still standing at the far end of the yard, staring at the ground.

Francesco tried to speak, and found his throat was suddenly choked. Emilio stood up. They looked at each other for a moment, and they might have been back in the city, were it not for the silence around them.

'So. You're here,' Emilio said flatly.

'Yes.'

He took a long drag on his cigarette and breathed slowly out, his eyes never leaving Francesco's. Then he flicked the stub aside and took a sharp breath in.

'Jesus Christ, Cesco.'

Francesco heard himself sob at the sound of the familiar nickname, and tried not to cry.

'You all right?' Emilio stepped forward and put a hand to Francesco's forehead. His hand was cold. Francesco flinched away from him without meaning to.

'I'm all right. Are you—'

'Why didn't you run? Jesus, I told you to run.'

Francesco's breath shook as he tried to speak. 'I couldn't . . . My mother . . . You were gone . . .'

Emilio sighed heavily, and put his arms around him. Francesco felt a great lifting, the relief of being near him again.

'Does he know?'

It was lower than a whisper, hardly more than a carefully shaped breath. Emilio was looking over his shoulder towards Gio, still standing watching them. Francesco could feel the tension in his arms.

'No.'

'Are you sure?'

He felt suddenly tired. All the thrill of seeing Emilio again left him. This was why Emilio had embraced him. He hadn't missed Francesco at all. He was only worried about who he had been talking to.

He tried to keep his voice steady. 'He wasn't there. He doesn't know.'

'Are you sure?'

'I'm sure.'

He felt Emilio let out a breath, and repeated the words to himself in his head as he turned to see Gio still watching them. *He doesn't know. He wasn't there. No one was there.*

'Francesco,' Emilio whispered, shaking his head. 'Francesco, Francesca. My little idiot.'

Francesco smiled, but when he lifted his face, there were tears in Emilio's eyes.

'Francesco. Why didn't you run?'

Seven

Catania, June 1938

> The story of the detainees of Catania is made up of poverty, 'petty theft and prostitution; of ignorance, illiteracy, and interrogation statements signed with a mere cross; of hours and hours of work in the fields. It is also made up of love affairs, of the occasional late and drunken night. It is the story of a hidden world made up of particular streets, parks, dance halls and special movie theatres.' It is the story of individuals forced to deny their own nature, to report their friends to the police, accept the fact that they are condemned and despised and beg for an act of mercy.
>
> Lorenzo Benadusi, *The Enemy of the New Man*, quoting G. Goretti, 'Catania 1939'

'It is the third night, in one week, Francesco.'

Francesco stops in the doorway. Though the sun has set, a warm ripple of air carries in dust from the streets. Catania is breathing out after a day of searing heat, taking a moment to rest before the night begins.

'Francesco Caruso, where are you going?'

His mother steps out of the darkness of the kitchen. She stands in the doorway, arms wrapped around herself, a tight smile on her face.

He pulls his thick jumper down tighter. Beneath it he is wearing a shirt dyed bright red, a little patchy, perhaps, but it has been hanging in his room for days, drying for this evening. There is another stuffed in his bag. A birthday present for Gio. Gio loves to dress up. Coloured scarves, dyed shirts, garlands. Anything that is bright, that does not remind him of the darkness they constantly hide behind.

'Only to Ancello's,' he says, thinking quickly of a bar, one of the quieter ones, one no one could suspect of immorality. 'There is a man who might buy my bicycle there.'

She looks at him hard for a moment. She can always tell when he is lying. Always could. He remembers her in Naples when he was just a boy, pulling stolen sweets from his pocket, hitting him over the knuckles. She was larger then, or was it just that Francesco was smaller? But since Catania, she seems to have lost some of her old strength. Francesco has grown, into the image of his father, she tells him, and she has diminished. She hardly goes out now. Increasingly, in the city, women are not seen on the streets. They remain at home, out of sight, busying themselves with housework, children, food. Indoor work. He looks at her standing in the dark kitchen doorway. Margherita Caruso. She has her own shadows to hide in.

She crosses the room and puts her hands on his shoulders, kissing his cheek. Francesco draws back, surprised.

'You are not being truthful.' He avoids her eyes. 'But,' she sighs, 'there is no harm in it. If you are finding yourself a girl, so much the better.'

'Mamma . . .'

'It is time, Francesco. We cannot live alone together forever.'

'I promised not to leave you alone. Not ever.'

'And you won't. There is room.' As he looks doubtfully around their small apartment, her face takes on a more serious expression. 'You know the taxes are higher,' she says. 'If you stay single, we will not be able to afford it for much longer. Do it for me, Francesco.' She pats his cheek. 'Bring me back someone nice. You deserve a beauty. And I deserve some company better than that.' She gestures to the radio, quiet in the corner. For the last few days it has been nothing but rumours of war. They have stopped listening to it, silently consenting together to switch off news bulletins filled with speculation and warnings of action. It is hard for them both not to think of Francesco's father. Not to wonder where he is, if he is listening to the same news.

Francesco looks down at his bag. The red shirt is visible beneath his papers. He thinks of Gio, probably waiting for him on the street. Dante, Luca, Antonio, the *arvulu rossu* boys pressed together at the dance hall.

All the talk amongst them recently has been of the police. Six weeks ago, a new chief was appointed, and it was clear from the beginning that things would be different. Molina, everyone knows, was selected by the regime for his fervent belief in fascist ideals, for his resolve to act against those who oppose the regime. The anti-fascists and the anarchists have been growing in strength, especially here. Molina is the city's reward.

Molina's first act was to enforce the banning of costumes at festivals. His second, the appointment of his second-in-command, Diego Rapetti. A tall, thin-faced man who paces the streets in person almost nightly, armed with a gun, searching the faces of men he passes in the street. Francesco knows several who have been stopped already, simply for standing still for too long, or for defying the directions on costumes. Though it has not been acknowledged publicly, they all know Rapetti's role is to control the *arrusi*. *To cauterise this city's plague*, he said in his first public speech in the square.

He stares down at the shirt in his bag, feeling the one he is wearing tight about his neck as his mother watches him. He shouldn't go. What will it do to her if he is found out? He thinks about it: trying to meet a girl, bringing her home to his mother. *A new start*, she said to him when they first arrived from Naples, after his father had gone. *We can make ourselves over again. Caruso. Say it again. Francesco Caruso.* Can he now? Can he make himself over again for her? A wife. He tries to imagine it. He can only think of Gio, Gio's arms around his waist, his lips . . .

'Go on!' She puts a hand on his arm and pushes him out into the street before he has time to turn back. 'Go and talk to some fathers and brothers. See what you can find for us. Though I don't know why you are wearing that old jumper.' She swipes at him affectionately. 'It will stifle you in this heat.'

He hears her laugh softly as she closes the door behind him.

Francesco stands for a moment in the dark street, waiting for Gio to appear, wondering whether to go back. Voices rise around him: women calling across balconies, the shouts of children running home, chasing each other over the cobbles. He looks up and sees Lucia leaning over the edge of a balcony, spreading out damp sheets and shirts. Her father owns the restaurant Gio and Francesco both work in; he knows her from the days she comes in to help with the waiting, when they are short. He has known her since she was a child. Only now does he notice how she has grown, how her body has softened into curves. He watches her hands smoothing out the cloth, her hair hanging damp across her shoulders. When their eyes meet, she smiles at him, before quickly turning away.

A girl. It would be the right thing. What his father would have wanted. He has only ever wanted to make his father proud. He looks down again at the edges of the coloured shirt in his bag. He cannot linger in the street too long; he will be stopped and questioned. If they find the shirts, even worse for him. They are hardly extravagant, but it will start suspicions against him. He looks up again at the balcony, and turns to go back inside.

'Francesco!'

He turns quickly, but the voice is not Gio's. Antonio is at the end of the street. Francesco watches him approach, his slight body almost invisible in the darkness. He is the youngest of the *arvulu rossu* boys by several years. Barely eighteen, but looking at his face, his glowing skin and deep brown eyes, he might be younger still. He grins at Francesco from beneath his untidy dark hair. Of all of them, Antonio is the least likely to show fear. Perhaps it is his youth that makes him unafraid. Perhaps he does not yet realise what he has to lose. Francesco should have known the talk of police would not have deterred him tonight.

He gives Francesco a shove as he catches up with him, grinning. Then, in a lower voice, says, 'Are you going?'

Francesco hesitates. He looks up, but the balcony is dark and empty now. Lucia's washing hangs listlessly in the still air. He pushes his hands into his pockets and gives Antonio a quick nod, keeping his head down as they walk together in the direction of the Piazza San Antonio.

The dance halls are not exclusively for *arrusi*, but it is known that this is a place where they gather. The first time, he and Gio were both sixteen, and the idea of it terrified Francesco, to be so open, all together in one place where anyone could round them up. Now, he understands the risks are not so great. It is not unusual, all these men together in one room. It has even become easier; by now, women almost never go out on the streets at night, certainly not to dances or gatherings such as this one. The absence of women is, it turns out, the best disguise they could have been granted. All over Sicily, across the country, men are gathering together in the evenings to trade their daughters, sisters, girlfriends amongst one another. The only difference is, the *arrusi* have nothing to trade but themselves.

When they reach the piazza, they can already hear the music through cracks in the windows, feel the vibration of feet on the uneven floor. They move quickly across the unlit square, keeping their heads down until they are safely inside the tiny, crowded space.

It is not like the dance halls they have seen in films, and not just because there are no women here. The room is bare, without furniture. At the far end, on a raised step, a small orchestra is assembled, tunelessly scraping its way through a waltz. The music is always slightly dated, as though the room is a snapshot of another era. He recognises Luca, who lives a few streets away and works in his father's grocery shop, his face bright and smiling, already flushed with wine. And Claudio, moving between the groups of men as easily as an eel in water, putting his arms around some, brushing past others, laughing at the hands that catch him, swing him around and let him go.

Though it will have opened its doors just a few minutes earlier, the room is already full. Couples dance in slow, lazy loops around the floor, sliding past men standing in groups around the edge, eyeing each other from a distance, or talking in low voices. Most are dressed in neatly tailored suits, though Francesco can see where they have been patched up and coloured in; some more garishly – brightly coloured shirts and jackets lined with lurid silk. Some wear an androgynous mixture of styles, scarves wound around their waists or hair, their faces painted, cheeks bright with rouge. He searches the faces for Gio, wondering if he has arrived before him. Antonio pushes a glass of wine into his hand and reaches an arm around his waist, which Francesco is quick to remove, in case Gio has walked in behind them. He sips at the wine; it is warm and sour, but enough to take the edge away from his nervousness. He always begins these evenings apprehensive; all of them do. By the end, they are laughing together, the threat forgotten. Drinking helps to speed the transition.

They have not always been so afraid. In Francesco's first few years of dancing, they were fearless, the dances spilling into the streets, the *arrusi* joining in with festivals dressed in brightly coloured skirts, their faces painted, flowers woven through their hair. Since Molina and Rapetti, everything has had an edge of fear. There have been rumours that Rapetti plans to clear the dance halls. He is starting with the streets, and then he will look for them in salons, in the squares, in their homes. No one is sure whether to believe the rumours. No one wants to be the first to admit to fear, to stop gathering, so they have all carried on as though nothing is happening, as though the regime is not tightening its net around them.

The red shirt is still in Francesco's bag. It looks pathetic now, against the costumes of the dancers. He sees Mattheo, dancing awkwardly with Claudio, who makes everyone look clumsy. Mattheo's eyes are ringed with kohl. He smiles at Francesco over Claudio's shoulder. He should have asked Mattheo to make the shirt. He would have done, if he could have afforded Mattheo's prices.

'He's not coming,' Antonio says, pulling him again towards the dancers, and this time Francesco allows himself to be led, gives himself up to the rhythm of the orchestra, the sensation of being surrounded by men like himself, like a safety blanket. Antonio draws him close and Francesco moves with him for a while, his feet clumsy on the floorboards. Antonio smiles at him, weaving their fingers together before spinning on to Dante, standing awkwardly in a corner. Luca takes Francesco's hand and they swing together, laughing, swigging at their wine, tripping on other men's feet.

A door at the far end of the hall is open, letting out some of the sticky heat of the dance. Through it, Francesco can see more dancers, though outside it is dark now, save for the flicker of their cigarettes in time with their breath. They are moving more slowly than the crowd inside. They look, some of them, almost asleep in each other's arms as they slowly turn.

He untangles himself from Luca and weaves his way through the crowds until he reaches the doorway. He can hear the music they are dancing to now, guitar music, slow and soft, notes falling over one another. He wonders how they have the nerve to be out here, where anyone can see them, but looking up, he sees they are in a courtyard, surrounded on three sides by high walls, on the fourth by the facade of the dance hall. They are completely enclosed.

A man is sitting on a step to one side, a guitar resting on his knees. His eyes are closed. He looks older than most of the boys who gather in the dance halls. His long, pale fingers stroke the strings as though he does not need to think, and when the music stops, he sits perfectly still, his hands resting over the guitar, his face woven in contentment.

'He's been coming every night for a week now,' Luca says behind Francesco. 'I don't know why.'

Francesco doesn't know either. He knows the man by sight, but he has never spent time with the *arvulu rossu* boys before. They have gossiped about him, the man with the beautiful forehead, the dark eyes, who lives alone and never associates with any of them. They have joked about taming him.

Francesco takes one last look back across the hall: Gio is still not here. He takes a sharp breath in, feeling the wine lightening his thoughts, making him bold, and walks over to the man.

'I like your playing.' It is the first thought that comes into his mind. He feels himself flushing. The man's eyes open. He smiles at Francesco, and indicates the space next to him on the step.

'You play?'

'No.'

Francesco realises that, while the man has ceased playing, the dancers have continued to move in imagined rhythms, occasionally knocking softly into one another and turning away. The man smiles at them, and puts the guitar to one side. Through the open doorway, Francesco can still see men moving in what seem now to be exaggerated, ridiculous shapes. The orchestra has begun a polka. He sees Antonio and Dante spinning together, holding each other close.

'I hate this courtyard,' the man says. He is examining his hands with close attention, weaving his fingers through his palms, flicking dirt from the edges of his nails. 'All these places.'

'You could go in there.'

He smiles. 'In there it is worse. Wherever we are, we are trapped.'

Francesco looks up at the sky, black and starless, and remembers what his father used to tell him. *You are never trapped if you can see the sky. There is always a way out.* 'I don't feel trapped.'

The man laughs quietly. 'You should. You live on an island.'

He thinks of the roar of the flames as his father ran from the house in Naples. Balancing on his shoulders, holding onto his father's hair, struggling not to fall as his father stumbled, all the time staring up at the dark sky. His mother screaming behind them. *Run.* He is so used to feeling trapped, to pretending to be someone he is not, he hardly notices it any more.

'Why are you here, if you hate it?'

The man smiles, and looks directly at him. 'I was hoping you would be here.'

Francesco feels his cheeks flame, and looks away. He cannot disguise his smile. He looks at the walls enclosing them on four sides, and the open doorway, the bodies spinning together. 'I came here for someone else,' he means to say, but instead he hears himself saying, 'So, how do we get out?'

The man smiles, picks up his guitar and starts another dance. There is a shifting amongst the bodies in the courtyard as they adjust their rhythm to his. 'You could swim,' he says. 'But then you'd just find yourself on a different island.'

He stays there, beside the man, the guitar eventually discarded between them. They talk about the city, war, music, and at some point Francesco looks up and sees Gio standing in the doorway, holding two tumblers of wine and watching them. Always the most colourful of all of them, he is wearing bright red scarves, tied in loops around his waist over torn brown trousers. His cheeks are flushed with running. He has drawn a beauty spot beneath one eye. He looks beautiful, Francesco thinks, watching him in the dark.

Francesco stands up. The man beside him stands too. Gio stares at them both, confusion in his face.

‘Happy birthday,’ Francesco begins, and then everything is noise, the doors to the dance hall slam open, and there is shouting, a single gunshot, screams.

Francesco feels someone grip his hand. Gio is still staring at them, as though he cannot hear the chaos behind him. Men in the courtyard push their way past him back into the dance hall, trying to escape, running directly into the path of the police. ‘Rapetti!’ someone screams, and then Francesco sees him, striding through the crowds, smiling, watching them run. Francesco breathes hard, remembering Rapetti’s words in the square. *This evil must be cauterised, burned to the core.*

He moves towards Gio. Then thinks of his mother, waiting for him at home. All her plans for him. Lucia, smiling at him over a balcony. The pull on his hand is stronger. The man has pushed a piece of corrugated iron to one side in the corner of the courtyard, revealing a dark strip of alley behind it. His guitar is strapped to his back.

‘Come on!’ he shouts harshly. Then, as Francesco looks over his shoulder, ‘You can’t help them now.’ For a moment, Francesco pulls him back towards Gio, as though he and the man are chained at the wrist, then he sees Rapetti stop behind Gio and put his arms around his waist, and Gio is lifted into the air, kicking his legs absurdly like a child, and carried away. Francesco turns, allowing himself to be pushed through the opening, feeling the edge of the sheet metal tearing at his arm, and then they are standing in an alley, breathing hard.

He looks down at his arm. A crescent of blood is soaking through his shirt. They pause for a moment. The man puts out a hand to the bloodstain, lightly touching it. Then, in a quick, sudden movement, he seizes Francesco’s hand and they run harder, towards the sea.

‘Emilio!’ the man shouts, turning to Francesco as they run. ‘And you are Femminella. Beautiful Femminella!’

Francesco laughs. They run on, through the back streets towards the dark line of the railway arches, the sea glinting with moonlight beyond them. They stop beneath an arch, pitch black and damp, breathing hard. Francesco is still laughing, hysterical with the fear of it, the surprise.

'I can help you.'

'What?' Francesco hardly hears Emilio through his own laughter and the sea, loud in his ears.

'I can help you,' Emilio says again. His voice is quiet and soft. 'And your mother.'

Francesco stops smiling. He is cold. He remembers the jumper, still in his bag with Gio's shirt back at the dance hall, and shivers. 'What makes you think—'

Emilio takes his hand. Grips it tight. 'It's all right,' he whispers. 'I have told no one. I have been looking for you.'

'Told no one . . .'

Emilio reaches into his pocket and draws out a paper, pressing it into Francesco's hands. Francesco unfolds it slowly, feeling his heart beat faster. He feels suddenly sick. He doesn't want to look down at the paper. There is a face on it. A photograph. He knows already; somehow he knows who it will be, even before he looks. He hears himself let out a low, stifled breath. His father's face is staring up at him from the paper.

Francesco has no photographs. No keepsakes. Nothing from that life. It was all burned, buried, destroyed. It is the first time he has seen his father's face in more than ten years.

'What . . .'

'Shh.' Emilio draws him closer, as a line of police officers march past them. 'Better to say nothing.' He puts his face close to Francesco's. In the dark, they are a normal couple, two shadows in a hidden, silent place, embracing. Francesco can smell cigarettes on Emilio's breath. The scent of engine grease on his skin. His voice is hardly audible over the waves.

'I know who he was. Who you really are. I can help you, Femminella.'

Eight

San Domino, June 1939

Confino is the regime's masterpiece: the fear of being sent there looms over everyone. It is much more efficacious for fascism than the actual infliction of the punishment. A punishment involves few people, a threat is for everyone. The law indicates various types of adversaries that can be condemned to *confino*. It is a sort of didactic game for the regime. The fact is that everybody can be sent there because not only the law is revolutionary but its interpretation is as well . . . What counts is not the text of the law but the possibility of applying it at will.

Emilio Lussu, *La Catena*, 1929

'No boats,' Emilio said, standing at the cliff edge with his hands in his pockets. 'None large enough, anyway.'

Below them, the beach was busy with tiny fishing boats, coloured with bright, peeling paint of blue, green and red. Francesco had watched men taking them out in the early morning, casting nets across the water between the islands before dragging them back along the shore, their catch bundled up in the shallow hulls. Emilio was right: a boat that small would never make it across the water to the mainland.

'If we could get across, though,' Emilio went on, 'on the other island there are more . . .' He stared towards San Nicola, lost in thought.

Francesco looked too. They had been kept on San Nicola for a few days before they were transferred to San Domino. Though they were so close together, the two islands could not have been more different. San Domino was a densely wooded plateau – a garden, the prisoners on the other island had called it, staring longingly across the water – whilst San Nicola was a barren, pale rock, rising in jagged peaks from the sea, its cliffs ringed with fortified walls enclosing the complex where they had been held. At the island's peak, the abbey rose high above the cliffs. Staring across at San Nicola, Francesco thought of his father, his hands clasping Francesco's ankles. He felt a familiar longing to climb, to try to find a safe route to the summit.

A cross mounted on the top of the abbey was silhouetted against the pale sky. Even from so far away, Francesco could see its outline clearly. When the sun was in the right position, it would cast a shadow across the sea towards him. *God sees all your sins*, a policeman had whispered to him, one night in the police station in Catania. *You cannot hide from him, or us.*

'If we could get to San Nicola and take one of the larger boats, then we might have a chance,' Emilio said, still frowning in thought.

Francesco looked sideways at him. Emilio had given himself a rough shave in the week that Francesco had been on the island. He couldn't help wondering if the timing was deliberate. He felt a flicker of excitement, that it could have been for him. He stared at the line of Emilio's jaw, his hair curling around his ears, the soft skin behind them. He found it hard to believe he was standing next to Emilio again. He didn't want to move, sometimes, in case it made him disappear.

'What for?'

'What do you think?'

'We can't escape, Emilio. There is nowhere to go.'

'This is ridiculous.' Emilio laughed out loud. 'I mean it! Ridiculous! What is their plan? Just to keep us here for five years, then send us home? What's the point of that?'

Francesco tipped his head back, staring up at the sky. His father had lied, as it turned out. There was the sky, wide and deep above him, and he had nowhere to go.

He had begun to map the island with his feet, from the overgrown seclusion of their two dormitories, back the way they had been marched from the beach through thick groves of pine trees, towards the cliffs that towered above the sea to the north. He had not ventured far in the other direction. That way lay a cluster of houses, lined in three short streets, which met in a small, secluded square. Beyond the village, thicker forests of pine trees, and beyond those, more rocks sloping gently towards the sea.

The village itself seemed almost deserted. In Sicily, a village had meant busy streets, markets, children running through gaps between stalls. People shouting from windows and beating the dust of carpets and curtains into the streets. Muddy water flowing in gutters, discarded fruit sweetening in the sticky heat. In San Domino, it seemed to mean silence, almost total, broken only by birds escaping the thickets or, rarely, someone crossing the empty streets on their way to the sea.

It had been a week, for Francesco. For Emilio, five. Time was moving maddeningly slowly. The *arrusi* could not help counting out the days in their heads: how many were in one year, how many in five. Francesco had spent the time writing letters to his mother, over and over. Each time he finished, he read the letter through, then screwed up the paper and began again.

In some of them, he told her the truth. Not just about himself, what he was, but all the things he had done. He burned those letters quickly, after deciding not to send them. He sat by the brazier pushing them into the flames, looking nervously over his shoulder, waiting for the paper to catch and curl. In others, he lied about everything. Told her he loved Lucia, he still wanted her; it was a mistake, she shouldn't worry about him. That Gio was only a friend he sometimes drank with. That he loved the state, even, the laws it imposed. Once, when his father was with them, he would not have dared to say anything in favour of the regime, but that was over now. They had never discussed it openly, but after his father was gone, Francesco and his mother had silently agreed between them that they would say nothing against the regime, in public or private. What was the point, now that it was everywhere?

'Better to do it from there.' Emilio raised a hand to shield his eyes from the sun, and pointed north towards the higher cliffs. 'It is unguarded. But how would we escape the rocks?' He frowned, then turned away from the edge and took Francesco's hand. 'Come on.'

He led Francesco back through the pines, turning right towards the north tip of the island. As they climbed, Francesco felt his pulse quicken. By the time they reached the edge, pushing their way through bushes and brambles that clung to the island like a thick jacket of wire, he was holding his breath. The sea was louder here. They edged closer to the great dizzying drop to the sea, where waves broke in thunderous applause before subsiding to reveal reefs and rocks sharper than teeth.

Emilio was right: there were no guards here. On the beach, two men were standing lonely sentry at a tiny wooden posting, their guns raised to the sun, but here, there was no need. There was nowhere to run.

Apart from the guards, Francesco rarely encountered people. On one or two occasions he had seen men working in the fields, bent over pitchforks and spades. If they saw him, they raised themselves and turned their backs to him. As he moved away, he would see them standing close to one another, and he could guess what they were saying. Whenever Emilio saw them, he had to be kept from approaching them, demanding of them what it was they feared. Francesco had to lead him away, his fists clenched, his face red with anger, and talk to him until he was calm again. He had not forgotten the guard's warning. Be caught talking to the islanders, and they would be punished.

He remembered people looking at him that way in Catania, as he was taken away. Through the window of the van that drove him to the hospital, when he opened his eyes it seemed that every face on the street was looking at him. He saw fear in some of the faces. Worse than fear in others. It had made him shake with shame. He had been alone then. He had not even considered trying to free himself. And now Emilio was here, talking again of escape.

Francesco remembered the night in the courtyard, a year ago. How effortlessly they had made their way through the fence of corrugated iron. How they had laughed with the delirious ease of it as they ran towards the sea. He still had the scar on his arm, from where they had pushed their way through. And then afterwards, under the arches. *I can help you, Femminella*. A terrible choice.

'You're not serious,' he said, turning away from the drop to stare at Emilio. 'You can't do it from here. Even if it was possible, where would you go?'

Emilio said nothing. Both of them worked over plans in their head. After San Nicola, the mainland, where they could hardly expect a warm welcome. To the east and north, nothing but open sea. No wonder the guards didn't keep them more secure during the day. Francesco had been surprised, at first, to see the *arrusi* casually duck beneath the wire fence of the yard and climb up to the village, or into the pines. But why should they keep them fenced in? The island was prison enough.

Emilio took a running kick at a clump of earth, watching it tumble over the cliff edge and land in fragments on the rocks.

'I can't stay here,' he said, kicking again at the earth. 'I know that. It will suffocate us, to stay here.'

Francesco shook his head.

'What?' Emilio turned to him. 'Don't you feel it? Don't you feel trapped?'

'Of course I do! I just don't want to make myself visible.'

'Visible?'

Francesco thought of his mother, alone in Catania. The night after the fire in Naples, when his parents had gone back and picked over the charred remains of their lives, looking for anything that could identify them, burning anything that was left, anything that bore his father's name. Francesco had only been ten years old, but he had felt their fear. He had known it was not a game, even though his mother had tried so hard to make it one afterwards. *We will pretend our name is Caruso. We are going to play at being new people, Francesco, with a new name. We are going to pretend your father never existed. You understand?*

Francesco had played the game well, since that night. He had been quiet, right up to the end. He had played so well, sometimes he forgot who he was too. When the police had come for him in Catania, he had been almost relieved that they were arresting him for pederasty.

Emilio nodded. 'Well,' he said, 'we all have things we would rather not go home to. But I still can't stay here.' He moved closer to the edge, staring out at the sea dissolving into a pale blue horizon. 'Will you help me?'

Francesco knew what he was asking. Knew what he should say. It was what he should have said before, back in Catania, that night under the arches at the very beginning, when Emilio had shown him the photograph of his father. *I will have nothing to do with any of it.*

'Yes,' he said, feeling his pulse quicken. 'Of course I will help you.'

He tensed as Emilio stepped closer to the cliff edge, until his feet were hanging over the lip of the rocks.

'Sometimes I think about throwing myself over.' His voice was almost lost beneath the sound of the waves clawing at the rocks below. Francesco held his breath. Emilio didn't look back at him, but after a few seconds' pause, he turned and smiled. 'Not really,' he said, with a short laugh. 'Of course not.'

'Do you think we will see it from here?' Francesco said, attempting to change the subject.

'What?' Emilio stepped back from the edge.

'The war. When it starts. From the other side, I mean.' They had not yet ventured to the south side of the island, facing the mainland. It lay beyond the village, where none of the *arrusi* dared linger for long.

There was a long silence. Emilio stared out to sea, his lips pressed tightly together. Eventually he said, 'What makes you think it will start?'

'Doesn't everyone think so?'

'No.' He shrugged. 'We wouldn't see anything. We might hear it, though. The guns.' He paused. 'How's the kid doing?'

'The kid?'

'Giovanni. Your Amazon.'

'He is not my Amazon, Emilio. Not any more.'

They looked at each other for a moment. Francesco traced again the line of Emilio's jaw with his eyes, the curve of his chin, the soft skin of his neck. He remembered the feel of Emilio's breath in his ear. *I can help you, Femminella.*

'I don't know,' he said. 'He's scared, I think.'

'He won't be much use to us if it comes to it.'

'If it comes to what?'

'Femminella.' Emilio smiled sadly. 'You only ever want to hide, and stay silent.'

'I don't want to fight.'

'We should go home and fight,' Emilio said, pushing his hands into his pockets. 'Fuck them. They will not even let us fight?' He shouted it over the cliff, at the steep drop, the knife edges of rocks, the sea foam. 'Fuck them! I promise you, Femminella. We'll find a way out of here.'

'We could swim,' Francesco said, smiling sideways at him. But if Emilio remembered that night in the courtyard, how easily they had made their escape towards the sea, he showed no sign of it now.

Food was the greatest concern, at first. Later, life would become more complicated, but those first few weeks were simply a question of survival. Four lire did not buy much. Most of San

Domino's food was imported, the prices inflated. The *arrusi* purchased supplies from the tiny shop close to their dormitories, run by two brothers. Some traded with villagers, when they were certain they were out of sight of the guards. The rest they took from the land. Luca devised rabbit traps, which never yielded anything but the occasional half-dead rat, or once, a pine cone trapped between its metal teeth. 'We could try roasting it!' he said, ever the optimist, holding it triumphantly in his hands. They had begun to dig out beds in the fields surrounding the dormitories, hoping to supplement their meagre supplies, but the soil was dry and pale. Nothing had yet grown. Francesco had tried to make bread, which sat flatly in their small stove and refused to rise. He kept it amongst his belongings, sharing out the loaves when the day's foraging had been unsuccessful.

A few found other ways to make money, adapting their expertise to the needs of the island. For some, it was simple. Mattheo's tailoring skills were easily suited to the mending of uniforms. In the mornings, after the doors had been unlocked and the roll call taken, they would often find a carabiniere standing outside, his head down, half dressed and holding a jacket or shirt, sometimes even trousers, in his hands. Mattheo would bound to the door and take the clothes from him, with a few coins, and then settle himself in the yard, angled towards the light, moving his hands quickly over the fabric and drawing a thread through it. A few days later, the same guard would return and shrug the clothing on, hand him a few more coins. Later, if he saw Mattheo again, he would be careful not to acknowledge him. Others traded objects they had brought with them: watches, jewellery, whatever they had been able to snatch as they were arrested in Catania.

That afternoon, lying in the sunshine of the yard, exhausted by taking his turn with a spade, Francesco thought through his skills in his head. Dishwashing, waiting on tables. Polishing silver. Reading and writing. It was laughable, how useless he had turned out to be. After Naples, his mother had worked so hard to make sure he knew everything he needed to survive, and he had learned all the wrong things. Emilio was even more at a loss: no one, not even on San Nicola, was in need of a car.

Francesco was beginning to doze when the sun was blocked by someone standing over him. He leaned up on his elbows, squinting at the light. Officer Favero, the guard responsible for the morning count, was staring down at him, a rifle strapped to his back. He was holding a spade in his hand. Its handle, black against the sky, made a twin with the point of his gun. As Francesco sat up, Favero held out the spade.

'I brought you a better one,' he said. A blush had spread across his pale cheeks. In the sunlight, his hair looked almost white. 'They are kept in the tool shed,' he went on, as Francesco stared at him. He had noticed a hint of a stammer in Favero's voice. Perhaps it was the reason he spoke so slowly when he addressed the *arrusi*. He wondered if the other officers had noticed it. 'It is kept locked. But if you ask, I . . . I can take you there.'

Slowly Francesco put out a hand and took the spade.

'You won't persuade anything to grow just now, though. Not without more water.' The guard attempted a smile. He thrust his hands in his pockets and gave a deep, affected sigh. It was as though they were simply chatting together in the street. Over his shoulder, Francesco saw Arturo standing in the dormitory doorway, watching them with his arms crossed. In the fields beyond the yard, Elio had paused his digging and was staring at them over his own spade. He sensed the growing silence around him.

'What's wrong?' Favero asked as Francesco began to move away. The guard looked almost offended. Then he glanced around at the faces watching them, and nodded. 'I see.' He thought for a moment, then, keeping his distance from Francesco, felt in his pocket and pulled something out of it. A bar of chocolate. Shielding it with his hand, he held it out.

'Here. Take it.' He smiled. 'They don't need to know.'

Francesco shook his head.

'It's all right. Just take it.'

'No. Thank you.'

The hint of a frown crossed Favero's face. Taking a step forward, he whispered, 'Take it, or I will tell them you tried to sell yourself to me.'

Francesco looked up quickly. The guard showed no sign of anger. His face was calm, though the hand still holding out the chocolate shook a little as he waited.

Slowly Francesco reached out and took it. They both seemed to breathe out with relief as he broke off a piece and pushed it into his mouth, the relief of sugar rushing through him.

'There is more.' Favero looked quickly over his shoulder at the two carabinieri officers standing by the fence, and moved closer to Francesco. 'You . . . you want more, don't you?'

Francesco shook his head. The silence in the yard was total now, every face turned towards them where they stood at its centre. He felt hot and uncomfortable under their gaze. He wanted to get away. He wanted to go back to the dormitory and lie in the dark. But he couldn't stop looking at the gun strapped to Favero's back.

'How much?' Favero said.

'What?'

'How much? There are . . . places we could go.'

It took a second or two for his meaning to dawn. When it did, Francesco almost laughed. It was so simple. In the end, it was always so simple. No different to the days of the dark streets in Catania, the way to get what you wanted. He could hear the carabiniere's breathing quickening, saw the flush spreading deeper across his cheeks. For a moment, Francesco was back there, in the quiet alleyways, the thrill of feeling hands reaching around him in the dark.

He leaned in closer.

'I am not a whore,' he whispered.

Favero drew back. Then he paused, and looked around again at the *arrusi* standing watching them in the yard.

'Do they know?' he said.

'Do they know . . . what?'

'I can see that they don't.' Favero smiled. 'The one thing that makes you different here. That singles you out. I know.' Their eyes met, and Francesco wondered if he really did. 'And . . .' he swallowed, as the stammer threatened to return, 'I think that I know why, too.'

Francesco looked over his shoulder. Emilio had joined Arturo now. The two of them were standing together, staring at him, motionless against the dormitory's dark interior.

'*Arrusu*. That's what you call yourselves, isn't it?' Francesco said nothing. He could feel Emilio's eyes on him. 'Well, I want you to know, *arrusu*.' Favero's voice was soft. Barely more than a carefully shaped breath. Francesco felt that same panic that he had felt so many times back home. The urge to run. 'I want you to know that I haven't said a word.'

Nine

> Our programme is simple; we wish to govern Italy. They ask us for programmes, but there are already too many. It is not programmes that are wanted for the salvation of Italy, but men and will-power.
>
> Benito Mussolini, October 1922, Naples

'What do you believe in?'

Francesco doesn't answer. His father is opposite him at the wide, polished dining table of their home in Naples, bent over a pile of papers, stuffing them into envelopes. From where he sits, Francesco can only make out the bold headline. *NON MOLLARE*. Do not give up. He is only seven, but he has already been taught those words.

The windows are open to the street, where crowds have been growing steadily larger and louder. Two days ago, a man everyone is afraid of gave a speech to a crowd of his followers in Naples' largest square. *The moment has arrived*, he told them, *when the arrow must leave the bow, or the cord, too far stretched, will break*. Now he is on his way, marching to Rome.

'What do you believe in, Francesco?' His father is staring at the open windows.

'God,' Francesco says, thinking this will be enough.

'No, something real.' The reply shocks Francesco. 'Something that is here, in this life.'

He knows the answer. They have this conversation often, while his parents fold the pamphlets and prepare the envelopes. His mother, at the end of the table writing out addresses, smiles to herself. She is wearing a high-necked white silk dressing gown. It glitters in the lights of the high library ceiling. Beneath the table, Francesco's legs swing freely, his feet not quite reaching the floor.

'Freedom,' he says.

'And?'

'Choices.'

'And?'

'Never strike first.'

His father laughs, and nods. 'Good. Never strike first. And what else?'

The three of them say it together, a chorus. 'Do not give up.'

Non mollare. The pile of envelopes grows taller until it threatens to fall. Francesco watches his mother add more to the stack, wondering where they are being sent. What people will think of his father's message, when they open them. 'They think we will,' his father says quietly. He is not talking to Francesco any more. He does this often, muttering quietly as though someone else is in the room with them. 'That is their weakness. They expect us to use the same weapons they do, and they expect us to give up when they would.'

Francesco looks at him while he speaks. His father's face is as familiar as his own. He wonders, when he studies it, if this is how he will look when he is older. He looks tired. There are deep creases across his forehead, around his eyes. But determined. Always determined. His mouth is set in a thin line of concentration, his fingers flicking lightly through the pamphlets. *Non mollare.* Francesco wants to grow up to be just like his father. A real man.

When the pile is finished, he takes Francesco's hands. 'I am going away for a few days.'

'Again?' He hears his mother sigh.

'You'll be all right, the two of you, while I'm gone?'

Francesco nods. He likes it when his father talks like this. It makes him feel like a man. Look after the house. Look after your mother. Take charge, do not yield.

His father stands up. Something is tucked into the belt of

his trousers, lifting his jacket as he walks to the door. Something dark and metal, the barrel pointing to the floor. Francesco stares at it, wondering what it means. *Never strike first.*

'Up, *recchione*!'

Francesco woke suddenly, feeling a hand heavy on his shoulder. He opened his eyes to Officer Santoro leaning over him, the hand shaking him roughly.

'Up!'

Then he was looking into the point of a gun, and sat up fast, flattening his hair with both hands, struggling to untangle himself from his blanket and stand in the cold half-light. The dormitory was nearly empty; the other *arrusi* were already awake and outside. He looked quickly to Emilio's bunk, at the far side. It was empty, like the rest. Behind Santoro and the gun, Francesco saw Luca doing up the buttons of his shirt, his hair equally untidy, his face blurred with sleep.

He stood for a moment in confusion. Were they being moved to another prison? Where could they be sending them that was more remote than San Domino?

Santoro marched the two of them outside, where they found the others already standing in lines. Arturo looked furious, like a chained lion, pacing up and down and kicking at the ground. He was joined at the wrist to Claudio, who had no choice but to walk with him, looking almost amused by Arturo's exaggerated displays of fury.

They chained Francesco to Dante, who was shivering with fear. He looked close to tears as they were marched through the pines towards the beach. 'They are taking us to be shot,' he whispered to Francesco, who shot him a warning glance in reply.

As they marched, Francesco looked for the girl he had seen on the road that first day, suddenly recalling the comfort of her smiling, open face. There was no one by the roadside. The fields were empty too. There were no figures standing watching as they passed. The island, which was always quiet, seemed entirely deserted. Then, as they were led down towards the port and ordered into two small fishing boats, he remembered. It was a Saturday.

Until four years ago, Saturdays had been no different to any other day. It was usually their busiest day at the restaurant, couples and families and holidaymakers pouring through the doors in an endless stream of dirty plates and coffee cups and scorched roasting trays. Francesco would finish work late, his hands red and wrinkled with scrubbing, his eyes stinging from the fumes of the caustic soap they used on the toughest pans. Sometimes Gio would stay to help him. Gio had found Francesco the job in the first place, and over the years had himself risen to head waiter. 'Why do you not try for something better?' he would ask Francesco often, coming to the kitchens at the end of the day. 'You have reading and writing. Do you know how rare that is here? You are *educated*.' He said the word with reverence. 'You can't be content with just washing pans!'

'Maybe I like it!' Francesco would reply, flicking a handful of soap suds at Gio. 'There are worse things in the world than washing pans.'

And the truth was, he had been content. He had preferred to stay in the kitchens, out of sight. It was rare for members of the police force or the regime to come to eat there, but there were only so many restaurants in Catania. And he bore his father's features.

Though the busiest, Saturdays had been Francesco's favourite day at the restaurant. He and Gio, alone in the kitchens, laughing together as they finished Francesco's work. Sometimes Lucia would join them and help with the washing-up, or stand watching them with one hand on her hip, enjoying the superiority of being the boss's daughter. Then Saturdays had been claimed for the regime, and no one worked any more.

It had been fun, at first, when it started. All of them gathered together on a Saturday afternoon to play games. They were given uniforms, and targets, and strove to outdo each other. Everyone attended, but the young men seemed singled out for special attention. Francesco was taught how to jump hurdles, how to march in time with other men, how to climb ropes and trees.

The women, meanwhile, were taken to the town hall and taught new ways to sew and clean. A nurse came to teach them simple healing and midwifery. Francesco's mother laughed about it in the evenings, that they thought to teach her how to birth a child when she had been present at the births of ten at least – not including Francesco's own.

Then, after two years of running and jumping and competing with his friends, they gave him a gun. He had taken it slowly, feeling the cold metal between his fingers, the unexpected weight of it. Remembering how his father had always forbidden him to hold one, had never allowed them in the house – except for that one day Francesco had seen one at his waist. But perhaps he had only ever dreamed that memory.

'A little too masculine for you, *femminella*!' someone had shouted loudly across the square. Francesco had frozen at the sound. The *arrusi* did not use their given names in the daylight. He saw some of the other *arrusi* look up too. A soldier marched to the man who had spoken and pulled him up roughly by the collar. He said something in the man's ear, and the man had pointed at Francesco.

That was his first arrest. For public disorder, they told him, for disrupting the proceedings of the Fascist Saturday. But he had seen how they looked at him as they shut the doors on him. *It is a pathology.*

After they let him out, Francesco saw Saturdays in a different light. It wasn't games they were playing. He saw a headline in one of the newspapers as he walked to the square. *Il Duce revives spirit of ancient Rome*, it had said, and he had understood. They were learning to be soldiers.

*

Francesco had not thought the tradition of the Fascist Saturday could extend so far. The islands had not seemed to be part of any civilisation; he had thought that was why they had been brought here. As the boats rounded the coast of San Nicola and drew up on its rocky beach, he looked up and saw the dark uniforms of the carabinieri lining the streets leading up to the fortress, heard their shouts, harsh and clear on the still air, and knew. There was nowhere the regime could not reach.

They walked up a steep cobbled road, passing briefly through cool shadows beneath the stone arches of the fortress's outer walls. When they emerged again into the sunshine, they were in front of four long, low dormitories, much larger than those they were kept in on San Domino. Their walls were stained ochre, their windows small and high. Prisoners were milling about in the open spaces between them, dressed in the same white uniforms that the *arrusi* wore. Ahead, up a series of low stone steps, was the entrance to the fortress, an archway between walls of stone and a round, flat-topped tower.

The yard was heavy with the stench of sewage, bringing back to Francesco the few days the *arrusi* had spent on San Nicola, when they were first brought to the islands. They had been kept separate from the rest of the island's prisoners, in a room beyond the archway, empty but for their narrow beds, the only windows boarded up. They had been too crowded there. In such proximity, they had fought, argued, gambled over tiny necessities. Water and food had been so scarce they had begun to forget the ties of friendship or love there might have been between them. When the carabinieri came to move them to San Domino, Francesco had not cared if they were going home, or to another prison, or to be shot.

As they walked between the barracks, the San Nicola prisoners began to move closer, gathering in groups to watch the *arrusi* pass. Their uniforms hung loose about their thin, malnourished frames. Their faces were gaunt, their eyes dark hollows. Francesco could feel their eyes following him as they marched on towards the fortress, and kept his own cast down. These were the anti-fascists, the men who had spoken out against the state. These were the men they had been taught to fear the most. They would destroy the country from the inside. They were a disease. A cancer on the state. Yet even they had been thought too good to be subjected to the *arrusi*'s company.

For a moment, the San Nicola prisoners watched them in silence. Then one of them shouted out, high and clear, 'How much?' The rest began to laugh, and there were more shouts: 'Dance for us!' 'How much, *recchione*, how much?' 'Where are your skirts, *femminella*?' 'Dance for us, *femminella*!' He felt Dante flinch beside him as a string of saliva touched his cheek.

Ahead of them, on the steps leading to the fortress, the carabinieri had lined up alongside other officials. To the side of them, the islanders had gathered in a large open space, watching as the prisoners drew closer. Francesco saw a woman pulling her two young children towards her, arms wrapped protectively around them, her eyes, turned towards him, narrowed with suspicion. On the other side of the officers, the older children had been separated from the adults into two ranks of girls and boys, wearing identical clothing and standing in neat rows. He felt self-conscious, walking towards the crowds, towards so many faces all fixed on his. He thought of the girl by the roadside the day they were taken to San Domino. Her shy half-smile. Her eyes following him with interest, even as Pirelli had whipped him to the ground.

Elena felt hot and uncomfortable in her uniform, too tight after three years of wear. Her hair was braided tight against her scalp. She stood in a row of other girls, all dressed identically in white shirts and black, pleated skirts, watching as the lines of prisoners were marched into the square. They were assembled before the steps, where the Director would take his place. The crowds shouted and jeered as they were brought in, but the children, standing in their rows, were silent. She tried not to fidget, tried to scratch an itch at her neck without moving her hands.

To her left, the boys were lined up, dressed in shirts and stiff felt trousers. Somewhere amongst them, her brothers would be standing to attention, arms tight to their sides, but she couldn't identify them amongst the uniform rows, their hair slicked to their foreheads, their faces blank. She imagined them for a moment lined up for battle, guns at their shoulders. *You think there will be war?* her father had said. *If it is God's will.* A single word, barked by the Director, and the boys would move as one, raise their guns, the first shot, the first strike . . .

She watched as the prisoners were brought into the square. The San Nicola prisoners, the anti-fascists, were slow to assemble, emerging from amongst the dormitories and ignoring the shouts of the carabinieri as they ambled towards the steps. She studied their hunched shoulders, their thin frames, trying to imagine them as the opposing army, facing the boys, her brothers. They would be blown over like dried-out trees in a strong breeze.

Elena thought of what the Director had told her father. They had money, some of them. Support back home. She could see the shadow of the mainland from here, a dark shade on the horizon, so close it seemed possible, if she stared for long enough, to see those crowded cities, the close-packed streets, the people moving anonymously through them. She watched as the San Nicola prisoners began to shuffle into rows in front of the steps. Some of them, surely, must be thinking of escape. She could not be the only one. But what could she offer them to help her?

The San Domino prisoners were brought in to stand beside them. There were only forty or so – hardly enough to form the ranks of an army. Elena had heard the rumours; they had spread across her island in hushed whispers. They were perverted. They had forgotten how to be men. She didn't know what that meant, to forget how to be men. She was too afraid of the answer to ask anyone.

Coviello was wearing his best white suit, adorned with medals. He looked bored, Elena thought, as he took his place on the steps before a large microphone. Later, there would be drills and exercises; Elena would go through the process of starching linen, looking after imagined babies, while her brothers would run lengths across the square, climb the pillars like monkeys. First were the speeches. The worst part. Standing hot and uncomfortable whilst the Director's voice echoed across the square.

When he spoke, his voice was surprisingly soft, audible only by the microphone's echo.

'I wish, as always, to thank the people of these islands for sharing their home with prisoners of the state.' The microphone screeched and wailed. 'To the prisoners' – he looked up – 'may you find here some salvation for your transgressions. You will receive nothing else. Not mercy, or forgiveness. But perhaps you may find peace.'

The prisoners stared back at him. Rows of faces, blank of expression. Coviello turned away from them, and passed his eyes over the group of girls standing to his right. Elena felt herself flinching at the memory of his cold eyes raking her skin. The undisguised hunger in the faces of men on the island as they watched her walk past. The way it made her want to hunch herself over, to disappear amongst the pine trees and the shadows. As she felt Coviello's eyes on the girls, she looked up, and saw several of the San Nicola prisoners looking over at them too, that same expression on their faces.

She stood for a moment under the shadow of their gaze, the Director's voice droning in the background, and after a while felt the shame and the fear replaced by something else. The way Coviello had looked at her, that evening at her house, as though he had been hypnotised. It had stalled his words. Made him, for a brief moment, forget himself. And she had done nothing, just stood there beside him. She had never known what it was like to have power, but now she wondered if this was what it meant. Was this how to get what she wanted? She wanted, suddenly, to test it. To see how far it could take her.

'For a long time, the state considered a more merciful approach to those of you who set yourselves up as its enemies.' Coviello had turned back to the prisoners. 'We tried to understand, to listen. This is what we see in return.' He was holding up a piece of paper. Elena recognised the same poster he had brought to the house that day he came for dinner, the image of the policeman with his gun at his side. His thin, angular face. His eyes, staring at her from the paper.

'Just a few months ago, on the fourteenth of January, a member of the Catanian police was killed for doing his duty.'

She watched as he stepped forward, holding the poster up, turning so that each of them could see it, though the picture was far too small, the crowds far too large, for anyone to make out the man's face clearly.

'Beaten. In cold blood. Is this the way to make our country great again?'

The San Domino prisoners were staring at their feet. She remembered the man her father had whipped on the road, how different his gaze had been. He was not alone; she had encountered more prisoners since on the island, and none of them looked at her in the way other men did. They had turned away from her, as though they were the ones who felt shame. Where was her power here? It was somehow absent, as though countered by something in them. Was this what it meant, to forget how to be men? And if it was, was there some way to remind them? If it was the reason they were imprisoned, perhaps it was the way to save them. There would be some power in that, in being the reason they were allowed to go free. What could she demand of them then?

Coviello bent to a crate beside him and took out a pile of the posters, flinging them into the air. She looked up, and watched them spin and whirl against the sky, settling in the square like a soft snowfall, the policeman's face staring up at them all.

As the papers rained down, Elena looked towards the prisoners. Only one of them was looking up. One of the San Nicola prisoners, an older man, about her father's age. He was staring not at Coviello, not at the papers lifting and rustling on the light breeze, but towards the small cluster of San Domino prisoners. His face was so strained, his expression so tense she thought he would cry out.

'And we *will* be great again!' Coviello's voice, louder now, filled the square. 'Beginning with this promise. We will find the man responsible for this outrage, and we will make him pay.'

Elena looked at the San Domino prisoners, examining their faces for a sign. *I want you to find out which of them did it*, he had said to her father. She tried to imagine any of them beating a man in cold blood, but she could only think of her father. The whip in his hand, sailing in an elegant arc through the air.

Coviello raised his hand in a Roman salute. The carabinieri responded as one, their arms raised high against the sun in perfect coordination. Elena tensed as she raised her own hand, the girls alongside her doing the same, the boys to her right raising theirs. She looked over at the prisoners. This particular battle had been raging for months, unspoken. For months, Coviello had been raising his hand in the salute, and for months, while the rest of the square responded, the prisoners had been standing resolutely still, their hands by their sides. Sometimes, at Coviello's order, an officer would take one of them into the square and beat him for it.

She looked over at the anti-fascists, her hand aching in the air, wondering if this was the week where one of them would give way and answer the salute. There was the usual restless movement amongst them; she imagined some straining to raise their hands, others pulling them back. No hands were raised. She waited for Coviello to give the order, wincing already for whoever it would be. But he said nothing. He looked for a moment as though he might speak, then the microphone picked up the faintest flicker of a sigh as he turned away from it, pulling his hat from his head and wiping a fist across his forehead. He said something quickly to one of the men beside him, and they all stepped down. Elena tried not to allow herself to smile. As she lowered her arm, she thought she saw the man amongst the anti-fascists smiling too. Their eyes met briefly, then there was a shout from the carabinieri, and they began to move away.

After the speeches and the exercises that followed, she walked with the rest of the girls towards the dock, where the boats for San Domino waited for them. The others were chattering excitedly, relieved to have been released at last from the gloom of the fortress's walls. The route back necessitated walking through the yard of prisoners, between the four low dormitories where they were kept during the night, beneath the full glare of the sun.

Elena hung back. She was still thinking of her realisation, as she had stood listening to Coviello in the square, of the power she might have. The yard, which had earlier been swarming with carabinieri, was largely empty of them now. It was her best chance to test it. To see if there was some way to gain favour with these men, the anti-fascists, who had money and supporters back home. Who might, even now, be planning a way to get back there.

She tried to walk so that her body was upright, her back straight and shoulders back, as she had seen girls practising when their mothers were paying no attention. There were very few prisoners in the yard now; the sun was still high and strong. But as she drew close to the last of the dormitories, she saw one leaning against a wall. It was the man whose eyes she had met in the square. The only man who had been looking up as the papers had rained down on them. He was standing alone, almost as though he had been waiting for her.

She slowed her pace further. The rest of the girls had reached the walls and the road leading down to the port. She watched them turn, then stopped close to where the prisoner stood.

She didn't dare look up. She could hear his breath beside her. Without meeting his eyes, she said, in a voice that didn't sound like her own, 'Do you want . . .' and then she stopped, not knowing how to continue.

She did look up then, and felt a flare of anger to see he was smiling at her, as an adult might smile at a child who has said something amusing that they could not possibly understand.

'No, *ragazza*,' he whispered, and she felt hot tears in the corners of her eyes. But as she moved away, she felt a hand on her arm, pulling her back.

His voice in her ear was quick.

'You come from San Domino?'

She nodded. Her cheeks were burning now.

'You know where they keep the prisoners there?'

She nodded again, though she did not. His grip on her arm tightened as he turned her round. The San Domino prisoners were marching towards them, on their way from the fortress to the port.

'There is something you can do for me, then.'

'Why give it to you?' Elena's mother said, frowning at the water as they drew closer to San Domino. The islanders were packed into four or five fishing boats. They sat silently in rows, shawls and caps covering their heads against the sun. Elena could see two other boats just pulling out from the jetty on San Nicola, the prisoners' white uniforms bright in the glare.

Her father, out of his uniform today, shook his head. Elena hardly recognised him now without his gun. He looked older. Tired. 'I don't know,' he said. He was holding one of the posters, staring at the grainy image of the policeman. 'I wish he had not. Looking after prisoners is one thing, but . . .'

'You are not a policeman, Felice. Or a detective.'

'Just so. But they will find someone else for the job if I do not do it.'

'And if war comes?'

Felice turned to her. 'What if war comes?'

'He said. Coviello. They might find a different solution for them.'

Felice sighed. 'I don't know.'

'What does he mean by that? A different solution? Another prison?' She leaned towards him, glancing at Elena, who tried to appear absorbed in staring at the fish darting against the underside of the boat. 'Or something worse?'

'What could be worse?'

'There are other ways, Felice. You know that. He can't keep degenerates locked away on islands forever. If war comes, at least it might force him to realise that. And why did it take you so long to come down?' She turned angrily to Elena. 'The other girls were already in the boats; what were you doing?'

Elena didn't answer. She was still thinking about what her mother had said about the prisoners. *He can't keep them locked away here forever.* Did she mean the Director? She watched the policeman's printed face creasing into folds as her father slid the poster into his pocket, and thought back to the square, Coviello holding the paper up: *I ask you all to be vigilant.* The papers, the man who had been killed, raining down on them, the soft rustle as they settled in the square. The prisoners standing in rows. Her brothers marching anonymously with the other boys, lined up like an army ready to fight. The prisoner's grip, tight around her arm, his voice urgent in her ear, the hope that had swelled in her with it, the promise of change. *There is something you can do for me.*

Elena looked up. Ahead of her, the jagged cliffs of San Domino rose like prison walls, cutting up the sun.

PART TWO

And if liberty is to be the attribute of living men and not of abstract dummies invented by individualistic liberalism, then fascism stands for liberty, and for the only liberty worth having, the liberty of the state and of the individual within the state.

Benito Mussolini, 'The Doctrine of Fascism', 1932

Ten

THE CHRONICLE OF DEEDS

May 1923

Genoa: at Marassi-Guezzi fascists strike workmen found in public bars, fire revolver and rifle shots, and set fire to the Friendly Society's premises.

Rome: workers distributing leaflets for May Day arrested. The fascist militia tear the red carnations from passers-by.

Milan: Chamber of Labour entered during the night, and an attempt made to set it on fire.

Parma: the worker Tosini Guido killed by fascists.

Milan: fascists attack a restaurant in the Strada Paullese, where dancing is going on.

Pompeii: several fascists ill-treat some young ladies who were carrying red flowers to the Madonna.

(Editor's note: This list continues for another fifteen pages.)

Giacomo Matteotti, *The Fascisti Exposed*, 1924 (assassinated 1924)

Francesco is standing in candlelight, in front of the tall curtained windows of his father's library. On the table, beside piles of books left open, their pages creased and annotated, is a stack of pamphlets. He holds the candle out to them, reading the familiar bold headings: *NON MOLLARE*. Ten years old, Francesco is the only boy he knows his age who can read. His father has been teaching him every night, after he has finished his own teaching at the university. It will make you free, he tells Francesco. If you can read and write, you can do anything.

Francesco likes the lessons. He likes to sit close to his father, rest his head against his father's soft woollen jacket, watch his father's fingers tracing words, reciting them together. *Non mollare* is his favourite. They say it together, when he finds the reading difficult. *Non mollare.* Do not give up. Do not yield.

It is three years since the day the man gave his speech in the square and marched towards Rome. Three years since his father first left the house with a revolver. He got what he came for, that man in the square that everyone feared. He governs Italy now.

Francesco has crept downstairs; the house has long since fallen asleep. He heard a noise in the garden. He thought at first that he should wake his father, but he is nearly a man now. He should learn to keep the house safe himself.

He takes his candle to the window and pushes open the heavy curtains. The garden is dark. In the tiny circle of light from the candle, he can see the beginnings of the lawn, the curve of it before it slopes down towards the river, where his father sometimes takes him to catch fish. The garden is empty. There is no one there.

As he turns away, he sees something in the corner of his eye. The smallest flicker of a light in the darkness. Then another, from the other side of the garden. He stands still for a moment, waiting. No more lights come. He looks down at his own candle. Moves it slowly from side to side, watching the patterns it casts on the lawn.

There is a sound of breaking glass from somewhere inside the library. The lightest ripple of sound, like the glasses he hears being clinked together when his parents hold dinner parties. Then, silence. For no reason he can think of, Francesco takes a deep breath.

Then everything is noise, a terrible, gushing roar. Francesco almost drops his candle, blowing it out just in time, but the darkness he expects is not there. The room behind him is filled with light and heat. He turns and stares into a wall of flames. He hears his mother screaming from somewhere beyond them. There is shouting from every direction; someone calls out his name, then he hears the glass of the window break behind him and strong arms lift him, and he is on his father's shoulders, and they are climbing a mountain together again, his father running with him across the lawn, away from the flames, into the darkness, everything behind them noise and heat and light, and he tries to look up to the sky, to feel free, but he can't see anything through the light of the flames.

'Night would be the best time,' Emilio whispered later in the dark. He had crept across the dormitory and lowered himself onto Francesco's bunk. Above the covers, but Francesco could feel his limbs pressed against his own, the thin blanket between them. He could smell Emilio's sweat, feel his warm solidity beside him. He wondered if Gio was still awake, watching them through the darkness.

'Best time for what?'

'To run.'

Francesco lay staring at the dark. He could hear the sea beyond the dormitory walls. Over it, birds called out with strange, high-pitched cries. He heard them every night, like the screams of trapped children, soaring overhead, silenced only when the sun rose.

Emilio shifted beside him.

'They'll expect us to try something in the day. Night, when they think we are locked in. I'll think of a way.'

Francesco could still feel the pressure of Favero's hand on his arm. The rest of the chocolate was hidden under his bunk; he was afraid to take it out. Afraid of what the others already thought of him. He thought of the two of them, he and Emilio, tossed about in a tiny boat, striking out across the sea towards the mainland. What waited for them there? Or tunnelling underground, like rats. Could he do it? Could he stand any more running, any more hiding?

'They're probably used to seeing fishing boats. By morning, we'd just be another fishing boat.'

'What would they do to us? If we were caught?'

Emilio shook his head, leaned across the bunk and put a hand to Francesco's lips. 'Just another fishing boat, Femminella. Then we can do whatever we want. Go wherever we want.'

Francesco shivered at that word, repeating the sound of it in his head. *We. We can go wherever we want. We. Us.* Did Emilio want him, then? Would he still want him after this?

'The difficulty is what direction to take.' Emilio was almost talking to himself now. 'We can't go east. And west—'

'You can't just run! Anyway, there are other ways. Safer ways – you heard what Arturo said.' *There are three ways to leave the island.* Francesco regretted saying it immediately.

Emilio turned to him. 'Yes,' he said, 'legitimate ways. Illness, punishment, or a petition. They will look for that. There will not be a way to . . . unless—'

'Shh,' Francesco whispered. They lay still as footsteps padded across the dormitory towards them. The creak of a bed frame, whispers, muffled laughter. Then, after a silence, an unmistakable, barely audible moan. Francesco shivered at the feel of Emilio's warmth against his.

'What was that, before?'

Francesco didn't look at him. 'What?'

'You know what. With the policeman, outside. The one with hair like straw.'

'Nothing.'

'It looked like something. He gave you something. What was it?'

'Nothing. It was nothing. He was just laughing at me. Like they all are.'

'They wouldn't be laughing without their guns,' Emilio said quietly. 'There are more of us. We would win easily, in a fair fight.'

Francesco thought of the story of Emilio throwing his plate of rations at the prison guard's face. He wondered how many attempts at escape Emilio had made, on the long journey they had all undergone from Catania. How many beatings and punishments he had taken. He thought of the poster Pirelli had pinned to the door. *Killed for doing his duty. Beaten. In cold blood.* January. The night Emilio was taken. He remembered the taste of the mud, as a boot pressed his face into the gutter in Catania. Rapetti's face, thin and dark-eyed, hunting them down.

'I don't think I can,' he whispered. 'Escape, I mean. I don't know—'

'Five years, Cesco. Imagine it. Can you be here for five years? Really think about it.'

'It could be worse.'

'How? A different-sized box, a different sky. We're still not free.'

Beside him, Emilio's face was set firm with determination. Francesco closed his eyes. When he opened them again, light was streaming through cracks in the padlocked door, and he was alone.

Eleven

Catania, June 1938

> Despite the large-scale measures and constant police surveillance, it has been impossible to put a stop to the scourge of pederasty; the unsatisfactory results of the measures adopted so far are due solely to the stubbornness and indifference of the most rebellious degenerates of this kind, who run any risk in order to satisfy their perversion and continue to infest their surroundings.
>
> A. Molina, report to the Prefect

Gio is absent from the restaurant and the dance hall for three days. By the second day, Francesco has convinced himself he will not see him again. The image of Rapetti carrying Gio away from the dance hall, his legs kicking uselessly at the air, returns to him in dreams. Already, since Molina took over, three *arrusi* have been taken and imprisoned, and no one has heard anything of them since. Gio must have been careless. Met someone in public, or dressed too conspicuously. There are a thousand reasons why they might have taken him.

He considers writing a petition. Or asking for help from Marcello, one of the older *arrusi*, the *primogeniti*. Marcello used to work as a lawyer, and lives in a large apartment on the Via Penninello. Francesco has never been – the *arvulu rossu* boys never go to the salons – but he has heard that Marcello's house is lined with books. That he is willing to help, for a price. That he is a fighter. Before he was a lawyer, Marcello had fought in the war. Some even said he had been at Caporetto.

He thinks about it: going to Marcello and asking for his help in arguing Gio's release. What reason would Marcello have to involve himself in the affairs of the younger *arrusi*? Besides hiding from the authorities, they have nothing in common, and no reason to care about one another's fate. Marcello would only laugh at him.

After three sleepless nights, he has almost given up hoping. But on the fourth day, crossing the castle square towards the restaurant, huddled against the corner of two narrow side streets, he sees Gio already there, wiping the outside tables. Lucia is with him, arranging chairs, an apron around her waist. Francesco is late. She has already begun his work for him. He smiles at her as he approaches, and she looks away, her cheeks flushing.

Above them, ivy trails across the bright red awning that shadows the restaurant's customers from the sun. The day has begun hazy and heavy with heat. Sunlight reflects from the table's polished surfaces, blinding Francesco as he walks towards Gio, who is already dressed in his pressed uniform, a red waistcoat over his shirt.

'You're here,' he says, looking quickly over his shoulder. There is no one by the castle. Its walls, usually dark, are burnished ochre by the bright sun. He squints, and turns back. He wants to hug Gio, but it is impossible, in the open. 'What happened?' He can feel Lucia watching them closely.

'Nothing,' Gio says tersely, moving on to another table. 'Nothing happened.'

He avoids Francesco all day. They do not even make eye contact. Then, as Francesco is finishing the last of the washing-up, preparing to walk home alone, he looks up and sees Gio watching him from the doorway to the kitchens.

'I'm fine, by the way,' Gio says quietly. 'I'm sure you were wondering.'

'I was. Of course I was.'

They walk together back towards the Via Calcera. It is their usual route, through streets busy with slow-moving crowds, shaded from the heat by tall, closely packed buildings. They usually stop at Francesco's flat first. Gio will come in for a few moments, sit with Francesco's mother and tell her stories of his day at the restaurant, while Francesco tidies the flat around them. Sometimes he thinks his mother loves Gio as much as himself. That is the joke of it: she would never suspect anything.

As they walk, Francesco thinks of the man in the courtyard. Emilio. What would his mother think of him? Coarse, and rough. After Naples, what happened to them there, Gio fits perfectly into the new quiet of their lives, into their low-ceilinged, silent rooms. She sees him almost as another son. What would it do to her if she knew the truth? Her heart would break.

'What happened?' he asks Gio, anxious to finish the conversation before they are home.

'You saw what happened. They carried me off at gunpoint, and you ran away.'

'It happened fast.'

'Fast enough for you to run off with someone else.'

'Sorry. I'm sorry, Gio. They already had you, and I thought—'

'You thought you'd found someone better.'

He hasn't seen Emilio again, though he has been back to the dance hall. Each time, he has found himself walking idly through the crowds, searching for Emilio's face, listening for the sound of his guitar. He still hasn't answered Emilio's question. The offer that has been made. He has the photograph of his father in his pocket now. A reminder that he must decide.

'Gio, I don't care about him.'

'After what I've done for you.'

'Are you all right? What happened?'

Gio looks away from him. 'Nothing. Nothing much. They took my photograph. Details. That sort of thing.'

'And then they let you go?'

Gio nods. Francesco frowns at him; he can't help it. How can he have been let go so easily?

'Without a fine? Or anything?'

'I was lucky.'

They are silent for a moment. Francesco knows what some of the *arvulu rossu* boys will think. What they will whisper about Gio, in dark corners. *He is one of them now.* Is he?

He shakes the thought away. No. Not his Gio. He puts an arm on Gio's shoulder. 'Poor *ragazza*,' he whispers. 'I'm sorry.'

Gio shrugs him away.

'Do you . . .' Francesco hesitates. 'Do you know anything about him? The man from the courtyard?'

Gio shakes his head. 'I knew it. I knew you were interested in him. He flirts with everyone, Fran. Don't you know that?'

'I just want to talk to him. Do you know where he lives?'

Gio says nothing.

'All right.' Francesco walks on ahead of him. 'I'll find him myself.'

'Marcello's.'

Francesco turns. There is an edge to Gio's voice. How does he know? He never goes to the salons. Francesco remembers his plan to ask Marcello for help. Did Gio do so himself?

'I don't know where Emilio lives,' Gio continues quietly. 'But he is sometimes at Marcello's apartment in the evenings. On the Via Penninello. You might find him there. Francesco . . .' He raises his voice as Francesco moves to his door. 'You should be careful.'

'Why?'

'Don't you know? Do you think Rapetti cares about our dances? Do you think he has time for that, really? Why do you think he came for us that night at the dance? It's never happened before.'

Francesco thinks back to the night at the dance hall. Rapetti's arms around Gio's waist, moving him aside, marching towards the courtyard. Their guns. The fierce determination in their faces. Emilio's hand gripping Francesco's tightly. How quickly Emilio had located a way out, and the edge in his voice. *Run.* If he doesn't know, then why should Gio?

'Gio . . .'

'They were there for Emilio. They were there because of him.'

The streets are quiet. Francesco moves quickly, feeling exposed as he moves closer to the centre of the city. In the dusk of early evening, a few men are gathered at street corners, sitting on the steps of churches. He feels their eyes following him as he passes. In a few weeks' time, these roads will be thick with crowds for the Ferragosto festival. The city will be taken over by the parades, the legitimate gatherings, the march of dignitaries and officials through the wider streets. For three days, the city will be brought close to a standstill while Catanians celebrate the arrival of the slow, hot days of late summer. He wishes the festival were already happening, for the safety of being concealed within a crowd.

He knows the Via Penninello, though he has been there only once or twice. It is not his Catania, those streets around the Piazza Stesicoro, where tall, wide-fronted houses line a bright square elegantly planted with trees and neatly paved. It is so different to the narrow, uneven streets around the castle, it might as well be another city.

The care that has been taken with the Piazza Stesicoro in part covers the excavations that are being carried out at its centre; a great, yawning hole has been opened up at the square's heart, revealing beneath it the lost layers of a former city. It is a theatre from the Roman age, people have been saying, and as he looks down at it, Francesco can just make out the shapes of roughly hewn steps climbing out of the dark cavern, scattered with workmen's jackets and tools. He stands for a while at the railing that has been constructed around it, staring down into the pit, and tries to imagine such a length of time passing. Hundreds, thousands of years. The Romans used the same materials the city is built with now: cooled volcanic rock and baked red bricks, cemented together with lime. He cannot make out a stage, but he imagines the crowds on the steps, their feet beating a rhythm against the rock, laughing at a performance somewhere still buried beneath layers of earth. All the long years that stretch between them and the ground he is standing on now. The thought of all that time makes him dizzy, and he steps back from the edge. He wonders what the excavation is for, who it is intended to please. What good can ever come of digging out a city's buried past?

The Via Penninello is a few turns away from the square, a narrower, darker street, but still far more respectable than Francesco's own. The walls are lined with balconies. A few people have come out in the last of the daylight, casting long shadows across the paved street. Two children watch him from between railings, their faces pressed against the metal struts. Further along the street, in the shadows, he sees a boy leaning against a wall, clutching his arm as though someone has hit him, before sliding to the ground in a strange, graceful movement, and settling in the dust.

He finds the door open, and steps into a narrow courtyard, open to the sky. Looking up at Marcello's apartment, he sees a light flickering in one of the windows, and hears the sound of voices, a guitar being gently strummed. He takes a deep breath, imagining the *primogeniti* inside. It is an unspoken rule that none of the *arvulu rossu* boys will ever visit the salons. Their two versions of the city are as separate as Francesco's and his mother's are. He doesn't even know for sure if he will find Emilio there.

In front of him, a narrow stairway leads up to the building's higher floors. As he climbs, he looks up. He can see stars, constellations he cannot name shining through the chimneys and parapets of Catania's close-packed buildings. He thinks of what a prison guard said to him once, the time he was arrested for public disorder, after they had been given guns in the square. *God sees all your sins. You cannot hide from him, or us.*

Marcello's door is ajar, but he knocks anyway. No one comes, and Francesco steps inside, hoping they will not register his arrival. The apartment is dark and low-ceilinged. The air is thick with cigarette smoke; through it, he can see the shapes of men lying on sofas, leaning against door frames or sitting on the floor in groups. No one looks up as he makes his way through them, searching in the gloom for a familiar face. They are drinking wine from cut glasses and pewter mugs. Books are piled everywhere, some being used as stools and tables, others lying open on the floor.

Francesco feels self-conscious as he moves through rooms, hesitating in doorways. It is so unlike the dance halls, where they spin and twirl and hardly talk to each other. Most of the boys there can barely read their own names. Something about the way these men are gathered, the sound of their voices, glasses clinking musically, reminds him of the parties his parents used to give in Naples. He feels like a seven-year-old boy again, standing in a doorway, looking in at a world he is not part of. The men move around him as though he were a shadow. He feels suddenly ashamed, as though they will know he is only a child, that he has nothing to say for himself other than the small things Gio has told him of politics. He thinks of the library in Naples, and wishes he could talk to them of his father. Of the life he once had.

He is about to turn back when he sees Emilio, sitting in the corner of a small room that has been laid out like a study. A desk has been pushed back against the wall to accommodate more people, and Marcello and Emilio are sitting in two armchairs by it, each with a cigar between their fingers. A man is sitting on the floor beside them, leaning against the desk as though worshipping at Emilio's feet. The rest of the room is packed with men listening to their conversation.

'It was beautiful,' Emilio is saying, his hands stretched out in front of him, as though stroking the lines of an invisible shape. 'Smooth, sleek edges.' Marcello grunts, a smile on his face. His skin is pale and paper thin. The glasses balanced on the end of his nose magnify his eyes, giving him an owl-like expression. Francesco looks at him, remembering the stories of Marcello fighting at Caporetto. It is hard to imagine now, looking at his lined, aged face. Hard to imagine, too, the thousands of men who died there, their faces pressed into the mud. Somehow, Marcello survived. He fought his way out, became someone significant in the city, rose above the dishonour of that notorious defeat, his country's greatest shame. Yet still, if the authorities were here, they would call Marcello weak. Feminised.

'She leans in,' Emilio continues, 'and says to me, if you can fix it, maybe I can fix you.' The room erupts in laughter. Emilio thrusts his head back as he joins in. He is wearing a pressed white shirt, open at the neck.

'And did you?' says the man sitting at his feet. They laugh harder. Francesco joins them, not wishing to appear out of place, and feels his cheeks grow hot as Emilio winks at the man who has asked.

'I was more interested in the car,' he says, taking a sip of wine. He winks again, and the man on the floor smiles. Francesco recognises him then, as he turns his face towards the door. It is Antonio, from the dance halls. Antonio, the youngest of the *arvulu rossu* boys. Francesco has never seen him at any meeting place besides the dance hall at San Antonio, yet he is here, sitting amongst the *primogeniti*, smiling at Emilio as though he has sat with him in Marcello's apartment many times. As though he belongs here, with these men, so much older than him. Francesco flushes, remembering his own certainty that he would not be welcome at a gathering of the *primogeniti*. What is Antonio doing here?

Antonio looks up and meets Francesco's eyes. Francesco recognises his own confusion mirrored there. And something else – a hint of shame. As though something has been discovered that Antonio would rather have kept hidden. Then Emilio turns around.

'Femminella!'

He stands up and holds out his hands. The rest of the room turns to Francesco and he looks down, embarrassed. Emilio crosses to him and kisses his cheeks, lingering a little longer than is necessary. Francesco can smell his breath, wine and cigarettes, and feels himself shiver involuntarily.

'You don't mind?' Emilio says, turning back to the room. Francesco imagines he is giving them another knowing wink, and feels his cheeks grow hot as Emilio's hand reaches around his back. As the other men shout encouragement after them, Emilio leans in to him and says softly in his ear. 'Come outside.'

'Why is Antonio here?' he whispers.

'Come on.' Emilio pulls him towards the door.

As they leave, Francesco turns back to the room, the air fogged with the fumes of cigarettes, filled with voices. Through the smoke, Antonio's eyes meet his again. His gaze remains fixed on Francesco, that same look of embarrassed confusion on his face, as Francesco follows Emilio into the hallway. They are still staring at each other as the door shuts between them.

'You have thought about it?' Emilio says when they are out of the apartment.

'I have thought about it.'

'Good.' Emilio pauses on the stairwell. 'I'm sorry,' he says quietly. 'I am just passing on the message. I don't—'

'I know,' Francesco says. 'I mean, I understand.'

They walk down the stairwell and into the street. Emilio looks up at the open window, through which the sound of the *primogeniti* can still be heard, and frowns. 'Come on,' he says, his hand still on Francesco's back, and leads him out into the Piazza Stesicoro.

'Emilio, what is Antonio doing there?'

'It doesn't matter. Come on.'

It is dark and empty now in the square. The excavation is

no more than a deep shadow at its centre. Francesco is thankful for the railings he knows stretch around its perimeter; it would be easy, in this darkness, to walk over the edge and into the pit.

'So, you agree? That must be why you are here.' Emilio draws him into the deeper shade beneath the trees. Francesco hadn't been certain of his decision, even when he agreed to come outside, even when he came looking for Marcello's apartment, but now he hardly thinks before he nods.

Emilio takes his hand. 'You must be sure. Once it is done . . .'

'I am sure,' Francesco says, and for that one, brief moment, he is. The relief of it.

'Good,' Emilio says. Then, after Francesco says nothing, 'You will be all right, you know.'

Francesco nods, and gives a small smile as if to say that he does not mind so much about the danger. But Emilio's face is serious as he squeezes Francesco's hand tighter. 'I mean it, Francesco. I will make sure of it.'

They stare at each other. Something has changed in Emilio, in the few minutes since they left Marcello's. Francesco cannot tell quite what, but whatever facade Emilio had previously adopted is gone. He feels as though they are meeting again for the first time. That Emilio is seeing him clearly for the first time. Neither of them can move their eyes away.

'Listen,' Emilio whispers. He reaches out and draws Francesco close to him, sliding a hand to his waist. At first Francesco can hear nothing. He is so focused on the feeling of Emilio holding him, he can hardly register anything else. Then he hears it: distant music.

'What is it?'

Emilio nods to the building behind them. 'It is the cinema.'

The music is a waltz. He knows it. He has seen the film many times. He imagines the screen inside: two tall figures, a woman dressed all in white, a man in black, dancing as though they were spinning on air. Something in the image makes him think of his parents, and he feels tears rising to his eyes. They used to pull back the carpet in the library, take each other's arms and spin around the room, laughing. He would stand in the doorway and watch them, longing for that closeness, that ease, while the gramophone crackled in the corner of the room, a low hiss like flames slowly rising. In Francesco's image of the film now, he sees his parents dancing, his mother's dress, feathers floating lightly with the movement as his father holds her close, his voice in her ear. *Heaven.* Flames, rising around them.

Emilio takes his hand. They move together slowly to the music from the cinema, slipping on stones as they try to keep time, laughing at their own clumsiness. As the music pauses, Francesco looks up and meets Emilio's eyes. A new tune starts, and as they turn again, Emilio leans closer, puts a hand behind his head and pulls him into a kiss. Francesco feels a shiver running through him at the energy, the heat that surges through him as their mouths touch. He wonders if this is all a part of Emilio's persuasion. He doesn't care.

They break apart at the sound of footsteps close to them. A couple walk past, leaning over into the pit and laughing. The heat is replaced by a shudder of fear. He stands rigid, hoping his figure will blend with the darkness and the shadows. When the couple have moved on, Emilio reaches for Francesco's hand, and Francesco pulls it back.

'I'm afraid,' he whispers, then feels Emilio's arms reach around him and lets himself be drawn back in.

'Francesco,' he whispers. 'Francesco, Francesca. My little idiot. Haven't I already promised to look after you?'

As they turn again to the music, Francesco longs for Emilio to kiss him again, but instead he pulls him close, resting his chin on the crown of Francesco's head. Francesco feels entirely surrounded by Emilio's warmth, his scent, the strength of his will. He knows it then, with a fear that thrills him. He might do anything for this man. Just to be close to him. There is nothing he would not do, no matter where it might lead him, what it would cost.

He looks up again, and meets Emilio's eyes. They stare at each other for a long time, still turning slowly in the dark, as though each of them is waiting for something. For a moment, Francesco forgets their agreement, forgets the *primogeniti*, Antonio, Marcello, everything but Emilio. When the music stops again, they both carry on. As they turn, he tries to remind himself he is doing this for his mother. For both his parents, to keep them safe. But he knows, underneath it all, that it is the thought of Emilio that makes him go on with the dance.

Twelve

San Domino, July 1939

At night, San Domino was so quiet Elena sometimes imagined she could hear screaming in her head, echoing the shrieks of the Diomedee birds that filled the air until dawn. In the evenings she sat with her parents and brothers in the parlour – her mother called it that, though it was hardly big enough for all five of them, and had only three chairs and a worn-out rug spread across the flagstones. Once, a carriage clock on the windowsill had ticked insistently, but it was gone now. The room's objects had been slowly and silently disappearing over the months her father was not working. Two small china vases that had belonged to Elena's grandmother. A tin jug in which they collected stray coins – the coins long gone too. A pair of brass candlesticks, one of them dented where Andrea had thrown it across the room in Elena's direction in a fight about something long since forgotten.

Her father's war medals had gone too. He used to keep them on the windowsill beside the clock. He had won them for bravery, he had said when she asked, which hadn't been often. He had fought at a place called Caporetto, years ago, before Elena was born, and been taken prisoner there. He never talked about that. Only the times before and after. The mud of battle, the noise, the strangeness of coming home afterwards. How quiet the island had felt. How quiet it still felt.

At least her father had found his work at the camp before the gramophone had disappeared. It was still in the corner of the room on a low table, gathering dust. She wondered sometimes why he had been more willing to give up his medals than an old gramophone that couldn't make a sound. Still, she was glad. The gramophone hadn't worked for years, but she liked to look at it, at the way the candlelight danced on its shining curved surfaces.

'What will happen, if there is a war?'

Elena's mother sounded as though she were continuing a conversation that had begun in her head. Elena had almost dozed off, leaning her head back against the chair.

'What have you been listening to?' her father said, turning towards her.

'Just news. The radio was working again.' She nodded to the kitchen, where she kept it. It was always stopping and starting. As though some days it didn't have the energy to tell them what was happening in the rest of the world.

He sighed. 'I don't know. I have asked the Director. There are no plans to move them. Not yet, anyway.'

'I don't mean the prisoners, Felice! I mean us. What will happen to us? Will you have to—'

'I don't know,' he said, more sharply, looking at Elena, then over at her brothers, sitting together on the floor, a deck of undealt cards between them. Elena thought of them running together on the beach, jousting with sticks, jumping through the surf. Marching through their exercises in front of Coviello. Then, horribly, she thought of all three of them sailing away, perhaps to the mainland, or to some battlefield hundreds of miles away. Herself, watching from the beach with her mother as they left. Walking back to the house, the two of them, alone.

'I wouldn't go,' Marco said, unexpectedly. They all looked over at him. 'They couldn't make me. I'd stay here. By the time everyone came back, I'd have farmed their land as well as my own. I'd kick those prisoners out as well.' He smiled, pleased with the idea. Elena looked nervously at her father, but he didn't seem angry. He leaned forward, folding his hands in his lap, and fixed Marco with a stare.

'Do you know what Caporetto was?'

Marco rolled his eyes. They had all heard the stories a hundred times by now.

'It was the battle that lost us the war,' he went on. 'Twenty-two years ago. Do you know how many Italians were taken prisoner that day?' His face hardened. 'How many ran, like dogs?'

'Thousands,' Elena said quietly. The sun was falling below the horizon. Shadows stretched across the floor towards them. Their own shadows, long and misshapen, shifted as the sun moved, as though they were dancing together. She remembered the days when the gramophone had still worked. Her parents, drawing back the carpet and dancing in this room, holding each other close, dancing like the couple in the film she had seen on San Nicola last year, the one where the woman wore a dress that floated with feathers, as though she would take off, as though she had wings. *Heaven.*

'Why do you think those men are here? The prisoners?'

Marco shrugged, but he was listening now, she could tell. This part was new.

'It is all part of the fight,' her father said. 'The fight to make our country great again. To make sure Caporetto never happens again.' He frowned, and she knew he was thinking about the time he was a prisoner himself. 'If there is another war, we need our armies to be stronger. We need to be sure we can win.'

'Why does that mean they have to be here?' she said, in a voice quiet enough to be silenced easily. She was never quite sure when it was her turn to speak. When a conversation was just for men, and she was expected to stay silent. But her father didn't silence her.

'They cannot kill,' he said, though he didn't turn to look at her. 'In a fight, they would run, as they ran at Caporetto. It is because of them that we spent months in the dark. That we were beaten.' His fists tightened at his sides. Elena saw that unfamiliar anger again in his face. 'They are not prisoners. Not like we were.' He closed his eyes. Elena thought of the image of the man on Coviello's posters. *They cannot kill.* But someone had been killed. A policeman, in Catania. And Coviello had asked her father to find the culprit, from among those men. How could he, if he did not believe they were capable of it?

'They are not kept in the dark. They are not beaten or starved. They are better off here than at home.'

'They are,' she said quietly. Her father turned to her.

'What?'

'They are beaten. Aren't they?'

There was something in his face now that she had not seen before. He was not looking at her like a father at his daughter. His eyes were blank and cold.

'Only when necessary,' he said. 'It changes nothing. What we are doing is part of the fight. So you see,' he said, turning to Marco again, 'the fight has already started. You will go, when it comes. Because you are both men. Not like them.'

'Not like them,' Marco repeated. Elena wondered if her brothers had been told what the prisoners had done. Why her father was so sure they would run, when it came to a fight. It made sense, she supposed, to separate men like that. But how could they know?

'Elena will marry, and give her husband children. That is how she will make her contribution.' She could feel him smiling at her, and could not meet his eyes.

'Who will it be, Lena?' Andrea said, grinning at her. 'Nicolo, from the store?'

'Or Matteo!' Marco said. They both laughed. 'He is older than you, Papa. Not many to choose from, are there, Lena?'

She turned away from them.

'And what would the two of you have done if you had been at Caporetto?' her father said, silencing his sons. 'What will you do when it comes again?' They looked up quickly then.

'Fight,' Marco said, at the same time as Andrea said, 'We will fight like men.' He smiled, his lips drawn back over his teeth.

'Good.' Their father smiled. 'Good. I only wish you had both been there with us then.'

*

She must have dreamed of the prisoner her father had beaten on the road, because when she woke the next morning, his was the last image to fade from her mind. His face, smiling at her. His skin, pale beneath a thin shirt, then the sight of him on the ground, the sound of him crying out as the whip fell.

She dressed quickly, pushing a few of her paper birds into the pocket of her skirt. About to leave the house, she saw through the open kitchen doorway a pile of the posters the Director had left there, the photograph of the policeman. No one was awake yet. The kitchen was empty. She walked quickly to the table and took a handful of them, feeling the weight of the paper, wondering if they would fly.

San Domino was already hazy with heat. Elena pulled off her shoes and walked along the path towards the village, feeling the soft earth cool on the soles of her feet. She exchanged a brief nod with a man who passed her, leading a donkey by a piece of twine around its neck, but besides that saw no one on the road. Beyond it, the cornfields had grown high and thick, their tips glistening in the sun. She stood still for a moment after the man and his donkey had passed, listening to the animal's slow huffing, its hooves echoing in the silence.

When she reached the village she paused for a moment outside one of the abandoned houses. In the yard, a cluster of bright red flowers was growing against the gatepost, clinging to the fence in an effort to reach higher. She picked a handful and threaded one through her hair, in doing so pushing on the gate, which swung open with a loud groan.

She stood still for a moment, as though she expected someone to come. One or two of the houses in the village were lived in, but they were on the street parallel to this, and their occupants likely to be out in the fields by now. She looked up and down the road, seeing no one, then walked boldly up to the front door, and pressed on it lightly. It, too, swung open.

Inside, it was dark and cool. Elena stepped into a low-ceilinged room, lined on one wall with shelves. There were three armchairs arranged in a corner and a low table in the centre. A thin film of dust covered everything. She moved through a doorway to her right and found a kitchen, a table at one end and a stove at the other, pots and pans lined up on the walls. She laid the red flowers at the centre of the table, hoping the flash of colour would make the room seem more alive. Moving through the house, she found every room was the same. Furnished as though still waiting for the occupants who had never come. As though waiting for her.

As she walked through the silent rooms, it was suddenly clear what would happen, where her future lay. It was here in this house. Or if not this, an identical one. In the living room, she threw open the shutters, hoping that sunlight would make the idea of it seem more real, more possible. A beetle scuttled across the floor and disappeared under one of the chairs. Far out to sea, a boat was tracking the horizon. She watched its slow passage until it disappeared into the haze.

Elena closed the gate carefully behind her and stood for a while on the street, feeling short of breath. She looked again up and down it, trying to imagine it as her street, her gate, her life. Why could she not do it? The rest of the islanders seemed content with their lives. 'A paradise', her mother often called San Domino, and it was. Thick groves of pine trees punctuated with bursts of flowers, red, purple, yellow and white. Clear green seas. A still, peaceful silence blanketing everything. How could it not be enough?

From the village, she turned left through the trees to her favourite place on the island, the Cala Tramontana. It lay beyond the Cameroni district to the west, where the pine forest opened out suddenly onto a great open space of land covered with low bushes of herbs and pale yellow flowers, sloping gently towards a patchwork of flat rocks leading down to the sea.

When she had emerged from the trees, she pulled on her shoes, crossed the shrubland and scrambled over the rocks until she was at the water's edge. The land curved around her on either side, enclosing the sweep of the cove. Above her, the sky was a brilliant blue, the sun directly overhead, lighting up the clear water. She could see white sand beneath it, fishes darting between weeds, leaving little trails of disturbed sand in their wake.

She pulled one of the posters from her pocket and studied, again, the words she could not read, wondering what was written there. Then, holding it up to the sun, she folded it into the shape of wings. They lifted slightly in the breeze, before she threw the paper in a straight arrow towards the horizon. It fell in a spiral to the sea.

As she watched it settle on the water, she heard voices behind her. Further along the shore, two men were running from the trees towards the water, shouting at each other and laughing. They were wearing the pale uniform of the prisoners. She crouched down among the rocks, watching them as they approached the shore. She could not help but hear her father's voice in her head as the two prisoners came closer. *A contagion.*

The men clambered along the rocks for a while, searching for a way down to the water, then stopped near where Elena lay hidden. She could see their faces now, and recognised one of them at once as the man her father had beaten on the road. His face was thinner now, but he was still beautiful, she thought, tracing the curve of his cheeks, the pale skin of his neck, the hint of curling hair at the opening of his shirt. For a second, she longed for him to see her, to look at her in the way other men did. She felt her dress clinging to her newly rounded figure, and for the first time did not want to hide herself away.

As she watched, her breath quickening, both men pulled off

their shirts. Beneath them, their bodies were thin and pale. Dark hair covered their chests. She felt afraid then. If she was discovered watching them, what would everyone think of her? But she found that she could not look away.

There was a pause while the two men stared at each other, before the taller man pulled off his trousers and slid himself down into the sea. The other, the one her eyes had remained fixed on since she had recognised him, hesitated for a moment before climbing slowly down after him still wearing his trousers, which darkened as the water soaked them to his skin.

Elena waited for a moment as they swam out from the shore. She looked back at the two piles of discarded clothing. It was a chance. Perhaps her only one.

She waited until the two men were no more than black specks in the water, so far out she could not make out their features, and then scrambled across the rocks to their clothes. Finding the shirt that lay on its own, she reached into her pocket and pulled out a piece of paper. Quickly, looking over her shoulder at the men in the water, she slid it into the pocket of the shirt, then ran breathlessly towards the trees.

Francesco lay back, feeling himself drift slowly away from the shore. The water soothed his sun-baked skin, and he felt the salt's sting on his blistered feet. He tried not to think of Emilio, floating naked close by; so close he could reach out and touch him. He allowed himself to drift, and San Domino began to recede on the horizon. He closed his eyes and felt himself move with the tide, wondering if, when he opened them again, he might find himself floating back through the muddy water of the port in Catania, the railway arches rising overhead, the air filled with soot and smog, his ears with the shouts of street traders and hawkers. But as he drifted further, he heard only birdsong and, from somewhere far away, Emilio calling to him.

They sat together on the rocks, allowing the sun to dry their skin. Francesco had pulled his shirt back on while he was still dripping wet, but Emilio had left his clothing in a heap, stretching his lean body out to the sun. Francesco allowed himself to stare openly at the curve of Emilio's body, the soft curls of hair on his chest, the line of his collarbone, his wiry arms. Emilio seemed entirely unafraid. There were no guards on this side of the island – there were no boats here, and only the open sea to welcome them if they tried to run. Still, he was studying the horizon keenly, as though searching for a route across.

'I can see why you'd rather stay here,' he said with a small, wry smile. Francesco did not reply. They hadn't spoken much since Francesco had refused to join Emilio in his escape attempt. He had noticed a change between them. Emilio spent more and more time alone. Twice now, Francesco had seen him talking with Pirelli, the older guard who had brought them the poster and its offer of a reward. He remembered the posters and their promise raining down on them in the square on San Nicola. He could not help wondering what Emilio was telling Pirelli. If Francesco came near to them, Pirelli would stiffen and stand straight, and Emilio would turn away, avoiding his eyes. When Emilio had suggested coming down to the shore, Francesco had hoped it was the start of a truce between them.

'What makes you think I would prefer to stay?' he said eventually, shielding his eyes from the sun. 'Just because I don't want to try to cross that, in a fishing boat.'

'There are other ways.'

'Is that why you have been talking to Pirelli? Don't look at me like that, I have seen you together.'

'That is nothing. You have seen nothing.'

'He is offering a reward.'

Emilio turned to him. 'You think I would do that?'

Francesco said nothing. He realised for the first time that he didn't know. He wasn't sure what Emilio was capable of.

He felt Emilio reach out and take his hand.

'You will come with me,' he whispered. 'I know you will. I know you.'

For a moment, Francesco felt himself yielding. It was such a familiar impulse, to say yes. He allowed Emilio's fingers to curl around his as they looked out together at the horizon, felt the words on his tongue, then swallowed them.

'You don't know me as well as you think.'

Emilio pulled his hand away and stood up quickly. 'All right,' he said as he began pulling on his clothes. 'But I won't ask again. And . . .' He paused and looked out again at the water. 'Maybe you will wake up one morning and find I am not here.'

'Are you coming?' Gio was waiting by the fence that surrounded the yard as Francesco and Emilio climbed back over it. He spoke in a low whisper. 'Luca has wine.'

'How?' Francesco asked, as Emilio raised his eyebrows.

'I don't know. He got hold of it somehow.'

Luca had always been able to get hold of things. Back home, he had worked in his father's grocery shop, but if you were on the right side of him, you could have anything slipped into your brown paper bag. When Francesco walked into the dormitory and found Luca standing at the table it was as though he was back there, Luca behind the counter, wearing the same blank expression as he slid the bag across, his gaze fixing you slightly too long, the bag slightly heavier than it should have been. Eight carafes of wine were on the table in front of him, almost black in the half-light.

Luca smiled at him. He looked thinner. They all did now. His shoulders sloped. They nodded to each other, as though Francesco had come by to make a purchase. For a moment, the dormitory was empty and silent, Francesco and Luca and the wine bottles still as a portrait, before the door was thrown open and the *arrusi* poured in, shouting at the sight of the wine.

Some of them had brought their own bottles, smuggled among their belongings or purchased along the way. Francesco saw Emilio go to his bunk and retrieve two small bottles of brown spirit, putting one on the table and keeping the other in his hand. He watched him taking small, slow sips from the bottle as Luca poured the wine into every available receptacle: mugs, bowls, egg cups, empty cans and tins. Francesco swallowed a sip of wine from an empty bean can and felt it graze against his lip, tasted the bitterness of his own blood with the wine.

They had taken blood from him in the hospital in Catania. They had drawn it from him with a needle, leaving behind a stinging, angry sore that did not heal for weeks. They could tell from the colour, they said. If he was one of the *arrusi*, they would know by the colour of his blood. Francesco had never asked them what colour they expected his blood to be, or what colour it should have been if he had been an ordinary man.

He put the can down and picked up a mess tin. The wine swam and flowed in its shallowness, pouring from the sides as he tipped it to his mouth. Arturo hit him hard on the back and laughed, whispered, 'Take it all down, isn't that what you do?' sideways into his ear as he poured more wine into the tin. Gio was dancing; he had wound something light and gossamer thin around his waist like a ballet skirt, and Claudio had his arms around him. They moved towards him and he felt Gio's arms around his neck, the familiar warmth of his grasp, and allowed himself to be drawn into the dance. He felt himself spinning. He heard someone cry out, 'To the dogs! Take us all to the dogs!' and felt Luca's arms around his neck too.

Someone pressed their lips to his cheek, then his mouth, their hot breath on his tongue. He saw Emilio again, leaning against the fence with Pirelli, whispering secrets, and drank more to shake the image away, heard himself cry out with the voices, 'Take us to the dogs!' then the breath in his mouth again, the warm taste of wine and saliva. Over someone's shoulder he saw Elio spinning, his arms raised, then Claudio pulling him into an embrace. He thought he saw Antonio, twirling and laughing through the crowd, but he couldn't have done: Antonio was dead; he had seen him bleeding into the dust in the square in San Antonio, he had heard the shots that killed him, echoing through the dark outside the dance hall. He stumbled into Emilio, leaning against a wall, and tried to pull him into the dance.

'We could do it now,' Emilio whispered, his voice slurring. 'Right now, before the guards come.'

'You're insane! They'd see us.'

'Not in the dark! We move fast.'

'I won't do it, Emilio. I have said already I'm not coming with you. They'll catch us, and then what would—'

'You said you'd do anything.' Emilio caught his arm.

'What?'

Emilio's whisper was strained, angry. 'That night. Outside Marcello's, the cinema. You said you'd do anything I asked you.'

Francesco shook his head, emboldened by the wine. He shrugged Emilio's hand away. Had he really said that? And how could he have known, even then, what he was really agreeing to? Who was this man, anyway? None of them had known him in Catania, not really. He had always kept himself apart from them. What reason had Francesco ever had to trust him? Hadn't everything they'd done led him here?

'I was wrong,' he whispered. 'I won't, not this. We're better off here.'

'I always knew you were a coward.'

'What—'

'Lucia! I haven't forgotten, Francesco. You always choose the easiest way.'

Francesco turned away and Emilio seized his arm. As he struggled, something fell from the pocket of his shirt. A piece of folded paper, still damp from his afternoon at the Cala. Before he could reach for it, Elio had darted over to them and seized it eagerly.

'Sending messages?' he said, unfolding it. Then his face changed. 'What is this?' He held the paper up. There was an image printed on one side of it, scrawled writing on the other that Francesco could not read from where he stood. Elio looked, suddenly, like his father. Francesco had met him a few times in Catania. He was a short man with a pinched, narrow face, who peered in suspicion at anyone not in a uniform. Elio's eyes narrowed. 'What have you been doing?'

'I . . .'

'You are collaborating with them?'

'Of course not!'

'Then why do you have this?'

Francesco stared at the paper in Elio's hands. 'I don't know. I don't know where that came from.'

'It is no surprise!' Arturo shouted. 'I have seen him taking food from the guards – the pretty blond one, wasn't it, Francesco?'

'So have I!' someone else shouted, and they all began to join in, fired up with wine and hunger. Someone reached beneath Francesco's bunk and found the loaves of flat bread he had been keeping there, raising them in the air and shouting, 'He has been hoarding, too!'

'And what do you think he does, to win favour from the guards?' Arturo shouted over them. Men began to offer their suggestions, laughing, snatching for the note as Elio held it up above his head.

'Nothing!' Francesco shouted. 'I have done nothing!' He looked for Emilio, but couldn't see him through the crowd. He felt someone kick him from behind, someone else push him in the chest. 'Are you a whore, Francesco Caruso? Is that what you do?'

'Stop it!' he shouted, turning on them. 'You don't know what . . . I have done nothing!'

'He has!' Elio shouted, holding up his hands. He sounded so certain, the chanting men fell silent. The room was suddenly quiet. 'Shall we ask him?' Elio said, turning to look at Francesco. 'Shall I, Francesco? Don't you think they would want to know?'

Francesco felt gripped by that cold fear again. The same

fear that had seized him as Favero, smiling, had drawn close to him in the yard. *I haven't said a word.*

'Please,' he whispered. 'Don't.'

'Luca.' Elio turned to the room. 'How many years is your sentence?'

'Five.' Luca sounded surprised at the question.

'Dante?'

'Five.'

'Emilio?'

'Five.'

He asked them all in turn. 'Five,' they all answered, looking around at each other, wondering where Elio was leading them.

'Francesco.' Elio took a step towards him. 'Tell them how many years you are sentenced for.'

'I . . .'

'Tell them.'

Francesco thought about lying. How did Elio know any different? Had his father told him? Was Elio's father really someone high up? Someone who knew about their sentences? Had he been talking to Favero? *The one thing that makes you different here. That singles you out.* He saw the threat in Elio's eyes, and knew that lying would be worse.

'Two,' he said quietly. 'Two years.'

For a moment, there was silence. Elio let the note fall to the floor, turning back to the men behind him. He spoke slowly. 'Two years and he will be back home. We will still be here, and he will be back home, tucked up in bed with some rich bastard policeman. He will have all the money and chocolate he wants. More than that. What has he done to deserve it, do you think?'

Francesco heard someone laughing, a low, quiet murmuring. Arturo was staring at Gio, a smile on his face.

'All this time,' he said, shaking his head. 'I thought it was you, Amazon. Turns out it was your bitch who sold us out.'

'No!' Francesco shouted, as they began to surround him.

He looked over at Emilio, but Emilio was leaning against the dormitory wall, watching with his arms folded.

'Was it you, Francesco? Did you tell the police where to find us?'

'I have done nothing!'

'How much did you sell us for? Was it just your sentence? Was there more?'

'What about him?' Francesco heard his own voice as though from a distance. He was pointing at Emilio.

'What about him?' Elio said. 'He has five years, like the rest of us. You just heard him say so.'

'Yes, but he knew something, didn't he? Before any of us, he knew what would happen, in Catania.' The sound of his own voice, its bitterness, surprised him. Emilio was staring at him from across the room, his face blank, devoid of expression. Francesco hated himself, hated the words as he said them. It was only an instinct. A kind of self-defence, a deflection. But still, the more he said it out loud, the more he realised he had always found it strange, how much Emilio had known in Catania.

'He knew, didn't he?' He felt months of anger, the frustration of hiding in shadows, rising in him. Wasn't it Emilio's fault, after all, that he was hunted, even here? Hadn't Emilio started everything? He could have stayed with Gio, they could have escaped the police together somehow. If he hadn't met Emilio, none of it would have happened. 'Before the rest of us, didn't he know that the police were coming? Didn't he warn us? How do you think he knew that?'

Luca waved a hand and poured himself another measure of wine. 'I don't care,' he said, shaking his head. 'It's all too late. I don't care what he does, what any of you do. It won't get us out of here.'

'It might,' Elio said.

'I was trying to warn you,' Emilio said quietly. He was still staring at Francesco. 'I was trying to help you. How many times did I warn you all, and you didn't listen?'

'You didn't warn *us*!' Marcello said, from where he was sitting at the table. 'The *primogeniti*, it was us who were taken first. Why didn't you warn us?'

'And how did you know?' Francesco said. 'Before any of the others, you knew something was happening. Do you know what that looks like?' The room was silent again. Emilio shook his head slowly.

'Be careful, Francesco.'

'I'm tired of being careful. It is your fault I have to be so fucking careful.'

'You should have run. Don't blame me for that. You always choose the safer way, prefer to hide. You should have run while you could. When I told you to.'

'How did you know?'

'Does it matter?'

'Yes,' Marcello said quietly. 'How did you?'

They were circling Emilio now, some of them clenching their fists. Emilio stood for a moment at the centre of the empty space between them, and Francesco felt a thrill of fear at what he might do. The moment felt frozen, as though time had stopped moving. Francesco looked towards the doorway, suddenly realising how late it was. The light around the door frame was gone.

The doors flew open and the guards were there, guns raised. Francesco saw Favero among them. As their eyes met, Favero looked away. The first blow sounded distant as the butt of a gun landed on a head heavy with wine.

Thirteen

The *arrusi* were confined to their dormitories for a week, as punishment. Inside, the doors padlocked shut, the temperature rose steadily. They had only two enamel chamber pots, which the guards took to be emptied each morning, the smell issuing from them hanging in the air long after they had gone. The atmosphere grew thick and stagnant.

Francesco spent the first night lying beside Gio on his bunk. Cups and jars were still scattered across the floor. Eight empty carafes stood on the table.

'Is it true?' Gio whispered. The dormitory was silent, but for the soft snores and sighs of sleeping men.

'What?'

'You know what. Your sentence. Only two years. Is that true?'

Francesco hesitated, then nodded. Gio lay back, staring at the ceiling, shaking his head. 'Why? You must know.'

'They didn't tell me. I didn't know about the rest of you, until we were here.'

Gio turned to him. 'You know what they will all think. Francesco, you didn't—'

'Of course not.' He took Gio's hand. 'I couldn't. You know that.'

Gio stared at him for a long time.

'Anyway,' Francesco went on, 'I believed you, didn't I? When Arturo told everyone you had betrayed us, I stood up for you.'

Gio nodded slowly. 'And what about him?'

'Who?'

'You know who I mean, Francesco. Do you think he really knew something, in Catania? What you said last night – do you think he knew this would happen?'

'Of course not. I mean, he warned us. But he didn't know . . .'

'You shouldn't trust him,' Gio said suddenly. 'Emilio. I don't care what you do with him. Just don't forget what he is.'

'What he—'

'He isn't one of us.' Gio took Francesco's hand and pressed it to his chest. 'He was hardly ever there – the dance halls, the *arvulu rossu*. He doesn't understand us.'

'He is not one of the *primogeniti* either,' Francesco said, staring over towards Emilio's bunk. 'He is not on anyone's side.'

'Be careful. That's all. I saw how they looked at you last night. You know what they'll think. You'll be out in two years, and the rest of us still here. You think they'll just let that go?'

'They'll forget about it.' Francesco lowered his voice further. 'In a few days, Arturo will be off at someone else.'

'Francesco, you must know why they only gave you two years.'

Francesco thought for a long time. Then, turning back to Gio and holding his hand tighter, he said slowly, 'I suppose it is because I gave myself up.'

'You didn't run?'

'No,' Francesco said quietly. 'I didn't run. I just sat there and let them take me. Maybe that's why.'

As Gio slept, Francesco lay awake, imagining the possibilities. A knife in the dark. Waking to cold steel against his throat. A rope, to make it look like he had done it himself. Something in his food, or just enough beatings the guards chose to ignore. The cliffs. Emilio couldn't stop them forever. He thought of Emilio sitting beside him on the rocks beneath the midday sun. *You will wake up one morning and find I am not here.*

The paper that had fallen from his shirt pocket was still lying in the centre of the room where Elio had dropped it. Easing himself out from beside Gio, Francesco crossed the dormitory barefoot and picked it up, taking it back to his own bunk. A few of the *arrusi* stirred and grunted in their sleep.

He unfolded it slowly. Rapetti's thin, dark-eyed face stared up at him. It was a torn scrap of the poster Pirelli had pinned to the wall, weeks before. Francesco looked up at it, remembering Pirelli's voice. *You will tell me everything. Five years is a long time to stay silent.*

He turned the paper over. The words on the other side were written in a tight, neat hand. Not the semi-literate scrawl of the *arrusi*. The writing was fluid, easy. Though the ink was slightly blurred, he could still make out the words.

> *Man is man only by virtue of the spiritual process to which he contributes as a member of the family.*

He stared at the paper. Was it a threat? If so, who was it from? Almost none of the *arrusi* could write like that. None but Marcello, Elio and perhaps Michel, who had studied at the university. But why would they leave him a message? He turned it over again. In the bottom left-hand corner, drawn on top of the photograph, was a tiny rough sketch. A rose, its stem dotted with thorns.

'Tell me something, *arrusu*. What will you do?'

Francesco pushed the paper hurriedly into his sleeve, and looked up at Arturo standing beside him.

'What?'

'With your three years? The three years you will have back home while the rest of us are still here. I am interested to know what you will do with them.'

On the other side of the room, Emilio sat up in his bunk.

'I hope it was worth it. Whatever you had to do for it.'

'I didn't do anything.'

'Really? Elio says he has seen you taking food from them. Did you do nothing for that either? And the bread – the rest of us starve, while you have all you want.'

'I could teach you to make it.'

'What?'

'The bread. I could—'

Arturo laughed. 'Where I come from, *arrusu*, it is the women who make the bread.'

'Do you see any women here?'

Arturo leaned down and put his face close to Francesco's. 'I'm not one of yours, *arrusu*. I don't bake, or sew. I take what I want. I take the women I want. That's what real men do.' He spat at the ground.

'If you are a man, then why were you taken? Why are you here?'

After a pause, Arturo turned and looked over at Emilio, sitting up in his bunk and watching them.

'It is his fault,' he said. The two of them stared at each other across the dormitory, as though at opposite ends of a ring. 'I spent too much time with him, back home. I thought he was a friend. I didn't know, did I? I didn't know I was hanging out with a *recchione*.'

Francesco stood up and felt himself raising a fist without thinking. He was thrown backwards, the rough plaster of the wall at his back. He closed his eyes, waiting for the blow to fall, but when he opened them, Emilio was holding Arturo by the collar.

'I told you,' Emilio said quietly. 'You touch him again, and I'll kill you.'

Arturo laughed. 'But you haven't.'

They both looked at Francesco, still pressed against the wall.

'You think you can keep us from him?' Arturo shook himself free of Emilio's grip. 'You think we won't make him tell us what he did, to get two years? Two years!' He kicked at the floor. 'We will beat it out of him, if we have to!'

'You will leave him alone. Or I will not leave you alone.'

For a moment, Arturo's gaze flicked back to Francesco. Then he shrugged, and walked back to his bunk. He laughed as he settled himself down on it, but something in the laughter felt forced.

*

When the week was over and the doors were opened, they stumbled into the sunlight, dazed and exhausted. Francesco sat in the shade of the trees in the far corner of the yard, watching the rest of the *arrusi* start up a lacklustre game of football, kicking a piece of black flint through the dust. A spade was lying beside him, but he couldn't find the energy to dig. When he saw Emilio leave the dormitory, he stood up.

'Planning a tunnel?'

Emilio didn't stop pacing. 'Maybe,' he said, staring at his feet in the dust.

'Maybe we should all live underground, like rats.' Francesco smiled, but Emilio said nothing. Francesco tried to keep pace with him, but Emilio was quick, as though trying to evade him.

'I'm sorry, Em. What I said that night. I was drinking.'

Emilio stopped. He still didn't look up. Eventually, he sighed. 'I've been thinking. You were right, the boats are a stupid idea.'

'Not as stupid as tunnelling.'

'There are other ways. You were right about that.'

Francesco remembered Arturo on his first night. *There are three ways to leave the island*. 'What are you going to do?'

'If you have a sick relative, they let you go home.' Emilio raised his hands. 'Simple.'

Except it couldn't be that simple. It couldn't possibly be.

'All we have to do is write a petition.'

'They'd go with you. Make sure you didn't run.'

They'll give you hell if it turns out not to be true.

Emilio laughed. 'Are they Catanians? Do they know that city like we do?'

Francesco looked up. Above them, a single bird was circling lazily against the bright sky. He tried to picture home: the Via Calcera, the castle, the restaurant, Lucia leaning over her balcony. The port, busy with tugs and fishing boats, children wading barefoot through the shallow muddy water. He had begun, already, to forget the city's details. It came to him in grainy, washed-out images, like underdeveloped photographs. It was lost to him, whatever they did now. The dance hall, the shadows beneath the railway arches, the *arrusi*'s hidden world. They could never go back, whatever happened to them.

'All we have to do is wait,' he said quietly.

'Five years. For some of us.'

'If we just wait . . .'

'That's what you said then!' Emilio punched his palm in frustration. 'When I told you to run. You didn't want to know what was happening. You are always choosing safety, always—'

'A coward?'

Emilio put up a hand in warning. Santoro was pacing the fence close to them.

'Will you help me?' Emilio said in a lower voice.

'I'm not going with you.'

'All right, but will you help me? I need someone to write my petition.'

'Em, why are you so desperate to leave?'

'Will you help?'

Emilio's poor writing skills hadn't mattered much back home. It had never given Francesco any power over him before. He had enough to write out receipts at the mechanics' yard, sums and names, his own signature, and that was enough. Francesco's own literacy had never seemed much use to him until now. What need did a dishwasher have of language? *You never know when you might need it*, his father used to say as they sat in the library in their house in Naples, reciting the alphabet and constructing sentences. *You never know.* Flicking through books, his father's arm around him, drawing Francesco so close he could smell the cigarette smoke on his breath. His mother was always there too, sitting across from them, folding the pamphlets, addressing envelopes. Always working, always fighting. If someone had asked him then which of them would push the fight too far, which of them he thought he would lose to it, he would have chosen her.

Slowly, he nodded. 'All right. But it's just a petition. I don't know anything about the truth of it, you know?'

Emilio put his hands on Francesco's shoulders and sighed. 'I didn't know anything more than you. Back in Catania. I just wanted you to be safe. You believe me?'

'How did you know I would be there, that night at the dance?'

Emilio smiled. He did remember, then. 'I told you then. I was looking for you.'

'We hadn't even met.'

'I saw you, though. All the time. In the park, under the tree, in the dance hall. You came to the mechanics' yard once, with your bike, do you remember? You spoke to Arturo.' Emilio shook his head. 'You didn't even look at me.'

'I didn't know.'

'You were always with him.' Emilio looked over his shoulder to where Gio stood bent over a spade, digging the soil of their vegetable garden, his face red with exertion. 'I swear,' he said, turning back to Francesco, 'I just wanted to talk to you. Everything else, your father, all of that, it came later. At first, I just wanted to talk to you. I didn't want things to go the way they did.'

'I know.' Francesco wondered if he was as sure of it as he sounded.

'I asked everyone,' Emilio said, smiling at the memory. 'They all called you Femminella. Beautiful Femminella. And you were.'

He looked suddenly sad. He put a hand out to Francesco's face, tracing the curve of his brow, his cheek, as though searching for something he had lost.

'I'm sorry, Francesco. For what I did to you. For what it cost.'

Fourteen

Catania, August 1938

Francesco sits beneath the railway arches by the port, dangling his bare feet in the water. It beats against his calves with the motion of ships in the docks. The sun is high over his head, pooling on its rippling surface.

The railway arches don't feel so safe in the daylight. He can hear the crowds behind him, the rattle of carts on their way to the fish market. He isn't used to seeing the brickwork in the sun; the arches are not black and shadowed, but a deep, soot-stained grey, marked by the passing of so many trains overhead. He puts out a hand and runs it across the rough, curved wall beside him. Wonders if the arches were once clean, the colour of sand and stone.

More footsteps; he hunches his shoulders, drawing his damp feet up onto the wall, as if making himself smaller will help him to hide. Anyone passing would see him sitting here, would question what he is doing, who he is. He always feels exposed, in the sunlight.

The streets are decked with flowers for Ferragosto. He has agreed to meet with Emilio tomorrow, during the festival. The streets will be thick with people; easier for the two of them to move unseen about the city. But now that what they have planned is only a day away, he doesn't know what to do. He has the photograph of his father in his hands, the photograph Emilio gave him that night after the dance hall, its edges soft and frayed. He stares into his father's face as though expecting the image to look back at him, the expression to change, to recognise him here in this new city. As though his father will tell him what he should do. He has already given Emilio an answer, but now he is away from him, away from the strange, helpless obedience he always feels when they are together, he wonders if he should change his mind. Whether there is any other way to keep his family safe.

He hears voices over the footsteps, somewhere close behind him, and turns quickly, thinking of Rapetti at the dance hall, his arms around Gio's waist. But it is only a couple, walking past the arches, arm in arm. The woman is wearing a dress of light blue linen, the man a crumpled shirt, unbuttoned at the collar. As they pass Francesco's arch, the man stops, looks around him quickly, then pulls her to him and kisses her lightly on the mouth. She pushes him away playfully, and they move on, laughing. Francesco watches them go, their footsteps perfectly in time. After they have left, he breathes out, and turns back towards the sea.

In his darkest moments, moments he would never confess to his mother, or to Gio, he wishes he could have someone else's life. That man's, perhaps, walking with a woman on his arm. The woman, her face calm and untroubled. Or even one of the police, Rapetti or his men. The simplicity of their goals. It should be so easy to change, to slide into another fabricated life – he has done it before, more than once. He wonders if Emilio would ever consider such a change. He would think it cowardice, what Francesco is contemplating.

He turns again, letting his feet slide back into the cool water. He holds the photograph up and remembers the day he came to Sicily with his parents, so long ago. Climbing the volcano with his father, the hot steam on his hand, the water bottle, winding his fingers through his father's hair as they climbed together, balancing on his father's shoulders. He could have that life back, perhaps. If he could find his father again, if he could just know where he has gone, what happened to him, that would be a way to change.

In the corner of his mother's room, tucked behind the curtains, is a metal box, padlocked shut. She has the only key.

Inside it is everything they still have from their life in Naples. There isn't much. Nearly everything was burned, to keep them safe. He knows there is a photograph inside a tiny locket, and a bundle of letters. A ring his father used to wear, which could hardly be used to prove anything. He has never seen the rest. His mother opens the box sometimes when she is alone; Francesco has seen her through her open bedroom door, sitting on the edge of her single bed and sifting slowly through its contents. Sometimes he wonders whether, if the police ever come for them, she will have to open the box and throw away everything inside it.

He wants to keep his father's photograph. He has no idea how Emilio came to have it, but now it is the only one he has. All he has left. But it isn't safe, he knows, to keep such reminders of the past.

A voice behind him says, 'Who is he?'

Francesco turns quickly, and breathes a sigh of relief to find it is only Antonio, standing in the shadow of the archway. He sits down beside Francesco and pulls off his shoes, then begins to roll up his trouser legs.

'We missed you at the dance last night,' he says. 'That man was there again, looking for you. Emilio. He said it was important.'

Francesco doesn't answer. He is thinking of the night at Marcello's. Antonio, sitting at Emilio's feet. The men, turning to look at him where he stood awkwardly in the doorway. Antonio's voice grows quieter. 'What do you know about him? Emilio?'

Francesco shrugs. 'Nothing.'

'Really? I thought, that night at Marcello's . . . I thought perhaps you knew.'

'Knew what?' Francesco turns to him.

'Nothing,' Antonio says hastily, turning away. 'Nothing. What are you doing with that photograph?'

Francesco looks down at his father's face. He remembers,

suddenly, an argument with Gio a few weeks back over a photograph taken of the *arrusi.* It was Antonio's birthday. Dante had taken the photograph in the restaurant, capturing a moment when Antonio turned from the table and beamed at him, in the middle of a joke. All of them, together. It wasn't safe, Gio said, to keep the photograph. Dante should burn it. What if the authorities came to his house and found them; what if they knew about one of the men in the pictures; what if it condemned the rest? Francesco remembered the look on Antonio's face in the picture; he was just a child, grinning into a camera. If you looked closely, you could see the dark lines pencilled around his eyes. Evidence, Gio had said. Francesco had hated him for saying it, because he knew it was true. It wasn't safe to keep photographs. It is never safe to keep anything from hidden lives. He wonders if Dante ever listened to the warnings, or if he kept the photograph after all.

He looks down into the water. It is thick with oil and sediment churned up in the wake of ships, but he can see his ankles through a few clear centimetres. See the darting of dull-coloured fish through tendrils of mud-dark weeds. It must be quiet down there. Peaceful. It would be so easy to disappear himself, to loosen his grip on the wall, to allow himself to sink down with the fish and the weeds and the dark.

'Is he someone you know?' Antonio asks, easing his feet into the water.

Francesco shakes his head. 'It's no one.' He lowers his hands, lets his fingers open and watches the photograph fall. It settles on the surface of the water for a moment, the sunlight still reflecting from its edging, the whites of his father's eyes, and then it is lost to the dark.

Fifteen

San Domino, August 1939

'What do you want to say?'

Francesco was bent over a sheet of paper, a blunt pencil in his hand. The door to the yard was thrown open; the dormitory was lit up with sun. Most of the *arrusi* were inside, sheltering from the midday heat. Francesco was relieved to find Arturo was not close by; he had been taken away early by Pirelli, who had begun to interview the *arrusi*, one by one, about what had happened to Rapetti. All of them were waiting anxiously for their own turn to come.

'I don't know,' Emilio said, pacing behind him. Francesco didn't need to say it; the truth was in the air between them. Emilio had no family in Catania. Francesco had agreed to go along with his plan, to help him write his petition asking to be allowed to go home, but he had always known it would come to this. The admission that there was no one at home to attribute his lie to. In Catania, Emilio had been alone.

'Say it is my brother.'

Francesco looked up from the paper. 'You don't have a brother.'

'You think they are going to take the trouble to check?'

Francesco sighed and put the pencil down hard on the table. 'Do I think they would take the trouble? Let's see.' He marked the points on his fingers. 'They took the trouble to make a list of *arrusi*. They took the trouble to research where we lived, where we went. They took the trouble to take us to the hospital and do those tests, and then they took the trouble to ship us out here, at God knows whose expense, and keep us here for the next five years.' Emilio raised his eyebrows. 'All right, two years, for some of us. But still. Do I think they would bother to check? Yes, I think they would bother to fucking check if you have a brother. I think they probably have already.'

'Fine. Say it is a cousin.'

'I don't think you should do this.'

'I'll get someone else to write it. Michel – I'll do his digging for a week. Or Marcello would, if I found something to pay him with.'

'If they find out . . .'

'Why didn't you tell me?'

Francesco looked up. 'Tell you what?'

'About your sentence. Two years.'

'This again.'

'Yes, this again.'

Francesco looked around the room, feeling the eyes of the *arrusi* on him. He had felt watched ever since Elio told them. He knew what they were all thinking. He knew what they would do to him if Emilio was not here to stop them. 'Because of this,' he said, gesturing to the room. 'Because of the way you all look at me.'

'I don't care. I know you. Better than any of them. You should have told me.'

Francesco sighed, and bent to the paper again. 'What are we calling your cousin?'

Emilio was not the only *arrusu* Francesco was helping. They had all begun to compose petitions. They had laughed at Elio Duchessa and his talk of letters from his father, that first day. Now, there was hardly a man among them who did not sit at the table long after the sun had set, dictating words of supplication that Francesco wrote out for them, showing them how to shape the words. 'My father's shame,' Luca said. 'I long to serve my country in battle' – Arturo. *My mother*, Francesco wrote, in letters that had grown increasingly desperate as the heat of summer intensified. Please. My mother.

In the prison in Catania, a lawyer who had been held for soliciting male prostitutes had helped the *arvulu rossu* boys to draft their appeals, writing out arguments in complex, elliptical sentences Francesco could make no sense out of. He wished he had learned more from the man now. He didn't know what had happened to him, but he was not with them on San Domino. Perhaps he had been more successful in pleading his own case than theirs.

Marcello sat at the table beside him, composing petitions for the *primogeniti*. They did not speak, but as he wrote out Emilio's petition, Francesco watched the lawyer at his work, the clean, elegant curve of his handwriting, and a thought came to him. Leaning forward towards Marcello and keeping his voice low, he said, 'Was it you?'

'Was what me?' Marcello said without looking up.

Francesco reached inside his shirt pocket and pulled out the sheet of paper that had been left there. Marcello took it, peering over his glasses. He stared for a long time before handing it back.

'Why would I write out passages from the Doctrine? I have better things to do.'

'Someone wrote it. It was left for me.'

Marcello shrugged. 'One of yours, then.'

'They don't write.'

'One of the guards.'

They stared at each other for a moment. If Marcello was lying, there was nothing to give it away in his expression.

'Why would it be one of the guards?'

'I don't know,' Marcello said, bending to his work again. 'Anyway, I doubt it was one of them. They have other things on their mind. War, for example.'

'You think it is coming?'

Marcello said nothing, but balanced his glasses back on the end of his nose, peering at the petition he was working on.

'What is it like? Being in a war, I mean.'

The old man stared back at him for a long time without saying anything.

'It is loud,' he said at last. 'And fast. Dirty. There is not much time to notice anything else.'

'You were at Caporetto.'

Marcello's face became hard and unreadable. 'Yes, I was there.'

'Was it . . . as they say it was?'

He had heard stories of German troops firing canisters of poison into Italian trenches. Men in their thousands smothered by thick clouds of gas. Those who were left killed with mines, machine guns, even flames.

Marcello shook his head. 'You should ask him,' he said, indicating someone behind Francesco. 'He knows as well as I do.'

Francesco turned. Emilio was standing by the open door, staring out at the sun-baked yard.

'You were in the war?'

Emilio didn't move. Francesco stood and put a hand on his shoulder. He shrugged it off.

'You never told me.'

'What should I have said?'

'You never said anything!'

'It was a long time ago.'

'Were you at Caporetto?'

'It was a long time ago,' Emilio said again. 'I don't remember. I don't try to remember.'

'But if you were there, Em, you must have been . . .'

'Fifteen,' Emilio said quietly. 'I was fifteen.'

In the early hours of the morning, Francesco woke from a dream of Emilio at Marcello's apartment, smiling, perched on the edge of Marcello's chair, exchanging stories of the war. They were dressed in uniform, their hair slicked down beneath felt caps, guns strapped to their backs. In the dream, Francesco's father was there, uniformed too, laughing at something Marcello said. When he saw Francesco standing in the doorway, he stood up and calmly closed the door, leaving Francesco alone in the stairwell, exposed to the open sky.

As the sun rose, Francesco was woken again by the sound of crying, somewhere close to him. Dante was lying curled in his bunk, a photograph beside him on the pillow. Francesco knew which photograph it was. The image of Antonio in the restaurant, the day of his birthday. Dante had kept it, despite all Gio's warnings.

He looked up, and met Francesco's eyes. Francesco slid from his bunk and went over to him. Around them, the *arrusi* were beginning to stir.

'It is his birthday,' Dante whispered, nodding to the photograph. 'Today is Antonio's birthday.' He lay back, staring blankly at the ceiling.

After the morning count, the boys of the *arvulu rossu* gathered around the table, the photograph of Antonio laid out in front of them. The doors to the yard were open, the sun so brilliant it had found its way through every crack in the dormitory roof, filling the room with a thick, humid heat. Outside, the yard was a furnace, pale dust open to the sky. Around them, the *primogeniti* were moving disinterestedly about the dormitory.

'We should do something for him,' Claudio said, staring at the photograph. 'We never really did.'

Luca shook his head. 'We should have done something then. We should have found out who killed him, for a start.'

Francesco thought of the night Antonio had died. Standing in the square, watching a thin river of blood weave its way towards him. Gio and Emilio standing on either side of him, urging him to run. Screams, rising in the night air. It felt like so long ago.

'It doesn't matter now,' Dante said, putting a hand to the photograph.

'Of course it matters!'

'Do you think it's true?' Gio said quietly, looking over his shoulder at the *primogeniti*. 'What they say – what Antonio did.'

'Of course not,' Dante said with finality. 'He would never have turned us in, given them our names. I knew him.'

Later that day, when the guards were not with them in the yard, some of the *arvulu rossu* boys ducked beneath the wire fence and walked across the island through the pines, to the cliffs at the north edge. Dante led them, carrying Antonio's photograph. As they followed the path through the trees, Francesco looked back and saw that Favero and Pirelli were following them, wary of their sudden pilgrimage. He had been trying to avoid Favero as much as he could, since that day in the yard, but always when he saw him, he felt the guard's eyes fixed on him. He wondered where they imagined the *arrusi* would run to. How they would stop them if they all hurled themselves over the cliffs together.

The hole in his boot had widened, the grass soft and cool through it. As they walked, crossing in and out of shadows cast by branches overhead, Emilio edged closer to him.

'At least Antonio was spared all this,' he said with a small smile.

'How can you be so—'

'The police killed him,' Emilio said firmly.

'Did they?'

'Francesco . . .'

'It's our fault. You know it is.'

'Stop it. We agreed we wouldn't talk about that.'

'Don't you want to? How can you bear it? Sometimes I want to tell everyone. At least then—'

Emilio seized his arm. Francesco winced at the strength of his grip. 'This isn't a game, Femminella. You understand? We say nothing. They'll kill us. They'll throw us off a cliff, or something worse. Wouldn't you?'

'It's finished,' Francesco said as they reached the edge of the pines. Beyond the trees was nothing but a thin band of rocks, then a sudden drop to the sea below. 'Your petition. You have a sick cousin at home who needs you.'

Emilio nodded. 'I'll have to move fast, once I'm there. If there's anything you want me to do, I'll have to be quick.'

Francesco knew he meant his mother. He had been trying not to think about her, these long weeks, because there was nothing he could do. She was alone. He tried not to think of how it would be for her now. The neighbours would not speak to her. The story must have spread through the city like fire. Would she even be able to go out, after the shame he had brought her? Would it mean closer scrutiny, someone eventually coming across a paper, a hint in a police report, something that would lead them back to Naples, or worse, to his father?

'Would you try to see her?' he said quietly.

'Of course.'

'I've written something.' He tried not to think of its contents, denying everything, denying what he was. 'If you could give it to her . . . tell her I'm sorry.'

'Do you think it will work?' Emilio said, looking over his shoulder. 'The petition, I mean.'

'I don't know.'

'Do you want it to?'

'It's not fair to ask me that.'

'I must think of something else if it doesn't.'

'You would try again?'

'Why? Would you stop me?'

There are three ways to leave the island.

'Em. Don't.'

Emilio flicked a cigarette from behind his ear. Francesco held out his lighter, as he had done so often in the dark. They stood together, hands cupped around it as the flame took.

Emilio took a long breath and breathed out wreaths of smoke as thin as sea foam. 'Have to,' he said, and Francesco felt the smoke in his own mouth, filling his throat like drowning.

The prisoners gathered together at the cliff edge, staring down at the drop. Emilio stood a little apart from them as Dante stepped forward and held out the photograph of Antonio.

They had no instruments. Some of the *arrusi* had been members of the dance hall orchestra; they might have played a solemn march to honour their friend. Instead, Francesco heard them trying to hum a tune together, a funeral march. Most didn't know the notes, and those that did hummed them too low, so that they were lost in the wind hurrying across the water as Dante let the photograph fall.

As they watched it twist on the air, Francesco felt the ground begin to shake. It started as a tremor beneath their feet, as though something deep within the earth was trying to speak. The edge of the cliff was visibly moving against the sea; particles of earth and larger clods shook themselves over.

Some of the *arrusi* threw themselves suddenly to the ground and lay flat, arms over their heads as though avoiding gunfire. Others ran from the cliff edge, afraid of being thrown over. Francesco sat down, laying his palms flat against blades of grass, feeling the shaking intensify beneath him before stopping with a sudden stillness. He looked up. Emilio had remained standing. His face was expressionless, as though he had not even felt the earth moving beneath him, or had known all along that it would happen. There were so many things he didn't tell me, Francesco thought, studying Emilio's face, how calmly he stood there amongst them as the tremors subsided. So many things Emilio had concealed from him. So many things he had hidden himself, in return.

He looked at the other *arrusi*, crowding together at the cliff edge. What would they think of him if they knew what he had done? Would he change before their eyes? Would everything they had thought about him up until that moment fall away? And when it had, would it be the real Francesco they were seeing beneath it, or was that only another fiction?

He clutched at the ground and closed his eyes, feeling weightless, untethered. He thought of the night he had found Emilio in the courtyard. *I was looking for you. You were so hard not to notice.* How could you ever be sure about anyone, what was really underneath the surface, why they did what they did?

The land felt changed, after the quake. Francesco wondered if San Domino was a fraction taller, or lower, or if the sea had risen higher around its edges.

Nothing is as safe as it feels, he thought, watching Emilio stamp hard on the ground, as though testing his weight against it. Not even solid ground.

Sixteen

Catania, August 1938

> Probably Judas belonged to the group of feminised males . . . who betray just like jealous females.
>
> A. Signorelli, *Sesso, intersesso, supersesso*, 1928

On the morning of the Ferragosto festival, Francesco is so surprised to wake with someone beside him, he almost jumps from the bed. When he remembers, he leans back and pulls Gio to him, feeling their damp skin press together, their legs tangled beneath the thin sheets. Gio smiles against his shoulder.

'Shh,' he whispers into Francesco's skin, still half asleep as Francesco opens his mouth to speak. 'We're not as alone as you think.'

Gio's parents were called away just before Ferragosto, and work kept him from going with them. The rest of his family were all gathered in Taormina. It was Francesco's mother who had offered, when she heard. 'He can stay with us,' she said, patting Francesco's hand. 'He is your friend. Ask him to come to us.' Francesco hadn't wanted to. Not this day, of all days. She thinks he is sleeping in the small box room beside the kitchen, but early in the morning he had crept into Francesco's room, sliding himself silently into the bed beside him.

Francesco glances at the clock: Emilio will already be waiting for him. Francesco chose the day himself. The city will be packed, but mostly with travellers from other cities, taking advantage of the special fares offered by the regime. Ferragosto is a time for taking trips. Many of the *arrusi* have already left the city, and those that have stayed will try to remain out of sight.

It has not always been this way. In the early days, after he first started frequenting the dance hall, he remembered joining in with the parades. The *arrusi* revelled in their public displays, dressing themselves in skirts and sequins, painting their faces, twisting ribbons and tassels through their hair, defying the laws that banned the wearing of costumes in public. Suddenly, for a day, their whole selves could be exposed to the sunlight. When Molina began enforcing the ban more harshly, some of them continued anyway, revelling in their defiance of the regime, until it beat them to the ground.

Gio is still half asleep, murmuring with his eyes closed. Francesco looks down at him, his hair matted against his cheek, his skin soft and tanned deep by the sun. He looks so young. The contours of his skin are so familiar. We have to stop this, he thinks. He wants to love Gio, as he did once, as Gio still loves him, and strains for the familiar ache, but there is nothing there any more. Gio may blame the man from the courtyard, Emilio, the night the police came, the night he and Francesco were pulled in different directions, but it started long before. Perhaps years.

It does not make it easier. What Francesco has decided to do, what he has agreed to. He sometimes wishes he had never sought Emilio out again. That he had never known the choices he has. He hears his mother coughing in the next room, and holds on to the sound, glad of it for once. She is his reason. He is already hell bound, if the police and the churchmen are to be believed, but this will not be another millstone to weigh him there. His reasons are pure. *God sees all your sins.*

Gio presses closer to him and smiles, falling in and out of sleep. Francesco watches him, stroking the soft skin at the nape of his neck, thinking, all the time, of Emilio. Emilio's arms around him in the Piazza Stesicoro. His voice, whispering in his ear: *I can help you, Femminella.* The scent of his skin. How much simpler everything would be if he had never met him.

*

It is easy to move unseen through the Ferragosto crowds. Francesco walks quickly, trying not to look at the procession, at the bright clothing and the rows of men from the cathedral, dressed in white robes, in case there are faces he recognises. They are moving in thick, winding threads towards the sea, drums beating in time with their feet, children hoisted on their parents' shoulders to watch, women dancing and laughing through the crowds. Francesco weaves his way between them, the crowds so dense he is sometimes lifted almost from the ground. He sees men marching in regimented step, their arms stiff and straight, their uniforms crisp. He tries to imagine what it would feel like to be one of them, to be a soldier. He tries to draw strength from them, for the war he is about to enter, for what he is about to do. Do they feel fear before a fight? If they do, they must press it down somewhere inside them. He wishes he knew how.

Emilio is waiting for him in the castle square, outside the restaurant. It is closed for Ferragosto, all of its staff and most of its patrons already on trains or boats on their way to the mainland. Emilio is sitting at a table, three of its four chairs still upturned on it, drumming his fingers against the wood. Despite what is coming, Francesco feels a jolt of excitement at the sight of him. Emilio stands quickly when he sees Francesco.

'Ready?' he says, taking his hand. Francesco feels stronger in his presence. There is something about the way Emilio looks at him, the faith he has in him, that makes Francesco braver. Still, he shakes his head.

Emilio smiles sadly. 'Let's go anyway.'

The office is dark and cold. Francesco feels an immediate instinct to turn from the door as it opens, and he sees the flash of a pressed uniform, medals shining on felt. Behind the uniform, a wide, polished desk, papers piled neatly, a clock, its pendulum swinging lazily against the flagstones. The blinds are closed. Thin fingers of light have forced their way through the gaps, patterning the floor. Francesco cannot help imagining his cheek pressed against that floor, a boot on his fingers, cuffs around his wrists. The rush of flames behind him in his father's library. *Non mollare.* Never give up. Never strike first. He shakes the thought away.

'You have brought him?' the man inside the uniform says to Emilio. Emilio inclines his head slightly. Francesco does not like this evidence that he defers to someone. He has never known it before of Emilio.

'Yes. Francesco Caruso,' Emilio says as they walk into the room. That's it, Francesco thinks. They know my name. No going back. 'He frequents the dance halls.'

Francesco feels Emilio's hand on his back, pushing him forward. Is it reassurance, or impatience? Their shoes are loud against the flagstones.

The man looks at Francesco searchingly, his eyes moving over every inch of him. The corners of his mouth curl, his nostrils pucker as though he is smelling something unpleasant.

'Does he?' he says slowly. His hair is slicked back neatly against his skull. 'Well, not for very much longer.' Francesco feels as though he is being stripped.

'Anything else?' he says, turning to Emilio. Emilio, his eyes cast down, shakes his head.

'Well then.' He motions to the door. Francesco feels a thrill of cold fear as it shuts behind Emilio. As his eyes adjust to the darkness, he feels the man in the uniform lean closer to him, and finally looks up at his face. Rapetti, his hands behind his back, smiling a thin smile.

'Your friend thought you would not come,' he says, looking at the door. 'He said we could never convince you. But I know you. I know what an *arrusu* is. You betray. You turn against your own. Like women.'

Behind Rapetti, above the desk, hangs a metal plaque inscribed with italicised words:

Man is man only by virtue of the spiritual process to which he contributes as a member of the family.

'At least this way you can do something of use to your country. That is a consolation, I imagine. You can even atone for your father, perhaps.'

Rapetti sits down behind the desk. He looks too young, Francesco thinks, for such an office. Barely older than the boys of the *arvulu rossu*. He leans forward and picks up a folder. Opening it, he turns it round so Francesco can see. The photograph of Francesco's father. Beneath it, a paragraph of text, and below that, printed in bold capitals, *FILIPPO AMELLO. MANCANTE*. Missing. There are more papers. A birth certificate bearing Francesco's name. His parents' marriage certificate. A photograph of his mother that makes his insides lurch with fear.

'You understand what this means?' Rapetti says slowly. 'You understand what I could do with it?'

Francesco, not taking his eyes off the image of his mother, nods. He has always known. He had thought all the evidence had been burned, that there was nothing tangible left of that life.

'You are lucky, in a way,' Rapetti says. 'You, and your mother. Though I imagine she knows nothing of your . . . condition.' He smiles conspiratorially, and Francesco feels suddenly sick. 'If you were an ordinary man, I would simply share this information with my colleagues, and bring you both in. As it is, I think you can be of more use to me this way.'

Francesco has an image of his mother sitting in a jail cell, standing trial before a room of strangers, after everything they have endured. He knows then he will go on, no matter what it costs.

'So, Francesco Amello,' Rapetti says, beginning to leaf through the papers. Francesco flinches at the sound of his own name. Rapetti leans forward and draws another sheet of paper from his desk. This one is blank. He picks up a pen. 'San Antonio. The dance hall. Tell me names.'

Seventeen

San Domino, August 1939

There had never been a Ferragosto like it. Francesco woke early to the scent of flowers, and opened his eyes to see the dormitory filled with them, as though it had been flooded with petals in the night. Dante, Michel and Mattheo were running between the bunks, laying out more, laughing as men sat up sleepily, rubbing their eyes, breathing in the heavy sweetness.

'We are supposed to take trips, on Ferragosto,' Dante said, as he pushed a handful of flowers into Francesco's hands. 'Well, we have. Here we are! Six hundred miles from home.' He laughed, an edge of hysteria to his voice. Francesco stared at him, thinking of the day he had written Dante's name on a sheet of paper, Rapetti, leaning over him, casting a shadow across the words.

Gio was sitting alone at the table. He turned as Francesco sat up. Francesco tried to return his smile, but found his mouth was dry. Gio was already wearing his costume for the performance they had planned, a red dress Mattheo had made for him. Mattheo had dyed a cotton sheet himself, squeezing the dye from berries that had fattened in the San Domino sun, pushing the cloth into the sticky puddle of juice. Looking at it, Francesco remembered the shirt he had tried to dye for Gio, so long ago, which had come out streaked and patchy. That was the night in the courtyard. Gio's birthday, and the first raid.

Mattheo pulled him up and threw a garland around his neck. When Santoro came to unlock the doors and count them, there was not a man lined up before him who had not been decked in flowers. On any other day they would not have dared, but they felt emboldened by the festival. In Catania, it would not even have been legal, this wearing of costumes. Such laws no longer mattered.

Still, they stood opposite Santoro for a moment in tense silence, before the guard laughed, lifted Francesco's garland with the tip of his gun, and spat on the floor.

'You may have your festival,' he said, raising a hand as though to strike Gio, standing defiantly in his red dress, before letting it fall. 'But if you are not back here at eight, do not think we will not be waiting for you.' He moved towards the door. As he went to open it, he stopped, and turned around. 'Something else,' he said, smiling now. He approached Emilio. Francesco saw, for the first time, the piece of paper in Santoro's hand. 'I have heard from Molina, in Catania.' His voice was casual, as though he were sharing an anecdote. 'He tells me you have no family there. No one at all is waiting for you.'

Emilio stood rooted to the spot. Francesco could see his shoulders shaking with the effort of it. Santoro moved closer to him and put the piece of paper in his hands. Francesco recognised his own handwriting.

'Do not try that again, *ragazza*,' he whispered. 'I will not tolerate lies, from any of you.'

Emilio stared back at him, his fists clenching at his sides. When the guard had gone, he screwed the petition into a ball and threw it at the wall, kicking at a chair as he returned to his bunk.

Francesco picked up the petition and smoothed it out, staring at the words he had spent so long writing. He had known it was hopeless from the start. He couldn't help feeling relieved.

The yard was decked in flowers too. They were draped over the crates Claudio had gathered together for a stage, across the dry branches of the trees, even the fence. Walking out into the heavy sunshine, Francesco thought of his last Ferragosto. Emilio, waiting for him outside the restaurant. The cool darkness of Rapetti's office. The sound of his own voice, unrecognisable, reciting names. Friends. It seemed so long ago. He seemed, in his memories, to have been a different man. He caught Luca looking at him and heard himself saying *Luca Marracchini*, Rapetti's pen working across the page. He tried to concentrate, not to think about that day, what he had done, as though the memory of it all might somehow write itself across his face. But every pair of eyes that met his reminded him.

'Francesco! Help us with the stage,' Claudio called, dragging more crates across the yard. Francesco stared at him. How did they not know? Or did they – were they only waiting for the right moment? How could he stay with them, today of all days, and not give himself away?

He turned away from Claudio and climbed over the fence, walking swiftly up the path away from the dormitories before they could call after him. When he reached the pines, he turned north, towards the beach. He would bring them more flowers. He would gather flowers in the woods like an offering, and then he would go back and join in with the festivities, and no one would know. He tried not to think of Emilio's petition. What Emilio might try now that it had been denied.

Beyond the trees, the sea was still, the sun high and full above the water. On the beach, he saw islanders gathering around boats, ready to row them towards San Nicola, or towards the larger ships waiting further out to sea. These, he thought, must be taking them to the mainland for the Ferragosto celebrations. He wondered if anyone but the *arrusi* would be left on San Domino by nightfall.

He saw a patch of colour in the grass ahead of him and began carefully pulling small pink flowers from the soil. He laid them in his basket, where they looked like a bed of confetti, ready for a wedding, and thought of the church in Catania. Standing below an altar decked in flowers, listening to priests talking of shame and retribution. Lucia waiting for him there, dressed in white silk. The wedding day he had never had.

He heard something move behind him, a cracking of twigs

underfoot, and ducked behind a tree. From behind it, he saw the figure of a woman approaching his basket, peering into it, then around her, looking for its owner. He recognised the girl he had seen beside the road on that first morning. She was wearing a yellow cotton dress, her hair loosely plaited. There was a streak of mud across one of her cheeks, and a tear at the hem of her dress. Climbing trees, Francesco thought with a smile, as he stepped out from behind the tree.

She took a pace back when she saw him, and raised one arm as though in defence.

'It's all right.'

'What are you doing?'

'Collecting flowers.' He took one of them from the basket and held it out to her. She didn't take it. She knelt and pushed her hands into the basket, sweeping the flowers aside. Beneath them, he had filled it with anything that seemed to be edible: berries, mushrooms, late fruit fallen from the trees.

'Don't eat those,' she said, holding up a thin grey mushroom. 'They are poisonous.'

Francesco took it from her, nodding his thanks and tossing it into the trees.

'What's your name?'

She said nothing. She was staring at him, studying his face with eyes narrowed in concentration.

'Mine is Francesco.'

She smiled then, and repeated the name. 'Francesco. Where have you come from?'

'The Cameroni district. On the road towards the Cala Tramontana.'

'No, where have you come from really?'

He hesitated. 'That way,' he said, pointing towards the sea. She turned in the direction of his hand.

'The mainland,' she said, staring out to the horizon.

'Close. Sicilia.'

'Are there cities?'

'Yes.'

'Cathedrals?'

He laughed, and nodded.

'Are you going back there?'

'I don't know. I hope, one day.'

She looked as though she had been about to say something, then stopped. 'Elena,' she said after a pause. 'My name is Elena.' She was still studying his face. A blush spread across her cheeks as their eyes met.

'Where do you come from?' he asked.

Without moving her eyes away, she pointed back through the trees towards the village. Francesco held out the flower again, and she took it, looked at it for a moment, then pushed it through the rough plait of her hair. She smiled at him, then something in her face changed.

'Is it true?'

'Is what true?'

'They say things about you.'

Francesco shrugged. 'I don't know. What do they say?'

She hesitated, then shook her head. 'Just things. Why do you need so many flowers?'

'For the festival. Ferragosto.'

Elena nodded. 'We go to San Nicola.' Francesco thought of the square. Coviello. The children, lined up like armies. 'I wish I could stay here,' she said. 'For your festival.'

Francesco smiled. Suddenly, as though she had heard something behind her, Elena took a step back. He looked, but could see no one.

'You could take me with you,' she said quickly.

'What?'

'When you go home. Back to the mainland – will you take me with you?'

'I don't know if I'm going back. And,' he looked around him, 'why would you want to leave?' The sea was still and calm behind them, the air heavy with sun and the scent of flowers. Francesco could not think of anywhere more beautiful, even without the threat of war and imprisonment back home.

'Please.' She took another step back. 'Please don't forget me, if you go home.'

Before he could reply, she turned and ran back through the trees. Francesco stared after her until she had disappeared. In the thick, dull heat, he could almost believe he had imagined her.

He returned to the dormitories as the sun was at its highest. The yard was filled with flowers and costumes. Gio was pacing up and down in his red dress, the skirt fluttering lightly in the breeze. Most of the other *arrusi* were inside, avoiding the heat, but there was a figure standing by the fence. Favero, smoking a cigarette. He flicked it away as he saw Francesco approaching.

'There you are.' He smiled, and Francesco felt cold all over.

As he climbed through the fence, he felt Favero's hands on his arm, helping him through, untangling his shirt from the wire. He tried to shake the hands away as he stood on the other side of the fence, but Favero's grip tightened.

'Come with me,' he whispered.

He led Francesco to the far side of the dormitory, overgrown with creepers and vines, out of sight of the rest of the guards. It was dark and damp away from the sun. Favero pushed him against the wall, pressing his body against Francesco's.

'You wrote that petition, didn't you?' he whispered.

Francesco said nothing.

'The man with no family. I know he couldn't have written it himself.'

Francesco looked down. A spray of purple flowers was growing from the dry earth by the dormitory wall. He focused on their petals, their deep orange centre, as he felt Favero's hand on his chest.

'I asked you for your price. Why do you not ask to go home? You write petitions to some office you have never seen, when you have only to ask me.'

'I am not a whore,' Francesco whispered.

Favero smiled. 'Everyone is, for the right price. Do you want them to know about your sentence? Only two years, when they all have five.'

'They already know.' Francesco smiled at the look of irritation that flickered across Favero's face. 'I told them.'

He gasped as the guard pushed him against the wall, an arm against his throat. Favero's face, usually calm and smiling, was suddenly red with anger. 'Do you think that's all I can do to you? Decide for me how much you are worth, *arrusu*. All right?'

He pulled Francesco forward and slammed him back against the wall.

'All right?'

Francesco nodded slowly.

'It will be better for you. I have seen the way they all look at you. I think your friend will not be able to protect you forever.'

Francesco flinched again, expecting the blow to fall, but the anger in Favero's eyes had cooled. He smiled, leaned forward and kissed Francesco lightly, letting his hands reach around his waist. Francesco found he couldn't move. He stood still, allowing Favero to run his hands over his body, before the guard pushed him to the ground and walked away.

Francesco sat in the alley, waiting for the yard to empty as the prisoners went back inside to prepare for their performance. His palms were grazed where Favero had pressed them against the wood. The dampness of the leaves was soaking into his clothes. He heard the laughter of the men, thought of Emilio and Pirelli, standing so casually together at the fence. Favero's arm against his throat. *Decide for me how much you are worth*. He was alone. All it would take was for Emilio to leave, to find some way out. He wouldn't last long after that.

Elena watched her mother carefully pinning a hat to her perfectly rolled curls. She was squinting at the cracked mirror that hung by the open doorway, pursing her lips and alternately frowning and grinning at herself as she brushed the final hairs into place. The two of them were alone in the house. For the first time Elena could remember, her father was not coming with them to San Nicola for the Ferragosto celebrations. He was staying with the prisoners at the camp. Her brothers were staying too; using the excuse of wanting to learn more about his work to avoid the festival.

Elena didn't ask him why the prisoners were not being taken to San Nicola. She thought of the man she had found picking flowers, Francesco, his pale skin gaunt and tight over his face, so much thinner than the last time she had seen him up close, the day they were brought to the island. *I don't know if I'm going back*, he had said. She had felt a sting of fear, that no one was ever able to leave San Domino, once they had found their way here. But then she had thought about him staying. They could not be prisoners forever. She remembered the empty house she had found, the furnished rooms beneath layers of dust, waiting for her. Imagined herself in the narrow kitchen, Francesco moving behind her, his hands on her waist. She felt again the softness of the petals between her fingers as she had pushed her hand into the basket he had been carrying. The cold, furred edges of the mushrooms he had gathered. She thought of the strange, quiet way he had looked at her, so different to the way other men did. Imagined a bed, soft sheets, silk against her skin. She had saved him. He might have eaten the mushrooms otherwise. Already, she had made him a gift.

Her mother hummed a tune as she smoothed out the last of her stray hairs before the mirror. Something had changed in her in the last few days. There was a new lightness to the way she treated Elena, a carefulness, as though her daughter had suddenly become more valuable. Elena would find her clothes had been washed and pressed for her, where once she would have done it herself, and her share of food suddenly equal to her father's and brothers'. She could not account for the change, and something about it felt unwelcome, as though another part of her childhood self had gone missing.

She waited for her mother in the yard, dressed in her too-tight uniform for Ferragosto. As she paced the dry earth, she saw something flash white in the sunlight, buried in the soil. It was one of her paper birds, pressed into the earth. She bent and pulled it out. The paper was yellowed, dry and cracked. It must have been one of last summer's birds. She smiled at the thought of it waiting here all this time for her. She folded it back into shape and threw it into the air, where it seemed to hover for a few seconds before falling back. As it landed, she kicked at it, as though that might encourage it to fly.

When she heard her mother calling, she found she didn't want to go back in. The calls grew louder, until Elena was surprised to hear an edge of fear in her mother's voice. Still she didn't move. She sat on the ground beside the bird, folded up and useless, hidden by the shadows of the house. She sat without moving, until the shouting stopped, and she heard the slamming of a door.

After a few more minutes of stillness, she stood up. Brushing the soil from her knees, she went back inside and stood at the mirror she had watched her mother at. She frowned at her face. Her cheeks were pale. Her hair static and unbrushed. She scraped it back against her skull, teasing out the tangles, flattening it with her palms, and pinched at her cheeks until they were faintly pink. Then she left the house in the direction of the Cameroni district.

A haze of heat had settled over the island through the early afternoon. It rose from the pale paving slabs of the village, thickening the air. Elena's feet were loud in the emptiness, stepping between pools of sun. Beyond the house, the fields of wheat had been stripped bare of their crop, bundled together in islands amongst a sea of gold.

She walked quickly past the empty houses of the village without pausing to look inside them, and on to the square. The fascist headquarters, a two-storey ochre building, stood along one side of it, its windows staring over the square like empty eyes. At times, the square was filled with police officers, but today there was no one. The island had been emptied for Ferragosto. She might be the only one left, but for the prisoners and their guards.

She turned left after the village, taking the road towards the Cameroni district. She knew, as soon as Francesco had told her, where it was the prisoners were being kept. There were two low huts, long since abandoned, on the road towards the sea. She had walked past them many times, and seen men there, police and prisoners milling about, but she had never dared to move closer. Today, something about Ferragosto, the emptiness of the island, the way her mother had begun to treat her as an equal, emboldened her.

The huts had been there, sinking into the earth, for years, but they had been patched up and the land around them cleared to make a yard, ringed with barbed-wire fence. Their roofs had been remade with terracotta tiles, bright orange against the sky.

She edged closer, using the shadows of trees and bushes to hide herself. Most of the prisoners were out in the yard, gathering around a pile of crates that had been dragged to the centre to form a low platform, covered in flowers. A few guards were standing around watching them disinterestedly. Elena didn't recognise her father at first. His cap was drawn low over his eyes. He was standing strangely, stiff and upright, his chest puffed out. She stared at the gun strapped to his back. His hands were hidden within dark leather gloves. His face was empty of expression. Unrecognisable.

As she watched, four of the prisoners stepped up onto the makeshift stage. She recognised one of them at once as Francesco. Their faces had been painted, bright streaks across their cheeks, over their darkly lined eyes. One of the other three was wearing a dress of red material, which hung ill-fittingly from his thin shoulders, and trailed in the dust. He was holding an apple in his hand.

She stared at them. She had never seen men dressed in anything but shirts and trousers before. She had never seen a dress like it before, not even worn by women on the island. She watched the man moving, poised, elegant, and thought of all the times she had imagined herself in such a dress, walking through crowds along elegant tree-lined streets on the mainland.

He held the apple up and stood in front of the three other men in turn. Elena studied their faces; they were costumed too, not in dresses, but with strips of white linen looped around their waists, across their chests, like sashes. One of them had wound a red scarf through his hair. It hung from his shoulders like a turban. Francesco was wearing a piece of cloth around his neck, a pale scarf, wound once about his throat.

The man in the red dress stopped longest in front of Francesco. Everyone in the yard watched them as they stared at each other. Even the guards were paying attention now. Elena saw her father standing a little way off on his own, his arms folded tightly across his chest.

The man in the dress took a step forward and held out the apple. 'For the fairest one,' he said in a soft voice, and she remembered the story, the goddesses, the competition. It didn't make sense; they were supposed to be three women, and the man with the apple wasn't supposed to be wearing a dress. None of it made sense. She watched Francesco hold out his hand and take the apple. Held her breath as the man in the dress leaned forward and kissed his lips.

It only lasted for a second or two. A second through which she couldn't breathe. Everyone else was silent too. Then she heard a cough, and a stifled whisper, laughter hidden behind hands. Turning her head, she saw her brothers crouched behind a tree close to hers. Marco was holding back the leaves, and both of them, their heads pressed together, were watching the yard with eyes as wide as her own must have been.

She didn't see how it began. One of the men in the crowd threw something, which struck the man in the dress on his cheek. He turned quickly, a hand raised to his face. Then another of them called out, '*Recchione!*' and they were all shouting, rushing at each other. A tall prisoner built like a bull seized Francesco and pulled him back, throwing him to the ground. The man in the dress watched them for a moment, then turned and ran to the fence, ducking under it and away towards the trees. As he ran, the tall man, still holding Francesco by the arms, shouted after him. She could not make out any of his words except the last, which he shouted in a clear voice that carried across the still air. *Caporetto*.

As he shouted, another prisoner collided with him, pushing him to the ground and striking his face, again and again, until Elena could hear the man's groans echoing across the clearing.

The guards rushed towards them then. Elena remembered her father on the road, the whip raised. She closed her eyes.

'What's the matter with you?'

Emilio didn't move. He was handcuffed, the chains looped around the metal leg of his bunk. He lay on his back, looking up at the ceiling. Cracks of sunlight streamed through spaces in the roof, lighting up the lines of his face. His eyes, swollen with bruises, were closed.

'For God's sake, Emilio! At least wait until the guards aren't around. Are you trying to get yourself killed?'

'Leave me alone, Francesco.'

He sat on the bunk and tried to take Emilio's hand. The chains rustled as Emilio moved his hands away.

'Would you just stop? He won't keep going at me if you just leave it alone.'

'Is he alive?'

'Arturo? Yes, he's alive. They've taken him to Foggia.'

Emilio opened his eyes then. 'Foggia?'

'Yes, there is nothing they can do for him here. He is too . . .' Francesco shut his eyes, remembering the blood, the mess of Arturo's face. 'Why did you do it?'

Emilio turned away.

'Is it because of what Arturo said?'

'What?'

'Caporetto. He said Caporetto, when Gio ran.'

'He was going to hurt you.'

'No. He wasn't. Tell me why, really.'

Emilio lay still, his face turned to the wall.

'You were there, weren't you? Caporetto – you saw it.'

Emilio was quiet, but Francesco could hear him breathing. It did not sound like the breathing of a sleeping man. He reached into Emilio's pocket and found a cigarette, bruised and bent. He put it to his lips and lit it with his own lighter, then passed it to Emilio, who took it without looking round.

'Em, what was it like?'

'It was a long time ago. I was young.'

'You could use it!' Francesco said, trying not to speak too loudly in his excitement. 'In your petitions. Wouldn't they think about letting you go home if they knew you had fought? If there is another war—'

'Go away, Cesco.'

'What was it like?'

'Hot. Go away.'

As he turned to leave, the doors opened. Santoro crossed the room and stood at the end of Emilio's bunk, Pirelli a little way behind him.

'I hope you have had time to think' Santoro said quietly, ignoring Francesco. Emilio did not look at them. 'I will not tolerate acts of violence. But if you think this will get you sent away, you're wrong.' He knelt down beside Emilio. 'I will keep you here for as long as it takes to burn your perversions out of you. You will not be sent to Manfredonia, or any other prison. You can start as many fights as you want. Understand?'

On the other side of the room, Pirelli took out another of his posters and nailed it to the door. Francesco stared at the image. The dark, piercing eyes he knew so well. He remembered the first time he had seen them, standing in the square in Catania, watching Rapetti speak. Rapetti's eyes had swept over the crowd as though he could tell an *arrusu* with a single glance. Francesco remembered the anger that had flamed in him, the fear. *This evil must be cauterised. Burned to the core.*

Eighteen

When they finally let Emilio out, pale from lack of sunlight, his wrists bruised by the chains, Francesco took him out across the island, north through the cool shadows beneath the pine trees, trying to encourage the life back into him with sunlight and air.

He didn't speak. He allowed Francesco to lead him where he wanted to without showing any sign of interest.

'Are you angry?' Francesco said, when they had reached the cliff edge. It was the place where they had gathered to say goodbye to Antonio. He remembered how Emilio had tried to persuade him they were not to blame. *The police killed him.* I am not alone in being naive, Francesco thought. He thought of how the ground had shaken beneath them, how Emilio had stood still while the others threw themselves down. Emilio, standing at the edge of the cliff. *Sometimes I think about throwing myself over.*

'Angry?'

'That they didn't send you away. That's what you wanted, isn't it?' *Piss them off badly enough, and they'll take you to the prison in Manfredonia.*

He felt Emilio take his hand.

'I'm not angry,' he said. Then, after a long silence, in a different, quieter voice, 'I'm afraid.'

They stood together at the cliff edge. The sun was searing, beating fully on their faces. The sea was calm below them, breaking against the rocks in a quiet ripple of song. It had seemed like such freedom, at first. Francesco had thought he was safe on this island, that he was leaving everything they had done behind him. But it was all trapped here with them.

'They know,' Emilio said quietly.

Francesco swallowed, and felt a hard knot in his throat.

'They can't. You don't know—'

'Of course they do.' Emilio kicked at the grass, sending a hail of stones over the edge. 'They know someone has betrayed them, anyway. They already suspect you. They'll work out the rest sooner or later.'

'What do we do?'

Emilio sighed, and lay down in the grass. Francesco lay down next to him. He wanted to lean closer to Emilio. To feel Emilio's arm around him.

'We wait,' Emilio said. 'You have less than two years now.'

'What about you?'

'I fight.'

Francesco looked up at him, unsure what he meant. 'And when we get back?'

Emilio shook his head. 'We might as well not talk about that now.'

'I do remember, you know.'

'What?'

Francesco turned to him. 'That day, in the mechanics' yard. I came with my bike – you said I didn't notice you. I did.'

He had wheeled it in, holding the broken chain, and stopped beside Arturo, who was leaning over the open bonnet of a shining black car. As he waited, he had seen a man standing by another car, taking money from a customer. He didn't know why, but there had been something about him, the way he spoke to the woman, the easy, patient smile he gave her, which asked nothing in return. Something, too, in the way he stood, in the shape of his body, the way his hair fell across his eyes. As he watched, the man looked over at him and their eyes met briefly. Francesco had flushed, and looked away.

'You were wearing blue overalls. There was a streak of oil on your face. I wanted to wipe it away.' He flushed again now, and began studying the tiny pale yellow flowers that dotted the grass between them.

'Why?' Emilio asked.

'Why? I . . .' Francesco stopped. He had never wondered why. The truth was, he didn't know. Only that he wanted to be with Emilio, to talk to him, to be close to him, always. He wondered if this was a part of his perversion too. Maybe others, those who loved naturally, always knew why.

Later, as they walked aimlessly through the deserted streets of the village, Francesco saw a flash of yellow cross their path. He thought it was a bird at first, then saw Elena's face staring at him from behind a pine.

'Come out,' he said, holding out his hands. 'It's all right.'

She crossed the path and stood in the road in front of them.

'You shouldn't be here,' she said, her arms folded.

Emilio smiled at her. 'Yes,' he said. 'I know.'

They walked through the village together, past the rows of empty, unlived-in houses. Francesco stared at their shuttered windows, thinking of all the families that could have come here. The rooms that could have been filled, the children that could be running through the streets.

In front of him, Emilio stopped, then walked forward slowly, as though the silence that hung in the air was something temporary, timid, as though a sudden movement might scare it away. They looked at each other in the sunlight, the shadows chased back by it, and smiled. Who put out a hand first? Francesco thought it was him, but as he did so, he found Emilio's already there, and they pulled themselves into each other easily, as though drawn by magnets, tied together by their secret. They found a rhythm as if there was music around them, and danced through the silent, empty streets as though people were watching them from every window.

Elena led them south from the village towards the thick belt of pines Francesco had never explored before. The land sloped steeply downhill. As they followed her, the path became increasingly narrow, until they were pulling away branches and pushing through closely knotted thickets of thorns and brambles. Then they were climbing again, steeper and steeper, until they came through the last of the trees and found themselves suddenly surrounded by empty air, standing at the cliff's edge. Elena was gone.

They stood for a moment listening to the low hum of insects, the rustle of leaves. A tiny green lizard darted out from the undergrowth and crossed their path, dancing close to the edge and then back. They heard a cry from somewhere below them, and Francesco saw a narrow path leading down through the rocks to the water below.

Elena was standing at the bottom, where the rocks flattened out into a platform above the sea. They scrambled after her, their feet sliding on the uneven path. 'Look,' she whispered as they reached her, pointing. In front of them, flat dark shapes were laid out on the rocks, glistening in the sun. As Francesco stared, one of them moved, rolling over close to another beside it. They were seals, lying fat and contented in the sun. They didn't seem to be alarmed by the proximity of men. They weren't used to it, he realised. Men never came here.

As they stood watching the sea ebb and flow in the spaces between the rocks, Elena took a piece of paper from her pocket, folded into the shape of a bird, and flung it at the water. It sat for a few seconds on the surface, drifting slowly away from the shore. Francesco thought he recognised the face on the paper, in the seconds before it sank beneath the waves.

Ahead of them, past the still blue-green sea, the shadow of the mainland was just visible amongst the clouds.

Elena turned and looked at them. 'Can you get there? The mainland.'

They stared at her, unsure what to say.

Eventually Emilio said, 'Of course we can get there.'

'I doubt they would have us back again,' Francesco said, looking at him.

She studied them both, as Emilio lay down on a flat rock, stretching his arms behind his head.

'Is it true you have forgotten how to be men?' she said, squinting at Francesco against the sun. 'That's what they say about you.'

'I don't know,' he said. 'I think so.'

She nodded. 'That's why you are here. Like the Diomedee birds.' She pointed at the sky, where dark shapes circled.

'How like them?'

'They are not really birds.'

'Aren't they?'

She shook her head. 'They are men. They were trapped here on their way home from the war at Troy. They have forgotten how to change back.'

Francesco smiled, and she looked indignant. 'You can hear them,' she insisted. 'Haven't you heard them calling out at night? Screaming? They want to be rescued. They want to remember how to change back.'

He lay beside Emilio in the sun, watching Elena pace the shoreline. The day seemed to be stretching out forever, as though someone had stilled the sun's progress through the sky. He wanted it to be always like this, always noon, always bright sunshine, always Emilio beside him. For a moment, he allowed himself to imagine they were the only two souls on San Domino. If he could have Emilio with him, he would wish for it. He didn't care about going back any more. If the world hated him, wouldn't it be better to live in a place like this, where there was only sea and sky? He felt Emilio take his hand, and turned towards him. Their eyes met, and Emilio smiled, as though he was thinking it too. He put out a hand and traced the outline of Francesco's cheek, his forehead. His fingers moved to the soft skin of Francesco's throat, down to his chest, feeling their way between the buttons of his shirt, making him shiver. Then they heard Elena's footsteps close to them, and Emilio drew his hand away.

As they lay there, Francesco remembered the night he and Emilio had stood beneath the railway arches, clinging to each other to hide from the passing police. It had been dark then. The sea had been loud beyond the arches, and Emilio had turned to him, shown him a picture of his father and whispered a question. Sometimes Francesco felt he had not been the same man since he heard it. *I can help you*, Emilio had said, fighting Francesco's reluctance to answer, to consent. *And your mother. All we have to do is help them.*

'What have you been doing with Pirelli, Emilio?'

At his voice breaking the silence, a flurry of birds flew up from the trees behind them. Emilio did not flinch from the question. Francesco was almost disappointed. It was as though some small part of Emilio's spirit, his defiance, was gone.

'He offered me a trade,' Emilio said flatly. 'My freedom if I told him what happened to Rapetti.' He looked away from Francesco, out towards the sea.

'And did you?'

'How could I?'

'But you could have said something . . . anything. Made something up, even.'

'I couldn't,' Emilio said, raising a hand over his eyes against the sun. 'It wouldn't be fair. I just couldn't.' He looked at Francesco, and Francesco was surprised to see tears in his eyes. 'I'm sorry.'

'Why?' Francesco almost laughed. 'I'm glad. Why be sorry? You're still here.'

'He told me there were other ways, he would do what he could for me, but I knew it was a lie.'

'Of course it was. It's all right.'

'He probably wouldn't even have kept his word.'

Francesco nodded. 'You're probably right.' But as he said it, he thought of Favero, offering him the chocolate, smiling at him as though they were equals. *Decide for me how much you are worth.* What could he demand? What would he be willing to ask?

'They are going to be extinct, you know.'

Elena was behind them, pointing at the rocks where the seals lay fat and unafraid, their soft bellies exposed to the sun.

'No,' Emilio said quietly from where he lay, 'I didn't know.'

'Soon,' she said, turning to him, 'one day, everything on this island will be dead. Gone.' She made a slashing motion with her fist. The violence of it surprised Francesco. 'Wiped out!' she said, smiling towards the sky.

This time, the note was in his trouser pocket. He didn't find it until he and Emilio were walking back together, dulled and happy with sun. Elena was ahead of them. He hoped she had not been seen with them. As he slowed his pace, allowing her to move further away, he put his hand into his pocket and felt a piece of paper there. He drew it out without much interest, and unfolded it.

He recognised the neat, italicised handwriting at once.

War alone keys up all human energies to their maximum tension and sets the seal of nobility on those peoples who have the courage to face it.

The paper was the same, too, the poster of Rapetti, the offer of a reward. Beneath the quote, the drawing of a rose, its stem studded with thorns. But it was what was written beneath, almost as an afterthought, that made Francesco's breath catch in his throat.

He glanced at Emilio. He was staring up at the sky, his face furrowed in concentration. Always thinking of escape. Always planning something.

Francesco looked down at the paper again, read the final words on it over and over, his head pounding. They were printed in capitals.

NON MOLLARE.

Do not give up.

PART THREE

War alone keys up all human energies to their maximum tension and sets the seal of nobility on those peoples who have the courage to face it. All other tests are substitutes which never place a man face to face with himself before the alternative of life or death.

Benito Mussolini, 'The Doctrine of Fascism', 1932

Nineteen

The moment has arrived when the arrow must leave the bow, or the cord, too far stretched, will break.

Benito Mussolini, Naples, October 1922

Francesco is standing at the top of the staircase of the great house in Naples, staring at the library door. He can hear voices behind it. His parents' voices, and another, a man's voice, talking in low whispers. He remembers what his father said earlier, before Francesco was sent to bed. As they sat in the library folding the pamphlets, *NON MOLLARE* written across them in bold, heavy type. *I am going away for a little while.* And he saw something, tucked into his father's belt. Wondered what it meant.

He knows what they are talking about. He is only seven, but he is not as stupid as they think he is. The man they are all afraid of has given his speech, and soon he will be leaving. Marching towards Rome. To rule the world, his father says.

He knows it was a gun he saw. He has been lying awake thinking about it, filling in the space in his memory until that is what is left. His father has a gun. Not pamphlets or books or words. A gun.

A door is banging somewhere in the house. He listens to the voices, trying to make out words. It is not so unusual. His parents often have gatherings late at night. But something about this one sounds different. There is no laughter, no clinking of glasses. Only whispered, urgent voices. Doors being opened and shut softly, footsteps attempting to be silent.

He descends the staircase slowly, barefoot. The door to the library is half open. Shadows are moving inside. Putting his eye to the opening, he sees his father pouring a measure of something into a clear crystal glass, handing it to someone and pouring out another for himself. His mother, in her white silk dressing gown, is frowning over the glass already in her hand.

'They have no suspicions,' the other man says, swallowing the contents of the glass. He is young. Shabbily dressed in a shirt and coarse brown trousers. Not like the people they normally bring to the house.

'Perhaps,' his father replies. He empties his glass in one. He is staring at his hands; they are shaking. He wipes them on his shirt.

'I need to know if we can count on you,' the shabby man says.

'Filippo—' His mother's voice is quiet. Francesco recognises the warning tone.

'I know.' He cuts her off.

'What have you always said? Never strike first.'

'I know.'

She crosses the room and puts her hands on his face. Francesco has never seen her look so urgent. Her eyes are open wide. 'There are other ways,' she says slowly. 'The pamphlets. Soon there will be a manifesto—'

'A manifesto! Another document. More words.'

'Words are what he uses.'

'It is what they expect of us,' the other man says. 'We have to fight them with something new. Something bolder.'

'And you will use my husband to do it.'

'We use the best tools we have.'

'He is a teacher! He knows nothing of war.'

Francesco is waiting for her to say his name. What about your son? What about Francesco? Although he doesn't know what they are planning, he knows he feels afraid. But she doesn't say his name.

'It's not right,' she says quietly. 'How can I stand by you if you do this?'

He puts his arms around her and pulls her close. Francesco

can hear her crying against his shirt. 'How can I face you if I do nothing?' his father says. He is crying too. Francesco has never seen a man cry before. 'It is a war, Margherita. I am only doing what I have to, to survive.'

A clock strikes somewhere in the house, and they all look towards the door, towards Francesco. He draws back. Presses himself against the wall. It is best to hide. It is safer that way. A channel of light from the library is stretching across the carpet towards him, another of moonlight from the uncurtained hall windows. He slides into the shadow between them. Presses his arms against his chest until none of the light can touch him, until he is hidden completely, holding his breath in the dark, saying a prayer in his head that he will not be found.

Twenty

San Domino, September 1939

It happened on the first day of September, but San Domino knew nothing of war for another two weeks. By then, according to the voice on the newly mended radio, Poland was overrun. The news passed a shiver of excitement through the island, to which no one was immune. Elena's father began to rise earlier to attend meetings at the fascist headquarters in the square, vigorously polishing his shoes before leaving the house. Her brothers practised sword fighting with sticks on the beach, and spent long afternoons sitting alert by the radio, grinning over it at one another as the voices told stories of attacks and counter-attacks, troops and marches and mutilating gunfire.

Elena watched the island, waiting for something to change, for this new state the world was in to manifest itself somehow in the air. Her mother's fussing had grown even more attentive; Elena had been made new dresses, had her hair styled and even been allowed to keep a small stick of rouge in her room, for festival days on San Nicola. She didn't understand what it was all for, why any of it mattered now. The war, so long promised, had finally come, and now nothing would be the same. At last there was something new to be excited about.

Her mother's principal source of excitement appeared to be the possibility that it might remove the prisoners from the island. A few days after news of the war came, Elena crept out of bed and listened at the kitchen door to her parents' hushed voices.

‘They cannot keep them now.’ Her mother was whispering, triumphant.

‘You should hope that they do,’ her father returned. ‘What will I do for work otherwise?’

‘There will be plenty of work now; you needn’t worry about that.’

‘Not if I can’t find out what happened to that wretched policeman. He will not let me keep trying forever.’

‘Then try harder.’

‘And what about Lena?’

Elena pressed herself closer to the door.

‘You needn’t worry about her, either,’ her mother said, a hint of pride in her voice. ‘I’ve seen to that. It will be fixed by Christmas. Sooner, if we join in the war by then.’

Elena lay awake that night thinking about what her mother had said. *It will be fixed by Christmas.* What did she mean? Or sooner – Italy had not yet joined the war, but everyone said it was only a matter of time, as though they could see into Il Duce’s mind. What would be done with her then?

And the prisoners – did they even know the war was happening? What would happen to Francesco, when it came? What would happen to the prisoner on San Nicola, who had promised her he would take her with him when he was finally free? She looked for him now every Saturday, as Coviello delivered his endless speeches. The last note had been passed to her as she arrived in the square, pressed hurriedly into her hands. It had not been difficult to pass it on as Francesco lay dozing in the sun with the other man, Emilio.

She had no idea what the notes were for, what they said, but a flicker of a promise had passed across the man’s face when he gave them to her, as though he understood her longing. He had promised her he knew how to get to the mainland. That he would not leave her behind if she did what he asked. She would have everything she wanted once they were there. A life free from expectations. Did he know, she wondered, that time was running out?

When she finally slept, it was long and dreamless, and the morning was half done by the time she woke. She got up hurriedly and took her usual walk around the island, but the air was humid and the sky grey. By the time she returned, she was shivering.

In the kitchen doorway, she found her mother waiting for her, looking tired and anxious. She put out a hand and pulled Elena roughly inside.

'Where have you been? We have been waiting.'

Elena shrugged, then looked up. There was a woman standing by the stove. She was plump and red-faced, her arms crossed over a shelf-like bosom. As Elena stared, the woman unfolded her arms and put her hands on her hips.

'Yes,' she said, not seeming to address either of them. 'She will do.'

Elena felt her mother pulling at her coat and sliding it from her shoulders. The woman was staring at her with narrowed eyes. She reached out with fat fingers and touched Elena's bare arms. Pulled them out to her sides, as though she were measuring the wing span of a bird. Elena's sleeves hung loose, allowing currents of cold air to reach in and settle around her skin. She shivered as the woman ran her hands along her waist, feeling the curve of her hips. She realised she had seen her before, among the crowds on San Nicola for the Fascist Saturday.

'Her cycles are regular?'

Her mother, standing in the background, nodded.

'My son will inherit his own grocery store,' the woman said, still patting at Elena's skin. 'And all the men in our family have several children.' She turned her head. 'You know the store, I think. Your husband—'

'Yes,' Elena's mother said quickly. 'Yes, we know it.'

'It was a pity, that,' the woman said, clearly enjoying her subject. 'So hard to keep people on, especially now . . .'

'Yes.'

'Well, perhaps if we can come to an agreement here, he will have a place there again!' She laughed, an unexpected burst of sound. Elena flinched at it. Then her face became serious again. 'But for now, he is doing well for himself, at the camp?' She wasn't looking at Elena now, but her hands were still around her waist, as though she had forgotten to take them away.

'We are comfortable.'

'Well.' Finally she dropped her hands. Elena found she was unable to move. She stood still, her arms sticking out like aeroplane wings. 'We can come to an arrangement, I think. Soon, I hope. Especially if . . .' The woman hesitated. 'My son will be anxious to take part, if we are to fight. There will need to be children first, if—'

'Yes. Of course.' Her mother wasn't looking at either of them now. She had turned away, leaning her hands on the stove.

The woman reached out again, and Elena felt her arms being lowered back to her sides. As she stood there, she remembered watching one of the women on the other side of the island sitting with a flock of pigeons one afternoon in the summer, slowly and patiently clipping their wings. The way, afterwards, they had stumbled on the ground, lifting their feathers, trying to rise into the air again, finding themselves weighed down at last. Defeated. She sat down slowly at the kitchen table.

'We will see you on Saturday?'

'Yes, of course.'

The women kissed each other's cheeks and clasped each other's hands. As her mother led her visitor out, Elena heard them talking in low voices, then the sound of the door closing softly.

When she looked up, her mother was sitting across from her at the table. They sat in silence for a long time.

'Is it Nicolo?' Elena said at last. She thought of all her

mother's attempts to encourage them to talk, on Saturdays. Nicolo, standing mutely, his eyes flickering between Elena and his feet, his cheeks reddening whenever she caught him staring at her.

'Yes.'

'Why now?'

'We have to be practical, *furetto*. If your brothers go to fight—'

'We have not even joined the war!'

'But we will. And if your father loses his job—'

'He won't,' Elena said quickly. Her eyes lighted on the posters Coviello had left with them. A small pile still lay on the kitchen table. She stared at the face of the man in the photograph. Someone had killed him, and her father was charged with finding out what had happened. Which of the San Domino prisoners had done it. Surely that was the way to keep his job.

'Even if . . . The prisoners won't be here forever, *furetto*. We need to think about the future. We need to think about it now, while your father is still working.' Her mother reached out and took Elena's hands in hers. Elena shrank back instinctively. The two of them rarely touched. Her mother's hands were cold and thin. Red from years of scouring and washing. 'Try to understand, Lena. You will be looked after. We all will be.'

'She said I would have children.' She pulled her hands away, clasping them instinctively around her stomach. Her mother sighed.

'There are . . . advantages. If you have children, the government give you more money. You will be helping the war effort.'

'I don't want to help the war effort.'

She took Elena's hands again, but this time her grip was firm. 'Sometimes we have to do things we don't want to,' she said in a slow voice, as though Elena were still a child. As though she could never understand. 'We have to, to look after the people we love.'

Twenty-One

'Thank God we are here,' Gio said, sitting beside Francesco. Most of the others had gone out into the last of the sunshine. Only Elio was lying on his bunk, flicking idly through a magazine he had traded for in the village. Francesco and Gio were sitting alone at the table, listening to a radio Michel had been building using coils of wire and pieces of silver-tinged rock. The *arrusi* had watched, fascinated, as he constructed it, hiding the pieces beneath a floorboard by his bed.

Francesco looked at him. 'You don't want to fight?'

The war was gathering pace. They had been listening to the excited voice of a news announcer, and a translator speaking over a recorded speech. Francesco could not help thinking of his father. Wondering where he was. Imagining war building back home; armies breaking over trenches like the passage of molten rock on the slopes of the mountain. In the confines of the dormitory and the yard, with the sea loud in their ears, it was hard to imagine battlefields, bombed cities, tanks rolling through streets.

Before Gio could reply, the voice began to fade into static. Gio tried fiddling with the wires, but neither of them knew how to begin, and Michel was not with them now. Pirelli had taken him away in the early morning, after the count. There was a renewed urgency to his enquiries about Rapetti now, as though the advent of war had made the question more immediate. Each morning after the count, one of them would be marched away to the fascist headquarters in the square to be interrogated, and would not be seen again until the afternoon.

'Of course not,' Gio said, still frowning at the radio. 'Frenchmen, English, what have they done to us?'

'Nothing, I suppose.' Francesco smiled. 'Remember how we

used to act out Caporetto, in the classroom? You always hid underneath a desk.'

'You ran about the room so fast no one could catch you!'

'Well, perhaps that says a lot about both of us.' He laughed, then realised what they were saying. Emilio had been there. Actually been there, at Caporetto. Marcello too. Until he had known that, Francesco had never thought of Caporetto as more than a story. A fable, to frighten boys into becoming men. What would it have been like, to actually be there?

'I don't want to fight either,' he said quietly. Abandoning the radio, Gio returned to his petition. Francesco had laid his aside and begun a sketch of his father's face, imagined as his own, thirty years from now. His father would be more than fifty now. *Non mollare*. He wouldn't give up. Not with less than two years to endure.

'Maybe they will make us, though,' Gio said. 'Maybe we won't have a choice, if they need men to fight.' He shuddered, as though he could hear the guns already.

'We haven't joined yet,' Francesco said. 'And anyway, we're not men.'

'Things might change, now there is a war. *We* might change.'

'It was written above Rapetti's desk, Gio.' He fingered the paper in his pocket as he recited the words. '*Man is man only by virtue of the spiritual process to which he contributes as a member of the family*. He actually had that hanging in his office, and you think those people ever believed we were men? That we could fight?'

Gio's pencil paused over his petition. He looked up.

'How do you know that, Fran? You have seen his office?'

Francesco swallowed. 'It's only a quote.'

'But how could you know it's there?'

He scrambled for words he couldn't find. He said nothing, long enough for Gio's eyes to narrow with suspicion. This was the game they had always played. Gio asking questions, and waiting long enough for Francesco to condemn himself.

As they stared at each other, the door opened and Michel stumbled in from his interrogation, throwing himself down on his bunk. Favero was standing in the doorway. He smiled conspiratorially at Francesco, and winked as he closed the door behind him. Though he didn't turn to look, Francesco knew that Gio had seen it.

'Well,' Elio said from across the room. 'Did you tell them?'

'Tell them what?' Michel asked, still lying face down on his bunk. 'There is nothing for me to tell.'

'We should tell them the truth,' Elio said, addressing the room, though it was almost empty. 'It is madness to keep it to ourselves now.'

'So you know something, Elio Duchessa?' Michel said, sitting up. As if they had overheard the conversation, Arturo and Marcello came in from the yard then, seating themselves at the far end of the table. Arturo's bruises had begun to fade since he had come back from the hospital at Foggia. But he walked with a pained limp, and one of his front teeth was chipped. He and Emilio seemed to have formed a silent pact to avoid one another whenever they were together in the dormitory.

'Of course not,' Elio said. 'But someone does. We would do better to help them.'

'To be traitors, you mean?'

'They should ask Francesco!' Arturo said, wincing as he stood up. 'He knows all about betraying his own, don't you, Femminella?' Francesco said nothing as Arturo moved towards him and took hold of his collar. 'Two years!' he spat, then turned Francesco to face the room, which was slowly filling now. 'Someone here must know why.'

Francesco met Gio's eyes. They stared at each other as Arturo pushed Francesco back into his chair.

Later, he stood with Gio at the far end of the yard, casting quick glances behind him as they spoke in low whispers.

The sun was almost down. In the shadow of the trees beyond the farmland, the air was cold.

'What have you been doing?' Gio demanded. 'Why have you been inside Rapetti's office? What reason could you have had?'

Francesco tried to speak, but found there was nothing to say. It was too late, far too late to deny anything. It had been too late for so long already.

'God,' Gio whispered, sitting down heavily in the dust. 'I've been so stupid.'

'No you haven't.'

'Francesco, what have you done?'

'It is a war,' Francesco said quietly, kneeling beside him, looking back over his shoulder at the dormitory. 'I have only done what I had to, to survive.'

Twenty-Two

Catania, September 1938

> The road of informers is paved with sordid desires and back-room rivalries, with the dreams of greatness of those who establish intimate relationships with the authorities in order to play out personal vendettas. Personal interests and less than praiseworthy feelings spurred many ordinary people to spread rumours and suspicions, arouse doubts, machinate tricks, insinuate slander, exaggerate village gossip, and throw discredit on personal enemies by cynically exploiting the act of reporting to the police.
>
> M. Franzinelli, *Delatori: Spie e confidenti anomini; L'arma segreta del regime fascista*

He is almost upon them before he sees them. Two dark figures in the shadow of the railway arch. Francesco has been walking the length of the railway line, from the fish market, still pungent with the day's catch, towards the docks, checking each archway in turn. The street alongside the arches is empty, though two turns away the city is thick with crowds. If he walks far enough, he will reach the *arvulu rossu*, the tree's branches webbed against the sky, and there will be six or seven *arrusi*, maybe more, gathered beneath it, sharing cigarettes, a bottle, secrets.

He almost turns back several times, appalled at what he has allowed himself to become part of. Each time, he sees again the documents on Rapetti's desk. Feels the sensation of falling, of the ground giving way beneath his feet, at the sight of the photograph of his mother. All he has to do is turn back, and everything they have worked for, all his efforts to keep her safe since Naples, will be for nothing. He will never see her again. He never had a choice at all.

He recognises Emilio's shadow beneath the fourth arch. There is a second figure with him, a shorter, thinner man. Antonio grins as Francesco approaches.

'I knew it,' he says, shaking his head and taking a cigarette from Emilio. 'I knew it would be you.' He is smiling as though they are embarking on a game together.

'All right,' Emilio says, silencing him. 'Let's get this done.'

Emilio runs through the instructions quickly. Antonio is to continue watching the men who gather beneath the *arvulu rossu* and in the park, as he has evidently been doing for months now. Francesco, the dance hall, the arches and anyone who comes to the restaurant. Emilio, the salons. Francesco hardly listens. He is too busy wondering what hold Molina's men have over Emilio. There must be something, he is sure. Emilio cannot be doing it simply for payment, or fear. What Antonio's reason is, he cannot guess.

'It is a war,' Emilio says, more than once. 'We all have to do what we can to survive. Think of your mother,' he says, a hand on Francesco's arm. 'What will happen to her if—'

'I know. You don't have to tell me. It's why I'm here.'

'They only want names. Anything unusual. Anything political they would not like.'

'What will happen?' Francesco says, feeling hollow. 'What will happen to them, when we have said their names?'

'Nothing. You have seen it already. They break up the dances, raid the cinemas. They take pictures and names, keep records. That is all.'

'What if that's not all?'

Footsteps echo in the street and they draw back further into the shadows. Two men walk past them, without seeing three shadows bent against the darkness. The men's coat collars are drawn up high, their bodies hunched. *Arrusi*, perhaps. Or perhaps two strangers who have lost their way. If so, Francesco hopes they do not wander too far towards the docks. The *arrusi* who gather there do not react well to being discovered in the dark.

'What will happen to us?' he says when the two men have passed. 'Or does this keep us safe from what they're planning?'

'We're not safe,' Emilio hisses. Francesco can hear the irritation in his voice. 'When will you learn, we are never safe. You can't keep hiding forever, Francesco.'

'It's all right,' Antonio says, sounding bored by the questioning. 'They never do anything. Some of us might get hauled in for a few days, nothing more.'

'You really believe that?' Francesco is still looking at Emilio. 'You think they'll leave any of us alone? People make lists for a reason.'

Emilio frowns. 'Look, I don't know,' he says, avoiding Francesco's eyes. 'All I know is, we are either with them when it comes, or we are on our own.'

On our own. Francesco would like to be on his own. If he was alone, no one could have any hold over him. He always thought Emilio was alone, that he kept himself separate. Now he knows the reason. He thinks of the dance hall, just a few streets away. Luca running to bring him wine. Gio swinging through the crowd, scarves trailing behind him.

'We meet here weekly, at the same time.'

'What about Molina?'

'We don't see him. Only Rapetti. And only if he asks for us. I take him the reports. We do not talk to each other about it unless we have to. There are places to exchange messages. I will show you where.'

'Why do you do it?' Francesco asks Antonio, as Antonio moves to go. 'They have something on you?'

Antonio shrugs. 'What do they need?' he says, walking to the edge of the arch. It has begun to rain. The paving stones glisten in the dim street lights. 'They know what I am, don't they? If anyone ever found that out – this is better than begging, isn't it?'

Francesco watches him meander back towards the city, his hands in his pockets, shoulders hunched against the rain.

They stand together beneath the arch after Antonio has gone. A train rattles overhead. Emilio lights another cigarette and stares out at the sea. The smoke begins to sting Francesco's eyes, but he can't bring himself to leave.

When the rain has stopped, Emilio flicks the cigarette away and turns to him.

'Come on,' he says, and takes Francesco's hand.

He leads him east through the city, a part of it Francesco hardly ever ventures close to. The police station is this way, and the wide, fashionable street leading up to the opera house. The last time he was here, during Ferragosto, the streets were packed with people and he had kept his head down, afraid of being seen walking towards the police station. This time, Emilio leads him quickly away from the main streets, through a series of narrow alleyways, until they are in front of a wide shopfront. The sign above it reads *Automobile Repairs and Parts*.

Emilio leads him down a side alley, to a yard filled with cars and pieces of machinery. In the darkness, they look like figures huddled together for safety.

'This is where you work,' Francesco says, recognising the yard.

Emilio nods. 'It was my father's.'

'Your father's?' Francesco has never heard him speak of his family before. 'So you own it?' He imagines a young Emilio running about the yard, following his father at his work.

Emilio shakes his head. 'The taxes got too high,' he says quietly. 'I sold it, after he died. Now I work here.'

'I'm sorry.'

Emilio shrugs. 'I should have married, I suppose, to avoid the tax,' he says, looking down at his feet. 'I don't know, I never . . .' He stops, and looks up at Francesco, suddenly embarrassed. To change the subject, Francesco turns towards a long black automobile with a curved body and large headlights, gleaming in the moonlight on the other side of the wall. Emilio smiles as he follows his gaze, and hauls himself up on the wall, pulling Francesco up after him.

'Do you like her?' he says as they jump down on the other side.

Francesco has never seen anything like it before. He runs a hand along the bonnet's smooth paintwork.

'She's Rapetti's,' Emilio says. 'So, if you want to leave a scratch . . .'

Francesco pulls his hand back quickly, and Emilio laughs. 'It is the safest way to explain his coming here. Strange, how often his car seems to need repairing.' He pats the car affectionately. 'She is my greatest work, this one. It is a true labour of love, to keep her always running, but always coming back for more. Here.' He runs to the shop and comes back with a set of keys. Unlocking the passenger door, he opens a sliding panel in the dashboard. There is a pile of papers inside. 'This is where I leave him messages, sometimes. There are a dozen places, all over the city. But here is easiest.'

'I thought you couldn't . . .' Francesco breaks off, embarrassed.

'I can write names,' Emilio says shortly. 'Numbers, simple things. I would not be much good in my job otherwise. If Rapetti needs anything more than that, we meet.'

'Of course.' Francesco wishes he had not brought the subject up. To change it, he says, 'Is this where I leave . . .' but this is an impossible sentence to finish too.

'No,' Emilio says, leading him back to the wall. 'I'll show you.'

On the other side of the wall, he takes Francesco's hand and runs it along the brickwork. Emilio's palm is soft and warm. They pause for a moment, their hands pressed lightly together, before Emilio moves his hand again until one of the bricks comes loose.

'Here,' he says, placing Francesco's hand in the space behind it. 'You can leave your messages for him here. Keep it short. Dates, names, behaviour. And anything political you overhear.'

Francesco nods. Then, without warning, his knees give way and he sinks heavily to the ground. Emilio puts a hand on his back as he shakes, fighting not to cry.

'This is all wrong,' he says through quick, shuddering breaths. 'How can you do it? How can I?'

Emilio waits until he has regained himself, then takes him by the shoulders and pulls him up. His face is serious.

'Look,' he says. 'You have to forget all that. I felt it too, at the beginning. If I let myself . . .' He stops. 'You have to focus on why you are doing this. What you are protecting. It is the only way to keep going.'

'What are *you* protecting?'

Emilio looks away. 'Trust me,' he says, 'it doesn't help, to think about what you are doing, who you are hurting. You'll lose yourself if you do that. Just remember, we don't have a choice.'

Francesco nods, taking a deep breath.

'It is a war, Francesco. Think of it that way. It helps, for when . . .' Emilio leaves the sentence unfinished, turning to look back at the yard that was once his. He lights another cigarette and holds it out. Francesco takes it and holds it between his fingers, watching the smoke curl into the darkness. When it has burned almost to the tip, he drops it, grinding it into the gutter. It is still lit. He feels it burning through the sole of his shoe, softening the sole. He looks up, and finds he is alone.

The following evening, Francesco visits St Agatha's. It has been years since he has been there. He still attends a small church close to the Via Calcera with his mother, and tries not to listen to the warnings against sin, the consequences of a life ill lived, but the larger churches, the abbeys and cathedrals, have kept him away. He never visits the Duomo. He feels afraid of its crowds, its lofty ceilings and luminous saints. But St Agatha's, next to the Duomo, is smaller. He likes the feeling of enclosure in its rounded walls. Even Agatha herself, a tall, imposing statue, seems to look kindly on him through eyes of blank stone. She knows what it is to be alone, to be despised. Now, she is a saint. He smiles, and bows his head to her. Nothing stays the same forever.

In Naples, he went to the cathedral often with his father. He loved it then: the cool stones beneath his feet, the ceiling so high it vanished in shadows. Churches are places where you are always welcome, his mother used to say, where every sin can be forgiven; but now he knows that was never true. He kneels in an empty pew, keeping his head down.

St Agatha's is busy. Crowds circle its perimeter, talking in exaggerated whispers. Francesco leans his head into his hands, feeling safest in the dark. *Forgive me*, he mouths, though he has never asked for it before. *I am doing it for my mother.* He tries to shut out the images of his friends, the dance hall. *And for my father, wherever he is. I promised him, I promised we would both be safe without him.* He thinks of the quotation on the wall in Rapetti's office. *Man is man only by virtue of the spiritual process to which he contributes as a member of the family.* Isn't that what he is doing? Has he not always striven to keep his family safe, no matter what the cost? Isn't that what it means, to be a man? If he doesn't do this, God knows what will happen to them. They will arrest his mother, certainly. Perhaps both of them. His father will be executed, if they ever find him. If he has not already been killed.

People pass him without noticing, whispering, kneeling, pressing their hands together in prayer. It is hard to imagine, sitting in the dark, that there are such things as guns and soldiers.

He tries to think of a prayer. One for his father, wherever he is. He prays that he is somewhere safe, among friends. That he will find a way to come back to them. That if he ever sees what Francesco has become, he will still be able to find a way to love his son. He knows, even as he whispers the words, that it is impossible. Filippo Amello would never have been capable of what he is about to do.

Before he leaves, he says another prayer, whispered so quietly he can hardly hear himself. A prayer for the friends he is preparing to betray.

On his way home, as he crosses the Via Garibaldi and makes for the safety of the narrower streets, he sees Gio walking ahead of him, in and out of shadows. Gio is walking with his head down, his fingers curled around a cigarette. Francesco watches him, feeling a pang of longing for the days when it was just the two of them, he and Gio kicking a stone across the street, unafraid. For those few short years, Francesco thought he had escaped. That there was no need for him to hide any more. Then it had started, the two of them apprehensively meeting in shadows, visiting the dance hall, clinging to each other in the dark. No wonder I have taken to it so easily, he thinks. All those years of practice. He thinks of Emilio's words beneath the arches. *You can't keep hiding forever.*

He tries to slow his pace, to avoid being seen by Gio, but his footsteps are too loud. As they pass through the Piazza San Antonio, Gio turns and sees him. He pauses, looking at the dance hall, its doors already open, and inclines his head.

Francesco knows what the gesture means. And although they have not danced for weeks, though he cannot bear the thought of being there now, of listing names in his memory and passing them to strangers, he nods his head in answer.

Twenty-Three

San Domino, September 1939

In late September, as the last hints of summer in San Domino were fading, new prisoners began to arrive.

They came singly, in small boats that landed late at night, after the *arrusi* had been locked in their dormitories. They came, it seemed, from all over Italy: Florence, Rome, Milan, Naples. Each time, the *arrusi* would wake in the morning to find that an empty bed had a new occupant, sitting up sleepily and gazing around with wide, confused eyes.

The first to be brought to Francesco's dormitory was an elderly priest from Palermo. He had a quiet, scholarly air that reminded Francesco of the priest at St Agatha's, who had always let him sit alone in a pew for as long as he wanted, without interfering or trying to offer advice. Francesco liked him immediately, though he hardly spoke a word.

When the *arrusi* had demanded the man's name on the morning they found him in the dormitory, there was an outcry when he replied, 'Father Eugenio.' Arturo laughed out loud, slapping the priest hard on the back. Elio asked if he was to become the new parish priest of the islands, since Father Rudolfo was almost always asleep or intoxicated when they arrived for his services. Throughout their interrogation, Father Eugenio remained silent. He sat on his bunk for the whole of his first day, staring blankly at the wall as though he could not comprehend what had happened, how he had found himself on San Domino. Francesco could not help wondering it too.

Autumn was settling around them. News, rumours, whispers of war spread across the island in ever-thickening clouds of fear. The *arrusi* pressed Father Eugenio for information:

what was happening back home, was the war likely to stretch that far, had he heard any news from the front? But the priest told them nothing. He only sat, clutching at his bible, his blue-grey eyes staring at the floor.

In those early days of war, Francesco and Elena seemed to meet each other more and more. Francesco was spending less of his time in the dormitory or the yard around it, afraid of Gio's accusing stare, of Arturo's threats and Emilio's restless pacing. Though he did not think Gio had said anything yet to the other *arrusi*, he could not bring himself to ask. He felt safer in the open, and spent most of his days walking the perimeter of the island alone, from the steep cliffs to the north, past those overlooking the beach, and south to the softer, rocky slopes, where the seals lay basking in increasingly short days of sun. Elena appeared to follow a similar route, and they would often encounter each other somewhere along it. Usually he would find her standing staring out to sea, flinging her paper birds into the air.

'Won't they fly?' he said to her as they stood together at the Cala Tramontana. It was the morning the priest had arrived, and Francesco had left the dormitory early, tiring of the *arrusi*'s ceaseless teasing. In front of them, the sea was heaving restlessly against a sky heavy with rain. The bright splashes of purple and yellow that had covered the plain during the summer had faded to rough sprays of green-grey leaves.

Elena looked up at him and smiled. She looked older than the girl he had seen by the road back in June. Her face was thinner, and there were lines around her eyes he had not noticed before.

Taking another paper from the pocket of her dress, she folded over some of the edges, held it out in front of her and aimed. It sank like the rest. She shook her head.

'Let me try.' Francesco held out his hand. He took the paper she passed him and turned it over. It was the poster of

Rapetti. He stared, for a moment stung with a mixture of fear and guilt. His balance wavered on the uneven rocks beneath his feet.

'You know him?' she asked. Francesco didn't reply. He tried instead to think of his mother's face. It helped, to think of her. He remembered Emilio, that night by the mechanics' yard, as he knelt breathlessly on the ground. *You have to focus on what you're protecting. It is the only way to keep going.*

'Why do you have these?' he said, holding out the poster.

Elena shrugged. 'There are piles of them at home. My father . . .' She stopped, and took the paper back from him. Francesco had folded it into a bird of his own, long and lithe, a strip left beneath it to scythe the air. She examined it carefully, then threw it in a swift, arrow-like motion over the edge.

They both stood still. The bird hovered for a moment, then twisted, tumbled and fell to the water.

As he watched, Francesco felt for the two pieces of paper in his pocket, the notes that had been left for him. They had been written on the same paper. Who had sent them? The quotations, he was sure, were only a cover, in case of interception. Every letter the prisoners received or sent was read by half a dozen pairs of eyes before it reached its recipient, and censored for the slightest of things. Francesco had seen a prisoner's letter taken from him simply for asking after his uncle, a known pacifist. A passage from the Doctrine, meanwhile, could attract no one's interest. The notes had to mean something more. Something he didn't understand.

Beside him, Elena sat down and edged towards the water, dangling her bare feet above it.

'Don't you ever think about just swimming away?' she asked, turning to him. He smiled. She lowered herself further into the water, until she was submerged to her knees, holding herself up on her elbows. 'I could just let go, and swim away.'

'You really want to leave?'

'I have to. Before . . .' She stopped, hauling herself back up onto the rocks and looking over her shoulder. 'I have to leave before the war comes. I think, by then, it will be too late.' She had wrapped her arms around herself, as though guarding against some unseen threat.

'Too late for what?'

'Don't you want to leave?' She was frowning up at him.

Francesco folded his arms too, hunching himself against the sudden cold. 'I'm not sure,' he said slowly. 'I'm tired of hiding. At least here . . .' He stopped, remembering that she knew nothing of his life, and looked at her. 'Your father.'

'What?'

'You said your father had those posters. Why?'

'Everyone has them. They are passing them around all the time. They want to know who killed that man. The policeman.'

'Do they know anything?'

She shook her head.

'But, what it says there . . .' Francesco gestured to the paper. *DIEGO RAPETTI. 14.01.39, CATANIA. REWARD.*

'I don't know,' she said. 'I can't read. I don't know what it says. I just know they want to find out.' She scrambled to her feet, her eyes suddenly wide. 'Do you know what happened?'

Francesco shook his head.

'They say it was one of yours, though.'

'Do they?'

'Some of them do. Some of them say you are not capable of it. That's why you're in prison. Because you can't kill people.'

He wanted, suddenly, to laugh. The gulf between what he saw and what others thought was so wide, he wondered how anyone could believe in it. Then he thought of Arturo. Arturo and all his women back home. Arturo wasn't like him. He was a real man, whatever that meant. What would they say about Arturo, what he might be capable of, if they knew about that?

'Do you think people have to end up the same as their parents?' Elena asked suddenly. She was staring at her hands, held out in front of her. He remembered her on the shore, making a slashing motion with her fists. He thought of his father's hands, shaking as he clung to a glass in the library. His mother, her hands on his father's face.

'Do you?'

'I just wondered,' she said slowly, 'if people can change. If the things they do can be changed. Or if we have to end up the same as them.'

'I don't know.'

She twisted her hands into fists, as though imagining she was holding onto something solid. He remembered the way she had seemed suddenly different, that day on the rocks with the seals. *Soon, everything on this island will be gone. Wiped out.*

'I can't stay here. I know that, anyway. I think I would do anything.'

He wanted to ask her what she meant. As they stood together at the water's edge, watching birds sink in and out of clouds, Francesco wondered for the first time what her life might have been like here. Not so different to his now, perhaps. The wind, the sun on the back of her neck, the dust, the empty streets, and surrounding her, nothing but sea. She had never seen a city. A cathedral. A train rattling on rails, Catania during Ferragosto, the festival of St Agatha, streets thronged with chanting crowds. The noise, the heat of being hemmed in by bodies. For one mad moment, he thought of telling her of Emilio's plans to escape.

'I should go back.'

Francesco nodded. 'So should I.'

'Be careful.'

He stopped.

'They are talking about war.'

'I know.'

'No.' She stepped forward and took his hand. Francesco was so surprised, he didn't pull it back. She held it tightly, pressing her other hand over it. She was staring into his eyes, her face pleading, as though she was expecting something from him. He could feel her hands shaking as she held him. When he did nothing, she let him go.

'I mean, they are talking about what will happen to you, when it comes.'

'Do you ever think about it?' Francesco whispered as the light began to fade. 'What we did?'

He and Emilio were lying on his bunk, sharing a cigarette between them. Outside, the wind had risen further, and rain had begun to spit at the dormitory windows.

'No,' Emilio said firmly. 'Do you?'

Francesco nodded. 'Sometimes I am afraid it will show on my face,' he said, and Emilio smiled.

'Little idiot. How could it?'

Francesco turned to him. He could feel Gio watching them through the darkness, and lowered his voice even more. 'Gio knows.'

'You told him?'

'No! Of course not. He just knows. Only about me,' he added quickly.

'Will he talk?'

'I don't know.' He considered. After he had told Gio everything, in the yard, Gio had hardly said a word. He had not been able to look at Francesco, and afterwards he had walked alone to the Cala, ignoring Francesco's calls for him to wait. Francesco had found it impossible to read in Gio's face what he was thinking. Whether he was considering revenge.

'It is a war,' Emilio said quietly, as he always did. As though, somehow, that made everything right. As though, in war, people were allowed to become someone else entirely. 'He doesn't know what that's like, what it means.'

Francesco gathered the courage to voice the question he had been wanting to ask for a long time. 'Tell me about Caporetto.'

'What do you want to know?'

'I don't know. But you were there?'

'Yes, I was there.'

'Were you taken prisoner?'

Emilio took the cigarette from him and drew in a deep breath of smoke. 'It was loud. I remember noise. And so hot.' He frowned at the memory. 'They would not let us take off our jackets. And the guns were so heavy. I remember my hands sweated too much to hold mine.' He shut his eyes, and passed the cigarette back.

'But at least you didn't run. You weren't a coward, like other men were.'

He thought of what they had learned about Caporetto in the schoolroom. Of himself and Gio running about the room and hiding beneath tables. It was the cause of his country's weakness, all those men who had run. Perhaps it was a sign, even then, that he and Gio would not grow up to be like other men.

'I've been wondering about your reason.'

'My reason?' Emilio turned towards him.

'You know what I mean. Your reason for . . . what we did. To the others. You never told me what it was.'

'You didn't need to know that.'

'You knew mine.'

Emilio winced as though with pain. Francesco wanted to ask more, but he knew it was useless. Instead, he lay silent, feeling Emilio's breath warm on his cheek. It clouded him, being close to Emilio. Sometimes he thought it turned him into someone else, someone he hardly recognised. He felt Emilio's strength, how it had always seemed Emilio could walk up to a police officer and tell them what he was, what he had done, and it wouldn't have mattered. He remembered the story of Emilio throwing his rations into a guard's face. If they had taken him prisoner at Caporetto, he would have fought them. He would have beaten at the door of his cell until they let him out.

Perhaps that was the reason for everything that had happened since they met. In only a short time, Francesco had begun to believe he was as invincible as Emilio. He had done things he would never have imagined himself capable of, all because Emilio had made him feel untouchable. Perhaps it wouldn't even matter if the other *arrusi* found out what he had done. They would never believe it of him. Not of their quiet, shy Francesco, who hated conflict above anything else, who preferred to blend into the shadows, to read books, who cared only about keeping his mother safe. Emilio had, if only for a brief time, turned Francesco into someone else, someone he hardly recognised. He had made him strong, as though he had known what was coming, what the *arrusi* would have to endure. In all the years they had been together, Gio had never come close to that.

'You were fifteen,' Francesco said. 'At Caporetto.' He tried to remember what he himself had been like at that age. I have done nothing with my life but wash dishes, he thought.

'Yes. I told them I was older.' Emilio shook his head. 'Stupid. I wanted to fight. Everyone did, back then. I didn't even tell my father. When I came back, it was . . . well, it was too late.' He looked away.

'How long were you a prisoner?'

Emilio shifted his weight in the narrow bunk. His arm pressed up against Francesco's. As their knees touched lightly, he flinched again.

'What's wrong?'

'Nothing. Just a stomach ache, that's all.'

'But, Caporetto – why do you want to leave here so badly if it was like that? We are safe here. If you leave, you might have to fight another war.'

'It would be better than this.'

'Stay and fight it here.'

'There's nothing here to fight, Francesco.'

Francesco took the cigarette back. It was burned nearly to the tip.

'At least you didn't run,' he said. 'Before they took you, I bet you fought them like a cat.' He smiled as he sucked at the last of the cigarette and flicked it to the floor, sitting up to grind it with the ball of his foot.

Twenty-Four

Catania, September 1938

The boy is young, perhaps no more than sixteen or seventeen. Francesco has him pressed up against the wall of the railway arch, a hand on his cheek, another at his waist. The boy grins as Francesco pushes his body against his.

'Tell me your name,' he whispers. The boy mouths it eagerly. 'Tell me again, what you told your friend just now.' The boy looks momentarily confused. 'About Il Duce,' Francesco prompts, and he grins. Several of his teeth are missing. He looks up at Francesco with excited, trusting eyes. Francesco tries to remember Emilio's warning, to press down the feeling of revulsion at himself that rises in his throat as the boy whispers, smiling proudly, 'I only said I would kill him if he ever came here. Him, and his blackshirts.'

Once he has the names, Francesco goes to a quiet street corner and scribbles them on a piece of paper, his hands shaking. Perhaps Rapetti already knows that the boys are *arrusi*. He knows he should tell them the rest, but now that the thrill had subsided he isn't sure he can bring himself to. He hesitates, then leaves the rest of the paper blank.

He walks quickly past the police station to Emilio's yard, and pushes the paper into the space behind the brickwork. He stands for a moment, once he has replaced the loose brick, considering the boys he has been talking to. Who their families might be. Their mothers and fathers. What might be done to them now. *They only want to keep track*, Emilio had said. Did they?

He almost reaches out a hand to take the paper back. Then

the image of his mother's photograph on Rapetti's desk clarifies in his mind, and he turns for home.

After dark, the city draws its battle lines. Crowds stay close to the Duomo, to the Via Etnea and the bright paved squares around it. There is music from bars, their doors wide open, crowds of men inside. Women are seen out of doors less and less now, police officers more and more. The *arrusi* press themselves into side streets and the darker squares. The railway arches, the docks, the Pacini Gardens, which stretch underneath the railway line – all this is their territory, fiercely guarded until the sun comes up. As he walks back through the city, Francesco can feel the streets charged with nervous energy, his own body humming with the fear and the thrill of what he has just done. Halfway home, he decides he cannot face the quiet darkness of the flat on the Via Calcera, or the bitter lie of the dance hall. He turns instead towards the port, and the Pacini Gardens.

This is a part of the *arrusi*'s territory he would not usually stray into, populated by men without employment who drink during the day as well as the night, but he feels he belongs with them now. He doesn't deserve the camaraderie of the dance halls or the comfort of the salons. Here, in the unkept, dank-smelling gardens, is where he belongs.

The gardens are unlit, moonlight patterning the pathways and beds of tangled weeds, filtering through trees woven tightly together overhead. He can hear the sea beyond their boundaries, but can see only a thick, heavy darkness in all directions. His footsteps, though, are loud enough to warn the men he knows are gathered in dark corners. Further in, he sees two figures sitting at the base of a statue, passing a flask of wine between them. As he watches, a young boy edges close to them, staring at them curiously. Eight, perhaps nine years old. He hears one of the men shout out, '*Ti va di fare un giro?*' You want to go for a ride? The boy stands frozen, his chest rising quickly with panic. Francesco watches, willing himself to go to the boy, knowing he will not move, and feels his cheeks redden with shame.

Gradually, over long, slow weeks of betrayal, it becomes easier. It is, after all, just another form of hiding. He is so used to keeping secrets, reinventing himself, that concealment of any kind is a familiar habit. He follows Emilio's advice, and becomes more skilled at pushing down that part of himself that wants to cry out each time he slides a note behind the brickwork, and after a while, he wonders if this is who he has been all along. The Francesco who would never have considered doing this, the Francesco of only a few weeks earlier, might have been no more than another disguise. *It is a war.* How can he be disgusted at himself when he isn't even sure who he is?

For weeks, he avoids writing Gio's name. He will have to eventually – they have arrested Gio before, so they will think it odd if he is not mentioned – but for now he cannot bear to. He gives them almost all the others. Luca. Dante. Mattheo. Claudio. Even Antonio and Emilio, for good measure, to show he is not on anyone's side. When he doesn't know a man's name, he finds out, drawing him into a corner of the dance hall or into the shadows of a side street and whispering in his ear: *you're beautiful, voglio te, what's your name?* They smile as they tell him, pressing their lips against his as he files it away in his memory.

That night, the night it all changes, he is at the dance hall. They rarely talk politics here, but now and again someone will launch into a diatribe against the regime, and Francesco will force himself to listen. He notes, too, any new faces, the wearing of costumes, the painting of faces, all of it evidence of subversion. He sees Gio, his eyes lined darkly, scarves around his neck, and feels an ache of pure despair, because this will be the night he tells them Gio's name. He can't keep it back any more.

The band is playing a slow waltz. Antonio is there with his accordion, his head bent over it, moving slowly in time to the music. The *arrusi* are quieter than usual. They stand in groups, a few couples moving lazily about the tiny space, arms around each other's necks. He looks for Emilio, though he knows Emilio will not be here. He will be at the salons with the *primogeniti*, where political opinions are fervent and unconcealed.

Luca comes forward and takes his arm. Everyone he passes greets him: 'Femminella!' 'We have not seen you for so long!' 'They say you only go with dogs in the docks now, Claudio saw you there, what were you doing?' 'We have missed you, Femminella!'

Through the crowds, he catches Antonio's eye. Antonio grins at him, so knowingly Francesco is afraid they will be suspected, and turns quickly away. Later, he sees Antonio talking in a large group of *arrusi*, his eyes moving from one to another, occasionally looking beyond them to sweep the room. Francesco wonders if he is enjoying the task as much as he appears to be. Or perhaps this is simply his own form of disguise.

Once, he goes to the doorway to see if anyone is in the courtyard beyond, remembering the slow, languid dancers, their cigarettes lighting with each breath, Emilio sitting against the wall, his fingers draped over the guitar. *I came here looking for you.* The courtyard is empty, two or three folding tables stacked against the wall, a rubbish bin overturned across the cobbles.

When he cannot bear to listen any more, Francesco drinks, and gives himself up to the dance. The room spins around him, the faces blurring into one: Antonio, Dante, Leonessa, Amazon, Duchessa. This is where he belongs, he thinks, laughing as someone drapes themselves around his neck. This is where he belongs, and he is destroying it from the inside.

He hardly hears the doors being kicked in, the shouting of police, until the dancing halts so abruptly he almost falls into the crowd. The music stops. The talking takes longer, but eventually that ceases too. He watches them fan out across the room. There are only four men; he is flooded with relief to find he recognises none of them. They are not Molina's men, the state police. They are carabinieri, dressed all in black, two lines of shining buttons on their chests reflecting the moonlight. The *arrusi* stand, frozen, as they spread out among them.

For one absurd moment, Francesco thinks of identifying himself, saving himself by telling the carabinieri who he is, what he has done for Rapetti and Molina. Instead, he shrinks against the wall, watching them move amongst the crowd, pushing back hats drawn down over eyes, pulling men by the collar from beneath tables and chairs. This is not a raid. They are looking for someone in particular. They move methodically until they have him by the arms. Antonio.

Francesco watches as he is pushed through the room, casting frantic glances around him. He is looking for me, Francesco thinks, and when their eyes meet, Antonio is pleading with him to do something. He is shaking, tears across his cheeks. Behind him, Francesco hears Dante screaming.

What can he do? He is surrounded by *arrusi*. What would they do to him if he revealed himself now? He watches Antonio being marched through the crowd, the *arrusi* silently gathering after him, and breathes a guilty sigh of relief as the doors bang shut behind him and they are left alone again in the dark.

'He is accused of prostitution,' Emilio says, when they meet later beneath the arches. It is cold, damp with recent rain. Francesco wraps his coat tighter around himself. His mother, already shocked by the change in him, by his bruised face and his silence, will be pacing the flat in a silent rage. He is hardly home in the evenings now. She has started smoking again. It is his fault, she tells him, when she speaks to him at all. He has left her alone for too long. She hears voices. Imagines men banging on the door, coming to take her away.

'Prostitution?' he says, confused. 'But they must know—'

Emilio shakes his head. 'They're not with Rapetti. They are carabinieri – they know nothing about us.'

'Then can't we go to him? Rapetti, or Molina. Can't we ask them—'

Emilio laughs sourly. 'What would you say? Please set an *arrusu* free? It is too late for that, Femminella.'

'You said they didn't want to take us. Only monitor. Were you wrong?'

'I don't know.' Emilio shuffles uncomfortably. Looks over his shoulder as though someone is watching them. 'I don't know, Francesco.'

'Will they come for us next?'

'Stop it!' Francesco takes a step back, surprised by the sudden change in Emilio's voice. Emilio's fingers shake as he lights a cigarette. 'Stop it, all right? I don't know any more than you do.'

'You're the reason we started all this.'

'I know. It has nothing to do with Antonio being arrested, though. If he chooses to make money that way, how can we help him?'

'We should try, at least. Speak to Rapetti.'

'And how would it look, do you think, if they did let him go? What will they all think? How many times has Antonio been seen talking to us? Gio, Luca – what will they think of us?'

Francesco remembers what he once thought of Gio, all those months ago, when Gio was taken away by Rapetti. After they had let him go, the suspicions he had. He rubs his hands across his eyes. 'I don't care,' he says eventually, feeling suddenly tired. 'I don't care who asks questions.'

'You will, if they ever find out what we have done to them.'

'I want to stop,' Francesco says. 'I don't want to do this any more.'

'Then stop.'

'Can I?'

'I don't know, Francesco! What did you think would happen?'

Emilio tosses his cigarette aside and lights another. Francesco watches the light from the first flare up and die in the gutter.

'What do you plan to do?' Emilio laughs a low, bitter laugh. 'Live out your life here, hiding? Live like the others, in the dark? Tell everyone you just couldn't get a woman, hope no one asks?'

Francesco says nothing.

'Better still, why not marry one?' Emilio continues, his voice rising. 'Why not find some poor, stupid girl who doesn't know you, and hide behind her? Is that what you plan to do?'

'What about you?' Francesco hears the shrill anger in his own voice. 'What are you doing to fight it, Emilio? Where are we standing now? You're no better than me. You won't even tell me what they are holding over you – if there is anything at all.'

Emilio seizes him by the collar and pushes him back against the wall. Francesco closes his eyes, but when he opens them, Emilio's head is bowed.

'All right.' He sounds defeated. 'Do what you want. Stop, if you want, and see what happens to you then. At least I'm brave enough to keep fighting.'

They stare at each other for a moment. Then Emilio lets go and pushes his hands into his pockets. Francesco, still leaning against the wall, watches him walk back towards the street.

'Good luck with your girl,' he says over his shoulder, as he disappears into the crowds.

Twenty-Five

San Domino, October 1939

Francesco's turn for interrogation came not long before the anniversary of the March on Rome. This was, traditionally, a time for clemency and forgiveness, though he doubted whether the custom extended as far as San Domino. Nevertheless, the *arrusi* had been working on their petitions with renewed fervour as the weather grew colder.

After the morning count, he followed Pirelli along the path from the Cameroni district to the village. They passed a grove of olive trees, the pale green fruit grown fat and ripe amongst the leaves, then the mulberry tree which stood at the corner of the turn towards the village, the ground beneath it stained black with long since fallen fruit. A number of villagers walked by in the direction of the beach, suitcases in hand. Francesco wondered if they were seeking a warmer winter than San Domino could afford.

The fascist headquarters stood at one side of the small village square. Pirelli strode up importantly to the two guards standing at its entrance and nodded smartly to them. He seemed, Francesco thought, to be enjoying himself.

Inside, there looked to be no one in the building but themselves. Their footsteps echoed loudly on the marble flagstones as Pirelli led Francesco to a small room at one side of a wide atrium, and seated himself at a table, indicating that Francesco should do the same.

'First, I want to talk about the anniversary.'

Francesco looked up, surprised.

'The March on Rome. We will, of course, go to San Nicola for the celebrations. Coviello has asked me to convey to each of you his . . . concern. That the prisoners do not join the others in the Roman salute. He has asked me to tell you that it will be easier for you if you do. He is tired of handing out beatings.'

Francesco said nothing. He was thinking of the *arrusi* standing resolutely every Saturday with their hands by their sides, each afraid that this week they would be the one to give in. So far, no one had. He did not like to think what would be done to the man who capitulated first.

'Now,' Pirelli said, a new tone of briskness in his voice, 'you knew this man Rapetti?' He pushed one of the posters across the table. Francesco nodded.

'You know what happened to him?'

'I know what people say.'

'I want to know what *you* say.'

Francesco sat silently. He had been expecting something more calculated than this. Pirelli rested his head on his hand. 'It is what you all say. You don't know anything. But one of you must.' He sighed with resignation. 'Look, I will make you the same offer I have made to the others. Tell me something useful, and they will let you go home for a while. For the winter, perhaps.'

Francesco looked up, suddenly interested. Did Pirelli even have the authority to make such an offer? He had already offered as much to Emilio, and been refused. He studied the guard, sitting across from him in his makeshift uniform, using words that sounded uncomfortable and forced in his mouth. Trying so hard to be part of something, to be one of them. Did he think his pretence had worked? Francesco doubted whether the other guards even knew he was using this room, in a building that seemed almost abandoned.

'He was using some of you as informants,' Pirelli said, leaning forward on his elbows. 'We know that. Do you know who?'

Francesco shook his head. What did that have to do with anything Pirelli wanted to know?

'It seems likely that one of those men was responsible. He was killed late at night, in a place your kind frequented. The railway arches by the port. Perhaps he was meeting one of his informers.'

'Perhaps,' Francesco said, trying to keep the image of Emilio and Antonio standing beneath the arches out of his mind. 'I wouldn't know about that.' He sat staring at Pirelli, hoping the questions were at an end.

'Tell me about Antonio Bianchi.'

The sound of the name shocked Francesco out of his silence. 'Antonio?'

'You knew him?'

'Yes. I knew him.'

'He was one of the informants, wasn't he?'

'How would I know?'

'You knew of his arrest? And . . . what happened to him after?'

Francesco nodded.

'His relationship with Marcello Ricci?'

'Marcello?'

He could not hide his surprise now. Pirelli saw it, a smile of satisfaction on his face as Francesco thought furiously. What had Antonio to do with Marcello, one of the *primogeniti*? Then he remembered that night he had gone to Marcello's flat, and found Antonio sitting at Emilio's feet. He had been so stupid not to have seen it then. It had been Marcello, not Emilio, that Antonio was there for.

'Theirs was . . .' Pirelli paused, as though his distaste at the words made them difficult to expel. 'A financial arrangement.'

If Pirelli had expected shock, he must have been disappointed. It was far from the first such arrangement Francesco had heard of. He thought of Antonio's arrest, back in Catania. Prostitution, Emilio had said. 'What do you want to know?'

'This man Antonio – did he have a reason to dislike Rapetti?'

Francesco laughed. 'We all did, didn't we?'

'I just wondered.' Pirelli leaned back in his chair, his confidence growing. 'If he did, and Marcello knew of it . . .' He let the thought hang in the air, looking pleased with himself. Francesco felt a sudden rush of pity for him. For how little he understood.

A few days later, the last bunk in Francesco's dormitory was filled. The new prisoner, like the rest, arrived in the early hours. Francesco opened his eyes that morning to the sight of a stranger pacing up and down the dormitory, muttering to himself under his breath.

He was a tall, thin youth, and Francesco knew at once that he was not from Catania. He walked quickly towards Francesco when he saw him sitting up, and stood at the end of his bed, studying him with his head tilted to one side. His high forehead and thin, pointed nose gave him an oddly regal appearance.

'You do not look like a *recchione*,' he said at last.

Francesco stood and extended a hand, which the other man did not take.

'God,' he said, looking around him and wrinkling his nose. 'How long have you people been living here like this? It is disgusting.' He spat at the floor.

His name was Carlo, and he had been brought alone from Rome. This was the only information he seemed willing to share, in the face of the *arrusi*'s eager questioning. He was more informative about what was happening back home.

'They flock to him,' he said, his face suddenly animated as he spoke. He was perched on the table, the prisoners gathered around him. 'I saw Il Duce give a speech to ten thousand men in Rome this year. It is incredible, to watch the crowds he draws. Impossible to believe, until you see it with your own eyes. They say we will join Germany in the war by Christmas.'

'And what about you?' Arturo said. He had been silent since Carlo had begun talking, but now he was studying the new arrival with narrow eyes.

'Me?' Carlo said, turning to see who had spoken.

'Will you fight? How long is your sentence?'

'I don't see how it is any business of yours, Catania.'

As Arturo struggled to think of a reply, Carlo picked up a pile of papers that lay beside him on the table. Francesco and Marcello had been working on a new round of petitions, with the anniversary of the March on Rome approaching. Some of the *arrusi* had begun to learn to write themselves, slowly sounding out the syllables. Helping with the petitions was the only way Francesco could find to atone for what he had done. It was too late, far too late. But it was something. With his help, the *arvulu rossu* boys had begun to learn elaborate phrases of supplication, long, heartfelt pleas and arguments, growing more confident as time passed with the language of humility. They knew no other. If they were ever sent home, they would be able to read and write nothing but entreaties for forgiveness, petitions for their freedom.

'*No educated person could doubt that the moral defect afflicting me is an illness of the spirit*,' Carlo read, in an exaggerated, high-pitched voice. '*An unwelcome gift, cruelly given to me by nature*.' He stopped. 'An illness of the spirit! Good God, is that what you all think?'

'I suppose you are here mistakenly too,' Gio said.

Carlo laughed. 'Mistakenly? No, I am guilty as they come. But at least I am not ashamed. An illness of the spirit!' He threw the papers down, shaking his head in disbelief.

'What should we say then, do you think?' Dante asked. It had been his petition Carlo had read aloud.

Carlo looked at him. After a long, studied silence, he said, 'I suppose you are all here for five years.' Dante nodded, with a nervous look in Francesco's direction. 'Then what is the point of your arguing? For the sake of your pride, why do you not tell them, yes, I am a *recchione*, a deviant, and I apologise to no one?'

They stared at him. None of the *arrusi* had considered such a thing before.

As they thought, the door opened and Elio strode in, returned from his interrogation with Pirelli. He stopped at the sight of the new arrival. Over the months spent in confinement, Elio's proud exterior had begun to falter. Where once he had walked with his head held high, he had begun to cast his gaze downwards and hunch his shoulders. The other *arrusi* were similarly worn. Carlo stood tall among them like a count amongst beggars. Elio was staring at him as if at a mirror of a man he had once been.

'Well?' Arturo said, as Elio stood in the doorway. His was the interview everyone had feared the most. They had no doubt Elio would tell everything, if he had anything to tell.

Elio smiled, enjoying the tension he had created. 'I wish I did know something,' he said, pulling back a chair. He was still staring at Carlo.

'Did he ask you about the salute?' Michel said.

Elio nodded. 'I think we should do it.'

'What?' Arturo stood up.

'It will be better for us. It might even help with our petitions, if we show allegiance. And we are here either way. Why not go along with them?' There were murmurs of agreement amongst the *arrusi*.

'What is wrong with you all?' Carlo stood up, scattering the papers across the floor. 'Why not also tell them you love your country, what it has done to you? Why not also thank them for locking you up, for teaching you to be ashamed of what you are?' He shook his head, and in a quieter voice said, 'How can you all be such cowards?'

'Some of us are not so proud of the accusation as you seem to be,' Arturo said. 'Or as willing to admit guilt.' He turned to the room. 'It is not nature, what you all are. It is not an illness.

You choose it, all of you. It is a perversion. Why be proud of that?'

'I am not proud,' came a quiet voice. 'How could I be?' They all turned to Father Eugenio, sitting on his bunk at the far end of the dormitory, his head bowed.

'I am not proud either,' Dante said, stooping to gather up the petitions from the floor.

Carlo shrugged. 'Then you will not have happy lives,' he said, looking pityingly over at the priest. 'At least I know what I am. And,' he stopped on his way to the door, 'if any of you dare to return their salute at the anniversary, you will pay for it.'

Outside, the rain had started again. The air was fresh and clean, smelling of sea and pine needles. As the few *arrusi* in the yard hurried inside, Francesco ducked underneath the fence and followed the path towards the Cala Tramontana, hoping to find Elena there. When tensions in the dormitory rose, he liked her quiet, thoughtful silence.

He soon sensed that he was not alone. Turning, he saw a figure following him. It was Father Eugenio, holding a coat over his head against the rain.

'I wasn't sure if there was a path this way,' he explained as he caught Francesco up. 'So I followed you. You don't mind?'

Francesco shook his head.

They walked together towards the shore. The rain had begun to ease, leaving a clear sky above the pale band of rocks. The sun was low, spilling across the water towards them in a haze of purple and orange light.

'What do you think, about the salute?' Father Eugenio asked as they emerged from the trees.

'I don't know,' Francesco said, thinking. 'I would prefer not to give it. But I do not see that it matters much now.'

The priest nodded. 'They are so important, these symbols. But no one knows why.' He stopped, and looked back towards the dormitory. 'Your friend is not well,' he said. 'Did you know that?'

'Gio?'

The priest shook his head. 'The tall one. I think you call him Emilio.'

'What do you mean by not well? Do you believe Arturo, what he said?' Francesco was not sure whether he even believed any more in the petitions he wrote. Was it fate, or an illness of the spirit, what they were?

He tried to remember what they had told him at the hospital, after his arrest in Catania. They had books, great thick textbooks from which they read passages to him as they carried out their examinations. At the time, lying on a cold metal table, hands pressing into his skin, he had tried to shut out their voices, but now he wanted to remember. Men should be fully men, they had told him, just as women should be fully women. Francesco was drifting somewhere in between. Lost. Something of the opposite sex, of women, was trapped inside him like a thorn, working its way in, closing on his heart. This was what fascism did, they told him. It pulled out the thorn. They had to start their work earlier, with children. When men were still boys, when women were girls. It was almost too late for a half-man like him.

He thought of Emilio then. What did it mean for Emilio, who was so much braver, so much stronger than Francesco had ever been? Emilio, who had fought at Caporetto, who had survived being taken prisoner there. Who had fought the guards in Catania as they took him. How could he be one of them, a splinter of feminine weakness cut across his heart? How could he have kept it so hidden?

Father Eugenio shook his head. 'I do not mean that. I mean what is usually meant by illness. It is his stomach, I think. He might need a doctor.'

'They are hard to come by out here,' Francesco said. 'I noticed a few days ago – do you think it is bad, then?'

The priest nodded. 'I used to assist the doctor in my parish. I will try to help, if I can.'

They had reached the shore. Francesco turned to hold out a hand, but Father Eugenio waved it away and followed him unaided, easing himself slowly and carefully across the rocks.

'Did you mean what you said before?' Francesco said, as they stood together at the water's edge. 'Are you ashamed?'

'Aren't you?'

Francesco thought. 'I don't know,' he said at last. 'I was, back home. Here . . . I don't know.' He turned to the priest. 'What happened to you in Palermo?'

'The same as happened to you, I imagine.'

'But you are—'

'I don't know what I am,' Father Eugenio said, cutting him off. 'I have no clue any more.'

A thought occurred to Francesco. 'Does it say anything in the gospels about us?'

'Of course not.' Father Eugenio looked shocked.

'About men, though. About . . . how we should be.'

The priest thought for a moment, then nodded. 'The gospels show us how to live. They show us the best examples of men and women. Paul is active, combative, he dominates. He is a pure man. Martha is submissive. Maternal. It is a guide, to measure ourselves against. Do you see?'

'I think so.'

'And the others,' Father Eugenio went on. 'Judas, the feminised man. The man who betrays.'

Francesco turned back to the sea. He had heard this talk before. *It is our task*, men had whispered to him in the prisons, *to turn Johns and Judases into Peters and Pauls.* He had known then that it was not about love. He could love who he wanted. They didn't care. He could even fuck who he wanted, if he did it in the right way. It was something within himself, something weak, something of women that should never have been there, so close to his heart, to the core of what he was. Something that made him a coward. A man who could betray his friends.

When he returned to the yard, Francesco found it empty save for a figure sitting beneath the tree. At first he thought it was Emilio. A dark, tall figure, his knees drawn to his chest. But as he came closer, he saw the pale yellow hair, and something propped against the tree beside him. A gun.

Favero's hands were resting on his knees, his fingers interlocked. His eyes were closed, his chest rising and falling in a regular rhythm. Francesco stared at the gun. Took a step forward. Felt his fingers flinch. *A splinter of weakness. Femininity, working its way towards your heart, like a thorn.*

'I would throw you to the ground before you could lift it.' Favero, his eyes still closed, laughed as he put out a hand and drew the weapon close to him. 'What would you do, anyway? Steal a boat and go home? Stay.'

Francesco hesitated. Favero held out a bar of chocolate. They looked at each other for a long moment, then Favero shrugged and slid it back into his pocket.

'All right. Sit, then.'

Francesco pushed his hands into his pockets and shifted on the spot. Favero laughed again. 'All right. Stand.'

He kept his eyes on the gun, on the guard's fingers around the trigger.

'You have not yet given me your price, *arrusu*.'

'I have it now.'

Favero raised his eyebrows.

'I want a doctor. For Emilio. He is unwell.'

Favero considered. 'There is no one close. He would have to be very bad, to bring someone out.'

'Will you try?'

A cloud passed over the sun. A cold breeze cast itself around them.

'Why ask that,' Favero said, 'when you could have anything? You could ask to be sent home.'

'To fight a war?'

'Do you think there will be war for us?' Favero said, his eyes closed again. 'And do you think you will fight it, if it comes?'

'I don't know.' He didn't want to think about it.

'It doesn't matter for me, anyway.' Favero smiled. 'I will be here whatever happens.' He gave a deep, contented sigh.

'Surely you would prefer to fight?'

'Perhaps.' He stood up suddenly, swinging the gun onto his back. 'I suppose I should be thankful I don't have to choose. What about you, *arrusu*?'

'Me?'

'Don't you want to fight? Wouldn't it be a way to atone?'

'What am I atoning for?'

Favero smiled again. Then, in a different voice, he said, 'Why haven't you asked me to pardon you?'

'What?'

'It would be a price worth asking. You could go home for good.'

'I won't ask you for forgiveness. I don't need forgiveness from you.'

'Well, clemency, then. The anniversary of Rome is coming. Now would be the time to ask. Think about it. No one would bother you again.'

Francesco stood still for a moment, looking at the guard. His hair was neatly brushed beneath his cap. His uniform perfectly pressed. He looked down at his own torn trousers, felt the hole in the sole of his shoe. The cold working its way into his bones. Why hadn't he asked?

'I thought real men showed no mercy.'

A smile spread across Favero's face. He nodded. 'You are right, of course.' He moved closer to Francesco. 'And I suppose you wouldn't want to go home now anyway.'

As he began to walk away, he stopped and turned back.

'I can't get him a doctor. You must think of something else.'

Francesco nodded, his mouth dry.

'Or I could just take you anyway,' Favero said, shrugging. 'That's what a real man would do.'

When Francesco looked up, Emilio was standing in the dormitory doorway, watching him.

Twenty-Six

Catania, October 1938

> Can a person approach a pederast, or is that an offence against decent behaviour? Does that mean he is a pederast or that he will become one? Well then, half of Italy should be sent to *confino*, because I think that any honest citizen can meet a serious and correct pederast without being sullied by the same defect.
>
> Catanian investigated for pederasty by Molina

Rapetti is leaning back in his chair. He doesn't move as Francesco walks in. His eyes are closed. His boots are resting on the table, a cigarette balanced in an ashtray beside them, the tip still alight.

'You should not have come here,' he says in a low voice. 'I have no wish to be in the presence of pederasts. Why have you come?'

Francesco takes a deep breath and steps forward. Rapetti opens his eyes. His office is dark, the curtains drawn. As Francesco's eyes adjust, he sees the quotation above the desk: *Man is man only by virtue of the spiritual process to which he contributes as a member of the family.* On the desk, there is a framed photograph of a woman sitting in a chair with a child on her lap. Her face is soft and smiling. The child is gazing up at her, the fingers of one tiny hand curled around a strand of her hair. He thinks, suddenly, of Lucia, leaning over her balcony.

'My friend. One of the other informants. He has been arrested.'

'Name?'

'Antonio Bianchi.'

Rapetti sits up and leafs through a pile of papers until he pulls out a file and opens it.

'Yes, unfortunate. Prostitution. Nothing we can do.'

'You can ask Molina to have him released.'

Rapetti raises an eyebrow. 'Can I?'

'Please. Will you?'

Rapetti laughs.

'The anniversary of Rome is coming,' Francesco continues. 'The March on Rome. I thought that might mean . . .'

'You thought it might bring you leniency?' Rapetti smiles at him. 'You thought the traditions of our state apply to you?'

Francesco takes a sudden step forward, and sees the alarm in Rapetti's face. *You are a contagion.*

'Please.'

Rapetti recovers himself quickly. 'This is carabinieri business,' he says briskly. 'We only have so much influence. And anyway, I will have no difficulty in finding others to fill his place. You were recruited easily enough, weren't you?'

'It will not be so easy when they know others have been arrested.'

'I never promised you immunity, *arrusu*. It is the nature of your kind, to betray.'

'No, but . . .' He takes a breath. 'You will lose our goodwill, eventually, if it keeps happening. If more of us are taken.'

There is a long silence then. Francesco holds the breath in, feeling his head grow lighter, the room begin to darken around him as he waits. He will be taken now, he thinks. What was he thinking, coming here, demanding so much?

'You know what I have wondered about you, *arrusu*?' Rapetti says slowly. He picks up the cigarette, burned nearly to the tip, and puts it to his lips, inhaling deeply. 'I have thought about you often. God only knows why.'

Francesco watches him turn over the files until he opens one that contains the image of his father. His birth certificate. A photograph of his mother. He can feel the blood pulsing in his head. He is so close, he could almost reach out and snatch them. Tear them into pieces. He wouldn't even care what was done to him after.

'Filippo Amello.' Rapetti looks up and smiles. 'I have been reading a lot about him. Everything there is.' He holds the file up. 'Do you know how I got these? You must have been wondering.'

Francesco shakes his head.

'I have not always been in Catania. I have worked in many places. And, like you,' he nods to the files, 'I was born in Naples.'

For a moment, neither of them speaks. Rapetti stares at the glowing tip of his cigarette. Francesco's mind is filling slowly with flames.

'How old would you have been then?' Rapetti says, as though he can see the flames himself. 'Twelve, thirteen?'

'Ten,' Francesco says. The memory of smoke fills his mouth. 'I was ten years old.'

'And you ran. Of course you ran. I watched you.'

The smoke begins to sting at his eyes.

'But you left things behind, *arrusu*. You and your family. Not everything burned in that fire.' Rapetti's smile widens. 'I could hand it all in, of course. But I find you are more use to me this way.' He shuts the file with a snap. 'No one else has seen this. Not even Molina. I like to keep my secrets, just as you do.'

Francesco stares hard at him, struggling to keep his balance. All he can think is that Rapetti is the only one who knows. If there were some way to get the papers back, to ensure Rapetti's silence . . .

'And I have wondered, sitting here with these pictures, these files, if this is the reason for your disease. In your particular case, if it is because you have had no father for so long. And your own father was a coward. A man who runs from the flames. It is no wonder you are how you are, is it? You have never seen a man be a man. You have known only girls.'

Francesco's fists clench. He can hear his breath, quick and shallow, trying to control an urge to scream. He holds it in. Rapetti has a wide grin on his face. He is enjoying himself.

'Sometimes I fear you, you *arrusi*; that you are too close to me, that you might do me harm. And then I remember. Everything is hereditary, in the end. The son of Filippo Amello can be no threat to me. You are not capable of it.' He gestures to the door. 'I have things to do, *arrusu*. You have taken up too much of my time.'

Only when he is on the other side of the door does Francesco allow his fists to unclench. Deep impressions of his nails are left behind, white against his palms. *You are not capable of it.* He wonders if Rapetti is right.

Twenty-Seven

San Domino, October 1939

> How many people have been sent to *confino*? It's about time we made it known, as abroad there is talk of 200,000 and in Milan alone reportedly 26,000 have been rounded up. Above all, this is stupid as well as base. In the meantime, let's make a distinction between two kinds of condemned: criminals and those sent for political reasons. I hope nobody wants to feel sorry for the delinquents sent to *confino*. Usually they are real scoundrels, thieves, pimps and drug dealers who must be removed rapidly from society, usurers, etc. The number of these *confinati comuni* (common criminal detainees) may increase. In all there are 1,527 of them. (Voices shouting: 'Too few! Too few!') Now let's look at the *confinati politici* (political detainees): 1,541 individuals have been warned, 959 have been cautioned, and 698 are on the islands. I defy anyone to say that these modest figures are incorrect. But none of these *confinati* wants to be anti-fascist, and some of them look as if they are fascists.
>
> Benito Mussolini, Ascension Day speech, 26 May 1927

'Seventeen years ago, our country saw the greatest revolution in its history since the Renaissance. We marched on Rome, and we took it, by glorious conquest!'

Coviello raised a fist into the air. The children, lined up in the square before San Nicola's fortress, raised theirs in answer. Elena felt a surge of excitement as she lifted her arm to the sky. Her hair was braided tightly against her skull. She was wearing a white dress saved especially for this day. Each year, it felt more constricting. Her mother had stayed up late into the night, pressing it until it was stiff and tight as cardboard.

The anniversary of the March on Rome was her favourite of the festival days. Men brought out brightly coloured banners and marched with them through the square. There was music, and feasting, and the speeches were not so long as they sometimes were. And she liked to imagine the march, the day Il Duce had taken charge of their country. She had seen photographs of him in magazines, and had one pinned to her bedroom wall beside the images of cities on the mainland she would visit when she was able to get there. Rome, Milan, Verona. She wondered what it was like in those places, on this day. Thousands upon thousands of people would be gathered to hear their own speeches. They would all be ready to welcome her, those surging, cheering crowds.

When her mind re-created the march, she saw soldiers wearing costumes like real Romans, glittering gold breastplates and leather shoes with straps wrapped around their calves. They carried spears, and there were thousands of them, filling the streets, the sound of their marching louder than any sound she had heard on San Domino. Crowds pressed in around them, waving banners and cheering until her ears were stuffed full. Because they were liberating her country. Because they had right on their side. She imagined herself marching with them, right over the sea from San Domino to the mainland, then on towards the capital, towards so much life and wealth and freedom.

She knew it hadn't been exactly the way she imagined it. She had always known the breastplates weren't real, that they would have worn uniforms like Coviello's, and that there hadn't been thousands of men, just hundreds. But she preferred her own, imagined dream.

She could see Nicolo standing amongst the crowd of islanders. He looked bored, his hands in his pockets. He was pushing at the earth with the toe of his boot. His hair hung limp around his face. A few days ago, she had met him for the first time since their mothers had planned a future for them. He had not met her eyes, but she had caught him staring at her when she turned away, his eyes travelling over her as Coviello's had, that day in the kitchen. As Francesco's never did.

She looked over at the prisoners, searching among them for Francesco's face. She sought him out now, whenever she walked across the island alone. She felt, she had realised, safer with him than she did with her own family.

The San Domino prisoners were standing where they always did, beside the ranks of San Nicola's. She saw Francesco at once, next to Emilio. He looked nervous, tired. She searched among the San Nicola prisoners for the man who had given her the letters. Today would be the perfect day for them to meet, if he had more to pass on. He would reach out and take her hand as she walked past the crowd of prisoners, or she would manage to slip unseen from the ranks as they walked back to the jetty, and find him in the crowds. Coviello tried, but it was impossible to keep order with so many packed into the tiny square.

It would be even easier today. Every islander in the Tremiti had come out to celebrate the anniversary. Hardly a white patch of paving could be seen amongst so many heads bowed to the sound of Coviello's voice. The square, once Coviello's speech was done, would be chaos, thick with crowds.

She still had hope, despite what everyone told her of the prisoners, that they were her way out. Coviello thought that they were weak, but he was wrong. He had visited that morning, before the ceremonies, to talk with her father about the Roman salute, the fact that the prisoners still refused to give it.

'They are cowards,' he had muttered. 'I know they will give in eventually.' They didn't see Elena at first, standing in the corner by the stove.

'But what can we do?' her father said. 'They are already threatened with beatings and they will not do it.'

Coviello shook his head. Then he looked up, and met Elena's eyes.

'Come here, *ragazza*.'

He held out a hand. When she was close to him, he put it around her waist.

'You have not spoken to the prisoners, have you?' Elena shook her head. 'What has your father told you about them?'

Elena swallowed. 'They are a disease,' she said in a quiet voice. 'They are a cancer on the state.'

Coviello laughed. 'She is a good girl, your daughter, Pirelli. We could use her, in our fight!'

'She is going to be married next year,' her father said, a hint of sadness in his voice.

'Well. That is right.' Coviello sighed. 'In another world, I could perhaps have found a job for your daughter as well as yourself.'

A job of her own. The thought of it gave her a thrill of excitement. As she stood with the Director's arm heavy around her, dreaming of the job he might one day find her, Elena thought of the prisoners. They would not give in to the salute. She knew them better than he did. They had resolve, like she did. They would fight.

In the square, Coviello's voice droned on, closer and closer to the moment when she knew he would give the salute. She felt tense, her pulse beating faster. She knew the prisoners would not reply, and if one of them was to be beaten, to be made an example of, it would surely be on this day, of all days.

When it came, she raised her hand so quickly it was almost ahead of Coviello's own. The carabinieri and the other islanders did the same. The sky was suddenly filled with arms held up against the gathering clouds. She looked through them at the ranks of prisoners. They stood, as she'd known they would do, with their arms firmly by their sides.

There was a long silence during which no one, not even the

islanders, dared move. Elena felt her shoulder aching as she kept her arm in the air. The sun had slid behind a cloud. The square was cold, dim with shadows, a brisk wind feeling its way amongst the crowds. Coviello stood motionless on the steps, his arm still raised, his head up. His eyes seemed to be searching the prisoners one by one, daring them to look up, to lift a hand.

The stillness was broken by a gesture from an officer beside him. One of the carabinieri moved forward, crossed the square and dragged one of the San Domino prisoners to its centre.

Elena strained to see which prisoner it was, breathing a sigh of relief when she saw it was not Francesco. It was a tall, slender man who held his face high as they drew him forward, as though he considered the carabinieri officers beneath his notice. He didn't flinch as they circled him. She could hear their taunts and laughter from where she stood. Behind them, the San Domino prisoners stood still, staring at the ground as the men began pushing the prisoner between them. One of them tore at his shirt, the other his trousers, until the prisoner stood shivering in his underwear, his hands raised to his face, his head still high. There was a still silence in the square, rows of prisoners and islanders watching mutely, until the prisoner fell to a sharp kick to his stomach, another to his face.

She was about to close her eyes when, in the middle of the ranks of the San Domino prisoners, a movement caught her eye. She stared with horror, even as relief flooded through her, as a hand rose slowly into the air. Coviello took a sudden step forward, his eyes straining towards their ranks. Elena recognised this prisoner. It was the man who had broken up the Ferragosto performance, the one built like a bull. He was staring at Coviello as though issuing a challenge, his hand still poised above his head. There was a pause. Then two more hands rose amongst the prisoners, and then more, and then there were hundreds of hands, chained in pairs, raised towards the sky in a unanimous Roman salute.

Coviello didn't move. He nodded slowly, sweeping his eyes across them, a flicker of triumph on his face. Then he turned and whispered something to the officer standing to his right. The man gave a shout, and the beating stopped.

She should have felt relief. Instead, she felt a surge of anger, as though she had been betrayed. Where was their courage, their defiance? They had held out for so long. They would surely not attempt to escape now. She looked to the anti-fascists, but there were hundreds of them, their faces hidden behind their raised arms so that they seemed like nothing more than copies of the same man repeated, nothing to distinguish them from one another at all.

Everyone was silent in the boat back to San Domino. Elio sat hunched at the end of one of the benches, his arms wrapped around his knees, avoiding their eyes. One of his was pressed shut by a heavy bruise where the carabiniere had struck him. It was a deep, dark purple, the colour of the mulberries that had spilled across the Via Cameroni all summer, staining the paving stones with their juices. He leaned his head back, shutting his other eye against the sun. Most of the buttons of his shirt were missing, others fastened in the wrong places. In Catania, Elio had taken more care over his clothing than any of them. His shirts were always perfectly pressed, neat creases ironed into his trousers.

'You are a coward,' Carlo spat, glaring at Arturo. 'Both of you. You betray us all, just to save that one's skin?'

Arturo said nothing. He was staring over the side of the boat, glancing occasionally up at Elio, then away. Though it had shocked him, Francesco didn't feel angry. Arturo's had been the first hand to be raised, but the others had been quick to follow.

'Where I come from,' Carlo continued, 'you would be killed for such a betrayal. We would wring your neck like a dog.'

'Just try it, Roman,' Arturo muttered. 'Just try it, and see what happens. As if I did it for him, anyway.' He spat at the floor in Elio's direction. Francesco watched him, wondering if what he said was true. Wondering how much of what Arturo said was only playing a part. That morning, he had helped Arturo to write a new petition, and afterwards, Arturo had sworn him to secrecy. They had sat together at the table, when no one else was in the dormitory, and Arturo had mouthed the words silently, glancing constantly over his shoulder.

I am an orphan. Fate and destiny have given me this disease – why am I to blame? Why punish me? Perhaps serving the sentence will cure me.

Elio looked up. Behind his bruised face, it was impossible to read his expression, but his eyes rested on Arturo, and his gaze did not falter until they rounded San Domino's jagged coast and pulled up on the shore.

Pirelli was waiting for them in the dormitory. As they staggered back to their bunks, exhausted by standing for hours in the sun, he took Gio's arm.

'It is your turn,' he said, indicating the poster of Rapetti behind his head. 'Let's go.'

As they left, Gio turned his head and met Francesco's eyes. Gio was wide-eyed, as though panic had frozen his thoughts. Then, at a bark from Pirelli, he stepped outside, and the door shut heavily behind him.

Twenty-Eight

Catania, October 1938

After their meeting, Francesco hears nothing else from Rapetti. Antonio's trial is scheduled for less than a week's time. Trials in Catania are a public spectacle; crowds gather in the Piazza Stesicoro, outside the Palazzo. Autumn has stripped the piazza of its colour; the buildings are grey and smoke-stained, shadowed from the sun by their own height and the trees that fill the centre of the square, rising high in search of sunlight. The half-excavated remains of the Roman theatre are a deep, shadowy pit. Since Francesco last came here, they have pulled out more rubble and left it at the hollow's edge, bricks and boulders, some carved columns, half-formed statues of men wearing breastplates and leather sandals. It is as though the city's past is rising up and bursting through its seams.

One side of the square is dominated by the Palazzo, a dark, imposing palace of volcanic rock. White marble columns, three storeys high, cut across its edifice, the only hint of light. During a trial, spectators loiter in the square, jostling each other for a glimpse of the proceedings through shuttered windows, passing whispered rumours, snatches of information amongst each other. Any trial would be sensational in the quiet, slow days of early autumn, but the trial of an *arrusu*, a *recchione*, a deviant, is cause for particular excitement.

When the final day comes, Francesco and Emilio stand together amongst the crowds. Most of the *arrusi* are there, taking care not to gather conspicuously. It has been a long time since the trial of one of their own. Gio is close to them, chewing nervously on his fingers.

'They say it was one of us,' he whispers as the crowds grow

around them. 'One of us, paying him and not being too careful who knew it. Do you think that's true?'

Francesco stares up at the entrance to the Palazzo, a shuttered gate two storeys high, and thinks of Antonio inside. What will he be saying, giving away?

'Boys as young as ten,' he hears someone whisper beside him. 'Paid them with sugar, we heard,' says someone else. 'They should be shot. It is contagious, isn't it? We should shoot them all. That would make sure they didn't come back, spreading their diseases.' Emilio spits at the ground as Francesco puts a hand on his arm. It is quickly shaken off.

They stand there for what feels like hours as the sun traverses the square, passing through the shadows of trees and buildings, stretching uselessly into the pit, failing to penetrate its darkness. A warm wind gathers itself around them, lifting the branches overhead, the rustle of leaves joining the whispering of the crowd.

'When he is convicted,' Emilio murmurs softly in Francesco's ear, 'when it happens . . .'

'If it happens.'

'. . . we have to run.'

'Run?'

He feels Emilio's warning hand on his arm, as a few people turn towards them. Emilio leans in closer.

'He will talk. He will tell them everything. It will be the only way to ensure a better sentence. He will talk about what we have done, the notes, Rapetti . . .'

'He wouldn't.'

Emilio smiles sadly at him. 'Wouldn't you?'

He thinks about it. Imagines standing in a courtroom, a judge proclaiming sentence. Would he talk, if it was him? He can't, for a moment, imagine doing anything else. He wonders if Emilio would do it too.

In a few hours, it could all be out in the open. Everything he and Emilio have been part of, everyone they have betrayed.

And not only that, but everything he has done, with other men. He feels the threat from both sides, as the crowds surge around him. How long will he last in this city, once the truth is known?

'All right. Run where?'

Emilio shakes his head. 'When it happens, we should separate. Meet me under the arches after dark. Talk to no one.' He is staring at Gio as he gives the last instruction. Francesco nods, trying hard not to meet Emilio's eyes.

Still the trial lingers on. It is nearly dark now, the trees no more than black shapes over their heads. Shadows lengthen further around them. The crowd grows restless. Some abandon the vigil, leaving others huddling together for warmth, leaning against trees, walls, street lamps. It is taking too long, he hears them whisper, the message spreading fast. Why is it taking so long? He feels Gio shifting close to him. Eyes watching them in the dark. A small child, huddling in his mother's skirts, is staring up at Francesco with what feel like dark, suspicious eyes.

He turns to Emilio.

'I can't wait here. I have to walk.'

St Agatha's is empty. Francesco walks along the cool flagstones at its perimeter, keeping his head down, feeling his father's presence beside him. He has never seen the place empty before; there should be a throng of Catanians whispering from every niche and vestibule. The trial has emptied even the churches of their congregations, spilling them out onto the streets like a slow, volcanic tide.

Why does he come here to feel safe? This is the last place he should feel protected, but something in the high walls, the stone faces of the saints, the long-dead civilisations that have built sections of the city in their turn – Roman foundations, Norman walls, Italian facades – reminds him how little in the world is permanent. Nothing, he thinks, staring up into the face of the dome. Nothing is permanent. Not even the regime.

He looks up at the altar. He can hear screams outside in the square. Agatha is looking down at him with blank, pupil-less eyes, her mouth open as though about to speak to him. The screams grow louder. He hears footsteps.

He turns. Emilio is in the doorway. He is breathing hard, hands on his knees.

'Femminella.'

Francesco flinches, and looks back towards the altar, that blank stare. To hear that name, here of all places. But there is no one here. The church is empty.

He takes a step forward, then stops when he sees how pale Emilio is. Already, Francesco's legs are tensed, ready to run. Already, he thinks, they know everything. The city is being turned against him.

'Did he talk? What—'

'They let him go, Femminella. He is free.'

Twenty-Nine

San Domino, October 1939

Francesco waited two hours in the dormitory, and Gio did not come back. Unable to stand the silence, he left the camp and walked north, through the cool shade of the pine trees, along the rough paths towards the cliffs overlooking the beach.

The anniversary celebrations over, most of the boats had returned to the port, tied up in a neat row along the sand. Across the water on San Nicola, he could see the black shapes of the carabinieri making their way back to the fortress, the paler figures of prisoners just visible amongst them.

Below him, two boys were running the length of the beach, leaping and jumping in the surf. They hardly seemed to notice the soldiers standing guard in their sentry box, their postures still as monuments of war. The boys picked up long pieces of driftwood, balanced them carefully against their palms and lowered them to their shoulders, squinting along their shafts and recoiling from each other in mock deaths that, from where Francesco stood watching them, seemed convincingly real. Returned from San Nicola, they had shed their constricting uniforms, replacing them with shorts and half-unbuttoned shirts, their hair escaping from the oil that had held it flat. Francesco thought of the day they had slid a gun into his hands in Catania. *All soldiers are athletes*, they had said. *First you learn competition, the taste of winning. Then they give you a gun.*

'They are afraid of being conscripted. My brothers.'

He turned. Elena was standing behind him, leaning against a tree, her arms folded. She wore an apron around her waist, starched a brilliant white. He remembered the dress he had seen her climb trees in, torn and streaked with mud. Her hair was covered with a white cap, like the one Lucia used to wear in the restaurant. As Francesco looked at her, she pulled it quickly off.

'The Director is visiting the village,' she said. 'For the anniversary. They have us serve the food. The girls, I mean.' She threw the cap onto the grass, then gave a gasp as it flew towards the cliffs. Francesco caught it just as it reached the edge.

'They are too young for conscription, surely,' he said, turning back to the beach to watch Elena's brothers miming their elaborate deaths.

'Andrea is,' she said, sitting down in the grass, 'but Marco is eighteen this year. They do not want to be separated.' She shook her head. 'They would not admit it; they say they want to fight. But I know they are afraid to be apart.'

'We have not even joined the war.'

'But we will. Everyone says we will.'

He sat beside her and handed her the cap. She took it, then closed her hand over his. Her fingers were cold against his skin.

'Perhaps they will not come this far to look for soldiers,' Francesco said, looking out at the flat expanse of sea before them. Below him, one of the boys shouted out a warlike cry, and lunged with his driftwood spear.

'And you would stay?'

He looked at her. 'I don't know. Would you?'

She shrugged, then gave him a shy smile. 'We could stay together.' Her grip on his hand tightened. 'If I don't . . . If you can't go home. If I never escape . . .'

'Why do you want to leave? Look at this place.' He waved a hand at the horizon. The sun was setting behind them. In the last of its light, the cliffs and fortress walls of San Nicola glistened a vivid, luminous white beneath a darkening blue sky. The light scattered itself on the still water between the islands, glittering a path between them. Over their heads, the first screams of the Diomedee birds had already begun to punctuate the silence. He thought, suddenly, of the first night he had met Emilio. *I don't feel trapped*, he had said, and what had Emilio replied? *You should. You live on an island.* There were only so many places to run to.

He looked down at their hands, still clasped together. Elena's fingers looked small, pale next to his. She put her other hand over his and held it there.

'Why did you give the salute?'

Francesco sighed. 'I don't know,' he said truthfully. 'It is not easy, when everyone around you is doing the same.'

'But you are different.'

'Am I? I think we are all alike, in the end.'

'You are not like them.' She looked towards San Nicola. The anti-fascist prisoners must all have returned to their barracks; the pale streets of the island were empty now. 'I don't know what you have done, why you are here, but you are nothing like them. If you were, you would be over there with them, wouldn't you?'

'Perhaps they have not done something so terrible either.' He thought of his parents, the pamphlets, the library. His father's shaking hands, the gun at his waist. *How can I face you if I do nothing?* How could he explain to Elena, who had never thought of them as anything other than criminals?

As he strained his eyes at the horizon in the diminishing light, he felt her lean her head against his shoulder. Instinctively he reached an arm around her. He could feel her shoulder bones through her skin. He watched the two boys on the beach, chasing each other through the waves and the shadows, and thought of Emilio, fifteen in the mud of Caporetto. They were children. Just children, bred for war.

'My father says you should take what you want,' Elena said. 'That's what real men do.'

Francesco smiled. 'What about girls?'

'I don't know. I think it is the same for girls.'

She looked up at him. Her eyes were wide, as though she were taking in every detail of him. He thought again how lonely she must be here. Whenever he saw girls in Catania, they were always in groups, walking to school or to the square, chattering and laughing. He had never seen Elena with anyone else. He tightened his arm around her. She was still staring into his eyes, an expression on her face he had not seen before. As he began to move away, she reached up and put a hand on his cheek, leaned forward and kissed him.

It was so sudden, he didn't move at first. Then, shocked, he pushed her away, more roughly than he had intended. She fell back heavily in the soft earth.

'I'm sorry . . .' he began, standing up and holding out a hand. Her cheeks flamed. He leaned down and tried to help her up, and she pushed his hand away, scrambled to her feet and ran from him into the trees.

He called out to her, running from the cliff edge through pine needles slick with recent rain, tripping on tree roots and soft earth. She was moving quickly, but her dress was bright in the shade, flashing in and out of the pine trees. In the dusk of early evening, it was hard to see amongst the shadows, but he kept running until he reached a clearing, and saw her standing still beside a tree, gripping it with one hand as though to hold herself upright, her chest heaving as she fought to catch her breath.

She didn't turn as he approached her. Not even when he said her name. She was staring at something. Francesco moved closer to her, following the direction of her gaze. On the other side of the clearing, there was movement against a tree: two people, two men, pulling at each other's pale shirts, their fingers in each other's hair. Francesco knew Elio from his narrow build, his thin shoulders and dark hair. The pattern of purple bruises spreading across his face from the beating the carabinieri had given him on San Nicola, his right eye still pressed shut. The other man was taller, broad-shouldered. He was kissing the bruises lightly, one by one, as Elio wrapped his arms around him. Francesco took longer than he should have done to recognise him, until he turned his head and their eyes briefly met. Arturo, his lips pressed against Elio's cheek, his hair, his mouth.

For a moment, Francesco forgot Elena. He could only stare at Arturo, remembering all the times he had spoken of the women waiting for him back home, all the stories he had told the *arrusi*, all the names he had called them. He had hardly seen Arturo say a word to Elio before, except in anger. As he watched, Elio turned his head too and stared at Francesco, who moved quickly behind a tree. He knew they must have seen him.

At his sudden movement, Elena turned. There was a look in her eyes Francesco hadn't seen before. A fierce, cold disgust.

'Is this what you are?' she whispered.

Francesco put out a hand to her.

'Tell me. Is it why you are here?'

'Elena—'

'Don't you touch me! You are disgusting.'

He tried to speak, but found he could not think of anything to say.

'What have you been doing? You must have been laughing at me. All this time . . .'

'I haven't laughed at you.'

'He was right about you. They all were. You are not a man at all. You are worse than them!' She pointed in the direction of San Nicola.

'Who was right?'

'I don't need you!' Her eyes filled up with tears. 'I have him now, he told me to keep away from you. Now I know why.'

'Who? Elena, did he give you these?' Francesco pulled the two notes from his pocket. 'Did you leave these for me?'

'Don't come near me!'

'Please! Tell me who gave them to you!'

'Leave me alone!' She pushed him away. He took hold of her arm as she tried to run, and she stumbled, throwing out a hand to steady herself, crying out as her knees struck the earth.

'Did he tell you his name?' Francesco felt his fingers shake as he held the papers out. 'The man who gave you these. Please, Elena, did he tell you his name?'

'You cannot say my name! You are the enemy, this country's enemy!' She scrambled to her feet, backing away from him as though afraid he would seize hold of her. 'I understand now. My father told me – you are what lost us the war, that's why they will never let you out! You are the reason my father was imprisoned. Why we are imprisoned still. You are cowards, all of you!'

'Is he paying you? Tell me his name!'

'*Recchione!* You are disgusting! He thinks so too. He hates what you are.' A cry fell from her, half sob, half scream. Francesco stood still, the question stalled on his lips. 'We know what you are, him and me!' She spat the words, her face red with anger. 'He told me himself. You are worse than a plague!'

Thirty

Catania, October 1938

'We should go home,' Emilio says, as Francesco pulls him towards San Antonio. Gio runs on ahead, screaming at them to follow.

'Why?' Francesco feels drunk, though he has not had a drop. Antonio is free. He stood up to Rapetti, and he won. He got what he wanted just by talking to him. How can Emilio not understand that? 'We are celebrating!'

'It's not safe, Cesco.'

'Why not? You said it would not be safe if Antonio was found guilty; now you say it is not safe that he is free. You must see danger in your sleep, Emilio Barone!' He spins Emilio round, trying to pull him into a dance. He stumbles, laughing, and Emilio catches his arm.

'For God's sake. This is still the same city, the same people. Watch what you do.'

'Come with me. Come with me and dance.' He leans in to Emilio, runs his hands down his chest, pressing himself into him. Emilio pushes him roughly away.

'At least wait until you are inside.'

'Until *we* are . . .'

'Go on your own, Francesco. If that's what you want, go on your own. Or, better still, go with him.'

Gio has run back to them, laughing, draping an arm around Francesco. As Emilio turns away, Francesco thinks of following him, or calling after him, but Gio pulls him on towards the dance hall.

He feels elated, running through the streets with Gio, the image of Molina signing a form, ensuring a release because of what he has said, burning into the backs of his eyelids. He has left Emilio behind, left his own deceit behind. As they run, he feels Gio pulling him towards a past he wants to return to, to the boy he used to be, who knew nothing of police, betrayal or Emilio. It has exonerated him, setting Antonio free. He would never have been freed if Francesco had not done what he did, known who he had known. It has all been worthwhile after all.

'Stop,' he calls to Gio as they pass a dark, abandoned doorway. Gio keeps running, and Francesco pulls him back. 'Stop here!'

They both look up at the doorway. Francesco remembers it, the narrow alleyway, the crumbling kerbstones. Gio, fifteen years old, turning back to look at him, surprise, then desire, on his face. Both of them shaking with apprehension as they drew each other closer, that moment, that first contact, burned into his memory.

He pulls Gio back into the doorway and presses his mouth against his. Gio gasps, and presses him closer. They reach for buttons, tear at them, their skin damp and hot beneath their shirts with the chase from the square. Francesco reaches into Gio's trousers, feels the heat, the hardness of him, grips him with both hands as Gio gasps and thrusts against him. He reaches for Francesco's face, kisses him, runs his lips across his skin. Francesco hears footsteps in the next street and moves his hands faster, thrilling at the thought of being discovered, of being caught, as Gio cries out into the dark and shudders against him.

The dance hall is the fullest Francesco has ever seen it. Every *arrusu* in the city, some from outside, it seems, has come to celebrate Antonio's freedom. There are shouts and screams as they enter, drinks pressed into their hands. Antonio is already here, being passed from man to man as though he were a trophy. The music is frantic, desperate, every waltz double speed, every polka triple, the ground shaking and thumping with hundreds of feet struggling to keep up with the delirious tempo.

'What's happened to you?' Gio shouts into his ear, and Francesco laughs, drapes himself around Gio's shoulders and spins him around, before throwing himself at Antonio, wrapping his arms round him. 'We are safe!' he shouts into Antonio's ear. 'We don't have to help them any more.' He waits for Antonio to laugh, for that familiar grin, but Antonio is pale and silent. His eyes move distractedly about the room. Sweat sticks to his brow. Francesco tries not to look at the deep, dark bruise above his eye.

Later, Francesco sees Antonio and Dante, their arms around each other, whispering in a corner. Their expressions are serious, their gazes darting about the room as though they suspect someone in it. Someone screams as one of the light bulbs explodes overhead and the men beneath it duck, laughing, spinning further through the crowds. Francesco can still hear Gio gasping in his ear, groaning as he thrust himself against him, and wants him suddenly more than he ever did, but he can't find him; the room is thick with faces he doesn't know, music he doesn't recognise. The door to the courtyard is closed, and though he knows it will not happen, Francesco looks towards it hoping to see Emilio walking in, wondering where he has gone. When he sees him, he thinks it is still part of his dream, until Emilio shouts over the noise of the crowd.

'Listen to me!' His face is pale. Francesco can see the tremor in his hands as he speaks. Did he follow them after all? Did he see . . .

'You have to run. All of you. They don't want us in this city. You have to run before they come for you.'

The music stops, and there is a long silence. It is broken by Gio, who gives a short, sudden laugh. Then everyone is laughing with him, the music begins again and the dancing, tentative at first, gathers pace.

'You have to fight!'

No one reacts. Emilio grasps Francesco by the arm.

'I mean it. You shouldn't stay here. The police will come for us, they are on the streets already. Come with me.'

Francesco shakes him off and drapes his arms around Gio. When he turns around, Emilio is gone. He moves to dance, but Gio stops him.

'Is he right?' Gio whispers in his ear.

'What?'

'Don't you think it is suspicious?'

'What is suspicious?' Francesco is shouting to be heard over the roar of the dance hall.

'Antonio; they just let him go.'

'What?'

'They just let him go!'

Antonio is behind them, spinning with Dante in his arms. Francesco laughs.

'They had a trial. They did not just—'

But Gio is shaking his head. 'Doesn't it make you wonder?'

'No!' Francesco shouts, trying to smile, to laugh it away.

'Fran, when have any of us ever been let go? They lock us up more than the Mafia!'

'Stop it. Not here.'

He pulls Gio into a corner. They lean against the wall together, panting.

'Fran, did you ever wonder if they are using us? Some of us, I mean?'

'Using . . .'

'To spy. Wouldn't it be useful for Molina to have information from us? Who we are, where we go?'

'Don't be so paranoid, *ragazza*.' He tries to draw Gio back into the dance, but Gio pulls him back.

'No, I mean it. What if he were helping him? What if Antonio is spying for Molina?' He pauses. 'I would kill him, if he was.'

Francesco stares at him. Absurdly, he feels a smile twitching at the corner of his lips. As it spreads, he sees the same beginnings of amusement in Gio's face, and suddenly they are both shrieking with laughter, with how ridiculous it is that any of them could be so monstrous as to betray their friends like that. Gio shakes his head, kisses Francesco roughly, and pulls him back into the dance.

As he makes his way through the room, Francesco loses Gio to the crowds. At some point he sees Antonio making his way to the door alone. Dante is standing watching him leave, his lips pressed tightly together, and Francesco remembers the photograph, taken at Antonio's birthday. The way Dante was staring at Antonio all that night across the table. How reluctant he was afterwards to give the photo up. He watches Dante turn slowly away from the door and rejoin the crowds, and then he forgets him, lost in the music, the pounding of feet on the floorboards, the heat of the bodies around him.

No one hears the first shot from outside. Only the screams in the courtyard that follow it, and then, in the silence after them, the second, and the third, and the fourth.

Thirty-One

San Domino, October 1939

Elena was woken by a scream. There were often sounds like that in the night. Birds, or some other creature alone in the dark. There was so much silence in San Domino, every noise was amplified.

She sat up quickly. It hadn't been a scream that woke her. That had been part of her dream; she had been running towards the cliff edge, and someone was behind her, trying to catch her as she ran on into the empty air. Francesco, panting as he chased her, his hands outstretched. She had run faster, the image of the two men pressed against the tree burning its way into the dream, terrifying her. In the dream, she was closer to them. She could hear the sounds they made, smell the sweat, the heat of them. She kept running, to shake the image away. When she went over the cliff edge, she hadn't fallen like her paper birds. She had kept going, on towards the mainland, nothing beneath her but air and sea and silence.

It had been a door shutting that had woken her. Outside her bedroom door, she heard footsteps, voices whispering, a muffled laugh. She crawled out of bed, pulling on a jumper, pushing her hair out of her eyes. She struck a match and held it out, found a candle stump beside her bed and lit it, leaning against the door.

She tried not to look at the long white cotton dress hanging from a rail in the corner of the room. The sight of it always took her by surprise. There was still no date for the wedding, but already her brothers teased her about it, holding the dress up against her and singing tuneless wedding marches.

She heard the laughter again. She had been expecting to

hear her parents; perhaps her father with one of his friends from San Nicola, out late and drunk on the acrid spirit they brewed up in their kitchens. But it was her brothers' voices.

The fear left her then. She opened her bedroom door quickly, not giving them a chance to run, and stood with one hand on her hip, the other holding the candle up to light their faces. Marco blinked, and put his hands over his eyes. Andrea turned away from her, but she reached out and seized his elbow, spinning him around.

'Stop it!' he said, as Marco hushed him. Andrea had a hand over his mouth. Elena pulled it away. There was something on his lips. Something red, smeared across his chin.

She remembered a day when she was very young, the two of them taking her out across the island to pick mulberries from the tree by the Cameroni district. How she had smeared the juice across her face, probing the sweetness with her tongue. She had used it to paint her lips as she had seen on the faces of the women in her magazines, shipped over from the mainland. Pretending she was different, someone graceful and elegant, someone far away from here.

'What are you doing?' She held the candle up to Marco's face as with the other hand she grasped his closed fist. Something fell from it. A stick of charcoal. There were dark lines across his eyelids, drawn unevenly beneath his eyes.

'Nothing. We went down to the camp, that's all.'

'What have you done?'

Marco snatched up the charcoal. 'Fuck off, Elena. It's nothing to do with you.'

She thought then of the day she had gone to watch the prisoners perform their play. The boy wearing the red dress, how it had flowed across his hips, the hem lifting in the wind. How she had longed for a dress like it. Her brothers, hiding close to her in the bushes, watching them and laughing. The fascination in their eyes.

'We were only playing,' Andrea said in a quiet voice. 'Please don't tell.'

'It's disgusting,' she whispered. They both stood staring at their feet. She felt hot with anger. Whatever it was, this contagion that took away men, turned them into something unnatural, it was winning. It had already taken Francesco from her. Now it was taking her brothers. It had to be fought, like any disease. If they could no longer be men, hold onto their own strength, she would learn how to do it herself.

She clenched her fists at her side as she thought of what Coviello had said to her father that morning. *We could use her, in our fight.* There was more than one way, then, to escape.

When morning came, she woke to find the determination had not left her. She could hear the Director's voice from the kitchen. He came more and more now. Almost weekly, he sat with Elena's father in the kitchen, drinking their wine, eating her mother's cooking.

She burst into the room without knocking.

'Do you know?'

Her father looked up. He and the Director were bending over some sheets of paper, laid flat on the table. They looked like plans for buildings. She wondered if they were expanding the camp, bringing more of those men to the island, and felt sickened. Behind them, standing by the stove, her mother shot her a fierce warning glance.

'Know what, *furetto*?'

Next to the plans on the table, the familiar posters were lying in their usual pile, the photograph of the man who had been killed, the man whose murderer her father had been tasked to find. Her father was failing. That was clear. Why else did the Director keep visiting? She would know by her father's manner if he had won a battle. That was why her mother feared for his job. Why Elena's life was being forced to change.

'Do you know who killed that man?' She walked into the

room, careful not to hesitate on the threshold. They needed to know she was serious. They needed to know she was not afraid.

'How do you . . .' Her father stood up, then looked at Coviello. 'I'm sorry. She is young.'

'No.' Coviello smiled as he stood, turning to face her. 'She is not so young. She understands.' He crossed the room and stood in front of her, studying her carefully with his dark, narrow eyes. 'Do you know something, *figlia*?'

Slowly she shook her head.

'But you would like to help?'

'Yes.' She looked quickly at her mother. 'I want to work. I want to work for myself.' She raised her chin, hoping Coviello could not see the tremor in her fingers, clasped together.

'You have spoken to them, haven't you? You have spent time with the prisoners.'

'Elena, I told you—'

Coviello raised his hand, silencing her father. 'It's all right. She is curious. That is admirable, even in a female.' He knelt down so that their eyes were level. She could see tiny black hairs growing from his nostrils. 'Have you spoken to them?'

She nodded again. Then everything went black, and there was a sharp, stinging pain across her cheek.

'That is for lying to me, and for not obeying your father. Fathers are to be obeyed always. You understand?'

'Yes.' She felt tears in her eyes, and fought to hold them back. She didn't want to cry. She didn't even mind the pain. The tears had come without her wanting them to, which only made them worse.

'You want to help? That is how you can make amends to your father.'

'I want to help.'

'Good girl. Then perhaps we could find a job for you, Elena Pirelli.' He smiled, so widely she could see his teeth. 'Would you like that?'

'What do you want her to do?'

'Just talk to them, as she has done already,' he said, turning to Elena's mother. 'Just let them talk to her. They will betray something in the end. They always do, men like that. It is in their nature.'

'It isn't safe. They are—'

'I know what they are. It's all right. They are not interested in someone like her. She is nothing to them.'

Elena saw again the two men pressed against the tree. Heard the sound of Francesco running after her, his breath heavy and quick. She put her hand in her pocket and drew out one of her paper birds. Slowly she unfolded its wings and smoothed the paper out, until the man's face was unfurled, his eyes darkly staring. She looked up at Coviello.

'What was his name?'

Coviello smiled at her. 'Rapetti,' he said, resting a hand on her shoulder. 'His name was Rapetti.'

Francesco was standing by the fence when Emilio fell. He had been digging all morning, but the rain had started up again, the earth beneath his spade becoming a muddy puddle. He dug the spade into it and leaned against the fence to catch his breath, pushing his wet hair away from his eyes.

He heard it before he saw anything. A heavy thud. He thought at first his spade had slipped over in the mud. Emilio was lying in the centre of the yard with his hands splayed out in the dust, his body twitching.

As Francesco ducked beneath the fence and ran to him, he saw Father Eugenio coming out from the dormitory. They reached Emilio together. Francesco knelt beside him, putting a hand on his shoulder, before he felt one of the guards hauling him away.

'He needs a doctor,' he said breathlessly, as Father Eugenio and Favero pulled Emilio up. 'He needs—'

'All right,' Santoro said, letting go of Francesco's arms.

'Take him to the infirmary.' Favero looked doubtfully at Emilio, who let out a low, muffled moan.

'It is not staffed,' he said. 'They have been called back to the mainland.'

'Fine. Send him back to Foggia then. I don't care.'

'I told you!' Francesco could not help shouting at Favero as they carried Emilio away. 'I told you this would happen!'

Emilio coughed, and something red and foam-flecked poured from his mouth.

'What have you done?'

'Nothing. I'm all right.' Emilio turned away from him. He was lying on his bunk, waiting for the guards to take him away. His skin was a sallow yellow, glossy with a sheen of sweat.

'Stop it.' Francesco put a hand to his forehead. 'You're not all right. What's wrong with you?'

'Leave me alone, Francesco.'

Francesco looked over his shoulder. The dormitory was full, but no one was paying them any attention. He pulled the notes from his pocket.

'Em,' he whispered. 'I keep seeing these. They are everywhere.' He pushed the papers into Emilio's hands. Emilio took them and stared at the image of Rapetti. Then he turned them over, studying the words written in their hasty, elegant scrawl.

'What do they say?'

'Nothing. It doesn't matter.'

'Is it a threat?'

'Maybe. I don't know. Emilio . . . what should we do? Pirelli will find out eventually.'

'What about Gio? Has he said anything?'

'I don't know.' After his interrogation, Gio had avoided Francesco. Francesco didn't know what he had said, how much he had given away.

'I thought that here we would be safe,' he said hopelessly.

Emilio smiled. 'You think that everywhere, Femminella.' He pressed Francesco's hand to his chest, and nodded towards the scraps of paper. 'I see it too. Not just on the paper. I see it all the time. His face. Ignore it, Francesco. There is nothing you can do.'

'It wasn't the police, was it?'

'What . . .'

'Antonio. Tell me the truth. The police didn't do it, did they? It was one of us. Someone found out that he was working for Rapetti. One of us.'

Emilio closed his eyes, and pushed the papers back into Francesco's hands.

'You don't need me any more, Francesco. You have to do this by yourself.'

Francesco opened his mouth to reply, but the doors opened, and Favero and Santoro marched in. He gripped Emilio's hand, clinging to it even as the guards pulled him away.

As they opened the door and helped Emilio out into the bright evening sunshine, Francesco caught his eye and thought suddenly of what Arturo had said, all those months before. The three ways to escape. *Illness takes you to the infirmary on San Nicola. If it is very bad, to Foggia.*

As the door closed behind them, he thought he saw a smile, just a hint of it, on Emilio's lips, and then he was gone.

Thirty-Two

Catania, October 1938

He is lying face down in the middle of the square. The *arrusi* gather in the doorway, the dance hall suddenly silent. The sun is setting behind the rows of buildings to the west, lighting up the sky with a deep orange glow, as though it is in flames.

At first Francesco thinks Antonio has just fallen. Then he hears someone cry out, a protracted wail; it goes on and on, boring through him, echoing from the high courtyard walls around him. He looks up at the wall behind the dance hall, searches for the corrugated iron, concealing the opening Emilio once pulled him through, a dark tunnel to safety.

The wailing will not stop. He wants to put his hands over his ears, but they feel too heavy, the image of the body in front of him shifting and moving in the dusk. Behind him, he hears one of the *arrusi* whisper something to another. Something about police, and guns.

'Fran?'

Gio's voice sounds far away. From Antonio's chest, a thin river of blood snakes its way through the dust. It meets his still fingers, pools between them, tiny red lakes, before trickling on towards the gutter, towards Francesco's feet. He feels the beginning of a hole in the sole of one of his shoes where Emilio's discarded cigarette burned through it, the ground still warm with sun beneath it.

'Fran?'

'Cesco?'

Voices from every side. One of them sounds like Emilio. He feels someone take his hand. Gio.

'Come on.' They seem to both say it at once. 'Come on.

Let's go.' The blood is running closer to him. He wonders if he will move his feet before it reaches them. How it will feel, soaking through the worn-out hole in his shoe. It will still be warm.

There is more screaming now. A woman – where has she come from? – is bending forward over what used to be Antonio, running her fingers through his hair, pressing them into the folds of his shirt. 'Who has done this?' She tries to pick him up. The hand, blood still collecting between its fingers, lifts a little, the body heavy and reluctant in her arms. Behind her, Dante stands motionless in the shadows, breathing hard, poised to run.

The screams catch light like fire, spreading through the square, echoing through the maze of crumbling back streets; Francesco hears them all around him, cries of 'Murder!' '*Arrusi!*' 'Plague!' Amongst them, he hears the voices of the *arrusi* crying out for revenge. Feet marching rhythmically, coming closer. The square is suddenly filled with police, holding back the crowds. Stones fly through the air towards them. Someone is reading from the gospels, shouting out above the crowd, 'God gave them up to passions of dishonour, committing what is shameful, receiving recompense fitting for their error!'

He feels Emilio pull on his hand. Gio is still holding the other. Who would win, he wonders, if they pulled him until he broke apart?

'Come on,' one of them says again, more urgently now. 'Let's go, we have to run,' the other. A stone whistles past his cheek; he feels the air move around it.

'Who has done this?' the woman wails, staring up at the police officers who are gathering around them. They all look the same in the shadows. They are uniform in the dark. Not like the *arrusi*. He would know each one of the *arrusi* in the dark, their real names and the names they have given themselves. 'Which of you did it?'

The crowds grow louder; he cannot hear individual voices in the din any more. Another stone flies, and one of the *arrusi* falls, a hand to his forehead, blood between his fingers.

Francesco lets one of the hands go. It offers no resistance. The other holds him harder. *I would go anywhere with you.* I still would, he thinks, and tries to convey it with a look, as though Emilio will read it in his face.

'You said we were safe,' he says slowly, not caring who hears him. He sees Antonio standing with Emilio under the railway arch, grinning at him excitedly as he walked towards them, as though it were all just a game. Emilio is breathing hard; he must have run back to the square, towards the dance hall, when he saw the police gathering. His hand tightens around Francesco's. 'You promised me we would be.'

'Cesco . . .'

He does not wait to hear what Emilio will say next. He turns to Gio. Tries to recognise in Gio's face the boy he met once, kicking a stone across the street. Gio's face is pale in the dim light of a distant street lamp. His long-lashed eyes are wide. His face is thin, deep hollows across his cheeks. There is nothing left of that boy. Francesco wonders if his own face is as unrecognisable. How can Gio not know what he has done, just by looking at him?

'Fran . . .'

And then, without expecting it, his mother's face comes to him. The sight of her standing in the doorway in the dressing gown he has patched up for her so many times. How many times has he promised her a new one? And she never complains. He left her alone that night, as he has so many nights. It had been Gio's birthday. Francesco had been wearing a red shirt beneath his jumper, another in his bag for Gio. And later, he had met Emilio.

'Leave me alone. Both of you.'

It is time, Francesco, she had said before he left that night. *Bring me back someone nice. You deserve a beauty.* Lucia's face, smiling at him over a balcony. He stares at the woman still bent over Antonio, her face covered by her hands.

'It's over,' he says quietly, unsure which of them he is talking to, and feels with it a swell of relief. Before either of them can reply, he turns and runs into the dark, towards home.

Thirty-Three

San Domino, December 1939

The *arrusi* lay on their bunks, staring as Pirelli reached up to the wall and fixed a series of images there, one by one. There was no sound in the dormitory but the rustling of the papers and the occasional short sigh from Pirelli as he pushed pins into the crumbling plaster.

There were four images when he was done, alongside the poster he had pinned there months ago. He turned, satisfied, to face them. Outside, the wind rose above the sound of the screaming birds. November had passed, and with it any last hopes of warmth. The days were short and rain-swept; the dormitories damp and claustrophobic. The *arrusi*'s petitions had long since ceased; they had sent out enough to fill entire files, rooms full of files.

No one spoke as Pirelli waited. All of them were transfixed by the photographs behind his head. Only Father Eugenio looked away, huddled in his bunk, his face turned to the wall.

'Quite a sight, isn't it?' Pirelli said, pleased with the effect he had had on them. Francesco felt cold. At the same time, he was unable to look away. The first photograph was of a man, lying face down in a gutter, his hands splayed out in front of him. The next two, close-ups of what was only half apparent in the first: a great bloody wound at the back of Rapetti's skull. The photograph rendered the damage in exquisite monochrome detail; the hair flattened and clotted with blood around a gaping, sharp-edged cavity. The final image was a face he knew well, though the expression was unfamiliar. Antonio looked wide-eyed and frightened as he stared at the police photographer.

'All of you from Catania know who both of these men are,' Pirelli said. 'This one' – he gestured to the image of Antonio – 'was an informer. Nearly all of you knew him, I think. Possibly he is a link to finding out who was responsible for this atrocity.' He pointed to the images of Rapetti. There was a long silence while Pirelli stared at them. Then he sighed, and turned away. 'I will leave these images here,' he said at last, 'to remind you of what you are protecting.' He turned in the doorway. 'And if anyone removes them, be sure you will all be punished.'

'Well,' Carlo said, walking over to the photographs and examining them closely. 'These are . . . impressive.' He studied them for a long time, while the others sat in silence. It was past eight; Pirelli had turned the key in the lock after him. Francesco looked over at Emilio's empty bed, feeling the exposure of his absence. Gio had hardly spoken to him in the weeks since he had made his discovery. Without Emilio, Francesco felt entirely alone.

'Someone has done the world a great service with this,' Carlo said, nodding his approval.

'With murder, you mean,' Dante muttered.

'With justice.' Carlo's voice was hard. 'What is one less policeman to you? Yes, a great service. I understand why you will not admit it to them.' He looked to the door. 'But, please. I must know who is the man. I must shake his hand.' He grinned at them. No one spoke. 'Come on,' he said more loudly, 'you should be proud! You should be revelling in this!' He gestured to the pictures, then looked over at Emilio's empty bunk. 'Of course,' he said, walking over to it and stroking the metal frame thoughtfully. 'Perhaps the man responsible is not here just now.'

The following day was a Sunday, and Carlo somehow persuaded Father Eugenio to set himself up in the second dormitory to take confessions. They would all disperse until the evening count, he said, and if anyone wished to confess to the crime, they could come alone. The *arrusi* obeyed him mechanically, without question. There was something irresistible in the command he had over them. It was easier, safer, to submit.

Francesco watched Elio and Arturo set off in opposite directions, Elio to the Cala Tramontana, Arturo to work in the fields. He had been watching the pair carefully since the afternoon he and Elena had found them in the clearing, wondering if there were any signs he had missed, but there was nothing. Except he saw now that their indifference to each other seemed studied. Knowing what he knew, Francesco could believe it was the product of many hours of practice, the way they moved around each other without their eyes meeting, never sat at the table at the same time, always settled themselves at opposite sides of the room. He couldn't recall ever seeing them together, until that afternoon in the clearing. He wondered how they had been able to stand it for so long. He thought of the night he had lain beside Emilio, and the muffled sounds they had heard in the dark.

He took himself north to the grove of pine trees, although he did not expect to find Elena there again. He was walking close to the clearing when the rain started. A wind came with it, forcing the drops into his eyes. He took shelter under the trees, sitting against a thick, rough trunk, staring across the clearing and remembering the shadows of the two men he and Elena had seen. Her voice, screaming at him. *Recchione*. When he heard it again, he thought he had begun to dream.

'Hello.'

She was there, watching him from a little way off, standing in the shadows of branches. Her hair was slick with rain. She wore a thin shawl around her shoulders, but no coat. She was twisting one of her paper birds in her hands.

He sat up. She surprised him by moving close to him and sitting down, crossing her legs neatly. Her hair was hanging loose, shielding part of her face. She seemed different. He thought of the last time he had seen her, screaming at him across the clearing. The anger seemed to have dissolved from her. She shifted herself to be closer to him, but she was avoiding his eyes, pulling at blades of grass.

After a while, she reached into the pocket of her skirt and took out one of her paper birds.

'You want to try again?' he said, holding out his hand, but she shook her head. Carefully she unfolded the paper and smoothed it out flat with her fingers against the grass.

'What was he like? Rapetti, I mean,' she said, staring at the image, stroking the flattened edges of the paper.

'Rapetti?' Francesco looked at it too. A fat drop of rain landed on the paper, blurring the lines of the policeman's eyes. 'I don't know. He was just doing his job.'

'But you hated him? You must have.'

'He hated us. I suppose that made us feel the same about him.'

'How did he die?'

There was a long silence. 'I don't know.' He didn't want to think about that now. Not while those photographs hung in the dormitory. The rain fell harder, crackling against the paper.

'Do you know who killed him?'

She said it calmly, but there was an edge to her voice now. Francesco felt something within him issue a warning flare.

'First Pirelli, now you as well,' he said quietly.

'Pirelli?' She looked at him closely.

'Never mind. I don't know,' he said, taking the paper and folding it up along its creases. He studied the bird he had made. 'We could try a new way,' he said, folding it into a shape like an aeroplane, two triangles of paper wings outstretched. Elena didn't even look.

'You never told me about those notes you left me,' he said carefully. He felt her tense beside him. 'You put them in my pockets, didn't you?'

She shrugged.

'All those questions for me, and I cannot ask my own? Who gave them to you, Elena?'

She stood up. 'I meant to tell you,' she said, as she crumpled the paper in her fist. 'I have made them fly. I don't need your help.' She took another paper bird out of her pocket and held it out. In a swift, sudden movement that seemed to recall the slashing motion she had made with her fist the day they stood on the rocks together, she threw it into the air. It soared in a perfect arc through the rain.

He only thought of it after she had gone. She couldn't read. She had told him that herself. How had she known Rapetti's name?

Francesco had forgotten about Father Eugenio, the confession, when he made his way back to the camp. Only when he approached the dormitory and saw Elio pacing in front of it did he remember.

'Something to confess, Femminella?' Elio said, looking triumphant as Francesco shook his head. 'What about your girl? He is not here to tell us what he knows.'

'He doesn't know anything either.' Francesco tried to push past him, but Elio seized his collar and pressed him against the fence. 'You miss him?' he hissed in Francesco's ear. 'You should. He is all that was keeping you safe here.'

Over Elio's shoulder, Francesco saw some of the other *arrusi* beginning to make their way back, figures in white scattered across the fields. The sun was setting behind them, lighting up the tilled soil.

'How long left for you now, Francesco?' Elio whispered. 'Eighteen, twenty months? Did you know that, Carlo?' he said more loudly to a figure standing behind him. 'This one only has two years for his sentence. Maybe I am not the one you should be accusing of being a traitor.' Francesco heard Carlo laugh, low and threatening. 'How long?' Elio said again.

'Eighteen. Eighteen months.'

'Eighteen. We have been thinking about what message you should take back, when you go.' Claudio and Luca were beside him now. Francesco tried to shake himself free of Elio's grip, but his hands tightened, one arm reaching around his neck. Then a shove from behind, and he was pushed to his knees.

'First, we thought they would wish to know how we are treated here.' Claudio struck Francesco's jaw, so fast it threw him sideways in the damp earth. As he lay gasping, Elio kicked him hard in the stomach.

'Then we thought they should know what *arrusi* are good for.' They pulled him up. Far in the distance, Francesco saw Gio standing by the fields. He was moving back and forth on the spot, as though trying to decide what he should do. Elio began untying his belt. 'In case they think you are good for war. You tell them, Femminella, when you get home, that this is all you are good for.' He reached for Francesco, his hands around his head, pulling him close. Francesco heard Carlo laughing behind him as he shut his eyes. Then he felt something pulling Elio back, and a roar of excitement from the men around them.

He opened his eyes and saw Arturo with his arms around Elio's waist. Francesco blinked in confusion. Elio struggled against Arturo's grip, the two men grappling together, as Claudio and Luca took hold of Francesco by the wrists, forcing him back down to his knees. Someone struck him hard across the face, and in the blackness that followed, he heard Elio scream. Then there was a sudden, dull silence. In the distance, waves sighed against the rocks, and the first of the Diomedee birds screeched a loud cry.

'I won't tell you again,' a voice said quietly. Francesco opened his eyes. Favero was standing at the centre of the group of men, his gun raised. Behind him, Father Eugenio had come to the dormitory door and stood leaning against it, watching them. Favero turned, taking them all in with the point of the barrel. 'Leave him alone,' he said slowly. 'Or I will make a message out of all of you.'

Francesco slumped down in the cool earth. From the corner of his eye he saw Elio shake Arturo's hand from his shoulder and spit at the ground. A hand reached out to him and he took it instinctively. Favero smiled as he helped him to his feet. 'You see what I can do for you, *arrusu*?' he whispered in Francesco's ear, reaching an arm around him. 'You see how much you need me?'

'You all right?'

In the dormitory, Gio sat beside Francesco on his bunk. He put a hand to Francesco's forehead, to the bruise that was rising there. Francesco shook him off. 'I'm fine.' He had been surprised to see Gio following him in, after his hesitancy outside. It had been so long since they had spoken.

Gio shrugged. 'I told you, didn't I? I told you they wouldn't let it go. Your two years.'

'I know. There's nothing I can do about that now.'

Gio turned and looked up at the photographs pinned to the wall, the poster of Rapetti. 'You know, don't you?' he said.

Francesco shook his head. 'Everyone thinks so. I don't know anything.'

'Come on, Francesco. You were working for him. You and Emilio. Maybe others too.'

Francesco stood up and went to the open doorway. Rain was starting to fall again. The *arrusi* who had not made it back to the dormitory were sheltering beneath trees, holding their jackets over their heads.

He heard Gio light a cigarette behind him.

'Where did you get that?'

Gio shrugged. 'The guards still have some. You're not the only one who knows how to get favours from them.' He passed it to Francesco, their fingers brushing together as Francesco took it.

'I know it wasn't you,' Gio said quietly, with a quick glance over his shoulder. 'Rapetti . . .'

'Who said it was?'

'You do know, though, don't you?'

Francesco looked at him. 'I don't know anything.'

'Look, I haven't said anything to them. You don't have to worry. But I know you're protecting him. It wasn't just Rapetti, was it?'

'Gio . . .'

'We were all there, at the inquest. You heard it too. Antonio was shot with a military weapon. An old model.'

'So?'

'Fran, you know what I'm saying.'

Francesco shook his head, trying to block out Gio's voice.

'A gun from the last war. A gun that belonged to someone who fought in the war. Fran, we have to consider—'

'He didn't kill him! He wouldn't do that.'

'Why are you protecting him? You know what he is. Did he do it for you? Is that why . . . Do they have something on you?'

'I don't know anything.'

'Antonio was working for Rapetti too, wasn't he? He must have been; how else would he have been released? Molina never released any of us, except him.'

'He released you once.'

'That was different.' Gio looked away from him. 'That was just public disorder, not a trial. That was nothing.'

Francesco shook his head. 'Why would he have killed Antonio? Rapetti, maybe, but why Antonio?' He closed his eyes, trying to think, and saw it again, the surprise in Rapetti's face as he staggered backwards. Emilio shouting at him to run. I knew, Francesco thought. I knew everything he had done, and I loved him anyway.

'Maybe Antonio was going to talk. Fran, everyone knows he was passing on secrets. Everyone thought it, after the trial, after he was released. Maybe Emilio didn't want him to tell us about the two of you.'

Francesco shook his head. 'He didn't,' he said, as the rain began to beat harder, the earth churning to rivers of mud. He remembered the day they had stood in the square, the whispers of the crowd, Emilio murmuring in his ear. *He will talk. He will tell them everything. Wouldn't you?*

The bruise on his forehead throbbed. His father had hit him there once, years ago, before the March on Rome, before the fire, before Catania. He had seen something he hadn't been meant to see. The blood streaked across his father's shirt. The gun. *I fucking thought we had him.* Francesco leaned forward, resting his forehead in his hands, closing his eyes. 'He didn't kill anyone.' He wasn't sure, as he said it, who he was talking about, but he felt the lie on his tongue. Bitter, and cold.

Francesco was asleep when they brought Emilio back. It was the middle of the afternoon. Rain was still beating on the dormitory roof. Inside, it was hot and clammy. The *arrusi* lay on their bunks, or sat with their feet resting on the table. No one spoke. They were drowned out by the rain, as though they were under siege.

Francesco dozed fitfully, dreaming of the night Rapetti died. It had been raining then, too. It was the last time he had seen Emilio, before the dormitories. He thought he would never see him again, as he ran through the streets, Emilio's shouts echoing after him, willing him on. They all began to bleed into one, those nights underneath the arches, beginning with the first, Emilio pushing a photograph of Francesco's father into his hands. *I can help you, Femminella.*

He had hardly slept the night before. He had lain awake, staring at the dark space in the dormitory where Emilio had once lain, thinking of him in the hospital at Foggia, wondering if they would ever bring him back. In the middle of the night, as the *arrusi* slept around him, a thought had come to him, and he had crept across the dormitory until he felt the cold metal of Emilio's bed press against his legs. He had knelt down, and groped beneath it. His hand had found dust, shoes, piles of clothing, then a small leather bag, one he had seen Emilio carrying often. He had pulled it out, and reached inside, felt the soft, liquid outlines of the mushrooms, remembered Elena's voice on the cliff edge: *Don't eat those. They are poisonous.* And Arturo's, always Arturo's, as if he had known what Emilio would do from the start. *Illness will take you to the infirmary.* What would Emilio stop at, to get home?

He was brought round in the afternoon by the sound of raised voices, the marching of feet on the pavement outside. The door opened, and rain poured in like a volley of arrows. He opened his eyes. Favero and Santoro were standing in the doorway, rain-soaked and dark in their overcoats, their hair matted to their foreheads. They held a man between them, his own hair long and dripping about his shoulders. Francesco watched from his bunk, only recognising Emilio after they had closed the door behind them, the bolts drawn heavily shut, leaving him shivering in the centre of the room.

Emilio walked slowly to his own bunk and pulled off his overcoat and shirt. Beneath it, his stomach was concave and bruised. Francesco got up and went over to him, putting out an arm as Emilio stumbled. He clung to Francesco, shaking as Francesco tried to lie him down. When he had persuaded him to lie still, he drew a blanket over him and knelt beside the bed, running his fingers through Emilio's rain-soaked hair.

'You have to stop doing this,' he whispered in Emilio's ear. 'Please.' Reaching beneath the bunk, he found the bag and held it out to him. The mushrooms were a rotting, wet paste. 'What will it take for you to stop this?'

Emilio turned his face away.

'Talk to me. What will it take? Sometimes I think you really are trying to kill yourself. That that's what this is all for.

Would you rather that than stay here? Is your freedom worth so much?'

He heard someone moving in their bunk, but when he glanced up, the dormitory was still and silent. The rain had stopped. He turned back to Emilio. He looked younger, his face gaunt against the pillow. For the first time in months, Francesco felt his own strength.

'Why do it this way, if that's what you want? You could just throw yourself over the cliffs.'

Emilio's eyelids flickered then. His lips twitched in a smile. After a pause in which Francesco thought he slept, he whispered, 'Next time.'

'All right.'

Favero turned around. He had been flicking at a cigarette that would not light. The rain had returned early in the morning, the air heavy and damp, the sky grey above the rain-soaked fields. Francesco walked out to where the guard stood outside the open dormitory doorway and held up his own lighter. Favero frowned at him for a moment before bending in acceptance. The end of the cigarette flared with his breath.

'All right what?' He blew a stream of smoke towards Francesco.

'All right. You know what.'

'Do I?'

Francesco moved closer to him and took the cigarette from Favero's lips. Putting it to his own, he drew in a long breath, and flicked it to the ground. 'Ask me,' he said, leaning forward to take another unlit cigarette from Favero's mouth. He held it out in the air. 'Ask me what my price is.'

Favero smiled. He leaned in close and reached for the hand that held the cigarette.

'How much?' he said quietly, and Francesco felt his fingers close around the cigarette. 'How much, *arrusu*?'

Francesco smiled. It was so easy. In the end, it was always so easy.

'The petition. He gave it to you in August. Do you still have it?'

'The cousin. The imaginary sick cousin. You wrote it, didn't you?'

'Sign it.'

Favero put the cigarette to his lips again and stood back, looking Francesco up and down. He was smiling too, as though he had always known the way it would happen. For a moment, Francesco hesitated. He felt himself exposed, Favero forcing his way into a part of his mind he had tried to keep safe for so long.

'You want him to leave?'

Francesco took a deep breath. 'Yes.'

'You know what they will do to you, if he is gone? I won't help you again.'

'I think he will kill himself trying if I don't help him.'

'I wonder if you know, *arrusu*, just how much he has protected you from.' Favero put a hand on his chest. 'I know violence. I know when men wish it on other men. You have only a few months to go. They will not let that pass.'

'I know.' Francesco thought of the few seconds before Favero had reached them, last night. Had he imagined it, or had he seen Arturo pulling Elio back? Was that enough to make him feel safe? He hesitated for a second, remembering the feeling of Claudio and Luca's hands tight around his wrists.

'He will keep trying,' he said. 'Emilio. It will kill him to keep trying. Let him go.'

Favero took a long breath of smoke, and smiled. 'All right,' he said, nodding slowly. He put his hands on Francesco's cheeks, leaned towards him until their mouths were close to touching. 'All right.' He smiled. 'It is a good price, *arrusu*.'

PART FOUR

The fascist accepts life and loves it, knowing nothing of and despising suicide; he rather conceives of life as duty and struggle and conquest, life, which should be high and full, lived for oneself, but above all, for others – those who are at hand, and those who are far distant, contemporaries, and those who will come after.

Benito Mussolini, 'The Doctrine of Fascism', 1932

Thirty-Four

He who is not with us is against us.
Either fascism or anti-fascism.
For the cause of the fascist revolution we are prepared to live, prepared to fight and prepared to die.

Aphorisms of fascism, painted in public spaces and recited regularly by schoolchildren

We are of the people – the unconquered ranks
They have on their collars the black flames
We are moved by a force that is sacred and strong
Death to death – death to pain.

Song of the Arditi del Popolo, the first militant anti-fascist organisation (1921–2)

The voices wake Francesco. His father, and the man who had been with him in the library. Outside, Naples is dark; they have been gone for hours. It is night, the house silent and still. After he had overheard them in the library, Francesco had crept upstairs and sat on his bed, determined to wait up for them, but it must only have been a few minutes before he had drifted into sleep.

He sits up, listening. They aren't whispering any more. They are loud, stumbling. They slam the door heavily behind them. He hears his mother's voice too, quick and hushed. Francesco goes to his bedroom door and opens it, until a thin splinter of light from the downstairs hallway spills into his room. He stands still for a while. They have gone into the library. He can't make out their words, but he can still hear the sounds of them moving about, the clink of glasses. He steps out onto the landing and slowly walks down, one stair at a time, until he is outside the library door again.

His father is pacing the room. He is wearing a thick black jumper over dark trousers. Francesco is used to seeing him in his university clothes, a suit over a light-coloured shirt. There is a small red flower pinned to his jumper. The other man is dressed similarly, with a black cap over his pale hair. His mother is sitting on the arm of a sofa in her dressing gown, perched like a bird, her legs tucked underneath her, her chin resting on her hands, watching him pace.

'We had him,' Francesco's father hisses. 'I fucking thought we had him.' He takes a drink from the glass in his hand. Francesco's mother stands up and puts a hand on his forehead. There is a streak of blood across it. She wipes it with a white silk sleeve. Then she turns her head, and she is looking into Francesco's eyes.

There is a sharp pain as he is struck across the face and dragged into the room by his ear. He opens his eyes and sees his father's hand raised above him, an anger in his eyes Francesco has never seen before. Then something lifts, and he lowers his hand.

'What did you hear?' he says slowly.

'Nothing.' Francesco has not yet learned how to lie. He has never needed to until now. He can hear the sound of the lie in his voice.

'What will you say? If you are ever asked about tonight, what will you say?'

'Nothing.'

Filippo Amello stares at his son for a moment. Francesco stares back. His father seems different. Harder. He can still feel the sting of the blow to his cheek. Then his father kneels down and takes hold of him, suddenly and quickly, in his arms.

'They will come for us now,' his mother whispers.

'No,' his father says over Francesco's shoulder. 'They would not suspect me, that was the point of this. Look around you, Margherita.' He sweeps a hand out around his head, shifting

Francesco in his arms as he does. Francesco looks up at the ceiling. It is painted with clouds. Sometimes he lies on his back in the library and pretends it is the sky above him, that he can feel the sun on his face as he stares at the plaster mouldings of leaves, the painted faces of saints. He shifts his head and looks at the walls of books, their spines dark and unreadable in the dim candlelight. 'We are not that sort of people.' His father laughs, high and breathless. 'They never saw me coming.'

'They burn the houses of people like us. Worse.'

He laughs again. '*Non mollare*,' he whispers. He draws his arms tighter around his son, and takes his wife's hand in his. In the warmth of his father's arms, Francesco closes his eyes and sees flames.

Thirty-Five

Catania, January 1939

'It is more than ten years now. Isn't it, Francesco?'

Margherita Caruso shifts in her chair and smiles at her son. It is a smile he doesn't recognise. Wide and still on her face, like a mask. He picks up his cup. There is a thin, almost unnoticeable crack in its lip. It grazes his skin as he drinks the lukewarm coffee. He thinks of Antonio's lips, cut and swollen after the prison. His fingers, pale against the blood already soaking into the gutters of the square.

'Thirteen,' he says, forcing himself to swallow the coffee. Thirteen years in this flat. These uneven walls, the low ceilings. He and his mother living so close together that he can hear the springs of her bed creak in the night. His room is filled with the clutter she has swept out of the kitchen, ready for this visit. A broken teapot balances on his pillow. Piles of books and magazines across the blankets.

The woman sitting opposite them smiles, and heaps more sugar into her cup. She is plump and red-cheeked. Francesco counts the sugar as she spoons it. One, two, three, four spoonfuls. She stirs slowly, her eyes never leaving his.

'And your family?' she says over the cup. Her fingers are perfectly curled around it. Francesco wonders if Lucia is finding her as unrecognisable as he finds his own mother today.

Margherita speaks quickly. Francesco wonders if it is noticeable to anyone who doesn't know her well. 'We came from Taormina. My husband passed away several years ago. It is just the two of us now.' She puts a hand on Francesco's arm. He has heard her say it so many times. So often that the lines between truth and fiction have begun to blur. Her lies are effortless, as though she has convinced herself of their reality. Sometimes he believes in it himself.

He looks at Lucia, sitting across from him at the table. He has known her for half of his life, but she looks suddenly like a stranger. He can tell she feels his gaze, is looking deliberately down, demure, her hands folded in her lap. Once, when they were too young to see the differences between each other, she would have smiled back openly. Was it her idea, for them to come here? He thinks of her sitting at her father's feet, eyes wide with pleading. *He is just a dishwasher, Lucia. Not even a waiter. He is beneath you.* And then, eventually, he would have given way. Most fathers do, in the end. Very few are so unbendable.

She hasn't touched her coffee. He wonders if she is afraid to spill it. He tries to imagine his arms around her. His hands tangled in her hair. He forces himself to go on. His hands on her waist, his lips on hers, pushing her down on a bed, pushing his hands under her dress . . .

'We don't plan to be here forever, of course,' his mother says stiffly. 'Francesco is saving. He works so hard. At the restaurant.' Her voice falters. She doesn't want to talk about his work. *Why don't you try for something better?* Gio always asks him. Perhaps this is the reason why.

There is a long, pained silence. During it, Lucia meets his eyes. He can see the searching in them, the yearning. She is trying to see if there could be a bond between them in this new context. Some connection that will break the tension, make them co-conspirators in a game others have designed for them. She is probably already imagining the two of them, years from now, lying in a bed together and laughing at this memory, the day their mothers bargained over coffee, decided what each was worth to the other, who should win. He tries to imagine it too. It is a warm, safe feeling, like a memory of childhood. Her skin is soft. There are children, their feet loud on the floor-boards upstairs. Sons and daughters, to make Italy strong again. He will never be alone. He will never be old while he has sons to carry on, to bear his name. His father will have fought for something real.

Beneath the table, Francesco reaches out a hand until it finds hers. Her fingers are cold. He feels them flinch beneath his, draw back a little, then lie still in her lap. He folds his hand over hers. In the background, he can hear his mother talking, something about his grandparents and a great house in Naples. He flinches at the mention of that house, and holds Lucia's hand more tightly, tries to feel the warmth in it. Her hand is cold. It hardly feels alive at all.

'I need to get my papers back.'

'Shh.' Emilio puts a warm hand to Francesco's lips. They are in the Pacini Gardens, sitting against the base of the fountain.

Francesco has been avoiding this meeting, trying to find another way out. But there is none. He has to get his papers back from Rapetti. And Emilio is his only link.

He has not been easy to find. After several raids on the railway arches, after the shooting, the *arrusi* have been meeting in less familiar places, the more dangerous open spaces, closer to the larger squares. Francesco has tried to stay away. Once, he saw two *arrusi* pressed together in a side street beside the Duomo, as though they did not fear the authorities at all. In the end, he went to the mechanics' yard and left a message for Emilio there, hoping it would not be intercepted.

'After I get them back, it's over. I'm not seeing you any more. Any of you.'

Emilio smiled. 'You have said that before.'

'I mean it.'

'And what will you do then? Hide for your whole life?'

'What can I do? I can't keep pretending. I don't want to be two people any more.'

Emilio shakes his head, brushing imaginary dust from his

sleeve. 'You are one person, Francesco. You've only ever been you. You've never understood that, have you?' When Francesco doesn't answer, he sighs. 'What do you mean, your papers?'

'The ones they have, the ones about my family. My father.'

'Francesco—'

'It's the only way to stop this.'

'They won't let you stop.'

'That's why I need my papers. Then they will have no hold on me.'

'You don't see! It's past that now. They know what you are, that's enough. After the shootings . . . I don't think they just want to monitor us any more.'

'What do you mean? You said—'

'I know what I said.' Emilio leans down and picks up a flask of wine, taking a long sip from it and wiping his mouth with the back of his coat sleeve. 'I don't know what they plan to do next. Rapetti won't see me any more.'

'Then maybe it's over.'

Emilio laughs. 'Over. Yes. Maybe it is. Or maybe they shot Antonio on purpose.'

'What do you mean?'

'The police,' Emilio says, rolling his eyes as though Francesco is a child. 'It is the perfect excuse for them, isn't it? Now they have more reasons to round us up.'

'Round us up? You make us sound like animals.' He shakes his head. 'They wouldn't do that. They wouldn't kill—'

'Wake up, Francesco!' Emilio drops the empty flask on the pavement. It skips and rolls into the gutter. 'We never had a hope in this city. They were always going to find a way. That's why we have to fight.'

'You said we would be safe. You lied.'

'I didn't have a choice either, remember.'

'I wish you would tell me why.'

Emilio looks away.

'I'm getting married,' Francesco says quietly. The second

flask, midway to Emilio's lips, pauses in the air. 'Lucia. Her father owns the restaurant. They have a lot of money.' He stops, hearing himself. 'It's for my mother,' he says, testing out the words. It sounds real. 'She gets lonely.'

A shadow shifts beyond the path, something moving in the undergrowth of the unweeded beds. They both tense, drawing themselves up. A cat darts out from the bushes, running lightly towards them, its green eyes flashing in the darkness. It stops to watch them for a moment, then runs on towards the docks.

'Say something.' He looks up. Emilio is drinking from the flask, hardly pausing to take in breath. His face is pained, his eyes narrowed. 'Please. Say anything.'

Emilio puts the flask down carefully on the step beside him, keeping a hand on it, his eyes fixed on it as he speaks. 'They're in his office. Not the desk; they're in a cabinet. I only saw them once. He locked them up afterwards. You can't get them back, Francesco.'

'I have to.'

'And after that, you'll be happy? Living with her? Pretending to be someone else?'

'I won't pretend! I can change.'

'You won't!' Emilio's face is red with anger. 'Do you think I haven't tried? Do you think I wouldn't do anything!'

'I can. I've done it before.'

'What does that mean?'

'You know what they say? The papers?'

Emilio shrugs. 'Only that it is about your father. They wouldn't tell me anything else. I heard Rapetti say something about the Arditi del Popolo, Mussolini . . .'

'My father tried to kill him.'

There is a long silence. Francesco has never said the words out loud before. It has been a long time since he has heard his own voice speaking the truth. He wonders how much Emilio really had known.

'When they came to Naples, before the March on Rome.

Mussolini, and the rest of them. The Arditi used my father because he wasn't like them. He was an intellectual.' Francesco hears himself say *was*, not *is*, and wonders why. 'I only remember it in pieces.' He rubs his head against his hands. 'It didn't make sense for so long. But that's what he was doing. He had a gun. There was a man, a younger man. They both wore a red flower. That's how I knew. When he came back that night, there was blood.'

'And that's why you came here?'

'They didn't come for us then. But he didn't stop. He and my mother – they just kept going with their pamphlets, their meetings. They caught up with him in the end – the Arditi were long gone by then. They burned our house. He ran, and my mother and I . . .' He paused. What had they done? 'We left ourselves behind.'

'But you didn't.' Emilio takes his hand. 'It's all here. You are still you. You have a different name, that's all.' He looks down, his voice suddenly quieter. 'We never change. It isn't possible.'

'I have to try.'

Emilio sighs. 'Where is your father now?'

'I don't know.' Francesco reaches for the bottle, finding it empty. He wants to drink. To go back to the dance hall and lose himself in a crowd of men. To decide for himself who he wants to be. 'They shoot men like him. They burn them. And their families.'

'And men like us?'

Francesco turns and looks at him. Emilio's face is shadowed, his collar drawn tight against his neck. He remembers the night they danced outside the cinema, their breath warm in each other's ears. The music, thin and distant through the brick wall beside them, the sound of a muffled voice singing. It feels like a long time ago. He puts out a hand and finds Emilio's, and it is warm, alive, despite the cold.

'It's over,' he says quietly. 'It has to be.'

'I'll get them back for you.'

'What?'

'Your papers. Don't go yourself. I promise you, I'll get them back. I'll think of something.'

'Emilio . . .'

'You'll regret it.'

'I know.' Francesco sighs. 'I have to try.'

'I don't mean that.'

He feels Emilio's fingers curl around his own, weaving in and out, under and over his palm, brushing against his wrist, slowly and softly, over and over to the rhythm of the sea beyond the railway arches, somewhere beyond the muffled silence of the gardens. He doesn't dare to move, to allow the moment to end. Everything about Emilio is beautiful. Even the way he holds Francesco's hand. Even the anger in his face, as he pulls his hand away and stands, turning away from Francesco, throwing the second empty flask onto the path, where it shatters the silence like a gunshot.

Everything is arranged with such speed, such precision, that Francesco suspects all the details, apart from the bride, have long since been decided upon. He tries to focus on the future, the plans for the wedding, and afterwards; to leave the old part of himself behind. Since the shooting, the *arvulu rossu* boys have been quiet. There have been no dances, no gatherings at the tree beside the port. It helps, to know he is not being missed. And it means there is nothing for him to report to Rapetti.

He sees nothing more of Emilio. There are rumours that the *primogeniti* are still meeting, safe in each other's houses. Francesco wonders whether Emilio is with them. At Marcello's, perhaps, all those men with wrinkled hands, sitting amongst piles of books, drinking from cut glass. He hardly sees Gio either, outside of the restaurant. At work, they say little, occasionally catching each other's eye as Gio brings dirty plates into the kitchen, but there is no time for conversation, and nothing to say. He feels Lucia watching him, when she visits, and does his best to avoid her. Occasionally he passes Gio on the Via Garibaldi, or sees him in church, but he feels as though they are strangers.

Once a week, as always, Francesco still walks to Emilio's yard and checks the space behind the brickwork for messages. He almost never finds anything there now. Just the occasional scrawled line, reminding him of his obligations, or a request to verify a certain name, find details on a certain *arrusu*. A reminder of the noose around his neck.

On a morning in mid-January, a month before his wedding, Francesco rises early and goes out into the silent streets. Catania has not yet woken. He can hear his own footsteps echoing through the narrow streets around the castle. He finds himself walking towards San Antonio, stopping outside the dance hall, now abandoned for so many weeks. The blood in the courtyard has been washed away, the square covered in fresh gravel, but Francesco can still trace the shape of Antonio lying there, his hands flung out at angles, the blood running in rivers between his fingers. He can still hear the crack of bullets, the roar of the crowd of *arrusi* inside, the silence afterwards.

He walks through the city towards the mechanics' yard, his feet following a pattern long committed to memory. So many times he has walked these streets, the papers bearing his friends' names heavy in his hands, and placed them reverently in the space behind the bricks, as though they were a votive offering. A prayer for his mother, to keep her safe. An offering for his father, to bring him back to them. Once, he would have left flowers at the statue of St Agatha, laying them before her dead stone eyes, kissing her cold feet.

Rapetti's car, which has been in and out of the yard since Francesco first came here, is not here now. Standing by the wall, he eases the loose brick free. The hole behind it is damp with recent rain. He brushes aside wet soil and feels something in the dark space. Something white, reflecting the sun from moisture gathering at its corners. A packet, wrapped in oilcloth.

He sits down in the gutter and unwraps it. He recognises the way it has been done, the material, the folds; he has wrapped many such packages himself, bearing the names of his friends inside them.

His fingers shake as he draws out the paper. It is a map. He recognises the streets around San Antonio, leading down to the railway arches, drawn in uneven curls of pencil. Beneath the fourth arch, someone has drawn an arrow, pointing to its centre. And beside that, a clock, the hands pointing to ten o'clock. The sky has been filled in, a circle of moon left paper white.

It is Emilio's drawing. He recognises the style of it at once. The drawing means ten o'clock, night not day, under the fourth arch. But which day? When was the message left? Perhaps he has been waiting there each night, hoping Francesco will find the note and come.

Then he sees another marking, towards the bottom of the paper. A sun, drawn as a child would. A circle, lines radiating from its centre. Sunday. It must mean Sunday. The fourteenth of January. Tomorrow.

He hears footsteps behind him. With trembling fingers, he wraps the paper in the cloth and replaces it in the space in the brickwork, sliding the loose brick into place just as three men turn into the alleyway. He nods politely, hoping his smile does not look forced, as they pass without acknowledging him.

He finishes work early on a Sunday. The restaurant has few customers; most Catanians observe the traditions and stay indoors with their families. A few young men sit alone at tables with coffee or glasses of wine. In a corner, beneath an alcove, two elderly ladies gossip for most of the day, each of them making their coffee last as long as they can manage. They have been coming to the restaurant every Sunday for as long as Francesco has worked there. They eat lunch, order two coffees and sit there until closing time. Francesco watches them from the kitchen, wondering how old they were when they first began their Sunday ritual. Barely more than children, perhaps.

When the restaurant shuts at five, he wishes it were later. He passes the ensuing hours pacing the streets behind the Duomo, trying not to meet anyone's eyes, waiting for the night to come.

At quarter to ten, he turns towards the arches. In the dark, he can sense the volcano shadowing him, its flanks enclosing the city, ready to flood the streets with fire. He remembers the day he watched it pour itself into the valleys, the screams as Catanians rushed to rescue livestock, houses, families. The slow inevitability of it, as the river of red rock spilled across the streets. There is a heaviness to the atmosphere now, as though the streets are waiting for something to break, holding their breath. It is the feeling Francesco imagines must come before an explosion, or the bursting of a dam.

The first three arches are empty. The smell of the fish market still lingers in the air as he passes them, alert to the shifting of shadows in the deeper darkness that collects beneath the railway lines. He reaches the fourth arch as the cathedral strikes the hour.

There is no one there. He steps into the darkness beneath the archway and stands still, listening to the silence behind the sound of the waves. Then he hears a footstep, and someone grabs his hand.

'Emilio! I thought you weren't coming.'

'What are you doing here?' Emilio's voice is a sharp whisper. He is still holding tight to Francesco's hand.

'What you told me to do.'

'Leave. Go, now.'

‘What—’

‘Francesco. Go.’

He pulls his hand away. Emilio’s face is barely visible above a high-collared coat, a scarf wrapped tightly around his neck. There is anger in his eyes.

‘I don’t understand. The note . . .’

‘What note?’

‘You left it by the yard.’

‘It wasn’t for you.’

‘What?’

‘The appointment.’ Emilio’s face is tight with rage. ‘It wasn’t meant for you.’

They turn together. The man is silhouetted against the light of a street lantern. Only when he moves towards them, his shadow resolving itself into a uniformed man, his face momentarily lit by moonlight, does Francesco recognise Rapetti.

Thirty-Six

San Domino, January 1940

> How beautiful this generation is of pure young men, their foreheads marked with virility! Seeing them is a joy. Their noble faces, their refined behaviour, the dignity of their lives make them seductive and attractive. Nobody can resist such beauty.
>
> F. A. Vuillermet, *Siate uomini, alla conquista della virilita*, 1930

Francesco stood, at the appointed time, outside the dormitory. The sun was fading above the trees. A breeze was stirring from the sea, whispering through the branches above him.

It wasn't too late. He could still go inside and close the door, stand in line for the count and lie alone in the dark. He thought of Emilio, lying in the dust, blood foaming in his mouth. His voice, quiet in the stillness, whispering, *Next time.*

It wasn't too late. He thought of the first time Favero had approached him, standing close, his breath on Francesco's cheek. *I am not a whore.*

Now, he was. In Catania, he had never been paid to do anything but wash dishes. There had been favours. Promises, the occasional drink. And there had been silence, from the police, in exchange for his services. But this was different. There was no ambivalence, no doubt about what this was. It was payment, pure and simple.

Many of the *arvulu rossu* boys had done it in Catania. Sometimes with the *primogeniti*, sometimes with rich men who would never have considered themselves part of the *arrusi*'s world. It was only taking what they wanted, like any real man did. The fact that they paid for it only widened the gulf between them. Real men paid, and got what they wanted. Feminised men, men like Antonio, men like Francesco, only took, and received.

But Francesco had never gone that far. Even when they had struggled for money, when he had had to rely on bringing home leftovers from the restaurant kitchens, he had never taken payment from any man. He had never sunk to it before. Still, now that the hour had come, he had not expected to feel so afraid.

He didn't hear Favero coming. He turned away from the rain as it started, facing back towards the dormitory, and when he looked back, Favero was there, his coat pulled up against his neck, his hands in his pockets.

'Come on.' The hint of a stammer had returned to the guard's voice.

Francesco looked back at the dormitory, where Emilio lay sleeping, gave one last thought to changing his mind, and followed Favero into the rain.

They walked in silence towards the village. By the time they reached it, the unlived-in houses standing dark against the sky, the rain was hammering hard against the paving stones. Front doors shone with fresh paint in the moonlight, raindrops illuminating shuttered windows that had never been opened. Favero stopped outside one of the gates and took a set of keys from his pocket. But when they pushed against it, the gate was already open.

Inside, the house smelled musty and damp. They stepped into a low-ceilinged room. The shadows of armchairs and a low table were just visible in the dim moonlight. A clock, the hands still. An empty grate. Somewhere within the house, a door was banging in the breeze. He felt hands on his arms, stroking them lightly.

'They were built for families to come here, but they never

came. This island was meant to be a place for families, for virtue. Real men.' Favero laughed quietly. 'You came instead, *arrusu*.'

Through another door, a kitchen table, four chairs arranged around it. A cluster of red flowers had been left in the centre of the table, dried out and paper thin. A stove, with pans hanging from hooks above it. Francesco thought of his parents in Naples. His father at the table, helping him to shape letters, to sound them out, while his mother watched them. He thought of Lucia, sitting at his kitchen table. Her hand in his. Her eyes, wide and questioning. A family. He would never have one now. It was the first time, standing in that lifeless house with a stranger's hands on him, that he had realised it fully. He was alone.

'So many houses,' Favero said, his voice soft. 'So many empty houses, for families who have never come.'

'You will sign it, after . . . Emilio's petition. You will sign it?'

Favero was still standing in the parlour, staring at an open door to the left of the room. 'There is a cot in there,' he said. 'They thought there would be children.'

'Shall we . . .' Francesco looked at the door, the corner of a bed beyond it. He wanted it to be over, but Favero guided him towards the armchairs and pushed open the shutters. Dust danced in the moonlight. Francesco looked through the glass at the moon, full and large in the window pane, focusing on it as Favero sat down on one of the chairs and flicked at a cigarette.

'Never could get this *bastardo* to work,' he muttered, flinging the lighter aside. He reached out a hand, and Francesco took his own lighter from his pocket without thinking and handed it to him. All those times, in Catania, he had done the same. All the boys he had offered his lighter to, their eyes meeting his, lips pressed to the cigarette, the taste of it on their breath. Had Gio minded? So many boys, and Gio had always come back to him. He had loved Francesco that much.

Favero held out the cigarette. Francesco hesitated, remembering the guard holding out the chocolate in the yard. Then he took it and inhaled deeply.

'Good girl,' Favero said. 'Good.'

Francesco sat in the chair opposite him and waited for Favero to speak. The guard had left his gun leaning against the wall by the door, as though, in the house, he had no fear of ambush, of Francesco trying to flee. He knew there would be no running now.

'Shall we . . .' Francesco began again, but Favero was frowning.

'I . . . I have a wife,' he said falteringly, staring straight ahead, concentrating on the still hands of the clock face. 'I love her.'

'All right.' He didn't know what else to say.

'We don't have children. But one day, I hope.'

'Yes.'

'Do you want children?'

Francesco didn't reply. He focused his thoughts on Emilio, sleeping in the dormitory. On his mother, alone and safe in Catania. All those empty rooms around her. He tried not to think of his father, wherever he was. *You are disgusting. He thinks so too. He hates what you are.*

'Of course you don't. God only knows what you want.' Favero looked up at Francesco. His eyes were shadowed, the whites flecked with red. 'They can't come with us, here. The wives. They have to stay on the mainland.'

'Oh.'

'So long. So long without her. I want you to understand . . . No, not you. You are not the point. I want God to understand that. That's all. God, and . . .'

He stood up suddenly, pulling Francesco with him. Francesco felt an instinct to resist as he was pushed against the wall, the unplastered bricks dragging against his cheek. He felt his whole body tense, ready to fight, then remembered why he was there and relaxed into the bricks, letting them graze his face, his palms, biting at his skin. He felt Favero's body pressed against his, his breath sighing in his ear, then his hands pulling at his trousers, dragging them down to his knees. He kept his eyes closed, trying to picture anything else as he felt his legs forced apart, Favero's breath on his neck, a sharp, burning pain as he pushed himself inside, gasping heavy breaths. He gripped at the wall, feeling one of his fingernails bending and breaking, the pain of it distracting. He tried to think of Emilio, safe in Catania, his reason for everything. The two of them laughing, running from the dance hall towards the railway arches, a guitar slung across Emilio's back. Emilio holding his hand beneath the fountain, winding his fingers over and under Francesco's palm. Each time he pictured Emilio's face, a jolt of pain brought him back to the present, and he saw Rapetti, smiling at him from his desk. Santoro, standing in the dormitory listing meaningless rules. Favero, holding out a bar of chocolate, whispering in his ear.

As Favero cried out, his forehead pressed against Francesco's shoulder, Francesco's mind was filled with the image of another night, the sound of Rapetti's head hitting rubble, his cry of surprise. His fists against the brickwork were clenched now, as though ready to strike. When Favero pulled away from him, he couldn't turn around, terrified that the face he saw would not be Favero's; that he would see dead eyes, rolled back in a pale face, blood pouring over the skin.

When it was over, Francesco bent slowly, wincing at the pain, and pulled his trousers up, hearing Favero behind him doing the same. As he moved towards the door, he felt a hand rest softly on his arm.

'Stay. You'll freeze out there.'

He had expected brutality, anger or indifference. This tenderness was worse. He shook his head, pulling on his jumper. His whole body ached.

'You can't get back into the dormitory, Caruso. Not until we come to unlock it. It's too late now.'

'I don't care.'

'I can't take you back there myself. Wait until morning.'

'I don't. Care.'

Outside, the rain was close to horizontal. Francesco stumbled through the darkness, feeling his way along the unlit streets. The wind screamed through the spaces between trees and houses, hurling dust and rain into his eyes. For a moment he stood still, thrilling at the feeling of space around him, reaching his arms out as if to grasp the rain as it fell. He had been outside every day since they were brought to San Domino, but there was something different to this darkness, the rain tearing at his cheeks, the freedom of it, a freedom he had learned long ago in Naples and since lost. He thought of Emilio's first absurd plans of escape, the boats. It would be easy, in the darkness, the wind, to walk himself off a cliff and into the sea. Perhaps he should. Perhaps that was what he deserved, after the things he had done. Perhaps that was the way to atone.

Thirty-Seven

Catania, January 1939

'For God's sake.' Emilio pushes Francesco back against the wall. A train rattles overhead, shaking the damp bricks of the railway arch against his skin. 'Get out of sight.'

Rapetti is not yet close enough to see them. There are two police officers with him, who stay standing in the street as he comes closer. Without time to ask questions, Francesco edges around the arch, climbing onto the narrow ledge between the sea and the wall. He feels the water seeping through the hole in the bottom of his shoe, soaking up the legs of his trousers. He stands with his back pressed against the bricks, concentrating on his balance. Beneath him, the sea is black and still, a deep pit of water and moonlight. His father's photograph is somewhere down there in the dark. He thinks of the digging at the Piazza Stesicoro. The long-hidden layers of the city's past, bursting their way up to the surface.

'Do you have them?' he hears Emilio say.

'Of course.' Rapetti's voice is calm and quiet. Francesco holds his breath, as though they will hear it over the sound of the water licking at the archway, the footsteps of men moving silently through the streets.

'Give them to me now,' Emilio says. His voice is quiet. Confident. There is a scuffling sound, and he hears Emilio gasp.

'After,' Rapetti says again. 'They are not here. I have left them somewhere safe. Give me what I want now, and I will tell you where.'

Emilio makes a choking sound. There is a terrible pause,

then Francesco hears him say through clenched teeth, 'They are all at Marcello's. Via—'

'I know where it is. Are you sure?'

'I arranged it myself. They think it is a party. They will all be there within the half-hour. I promised them wine.' Another pause. 'Marcello thinks I am bringing it to them there.'

The *primogeniti*. Francesco breathes hard, trying to stay silent, to keep his balance. Emilio is giving Rapetti the *primogeniti*. All of them.

There is another long silence then. Francesco risks peering around the arch. Rapetti has moved away to speak to the two men waiting on the road. After a short exchange, they hurry away into the night. He thinks of Marcello, the others, gathered in his flat, unsuspecting. Alone under the arch, Emilio glances back and sees Francesco. His eyes widen with fear. Francesco hides himself again. When Rapetti returns, he can hear the triumph in his voice.

'They are on their way. It will be done quickly, if you have told me the truth.'

'And what about . . .'

'They haven't seen you. I haven't named you either. You think I want them knowing I make deals with *arrusi*?'

Later, Francesco will remember those words. He will lie awake at night trying to remember the exact phrasing, the precise meaning of what has been said. Those words have been Rapetti's only mistake.

'They have the warrants with them,' Rapetti says. There is a sound of rustling papers. 'Do you want to hear them?' Emilio doesn't answer. Rapetti's voice becomes calm. Officious. It is the voice he uses in the square, to address the crowds on the Fascist Saturday.

'*Proposal for the confinement of* . . . and there we add the name. There are twenty-two for tonight. Thanks to you, we know where to find them.' He assumes the voice of an official again. '*The plague of pederasty in this province's capital is worsening and spreading . . . We must resort, in the case of the most obstinate offenders, to the use of* confino. You know what that means?'

'Now give me what I want.'

'Twenty-two. Would you like to hear their names? Would you like to know where they are going?'

'We have an agreement. Tell me where.'

There is a silence. Francesco's toes are clinging to the ledge. He can feel the soles of his shoes sliding on the wet brick.

'Would you like to see your own?' Rapetti says. Francesco stiffens. 'It is the first one I wrote out. Emilio Barone. Proposal for confinement.'

'That wasn't part of it.'

'Of course not. It was only for reserve, in case you tried to play me.'

'I have done everything you asked.'

'And what about your friend?'

'My . . .'

'He may as well come out.'

Francesco feels a cold fear spreading through him. He inches further into the shadows, as though they will somehow make him invisible.

'I was very clear, Barone.'

'I'm sorry . . . I didn't know . . .' Emilio sounds afraid now. Francesco can't move, even if he wanted to. Then he feels a hand close on his arm and he is pulled from the ledge and back under the arch. He looks down at his feet, afraid to meet Emilio's eyes.

'I should have known,' Rapetti says, still holding him. 'You are duplicitous, all of you.'

'It changes nothing. He was here by chance.'

There is a long pause. Francesco glances up. Emilio is looking away from them, staring out at the darkness of the city. Behind him, Rapetti breathes out a long, low breath.

'I was wrong to make this deal with you, *arrusu*,' he says, looking at Emilio. Francesco feels light-headed, panic rising in his throat. 'I cannot leave any of you behind.' He turns to Francesco. 'I don't care about these boys, not really. They are children. We will take you all in the end, but it is your kind, you older ones, who are the cause. You teach them your ways. If I strike at the heart, the body dies. I should have remembered that.'

'I'm not one of them,' Emilio says quickly. 'I'm not with anyone. I'm not a threat to you – surely I am more use to you here.'

'I can't trust you, *arrusu*. This one has made that clear.' His grip on Francesco's arm tightens, before he lets him go and reaches to his waist. He draws out a pair of handcuffs, clinking in the silent dark.

Something releases in Francesco's mind then. He is no longer standing beneath the railway arches in Catania. He feels the heat of the flames in Naples rising around him, hears his mother's screams, his father's ragged breathing. The heat intensifies until he feels as though his whole body is on fire. He looks at Rapetti, imagines him standing on the lawn in front of the burning house, watching his family run. All the years he has spent without his father. All the longing, the not knowing, the hiding. He hears himself cry out, and then he and Rapetti are grappling with each other, his arms around Rapetti's neck, clawing at him.

Behind him, he hears Emilio shouting. *Stop. Francesco, stop*. But he can't, even if he wanted to. Rapetti grips his arms and digs his nails into the skin, flinging him sideways against the arch. Francesco's face is in the gutter, dank water flowing into his mouth.

'Please,' he hears Emilio beg, 'it is a mistake, a misunderstanding. He doesn't know . . . Just tell me where.'

Rapetti reaches for something strapped to his waist. Something black and shining that fits perfectly in his hand. Francesco watches his fingers curl around it, then his senses return and he hauls himself up, screaming at Emilio to run, throwing himself at Rapetti, his fists clenched, everything in him straining to knock the gun from his hands.

It is only chance that helps him find his target. Francesco has never been a fighter. Never will be. His eyes are closed when he feels his fist connect with something hard. He hears Emilio scream his name. He reaches forward and grasps Rapetti's collar with both hands, throwing him back against the railway arch with as much force as he can find. Emilio screams again. There is a sound like rotting fruit bursting open. Dully, Francesco wonders why no one has come. They have made so much noise, half the city must have heard them.

When he opens his eyes, Rapetti is slumped back against the wall, his own eyes wide with surprise. The blood is slow to come, but when it does, it is more than Francesco believes one body could ever hold. Rapetti slides, almost gracefully, to the ground. Francesco cannot look at the back of his head, concave and broken, the gutter water running red. Emilio is staring down at it. He is breathing heavily. So loud. Surely someone will come for them now.

'Run,' Emilio says quietly.

Francesco doesn't know what he means. Nothing has meaning any more. Whatever it was that allowed him to do it, the fire in him, has gone. There is only blood, and fear. Then, finally, with something like relief, he hears them. Footsteps marching in formation, drawing closer. He tries to count how many feet must be making the sound. Hundreds, perhaps. Or just a few. He can't tell.

'Francesco,' Emilio whispers. 'Run.' He says it again, louder, and takes Francesco by the shoulders. The marching seems to be growing louder, vibrating through him as Emilio shakes him. 'It doesn't matter where, just run. Now.'

Francesco feels his knees give way, Emilio reaching for him as he falls.

'Cesco!' The sound of Emilio's scream fills his ears as the

marching grows louder. 'Cesco!' And 'Run!' But Francesco can't run. He lies in the gutter, the muddy water cool against his cheek, his eyes level with Rapetti's, which are still wide open, the pupils rolled back.

Then something heavy is pulling at his arm, and Emilio is hauling him up, and they are both running, out from under the arches, past the fish market, through the Duomo square, darting into the back streets, weaving their way through narrow alleyways and spaces between buildings, all the dark places they have hidden in for years flashing past them.

You are not the same again after you have killed. You are a true Italian then. One of the men in the square in Catania had said that to Francesco once, during one of those endless Saturday parades. The same man who had handed out guns, and arrested Francesco when someone had mentioned his true name. *Femminella.* If they had known then what he was, what he was capable of, they would not have given him such a name.

Francesco pulls up and stops to catch his breath. He puts out a hand and leans against a damp wall, pressing his cheek against the cool stone. It is a long time before he looks up and realises he is alone.

Thirty-Eight

San Domino, January 1940

He'd thought he could find his way back to the dormitory by memory and instinct, but standing in the deserted streets, Francesco hardly knew which way was west. He stumbled between the houses, tripping over fallen branches, pine cones, using the shadows of roofs to guide him until he felt the pavement grow rough beneath his feet, then turn gradually to soft earth and stones. He saw the webbed shadow of the bare mulberry tree above him and recognised the turning to the Cameroni district, half falling along the path until, with relief, he saw the outline of the dormitory against the sky.

They found him in the morning, after the guards had been and gone. He woke to hands under his arms, pulling him up, and someone tugging his wet clothing over his head and laying him down in his bunk. A blanket around his shoulders, and a mug of bitter, scalding coffee by his side. When he opened his eyes again, Arturo was bending over him, shaking his head.

'You are some kind of fucking miracle, *arrusu*. You are the only one of us who has managed to wake up outside the door instead of inside it.'

Francesco looked up dazedly at Arturo, remembering him beneath the trees with Elio, wondering if Arturo had known it was him watching that day. They stared at each other for a long moment. Then Arturo's mouth flickered with the beginnings of a smile as he reached out and helped Francesco to sit.

He felt the ache in his limbs, winced at the broken skin on his hands and forehead where they had been pressed against the wall. His eyes met Emilio's then, sitting up in his own bunk on the other side of the dormitory. There was something in Emilio's face Francesco did not understand. Did he know?

The guards said nothing during the day, though they must have missed Francesco at the morning count. In the evening, they came late to lock the doors. The prisoners shuffled into their lines slowly, eyes to the ground. Emilio was among the last to assemble.

'*Muovetevi!*' Santoro shouted impatiently. He struck his gun against the floor, glancing back quickly to Favero and Pirelli, standing by the door. Francesco couldn't look at Favero's face. When he did, there was no sign in it of a sleepless night, a restless conscience. Favero's hair was neatly brushed beneath his cap. His uniform perfectly pressed. Francesco could still feel the guard's fingers pressing into his skin. His hands around his waist.

Pirelli stepped forward. He was standing taller, his chin raised, but Francesco could see the dark lines around his eyes, the exhaustion. When he spoke, his voice was tired and weak.

'For weeks now, I have been asking, and still none of you will tell me.' His whip was coiled around his fist. He turned to the poster on the wall, looking into Rapetti's eyes as though pleading to him. Francesco tried not to look at the photographs. The bloodied mess of Rapetti's head. His hands, pale in the gutter. 'It is a simple question. One of you did it, or knows who did. Whoever tells me can go home.' There was a shifting amongst them. Pirelli drew himself up, sensing their interest. 'Now. A full pardon. All you have to do is tell me the truth.'

Francesco felt his breath tighten in his throat. He looked sideways and his eyes met Gio's. Gio raised his eyebrows as though he expected something of Francesco, as though he was waiting for him to speak.

Francesco remembered a day in Catania, long ago in the schoolroom. He had taken something from their instructor's desk, something small and inconsequential, a pencil, perhaps, or a sheet of paper, just to show that he could. The instructor had lined them all up after classes, a cane in his hand. Gio had known it was him. Somehow, just by glancing at him, he had known. Francesco remembered standing in the line, meeting Gio's eyes. Gio hadn't said a word. He had only stared at him, a question in his eyes, and somehow, under the force of that gaze, Francesco had found himself confessing.

Now, Gio's gaze had turned to Emilio. Francesco remembered their conversation in the rain. *Why are you protecting him? You know what he is.* Gio had understood everything, only his understanding was the wrong way around. He thought Emilio had done it, but it was Emilio who was protecting Francesco. Emilio alone who knew what he was.

Pirelli cracked the whip against the floor. Francesco thought he saw a flicker of movement then, Gio about to step forward. He wanted to cry out, to find a way to stop him. As he drew in a breath, wondering what he would say, he heard Favero's voice.

'Barone. Emilio Barone.'

There was a silence. Slowly, Emilio stepped forward. Francesco could see Gio's face tightening. He felt his heart beating faster. Emilio stood with his hands behind his back, meeting Favero's eyes without blinking. Francesco felt himself tense, as though to run.

'I have a petition for a temporary visit to Catania,' Favero said. 'You submitted it last summer.'

Emilio, his eyes wide, nodded.

With a quick glance at Francesco, a smile, Favero pushed the paper into Emilio's hands. 'Gather your things. You leave in the morning.'

'It won't work, you know.'

Favero was standing on the other side of the fence. The day was unusually mild, and Francesco had been walking the perimeter, enjoying the feeling of cool air on his face, dry soil beneath his feet. He stopped at Favero's voice. It brought back memories he was trying to forget.

'What?' He didn't turn to look at the guard. The breeze shifted, and he could smell Favero's sweat, the musty scent of him. He felt the rough wall again, the sting of it against his palms.

'You know what. Your petition. We aren't fools, Caruso. They'll catch up with him eventually. Bring him back here. If he's lucky.'

Francesco shrugged. He was never sure, now, whether his indifference was feigned or real, he practised it so often. 'Why do you care? You've had what you wanted.'

He felt a hand on his collar pulling him back, the wire of the fence pressing into his neck.

'You say a word, just a word about that, and I will make sure you never go home, *arrusu*. You will die here, on this island. I promise you that.'

Francesco coughed, clutching at his throat. But he smiled as Favero let him go. In the daylight, he was no longer afraid of men. It was those shadows that followed him through dark, narrow streets, put a hand around his throat in the night, that he feared the most.

Thirty-Nine

Catania, January 1939

At night, Francesco dreams of running. Narrow, uneven streets, the sound of Emilio's ragged breathing beside him. He tries to remember the exact moment their breath separated, became one instead of two, the exact moment he had left Emilio behind. He can't remember any of it. He has only snatches of how it felt, his neck still throbbing with the memory of Rapetti's hands around it, the feeling of Rapetti's collar still in his grip, the impact of his head against the bricks. The surge of energy that had pushed Francesco to do it, the thrill he had felt as he threw Rapetti back against the railway arch. The sound of it. The heavy, rotten sound.

He doesn't get up for two days. At first his mother tries to persuade him with patience and sympathy, but by the second day, she is shouting from the doorway, trying to shame him into rising. He hardly hears her. He only hears that sound, over and over. When he closes his eyes, he sees Rapetti's eyes, wide open and staring at him from where he lies in the gutter.

On the third day, something shifts, and he rises mechanically and walks to work without acknowledging her. He spends the day avoiding talking to the other kitchen workers. He suspects he has only kept his job, after two days of unexplained absence, because he is soon going to marry the owner's daughter. He speaks to no one until, towards evening, as he is starting on the last of the dishes, he looks up and sees Gio standing in the kitchen doorway. Gio has untied his waiter's apron. He looks older, dressed in a dark suit, his hair neatly flattened against his skull.

'I thought you weren't coming back,' he says, coming to stand beside Francesco at the sink.

'Where else would I go?' He buries his hands in the warm, soapy water. Remnants of food and misplaced cutlery slide between his fingers. He focuses on the water, unable to turn and meet Gio's eyes.

'Where have you been, Fran?'

'I was ill.'

'Then you don't know.'

He pauses, a plate in his hand. 'Know what?'

Gio looks back over his shoulder at the empty restaurant. One of the waiters is still drifting between tables, collecting glasses and folding up tablecloths. He speaks quietly.

'They're gone. The *primogeniti*. No one knows where.'

Francesco lets the plate slide back into the water, and turns around.

After he had stopped running through the back streets that night, he had gone back to look for Emilio. He had walked the streets between the Duomo and the sea, coming as close to the railway arches as he dared, and had seen no one. Now, he tries to remember how far he had run with Emilio beside him. There was a point, he thinks, when it had seemed Emilio was running directly towards the police station, and Francesco had taken a different path. Perhaps that was when they had separated. He hadn't been looking; he had stopped thinking of anything but getting away.

They will have found Rapetti by now. If that night had really happened, if it had been more than a dark, vivid dream, they will have found the body of a policeman huddled in the fourth railway arch, blood pouring into the gutter from a wound in his skull. Why has no one come for him? He remembers Rapetti's words to Emilio that night. *They haven't seen you. I haven't named you, either.*

'Fran? What do we do?'

Francesco looks up. Gio's face is pale and drawn with

worry. He wishes he could be that unaware, that ignorant of what is happening.

'Nothing,' he says, letting his hands sink back into the water.

'Nothing? We should leave. If they are arresting the *arrusi*, it won't be long. They will come for us too. You heard what Emilio said.'

Francesco feels suddenly more tired than he has ever been. He leans his head forward, feeling the water reach to his elbows, seep into his rolled-up sleeves.

'I can't. I can't run any more.'

They have taken Emilio. He knows that before he tries to find him. He knew it that night, walking the empty streets, searching alleyways and alcoves, all the familiar hiding places. He had run too far on his own. Emilio was gone.

When he comes home after work, his mother is waiting for him in the doorway, her face lined with anxiety. He knows it is the wedding she is concerned with. It is less than a month away now. It will be held a few days after the festival of St Agatha, when Agatha's statue will be paraded through the city, past the *arvulu rossu*, parallel to the railway arches and then back into the respectable streets, crowds of celebrants following her.

'You look better,' she says, holding a hand up to his forehead as though he is a child. Francesco shrugs her away.

'Lucia was here,' she says, nodding to the kitchen, where two empty teacups are still on the table. 'I'm so happy, Francesco.' She takes his hands and presses them between hers. 'It has made me so happy, after so long.'

He smiles at her, wondering how, after all their years of lies and pretence, she cannot see through his now.

Without Emilio, the city feels larger, unfamiliar. In the shorter winter days, the streets are shadowed, the dark volcanic paving stones reflecting none of the weak sunlight. Even the

Duomo square is dark. A few Catanians still linger there, sitting on the steps of the fountains, but most people move quickly, not pausing to allow the cold to settle around them. Night comes early, lights from shuttered windows flickering across the squares. The domes of the cathedral and the churches are black against the sinking sun.

Talk among the *arrusi* who are left has been of nothing but the arrests of the *primogeniti*. How many were taken, what was done to them after. There are rumours of medical examinations, of beatings, and worse. One of the men who works in a restaurant close to Francesco's had, to everyone's surprise, been released the following day. Afterwards, he was full of the story. They had taken him to the police station first, then to the hospital. Men had done things to him there. Things that made Francesco shake with fear. Tests. The man laughed it away now, back safe again. How he had tensed at just the right moment as the probe was inserted, and the doctors had declared it all a mistake and sent him home.

'They even shook my hand,' he told Francesco, smiling proudly. 'I didn't mean to do it; it was only natural, wasn't it? I was afraid.'

Through it all, Francesco thinks of what he overheard as he hid behind the railway arch on the night they were taken. *Proposal for confinement.*

On Sunday, Francesco walks down to the church of St Agatha and finds it full, every seat taken by a figure bent in prayer, their whispered pleading rising to the vaulted dome. It is as though the whole city is uniting in a cleansing act. As he walks towards the altar, he feels their eyes on him, whispers directed studiously away from him, eyes following him as he stares up at the painted windows. He imagines standing here, Lucia walking towards him, her face veiled, her body draped in white lace. He imagines taking her hand, that cold, small hand, and promising God that he will love her. He thinks of Emilio's hand in his beneath the fountain, weaving their fingers together. He thinks of what Gio said to him in the kitchens. *It won't be long. They will come for us too.* He knows Gio is right. As Emilio was.

Where is he? Francesco directs the question at the statue above the altar, the arms stretched out on stone carved to look like wood, the dead, pupil-less eyes. Where is Emilio? He would have fought when they took him. He would not have gone meekly, as Francesco would. He would have fought like a tiger, and what would they have done to him? Francesco should have waited for him. He should never have run so hard.

Why doesn't he run now? He knows it is what Emilio would tell him to do. He can still hear Emilio's voice screaming at him under the arches. *For God's sake, don't wait, just run.*

Francesco kneels on stone, pressing his hands against the cool flagstones, not caring that he is in the way of feet, not feeling them as they push their way past him, stepping over and around him. He is afraid too. So why does he not run? He could do it, he and his mother. They have done it before. It is what they will expect of him. To run as a woman would run, but he won't. He will stand still and let them come to him.

Is it defiance? He has never been strong enough to stand up to the regime before. He has always run. The real reason – the reason he will only wake up to months later, on a boat that slips between San Domino and its neighbouring rock as easily as a hand in the dark – is Emilio. The draw of the darkness, the same draw that has pulled him so often into the alleyways and shadows of Catania. *We should put bells on your ankles, like they did in the old days. So everyone can hear you coming. You are worse than a plague.*

But they haven't. One by one, the *arrusi* are disappearing as quietly as a shadow in the sunlight, and no one knows where. Francesco needs to know what happens next, to someone like him. He needs to know what has already happened to Emilio. In the end, the thought of not seeing Emilio again frightens him more than the thought of running.

Forty

San Domino, February 1940

Winter had brought with it a cold like the *arrusi* had never experienced before. It forced its way between cracks in the dormitory walls, seeped beneath the door, settled deep and heavy in their bones. They spent long hours of the day lying in their bunks, layers of clothing piled over them, praying for home, for the deep summer sunshine of Catania, pooling in the wide-open squares, soaking into the dark volcanic paving stones. Francesco lay in his bunk thinking of Emilio back home, wondering where he was, whether he had managed to escape the watchful eyes of the guards who had travelled with him. He had been gone nearly three weeks. Far longer than the few days he had been granted, even with the time it would have taken to cross the water. How long should Francesco wait, before knowing he was not coming back?

Sometimes, in the night, a vague fear of the men surrounding him led him through the darkness to Emilio's bunk, where he would sleep in interrupted fits, before crawling back to his own before dawn. Other times, he woke to find someone's eyes on him from across the room, or his belongings scattered over the floor. It was never anything worse than that. He wasn't sure whether it was the threat of Favero or Arturo that deterred them more, but sometimes, lying alone in the dark, he wished he had not done what he had done for Emilio. He wished Emilio was still here with him, and he had never gone with Favero to that dark house, allowed him to do what he had done.

In the evenings, they still gathered together around Michel's tiny radio, the signal fading in and out as they strained to listen for news of the war. They heard speeches, rhetoric, news of engagements and bombardments, most of it in unfamiliar languages. In Finland, a winter war was raging. Francesco had never imagined war happening in the snow; when he thought of it, it was always baked earth, a searing sun, sweating in a heavy uniform. Emilio, fifteen years old, in the mud of Caporetto. He couldn't imagine guns covered with snow, trenches deep with it, ice on triggers as men pulled them with shaking, frozen fingers.

'He is trying to escape the war,' Claudio said, as they listened. They all knew who he meant. 'He will have run as soon as they got him back to Catania, so he won't have to fight.'

'He wouldn't,' Francesco said from his bunk. 'He would want to fight.'

Marcello laughed. 'You forget, he has seen it before. He will run if he has any sense. I only wish the rest of us had the chance.'

'Maybe there is someone waiting for him there,' Dante said. 'Maybe someone escaped the police, and they are trying to be together.'

Francesco turned his face to the wall.

Talk of war and guns reminded him of what Gio had said to him once. What they had all heard at Antonio's inquest. *He was shot with a military weapon. A gun from the last war.* If not Emilio, then who?

'Deserters will be shot!' The voice on the radio was translating another, speaking German. Both sounded harsh and angry. 'Anyone found to be betraying the ideals of our nation will be shot!'

The *arrusi* were huddled together at the end of the long table, warming their hands around an oil lamp flickering in the dark. They looked at each other, as though afraid the voice was speaking to them. That was why they were here, after all. For betraying the ideals of their nation. Francesco looked at

Gio. He was pale, staring at his hands in his lap. When the voice repeated its warning, he turned his face away.

'I wouldn't last five minutes,' he whispered, as Francesco moved to sit beside him.

'You don't know that. You'd be all right.'

'That day in the classroom. I hid. I would always hide.'

'That was just a game, Gio. And anyway, we don't know that's what will happen to us.'

'It would be better to give me a death sentence now,' Gio said, his head sinking forward on his hands.

'What is it like?' Dante said, turning to Marcello.

Marcello smiled grimly, picking at a loose thread on the sleeve of his shirt. 'What is what like?'

'War.'

He did not pause before answering. 'Hell. It is like being in hell.'

They listened on as the list of countries under threat was read out, while Marcello sat with his back to the machine, his chin resting in his hands. Only Gio was not listening. He got up from the table and went to lie on his bunk in the dark, his arms wrapped around himself, flinching as the voice grew harsher. And still, as the voice spoke on, as the days grew longer, Italy did not join the maelstrom.

Elena did not dread the cold. It was her favourite time of year, when the earth no longer baked beneath the sun, when she could hide herself within layers of wool and fur. She still walked the length of the island whenever she could, muffled to her ears, enjoying the soft silence of the empty fields, the lull of the waves, quiet beneath a sky heavy with mist and rain. She hadn't seen the Director in weeks. He hardly ever come to San Domino in the winter. As she walked, she recited the list she had been compiling of the prisoners for him, sorting through what she knew of them, wondering which of them had something to hide.

She had had little chance to speak with them in the weeks since she had agreed to help Coviello. With the cold, the prisoners had shut themselves away in their dormitories, and Elena in turn had been kept to the house. Her mother had begun filling her days with a frenzied series of lessons on cookery, laundry, aspects of housekeeping she had already been shown a hundred times on San Nicola. The house began to fill with visitors; though Coviello was unlikely to return before the spring, others came more and more. The islanders spent the winter months huddled together in each other's houses, waiting for the sun to return. Elena cooked elaborate meals, serving them to families who sat with her mother and gossiped about the island's small dramas: who had been seen together in the square, what had been overheard at the grocer's, who had got a new job on San Nicola. They asked her about her marriage plans and she avoided their eyes, thinking of the long white dress still hanging in her bedroom, the sun lighting it up each morning like a cautionary flare.

There was little sign of her father, who was spending more time than ever at the camp. Her brothers, though, kept mostly indoors during the colder months, squabbling in the confines of the house. Apart from the two soldiers who never seemed to leave it, the beach was empty, the sky the same grey pallor as the sea.

February saw the slow, creeping return of the sun, and with it, the return of both islanders and prisoners to the streets and fields. Elena began to resume her walks across the island, slipping out of the house as the sun rose and returning in time to help her mother with the day's work. On one of these mornings, she returned to find her father slumped over the kitchen table. His head was covered by his hands. A half empty bottle of spirits stood on the table beside him. She stood in the doorway, unwinding her scarf and hanging her coat over a chair.

'Papa?'

Her father didn't move. Elena pulled out a chair and sat beside him, putting a hand over one of his. It was cold.

'I have failed, *furetto*.' His words were muffled against the table.

'How?' She looked up then, and saw her mother standing by the stove, her mouth open, her hands gripping a pile of dishes. Elena waited, but her mother made no attempt to speak. Eventually she looked away.

'How have you failed, Papa?'

Her father sat up. His face was red and puffy. He snatched at the pile of posters and crumpled one into a ball, tossing it across the room. A letter was laid on the table in front of him.

'The Director is returning. Soon. And I don't know which of them it was. I don't even care.'

Elena stood up and crossed the room, picking up the paper and smoothing it out on the table, stroking the lines of Rapetti's face. She could feel her conviction strengthening, even as her father's seemed to weaken.

She had seen films about detectives in San Nicola. They were always men, and they always knew more than everyone around them. Elena didn't feel like she knew anything. Nor did her father, she was sure. She thought of him on the road with his whip, and imagined him in the dormitories, shouting at the men, threatening them, waiting for one of them to break down. That was not the way. She knew that from the detectives in the films. People never talked if you threatened them. You had to be kind, and friendly. Make them think they had nothing to fear from you. Or trick them into giving something away.

'Will you lose your job?' she said, turning back to him. Her father nodded. She remembered the days after he had lost his place at the grocery store on San Nicola. How he had sat for days at a time, hardly moving, like a broken doll, his head slumped forward on his hands. She couldn't imagine Coviello ever allowing himself such weakness. Coviello would always look after his family. She thought of Nicolo, sitting across from her at the table, watching her with wide, expectant eyes.

The empty house she had found, silently waiting as dust gathered in its corners. They would not fail. They couldn't fail.

She looked at her father, his head resting on his palms. He looked defeated. She felt shame burning in her cheeks.

'It will be all right,' she said, putting a hand over one of his. 'We will find out the truth.' He gave a low, muffled moan. Elena wondered if she was the only one in her family who really understood how things were, how everything worked in this new Italy.

She marched purposefully towards the camp, searching for men among the trees as she went. Though the cold that had kept them indoors was waning now, there were still few of them outside. She no longer expected to find Francesco sitting on the cliffs, waiting for her. But she was wary. Wary of finding two of them huddled beneath a tree, that image still burned deep into her memory.

She turned towards the Cameroni district, passing the mulberry tree, its bare branches twisted and bent like an old woman's fingers after the long winter. The fields were bare too, the yard outside the dormitories empty and grey in the dull morning light. There was only one figure in it, wearing the white uniform of the prisoners. He was pacing slowly up and down, his head bowed against a thin drizzle of rain that had just begun to fall. She stood for a while watching him, trying to see something in his stance, his manner of walking, that betrayed what he was. He was thin, but they all were now, after months of imprisonment. She had seen men thinner than this one, on San Nicola. Men who had been imprisoned there for years, since the regime had begun to gather up those who opposed it. She had not known men could last so long on so little. In comparison, this man seemed strong.

As he turned and saw her, she recognised him as the man who had worn the red dress, the day last summer she had watched them perform their play. Ferragosto. So long ago, when the air had been thick with heat and flowers. He had fled from the fight that day. She had seen him duck beneath the fence and run, shouts of 'Caporetto!' following him. Her father had warned her that that was what they would do. When it came to a fight, they would always run.

She approached the fence warily. There were no guards, but even if she saw one now, it would not matter. Coviello himself had told her to talk to the prisoners. She could go where she wanted. They could not stop her. She stood by the fence and waited for him to reach her.

'What's your name?' she said in a loud, clear voice as he came closer. The man looked up, surprised. He was hardly more than a boy. His face was thin and angular, his eyes staring from deep hollows. He was twisting his hands anxiously, as though trying to come to a decision about something. She wondered if she was the first girl he had been close to in months.

'Giovanni,' he said eventually. 'Gio.' He resumed his pacing. Elena paced with him until he stopped, irritated. She studied his face, wondering if he was the sort she could persuade to talk. If he would betray one of his friends. That was what they did, Coviello had said. Feminised men, weak men, always betrayed one another in the end.

'My father is one of the guards,' she said importantly. 'He doesn't think you should be locked up. He hates to do it.'

Giovanni stared at her for a moment, then shrugged. 'It makes no difference to me,' he said.

'If you tell us who killed that man, you can go home.'

He was staring at the ground now. His hands were inside his pockets. She could see his breath, misting on the air, and shivered, drawing her coat tighter around her. He was not wearing a coat. His shoulders were shaking with the cold.

He will know that already, she thought. Her father would have promised him that months ago. It would make no difference to him now.

'Why are you out here?'

He didn't answer.

'It's because you know, isn't it? You don't want to be in there with a killer.'

'No.' He looked up at her quickly. 'He isn't here. The man who did it. He's not here any more. They let him go home for a while. Idiots,' he muttered, shaking his head, then looking back at her sharply, remembering who she was.

'So you do know.' She tried to sound indifferent, but she could feel her heart beating faster. They looked at each other for a moment, then Giovanni shook his head slowly.

'I don't know anything.'

'Wait!' she called, as he turned to go back inside. He stopped. The wind was rising now, and she thought of the folds of red cloth that had hung from his hips that day in the summer, lifting in the breeze like bright, brilliant wings. The thought came to her quickly, and she spoke before she could question it. 'If you tell us, you will not have to go to the war. They will not make you fight.'

He stood still for a long time. Elena tried to slow down her own panicked breathing, feeling her fingernails digging into her palms as she waited. This was what they wanted, wasn't it? To avoid the fight?

For a long time, he said nothing, then at last he turned around. He smiled, and glanced over his shoulder, back towards the dormitory. 'Yes,' he said. There was a look on his face like relief. Satisfaction, as though telling her would be the settling of a debt. 'It doesn't matter now, anyway. Yes, I know who it was.'

Forty-One

Catania, February 1939

He hears the roar of the crowds before he is even awake. Sitting up in bed, Francesco pushes back the curtain and looks down into the street. It is already thick with people, making their way down to the cathedral square for the festival of St Agatha. They are dressed in their finest, flowers wound through their hair and strewn across the streets. In a few minutes, the statue of St Agatha will be carried out of the cathedral and taken on a day-long procession through the city, followed by almost every citizen of Catania. They are thousands strong, hundreds more visiting especially for this day. Once, the *arrusi* had followed the processions in their costumes, camouflaged amongst the crowds, even after the ban was enforced. He wonders whether any of them will dare to be on the streets today.

It is nearly three weeks since the *primogeniti* were taken. For a few days afterwards, the boys of the *arvulu rossu* had been paralysed by fear, but slowly they have been returning to their usual meeting places. There have even been some dances. It is over, they agree among themselves. Whatever Molina had been planning, he has carried it out now. There is no need for them to feel afraid.

Francesco feels less sure. It was only Emilio who had spared the *arvulu rossu* boys, who had kept their locations secret. But Molina knows about San Antonio, the dance hall, the railway arches, the *arvulu rossu*. He knows it all, thanks to Francesco. He tries to remember what Rapetti said to Emilio that night. *We will take you all*. Is that what he said? If it was, then why hasn't Molina come for them?

His wedding is a week away. The flat is filled with his mother's preparations: decorations, cooking utensils, material she is sewing for tablecloths. He stands in his bedroom doorway, watching her as she works. She smiles as she looks up at him, a half-sewn cloth in her hands.

'Why aren't you in the square? I thought you were going to see the parade today.'

'I have seen it enough times.' He sees the disappointment in her face. She wants the flat to herself, to get on with her work. 'But I will go now, if it helps with . . .' He sweeps a hand across the room.

She laughs. 'It will be the most beautiful wedding the Via Calcera has ever seen.' As she bends over the cloth, he cannot help thinking of all the times she has refused to sew, has made Francesco mend his own clothes, telling him that the regime wants her to do it, so she will not. She has hidden within this new self so carefully, he can't even tell any more whether it is a disguise. He feels suddenly sickened by the thought of what he is about to do. It is just another betrayal, another layer of lies. He wonders if he has ever done anything that is an honest reflection of himself.

'All right,' he says, kissing the top of her head lightly. 'I'll go now.' Without looking up from her work, she puts a hand on his and squeezes it tightly.

He battles his way through the crowds towards the railway arches. All the places he is used to hiding in, the emptier, quieter streets, are suddenly thick with noise and bodies, fighting each other for space to see the procession. He can hear the distant clanging of bells, marking its progress from the Duomo. Then he sees it, the bright, glittering lights of the statue of Agatha, adorned with candles, floating serenely over the procession as though she is hovering in the air above their heads. The crowds hush as she draws closer to them, her blank eyes staring from a pale, painted face. He looks towards the railway arches, now busy with people, and tries not to think of what he left behind there only a few weeks earlier.

What would Agatha think of him, if her eyes could see? What would she think of this city? They had tried to marry her to a Roman general, Francesco read once. When she refused, and clung fast to her faith, they had tortured and imprisoned her, and she had died alone. He smiles to think that this city, of all cities, should have chosen her as its most venerated saint.

Only as Agatha draws close to him, the crowd around her parting to allow the robed priests passage, does he see the first of the police. They are dressed inconspicuously, not in their full uniform but in casual shirts and trousers, but he sees the guns at their waists, recognises their blank, official stares. He counts four, perhaps five of them, fanned out through the crowds. Across the pavement he recognises Dante, dressed anonymously in a dark navy jumper and black trousers. Further off, he thinks he can see Luca standing beside a woman he doesn't know. It seems, as he watches, as though the police are tightening in a circle around them, but suddenly he can't be sure if he is really seeing any of them, if it is just his mind suggesting a trap that isn't there. He feels invisible in these crowds, as though the police could brush past him without knowing him, as though he could do anything and there would be no consequences. Then someone pulls at his sleeve, and he turns to find Gio beside him.

'I can't find Claudio,' Gio whispers, then repeats the words louder as the crowds begin to clamour again, the statue turning a corner and moving in its strange, serene march towards the *arvulu rossu*. 'I can't . . .' He bends forward, hands on his knees. Francesco kneels beside him, feeling the crowd pushing and flowing past them. He puts a hand on Gio's shoulder.

'What do you mean?'

'We were supposed to meet – he didn't come.' Gio looks up with wild, frightened eyes. 'They're taking us. Aren't they? They're taking us too.' A tear slides across the tip of his nose and onto the pavement between them. 'Those tests – I can't do it. I can't let them.'

Francesco pulls him up. The crowds are thinning now, as the statue moves away from them. He looks for the police he thought he had seen, but they have moved on too. Or perhaps they were never there. He is shaken by a feeling of disappointment, and wonders why.

'Emilio was right, wasn't he?' Gio says, looking over his shoulder as though they are behind him now. 'They are coming for us, aren't they? Should we run?' He seizes Francesco's hand. 'We could run, hide, together.'

Francesco is about to reply. Then the image of his mother sewing tablecloths, of Lucia walking through the church of St Agatha towards him, fills his mind. The thought of all the long, slow days of deceit he will have to live with her, if he stays. He has been hiding for so long – half his life – and he will have to keep hiding until he dies if he marries her. He thinks of Emilio. The night they danced outside the cinema. It was the only truly honest thing he ever did, that night he had let Emilio dance with him. More than anything, he wants to be with Emilio again. Wherever he has gone. He wants to be honest, for everyone to know what he is. His mother, Lucia, everyone. To face the crowds openly, for what he is to be written down, to be part of the record of his life for anyone to read. He only knows one way.

'Yes. He was right,' he says, letting go of Gio's hand. 'They're coming. We should separate. Run, if you can. Go now.'

As he walks away, he hears Gio shouting after him. 'What about you? Francesco, what about you?' He doesn't turn around. He keeps walking, fighting back the urge to run back to Gio, to put his arms around him, to keep him safe.

As soon as he is out of sight, Francesco takes a detour towards Emilio's repair yard. When he is beside the low wall, he takes a piece of paper from his pocket and writes down his name and full address. He doesn't even know for sure if anyone is checking the hiding place now. Over the wall, the space where Rapetti's car once stood is empty. He remembers Emilio, smiling proudly over it. *She is my greatest work, this one.* His hand, guiding Francesco's over the brickwork. Looking over his shoulder at the empty street, he takes the loose brick from the wall and slides his paper into the space behind it.

He spends the next few days with his mother. He hardly goes out. Every sound makes him start, until she jokes that he must have wedding nerves, with so little time to wait. She sings to herself as she moves about the flat. He remembers her with his father, dancing in the library, so long ago. Half his life ago. He wonders how she has managed to survive so long without him, with the ache of it, the deep, insistent longing.

By the night before the wedding, he has given up hope that they will come for him. It is almost a relief, after everything. They sit together in the kitchen, sipping at small glasses of grappa, toasting his future. He thinks of the message he left, his own details, and wonders how he could have done it. It was as though a madness had overtaken him for a few days, the loss of Emilio distorting his logic. He doesn't want to leave his mother; he never did. How can he have wanted them to take him away, just for the sake of Emilio? He will find a way to survive. He always has.

Almost as he thinks it, as his mother laughingly refills their glasses, he knows. Afterwards, he can't think how. There is some change in the air; perhaps he hears a footfall on the street, perhaps it is the sudden silence outside. Something that reminds him of the moment in the library a lifetime ago, standing with his forehead pressed against the window, the few seconds of silence before the breaking of glass and the roar of the flames. The moment, standing in the hills, when he could sense the volcano waking, ready to flood the valleys with fire.

He knows. Before the loud, insistent knocking, the shouts, the sound of his name being called by a stranger, his mother's eyes wide with fear, he knows.

Forty-Two

> A typical pederast because of his deep-rooted depravity, his physical features and his behaviour . . .
>
> Lean face, deep-set eyes, flaring nostrils and thick lips, seems like a perfectly sensual type. He could be considered a fortunate male if his voice did not give him away . . .
>
> Born homosexual, he practises pederasty without restraint; it is a vice from which he can no longer break free . . .
>
> Police and medical reports on the Catanian detainees

As he feels the handcuffs close around his wrists, Francesco can still hear voices from the nearby restaurant, footsteps on the Via Etnea, a woman laughing, glasses being refilled. They walk quickly to a car, waiting for them at the end of the alley. Two men sit on either side of him, holding him by his wrists.

He closes his eyes. He keeps them closed as the car begins to move. The windows are clean, and through them he knows he will see the faces of people on the streets watching as they pass. He doesn't want to see them, the look in their eyes. He has seen that look before, fleetingly, from police and soldiers. In the last few weeks, he has been seeing it everywhere.

The drive is short. The cuffs around his wrists are tight, pinching at his skin as he feels himself being pulled to his feet and out of the car. He opens his eyes then. They are standing in a courtyard. Francesco tips back his head and looks up. The moon is fat and full above them, cut in half by the roof of the police station. Its light casts a sickly grey glow over the yard. Another car pulls up, and he sees a man being escorted from it, his hands behind his back. It is too dark to recognise who it is. He closes his eyes again and allows himself to be led, feeling the ground beneath his feet changing from smooth volcanic stone to a rough, uneven floor, shuffling forward in slow steps until he stops suddenly, the hands on his arms disappear, and he hears a door shutting heavily behind him.

The last thing he hears before they leave him in the dark is a voice, quick in his ear. He feels as though he has heard the words before.

'God sees all your sins, *arrusu*. You cannot hide from him, or us.'

After two days, they move him to the larger prison, on the outskirts of the city. Francesco keeps his eyes shut again as the car rolls through the streets, though the city is emptier now the festival of St Agatha is at an end. With them closed, he can't escape the image of his mother, staring at the door as the knocking and the shouts grew louder. The disappointment in her face, the fear.

Towards the end of the drive, he allows himself to look. The streets here are wider, brighter without the close-packed walls of the centre of Catania. Houses are larger, framed by tall, imposing iron gates. He imagines Molina must live in one of these houses, safe from the city's plague behind tightly locked gates.

He knows the prison at once, its ochre walls lined with barred windows, but the building next to it is unfamiliar. It is large and sprawling, without windows. Its walls are painted a pale sky blue. He watches as they drive past it, searching for a way to see inside it. As the car slows, he turns in his seat and sees a door open in the blue wall. A woman comes out. She is dressed all in white. A white cap is pinned to her hair. When she turns, Francesco sees the unmistakable sign painted on the back of her dress. A bright red cross. He remembers the stories of the *primogeniti*. The tests. The man who had been set free, and what he told them. He clenches his handcuffed fists tight behind his back, as though already bracing himself for what is to come.

The hospital floor is cold and damp against his bare feet. Men dressed in white move quickly about him, their faces covered with masks, as though to breathe the same air as him would be a hazard.

In the centre of the room, a metal table gleams in the light from the narrow window. It is on wheels. Francesco has an image of himself thrusting it towards the men, knocking them in all directions, climbing up onto it and smashing the window, pulling himself through it, his shirt tearing on the broken glass, Emilio waiting below to catch him.

He stands still. Even when they let go of his arms and undo his cuffs. A variety of instruments are laid out on the table, flashing with the passage of the sun. He looks at them, feeling the men's boredom around him; they have done this many times before, he thinks. They have done this to Emilio. He wonders why he does not run.

He had not known for certain, even up to this moment, what he had been arrested for. Only now, standing in the cold white room, can he be sure. There is, so far as he knows, no medical test for murderers.

'Remove your trousers.'

He stares at the men for a moment. They are not smiling. They mean it, he thinks, and unbuckles his belt slowly, his fingers catching in the loops.

'Lie down.'

He begins to lift himself up onto the table.

'No. On your front.'

It is not easy to turn himself around. The table shifts and slides under him. One of the men holds it still for him. There are thin white gloves over the man's hands. When he lies down, he gasps at the cold metal on his thighs, between his legs. Someone pushes his knees apart.

'We hardly need bother looking with this one,' he hears a voice say, as the gloved hands push his buttocks apart. 'From what I hear, she takes it more than a Roma whore.' As they laugh over him, he feels something cold and hard pressing against him, pushing and stretching, searching for an entrance. He clamps his mouth shut, biting his lips together. *I will not scream*, he promises himself. *I will not cry. I will not make a sound.*

When they slide it in, his closes his eyes and tries to imagine he is under the arches again on a warm, dark night, Emilio close by, stars swimming in the water spread out beyond the docks. He remembers the feeling of gripping the ledge with his toes, hovering above the darkness, poised and ready in case he needed to jump, to kick out and swim away. He lets himself tip forward, feels his stomach lurch. Behind him, he can feel Emilio moving further and further away. He takes a deep breath, and closes his eyes. And then he dives under.

Forty-Three

San Domino, March 1940

It was several more days before the Director returned. By then, Elena had been storing the knowledge so deep inside herself, it had begun to take root. She carried it as though it were a precious, breakable thing, an egg cradled in her palms. All she had was a name, whispered to her by the boy at the fence. She didn't even know if it was true. They lied, her father had told her. Prisoners always did, and these ones more than most. Francesco had lied to her, hadn't he?

It was only the thought of the mainland, the possibility of escape, a new life, that had kept her from forgetting the name. *Perhaps we could find a job for you*, Coviello had said. Now, when she imagined herself on the mainland, she was wearing a crisp tweed-coloured suit, sitting behind a wide, shining desk. She had seen a woman once wearing a suit, when some people had stopped by the island to carry out an inspection of the land, before the new houses were started. She had neat dark hair pulled away from her face, and the suit was fastened with big shining gold buttons. She had walked a little behind the men she arrived with, but Elena could tell by the way she held her head up that she was someone important. Someone who would sit behind a big desk, writing letters and giving orders to strangers.

What did people do who had jobs? All her father did was put on a uniform and make sure none of the prisoners ran away from the island. What did Coviello do all day? What would she be doing, when she worked for him? She smiled at the thought of it; anything, anything at all, would be sufficient escape.

*

She had dodged one of her mother's cookery lessons to walk across the island, taking in the fresh, budding colour that was spreading across it with the sun: tiny pink and purple petals unfurling from pale green buds, a scattering of tall-stemmed yellow flowers burnishing the scrublands. At the Cala, the sun was sinking behind the water, the colour of blood spilling across the sea towards her. Elena longed to know if such colours existed on the mainland.

She found her mother at the kitchen table when she returned, the long white cotton dress laid out in front of her. She stood in the doorway, staring at its pale, shapeless outline on the table.

'It needs taking in,' her mother murmured as she came into the room. 'You have lost weight since the summer, *furetto*.'

She stood still and quiet as her mother eased the dress over her head, running her hands along the contours of her body. She did not need to resist now. She had the means to escape within her own mind. All she needed was one more visit from Coviello, and she would be safe.

Her mother's hands were soft against her skin. She carried out the measuring in silence, pinning and pulling at the fabric, which weighed heavy at Elena's shoulders. When it was done, she stood back.

'Is it ready?' Elena whispered. Her mother nodded.

'You will be happy, *furetto*,' she said quietly. 'I promise you will.'

'How long?' The dress felt rough against her skin. Her mother moved behind her to make a final adjustment to the waist, lifting the skirt and applying additional pins at her side.

'We need to wait a few more weeks,' she said over Elena's shoulder. 'Nicolo must find someone to help in the store for a few days. June, perhaps.' She smiled, and wrapped her arms around Elena's stomach. 'He is taking you to the mainland for a trip, afterwards. Haven't you always wanted to see it?'

Elena felt her self-control give way. She blinked fiercely,

determined not to let her mother see her cry. They stood there silently, her mother's arms wrapped around her, pins biting at her skin. When Elena turned, she thought she saw tears on her mother's face too, which were quickly brushed away.

'I have been talking to the prisoners,' she said. 'There might be a way out, still.'

'What do you mean?'

'I know which of them it was. They have given me a name.' She spoke quickly now, thrilled by her unexpected triumph. *They never saw me coming.*

She had expected excitement, even celebration, but instead her mother sighed heavily. 'That again,' she said.

Elena nodded. 'Now Papa can keep his job. And perhaps . . .' But she stopped short at the next thought. Everything in its turn.

'What do you mean, a way out?'

'I thought, if he kept his job, it would not matter so much. If I . . .'

'Oh, *furetto*.' Her mother let go of the fabric, letting it fall about Elena's waist in shapeless folds. 'Do you still think it is a job worth keeping?' She smiled sadly. 'Then, you do not know what he has had to do for it.'

Elena thought of the first day she had seen the prisoners. How it had felt to watch her father beating Francesco on the road. How strange he had looked, how unlike the man she had grown up with, how new the world had seemed. She had hated him for his job, then, but so much had changed. At first he had seemed proud, as though the job had given him a new sense of his place in the world, but recently that pride had begun to dim.

'I know more than you think,' she said.

'I am sure of it. But Lena, you have to be careful with what you know about people, the secrets you find. Once you have told someone else, you can't ever go back.'

'I thought you hated them. Isn't it right, that they be punished?'

Her mother raised Elena's arms and lifted the dress carefully over her head.

'Right for who, *furetto*?' she said, replacing it carefully on its hanger and turning to the stove.

Coviello came as Elena's mother had begun the evening meal. Her father was sitting silently at the table, watching as her mother stirred a stew of vegetables on the stove. Coviello did not even knock. They just heard the door banging behind him, his boots on the flagstones, as though he had never been away.

He walked into the kitchen and stood behind Elena, putting a hand on her head as though it were he who was her father, not the man slumped opposite her at the table. After he moved his hand away, she still felt the weight of it, pressed against her skull.

'You have been making arrangements,' he said over her, nodding towards the dress hanging by the door. 'That is good. We need to increase the population here as much as on the mainland.'

Elena felt her cheeks grow hot.

'And children are a blessing, from Il Duce.'

'From God,' her father said suddenly, looking up.

'Yes, of course.' Coviello smiled. 'From God.' Elena looked up at his face. He was studying her father carefully. He looked amused, as though he had a secret joke to tell. 'It is a good thing,' he said, the small smile still on his face, 'because we are cutting back on men. From next week, we will not need so many at the camp. Only the carabinieri, I think.'

They were all silent for a moment. At the stove, her mother stopped stirring and stood motionless. There was no surprise on Felice's face. He nodded slowly. He looked almost relieved, as though a blow he had long been expecting had finally fallen.

'Are you moving the prisoners?'

'I am not allowed to say. But they will be gone. Not now,

but when the war comes.' He hesitated. 'If the war comes. We will need this space for other purposes.'

'What will you do with them?' They all looked at Elena, her voice unexpected amongst the others. Coviello smiled, and put a hand on her shoulder, squeezing it reassuringly. She flinched under it.

'You need not worry, *ragazza*. They will be looked after. I know you have spent time with them.'

'I have spoken to some of them. You asked me to. Don't you want to know what I have found out?'

She sensed her mother shifting uncomfortably by the stove.

'Why don't you tell me?'

'Will my father keep his job? Will there be work for me, if I tell you?'

'We will see. That was the bargain, I think,' he said in a voice tinged with undisguised amusement. He smiled broadly. Elena saw her father looking up hopefully from the table. She felt a desperate, hollow sadness at the imploring look in his eyes. Coviello had turned him into something lower than the man who had lost his job so many months ago. He would do anything for the Director now, she was sure. The stranger she had seen whipping Francesco on the road would take over entirely, and he would be lost within that new, strange self.

Coviello was watching her father too, a cruel half-smile twisting his face unnaturally. *He is enjoying it*, she was suddenly sure. She knew it then. Coviello didn't care who had killed the policeman. He didn't even care if they never found out. Now that the prisoners were going to be moved anyway, why should he? It was just a game he had played with them all. Hadn't he said it himself? *The truth. It is not so easy to know what that is.*

She wanted her father back. The man she had lost that day the prisoners had arrived. She met her mother's eyes, and saw the same fear in them. She swallowed hard.

‘They have told me nothing,’ she said slowly. ‘They don’t know anything.’

Coviello nodded. ‘It’s all right. At least now you see, Elena Pirelli, what deviancy looks like. You know what will happen if you do not follow the right path.’ He looked again towards the dress, his grip on her shoulder tightening. ‘I am sure you will be very happy, little one.’

She thought of the two prisoners she had taken down to the rocks at the south tip of the island, to show them the seals which lay in the sun. Francesco, and the other. His name, the name that had filled her head since she heard it. It didn’t matter now. It was a nice-sounding name. It had a light, lilting rhythm to it, like the beginning of a song. She had only heard it once, after that day on the beach. Standing at the fence with that boy. Giovanni. She remembered how he had frowned as he told her the name, as though it made him feel angry, or afraid. Emilio. Emilio Barone. She buried it deeper inside her memory, hoping it would be lost there.

‘I won’t talk to them any more,’ she said, staring at her hands, folded in her lap. She noticed for the first time how they were red and scoured, like old women’s hands, like her mother’s hands. The hands of a woman who had lived a lifetime in this kitchen, on this island. A woman who would never see the mainland, who would never do anything but work, and cook, and watch time passing slowly by.

After Coviello had gone Elena went to her room and sat on the mattress, hugging her knees, feeling as though the bars of a prison were rising high around her.

Forty-Four

'You are alone.'

Francesco looked up. Pirelli was standing over him. He had no gun. His shirt was buttoned unevenly, his trousers stained with dust. Behind him, the sun was low in the sky, silhouetting his face, which seemed to have aged in only a few days. He looked tired. The shadow of the dormitory spread across the yard, creeping closer to where Francesco sat beneath the tree, shifting his body to angle it into the last of the light.

Francesco looked around him, and nodded. The yard was empty. Earlier, one or two of the *arrusi* had been half-heartedly digging at the soil, but they had long since abandoned the task.

'Your friend is not back?'

As Francesco shook his head, Pirelli eased himself down beside him. They leaned side by side against the tree's broad trunk, their legs stretched towards the light.

'I have heard nothing,' Pirelli said. 'It is strange. He only went to visit a relative.'

They did not all know the truth, then. This one, at least, believed the petition was genuine. He thought of Emilio, somewhere in Catania. Perhaps he had already moved on. Where would he go? Did he even have a plan? How could he ever be free, if he was never able to say his own name? Perhaps Dante was right. Emilio might have had someone else waiting for him all along.

'He has been gone nearly two months,' Pirelli said. 'He should be back by now.'

'I imagine he is not in any hurry.'

Pirelli smiled. Pulling a cigarette from behind his ear and a lighter from his pocket, he looked up, frowning at the sun.

Francesco studied him, noting the new lines on his face, the flinch of pain as he shifted his position on the ground.

'You are wondering why it was me, aren't you?' Pirelli said.

'Why it was . . .'

'Why I was the one who had to find out what happened to that policeman in Catania.' He smiled, shaking his head. 'When I am not even one myself.'

'There must be a reason.'

Pirelli sighed. 'You don't have to worry, anyway. You won't see me again after this. They have no use for me here anymore.'

Emboldened by the way in which Pirelli spoke, as though they were men who had met casually on the street, Francesco said, 'Did you come with us from Catania? Or somewhere else?'

Pirelli smiled. 'Neither. I come from this island. I have always been here.'

Francesco stared. Apart from Elena, he couldn't imagine anyone actually living their whole life on San Domino. He realised that, until now, she was the only islander he had spoken to. He thought about telling Pirelli about her, and decided against it.

'Well,' Pirelli said, 'not always. There was the war. But that was a long time ago.'

'You fought in the war?'

Pirelli nodded. 'I was at Caporetto,' he said, his mouth a firm line. 'I was not one of those bastards who ran. I was a prisoner. A year, they took from me, those men who betrayed us.'

A year of imprisonment. He had never even asked Emilio about that.

'So why was it you?'

'I don't know,' Pirelli said. 'A test, perhaps. To find out my loyalty.'

'And did you pass?'

Pirelli laughed, loud and sudden. 'Yes, I think I did. But I think, too, that he never really wanted to know. I think he knew from the start that I would fail.'

'What will you do now?'

He shrugged. 'I will have to find something else to do.' He breathed out a steady stream of smoke. 'I used to dream of leaving this place. I used to long to get away. Now, all I want is to stay.'

Francesco wondered if that was what he wanted too. 'Why can't you?'

Pirelli shook his head. 'I have a family to support. There is nothing here. I will have to go away to the mainland if I can't do this any more. It is different for the rest of them.' He smiled. 'Santoro and the others. This is their life; there will always be something else for them. Me, it was all I had.'

'What about the war?'

'You think I want to fight?'

'I just mean that soon it won't matter what people used to do. If you have to fight.'

Pirelli sighed heavily and ground his cigarette into the dust. 'Of course I want to fight,' he said slowly. 'It is what I am built for. It is what we are all built for.'

'Nothing else?'

'I used to think . . .' He hesitated, then lit another cigarette. 'No. There is nothing else.' He handed the cigarette to Francesco and took another for himself. 'I would rather stay here, though. My sons would rather stay here, whatever they tell me they believe. And I could have done too, if things were different.' He smiled. 'You would have kept me from the war, *arrusu*!'

Francesco watched him leaning back against the tree, his eyes closed, the cigarette dangling from his lips. He wondered what Pirelli had done, how he had lived, before the *arrusi* had come. How he would live once they were gone, if war never came. *You will be given four lire each day for food and necessities.* Had it really been so simple, his life here? He wondered how he had never noticed that before. And why had it never been enough for Emilio?

*

Francesco woke in the night to a shadow leaning over him. He sat up fast, instinctively reaching for a weapon he didn't have, but the shadow put out a hand and pressed it lightly to his lips.

'Shh.'

He lay back, and felt the hand brush against his cheek.

'I did it.' It was Emilio's voice. He was dreaming, then. He closed his eyes, willing the dream to continue. It was so real, he could smell Emilio's scent, feel the warmth of the hand on his face. 'I promised you,' the shadow whispered. 'You're safe now.'

The figure knelt down and pressed something into Francesco's hands. A stack of papers, twisted into a thin roll. As the dream faded, he saw the shadow stand and watch him for a moment, before it disappeared back into the darkness.

When he woke, it was still early, the dormitory in half-darkness. Francesco reached out a hand, the memory of the dream still fresh. A roll of papers was pressed against his side, hidden beneath the thin sheets.

He looked over at Emilio's bunk. There was a figure in it, hunched beneath the covers. He stared at the shape for a long time, waiting for it to dissolve into the remnants of his dream, but it was still there even after he had closed his eyes and opened them again.

He sat up, uncurling the papers with shaking fingers. He stared at them for a long time, as the sun rose and men shifted and muttered in their sleep. He didn't look up as they began to wake, getting up to boil water over the spirit lamp, stretching out their limbs and pacing the dormitory. He was still staring at the papers as the first of them noticed Emilio, sitting up in his bunk, and began to crowd round him, plying him with questions: where had he been, why had he been gone so long, what was happening back home?

He was still staring at the papers as the guards came to

open the doors and line them up for the count. For a moment, he didn't think to hide them, he was so mesmerised by the creased lines of the photographs, the words on the documents, so absorbed he hardly registered the fact that Emilio had come back. On the top of the pile of papers was a face he had only seen twice in more than ten years. A face that looked increasingly like his own: dark, worried eyes, a lined forehead, a thin mouth. Three words were printed beneath it in bold capitals: *FILIPPO AMELLO. MANCANTE.*

'They were still there,' Emilio said. 'All your papers. In one of the places Rapetti and I used to exchange messages. I searched for hours, before I found the right one.'

They had climbed up to the cliffs beyond the pine trees to the north, where once they had been shaken by an earthquake. The ground felt solid now. It was hard to imagine how it could ever have been so unstable. Emilio was still dressed in his prison uniform of white trousers and shirt. Francesco wondered whether he had worn it all the time he had been back in Catania, or if they had returned it to him when they brought him back. He looked thinner. The shirt hung from his narrow shoulders. The hair on his face had grown beyond a hint of stubble into a rough beard.

'I would have burned them there, but I wanted you to know. That it's over now.'

Francesco stared at the pile of papers. It was difficult to believe they were the cause of so much that had happened. He weighed them in his hands. The wind rose and lifted their edges, and he thought of Elena's paper birds, soaring over the cliffs into the sea.

'It was a risk, bringing them back here.'

Emilio shrugged. 'They don't search us. Haven't you noticed that? I think they are afraid of the contagion.'

'No one else has them?'

Emilio shook his head. 'Not unless Rapetti lied.' He smiled. 'But I think we would know, by now.'

Francesco leafed through the papers one by one. Everything was there. His birth certificate, his parents' birth certificates, the record of their marriage. His father's arrest warrant. Photographs of them in Naples. All of it. Everything Rapetti had saved from the fire to hold against his family. He felt a heavy weight lifting as he thought of his mother in Catania. Safe.

He looked at Emilio, suddenly sure of something he had been wondering about for a long time.

'That's what you were doing, that night under the arches. With Rapetti.'

Emilio nodded.

'And when you ran – this is what you were running for.'

'I was too slow,' Emilio said, staring at his feet. 'I didn't know where to look first, if he had even told the truth. They took me before I could start searching.'

'And the *primogeniti*?'

'It was a trade.' Emilio looked back in the direction of the dormitory. 'They are all here for you.'

'And I ruined it.'

Emilio shook his head. 'It wasn't your fault.'

'If I hadn't been there, that night . . .'

'Who knows?' Emilio said, smiling sadly. 'Maybe they would have taken me anyway. Maybe that was always his plan.'

'But trying to escape. All this . . .'

'I promised you, didn't I? I said I would get them back for you. I said I would keep you safe.'

Francesco remembered that night in the Piazza Stesicoro, beside the ruins of Catania's past, when he had made his choice. He had thought Emilio's promise was nothing more than words.

'I thought you were going to run. When you got back to Catania – I thought it was to escape. That I wouldn't see you again.'

Emilio smiled, and put out a hand to him. 'Where would I run to, Francesco? You're still here.'

Francesco sat down heavily in the grass. He looked at the papers again, everything Rapetti had ever held over him. All of it had still been there, waiting to be found. If Emilio hadn't gone back . . .

'They would have found them eventually,' Emilio said, as though he could hear Francesco's thoughts. 'You don't know what it has been like, being here for so long and knowing they could be found.'

'Why didn't you tell me?'

Emilio shrugged. 'I didn't want you to worry. You were happy here. Happier than you were there, anyway. At least here you can be what you are.'

Francesco looked down at the photograph of his father. The only photograph of him he had now. Perhaps the only one he would ever have. He laid it next to the image of his mother, touching them lightly with his fingers.

'We have to do it,' Emilio said, putting a hand on his shoulder.

They built the fire using dried leaves and pine needles. When Francesco lit it with his lighter, the air filled with a smell that reminded him of that night in Naples, running through the garden as trees caught light behind them. He watched the edges of the papers curl and blacken. His father's face collapsing into the flames, the whites of his eyes lighting up with fire.

When it was done, they sat and watched the fire die as the sun went down. Emilio leaned back, putting his hands behind his head. Something had changed in him since he had come back with the papers. He seemed calmer, quieter. The urgency of the man who had found Francesco in the courtyard that night at the dance hall seemed far away. 'Look at that sky,' he whispered. He reached out a hand and found Francesco's, weaving his fingers under and over his palms.

'All this time,' Francesco said, leaning back with him and

staring up at the darkening sky. Against the glow of the last of the sun, the Diomedee birds dipped and wheeled.

'All this time.' Emilio turned to look at him. They stared at each other for a long time, the flames reflecting in their eyes, until the sun fell behind the sea and shadows settled around them.

Forty-Five

San Domino, June 1940

She knew, the moment she woke up. Afterwards, Elena couldn't say how she knew, but there was a heavy certainty in her tiny cupboard room that morning. A knowledge that everything was about to change.

Perhaps it was the Director's voice, loud and commanding from the kitchen. He hardly ever visited in the morning. Perhaps it was the sound of dishes being moved back and forth, her mother's anxiety transferring itself across the kitchen and back again.

She sat up, trying not to look at the door where the dress was hanging. The wedding, endlessly delayed and renegotiated after the loss of her father's job, was two days away. Two days to think of another way out.

Barefoot in her nightdress, she left her room and stood outside the kitchen door. It was open a crack. Coviello was standing by the stove, his hat in his hands.

'We expect the announcement in the next few days,' he said, his voice stiff and formal. 'I thought you would like to know.' Her father, standing opposite him, nodded. He was out of uniform now. His gun had been taken away. It was like the old days again. He spent long hours sitting on the back step, looking out at the patch of earth they tried to grow food in, his chin in his hands. His old clothes seemed too big for him. His trousers were loose around his knees, his shirts shapeless and ugly. Elena hardly recognised him. Sometimes she wondered if things would have been different if she had told Coviello the name. Somehow, she didn't think they would have been.

'And . . . them?' Elena's mother said hesitantly.

'We are clearing the islands.' Elena felt her breath quicken. 'They will be needed for prisoners of war, other purposes. We need as much space as we can find.'

Her father sat down slowly. 'So you are moving them.'

'Yes, we are moving them.'

'Where to? Another island?'

'As I said. We need as much space as we can find.'

'Then – clemency?'

The Director laughed. 'Clemency? For them? No.' He shook his head. 'If anything, the opposite of that.'

Still in her nightdress, she ran. The wet ground was sharp with stones beneath her bare feet. Her breath came fast and painful in her throat, her chest burning as she gasped in air. She ran through the village, trying not to look at the empty houses, one of which was standing waiting to claim her, and turned down the road that led towards the Cameroni district, towards the dormitories, imagining a gallery of images. The prisoners lined up against a wall, her father with a gun to their heads. A rope, hanging from the dormitory ceiling. All of them at the summit of the cliffs, blindfolded, stepping over the edge. For a moment she paused, staring at the empty yard, willing someone to appear so she could shout, so she could warn them. Then her courage failed and she turned, and ran towards the cliffs above the beach, faster and faster, remembering her dream of running towards the edge and taking off, leaving San Domino behind her, leaving her family, Francesco, the prisoners, all of it a distant memory as she flew towards the mainland.

Could she do it? She wasn't sure. She wasn't sure right up until the moment when she reached the cliff's edge, the beach a strip of golden sand against the still blue sea beyond it, and stopped without wanting to, stopped so suddenly she felt herself lurching forward, her arms out to keep her balance, her toes gripping the edge. A few tiny stones trickled over the verge, tumbling to the sand below.

She sank to her knees, her fists clutching clumps of grass, her eyes shut tightly, as she gasped through her sobs. There was no escape. She had run as far as she could go.

The theories were numerous. They had run out of money to pay the guards. The *arrusi* had all been granted pardons. They were not going home, they were to be executed. Or they were being taken to another prison, even more remote than this one. There were whispers of war. Of fields far away where they would be the first in line to face the guns. Over the doorway, a notice had been posted.

> All prisoners are to gather their belongings and be prepared to leave for the boats at dawn tomorrow.

They had sat in silence staring at it when it was first pinned up. Now, they were slowly shuffling around, gathering up their things, avoiding each other's eyes. Only Dante was not moving. He lay in his bunk, staring at the ceiling.

'He won't survive war, anyway,' Marcello said, stirring a mug of coffee. 'Or other prisons. If this was too much for him—'

'Shut up,' Elio hissed from his bunk. 'Just shut up.'

'He should never have been here,' Luca said.

'None of us should,' Carlo replied angrily.

'I don't know.' Michel was fiddling with the radio, trying to find a voice amidst the crackling static. 'Maybe it is right, that we are punished. What use were we to anyone back home?'

Francesco thought of his mother, of Lucia, and wondered if Michel was right.

'Well,' Arturo said, standing up. 'I for one hope to God they're taking us home. Even if it does mean we have to go to the trenches. Are you men or not?' Francesco recognised a flicker of the Arturo who had first been brought here, so angry, so desperate to prove that he was not one of them.

'They know nothing about real war, do they, Emilio Barone?' Marcello said, clapping Emilio on the back.

Emilio smiled, shaking his head. 'It was so long ago, I do not think I know anything of it now.' Francesco thought of the two of them, wading in the mud of Caporetto. He could never make that image of Emilio fit with what they accused the *arrusi* of being: cowardly, womanlike. Men who were no use to their country. Men who could not kill. Would they ever use them in the fight? Would they forget their idea of what an *arrusu* was, once they were needed in war?

'So, you think they are sending us to fight?' Everyone looked at Carlo. Some of the *arrusi* were nodding, as though it was what they had always anticipated, in the end.

'They might be sending us home,' Francesco said.

Elio turned to him. 'You better hope they are not.'

'Why?'

'We still don't know, do we?' Elio said, looking around the room. 'Who it was who betrayed us.' Francesco stared back at him, unblinking. 'And we still don't know why your sentence was half what the rest of us got.'

'Leave it alone, Elio.' It was Arturo who spoke. Francesco turned to him, surprised.

'What do we think?' Elio said, ignoring Arturo, his voice suddenly loud. 'Do we think that was a coincidence?'

Francesco felt all of their eyes on him now. Since Emilio had come back, he had felt safe again. Now he wondered if it was enough.

'Why do you care about that now?' he said, hearing the tremor in his own voice. 'Why do you care if we are all leaving anyway?'

Elio took a step closer to him. His fists were balled tightly at his sides. Around him, some of the other *arrusi* began to stand too.

'What do we do with traitors? With men who betray their own kind?'

'It was me.'

There was a silence. The voice was quiet. They all turned to Emilio, sitting on his bunk, staring at his hands. He looked up. There was no defiance in his eyes now. He looked tired.

'I did it,' he said. 'Alone. They paid me well.'

Francesco opened his mouth, but Emilio spoke over him. 'I did it alone. I don't care what anyone says, what you suspect. There was no one with me. I met with Rapetti, I gave him your names.'

Francesco stood up, and Emilio shot him a fierce warning look. Marcello was shaking his head. 'There are more of you,' he said, his face turned away as though he could not bear to look at Emilio. 'There must have been more.'

Elio moved towards Emilio. 'Tell us,' he said, his voice tight with rage. 'Tell us who else.'

'Even if it's true, why would I tell you?'

'You want to live, don't you?' Marcello said quietly. Francesco felt suddenly cold. 'If you tell us, perhaps we will let you.' They were circling him now, more and more of them, a tight group with Emilio at its centre.

'Traitors will be shot,' Marcello said in a quiet, matter-of-fact voice. 'Deserters and traitors. It is only right that it should be this way. It is justice.' Francesco thought of all the leather-bound books, the legal texts, lined up on Marcello's shelves in his study. 'Don't think we won't apply it to you too.'

A military weapon. A gun from the last war.

'If we ever go back to Catania, how long do you think you will last?' Marcello said. Francesco thought of Antonio lying alone in the square. Blood soaking through the hole in the sole of his shoe.

'Why do you care now?' Emilio still didn't look up. 'What does it matter to you? It is already done.'

'You think it will all go away?' Marcello laughed. 'Did the last war leave you alone when you came home? Did you never dream of it? Caporetto? All that blood? Did it never catch up with you? I promise you, Emilio Barone, Catania will be a prison for you if we ever get back there. Worse than this one. You will never stop running.'

'You shot him,' Dante said quietly. He stood up slowly and faced Marcello. Francesco could see the tremor in his hands, the strain of trying to hold back tears. 'Antonio. You shot him.'

'He was a traitor,' Marcello said dismissively. 'He deserved nothing else.'

Dante didn't move. He stood still in front of Marcello, his mouth forming words that never came. Then with a low howl, he collapsed onto his bunk. No one went to him. They watched him, curled in a ball, shaking with rage.

'But you and he . . .' Francesco didn't know how to say what Marcello and Antonio had been. He didn't know the words.

Emilio stood up. 'I could tell anyone that, if I wanted to,' he said.

Marcello laughed again. Some of the other *arrusi* joined in. Francesco almost joined in himself, because he saw at once there was no point in it. Why would the authorities care about avenging one dead *arrusu*? Why would it matter to them at all?

Emilio looked at Francesco, meeting his eyes across the room. Francesco felt his cheeks grow hot with shame. He should speak. He should confess too, but he found himself frozen, the image of the body in the square too bright in his mind to risk speaking. The thought of Marcello in the dark, waiting outside the dance hall, his gun resting heavily in his hand.

'And what if we aren't going back to Catania?' Emilio said. 'You can't catch up with me then.'

Marcello shrugged. 'We will have to go home eventually. They cannot keep us on islands forever. Either that, or they will deal with us another way. Then, I do not need to take my revenge.' He stood up and crossed the circle of empty space around Emilio, staring him down. 'God will do it for me.'

Emilio drew in a breath. As he opened his mouth to speak,

the bolts were drawn back and the guards opened the doors, giving the signal for the morning count. The *arrusi* shrank back and took their places in the line.

'Is it another island?' Arturo said, as Santoro marched along the row. Francesco saw the guard's eyes narrow. 'Or another prison?'

Santoro said nothing. Favero was standing by the door. He looked away as Francesco met his eyes.

'Tell us!' Arturo said. 'We deserve to know.'

Santoro turned then, and struck Arturo across the face. He reeled backwards. The guard waited until he had recovered himself, then faced them and spoke.

'You will be ready for the boats at dawn.'

'He's right,' Emilio said as Francesco joined him afterwards in the yard. 'Marcello. There's nothing for me back there. I'll be shot as soon as they can load the bullet.'

'You could tell them everything,' Francesco said, not knowing, even now, what he wanted Emilio's answer to be.

'So they can shoot us both. You think I would do that?'

Francesco stared at him. His Emilio, who had rescued him from a dance hall raid and pulled him towards the sea. Who had fought, month after month, to go home, just to get Francesco's papers back. Emilio, his long, pale fingers stretched over guitar strings, his hands on Francesco's cheeks, pulling him into a dance. His voice, reciting names, Francesco's name, in a dark police office in Catania. Why had Emilio done it?

'I would understand.'

They were walking out of the yard now. Francesco had followed Emilio without thinking. They ducked under the fence and kept going, past the mulberry tree that marked the turn towards the Cameroni district, past the last few houses of the village towards the groves of pines that covered the island's north side. The air was thick with their scent, the ground sprung with fallen needles.

'Why did you tell them it was you?' Francesco demanded, as Emilio quickened his pace towards the cliffs. 'Why did you do that?'

Emilio shook his head. 'They will suspect something forever if you go home. If they have no one else to blame, they will always suspect you. Now, they can blame me instead.'

'But you're coming with me. If we go home, we go together.'

'I can't. I have to go now.'

'Where?' Francesco tried to take his hand, and Emilio pushed it away. A sharp wind began to tease at them as they climbed. The sun was falling low behind a horizon of clouds. 'Em, you did it, you went back for my papers. You saved me! You don't need to escape again.'

'I can't go back there. Catania. I can never go back.'

'You can! Your yard – it's still there. Maybe, one day, you can buy it back. You can carry on your father's work. Em!' Emilio was walking faster and faster, Francesco shouting as he struggled to keep up.

With a sudden rush of heat and blue sky, they emerged from the trees at the edge of the cliffs, only a few feet away from the dizzying drop to the sea. Francesco took a step back towards the pines, but Emilio walked up to the edge and stared over it, his hands in his pockets. Francesco remembered the day of the earthquake, how Emilio had stood through it all, unafraid. The wind was rising now; Emilio was so thin and pale, Francesco half feared he would be thrown over. Ahead of them, the blue-green sea stretched to the horizon, broken only by patches of sunlight mirrored on its surface. He took a step towards the cliff edge, and tried again to take Emilio's hand.

'What do you mean, you can't go back?'

'I wish we could stay here.' Emilio turned, smiling sadly at him. 'Just us.'

'Emilio, what did you mean?'

'Is there really a hell, do you think?' He sounded suddenly afraid. 'Do you think we can escape it?'

Francesco had never seen Emilio cry before. The tears were heavy on the contours of his cheeks, glistening in the last of the daylight. Francesco looked down. There was a small circle of scorched earth between them, the remains of the fire they had built to burn his papers. He saw again his father's face, his mother's, melting into flames.

'You wanted to know what my reason was,' Emilio said quietly. 'Everything we did. Why I let them use me like that.' He was speaking quickly, as though desperate to rid himself of the words.

'Why did you?'

'I'm not what you think.'

'Emilio, why did you do it?'

'You said I must have fought them like a cat at Caporetto, remember?'

Francesco smiled. They had been lying together on Emilio's bunk. It had been raining that night, pounding on the dormitory roof like a siege.

'You were wrong. I let you believe they took me prisoner there. It wasn't true.' Emilio sat down heavily in the grass. Francesco knelt beside him, gripping tight to his hand. 'I ran.'

'You . . . ran?'

There was a long silence. Emilio's head was bowed. When he spoke, his voice was quiet. 'We were in the trench for two days, waiting. It was so cold, it hurt to move my eyelids.' His words came faster and faster, as though he had been keeping them trapped in his throat for a long time, as though they had been choking him. 'Then the gas came. I remember how it sounded. Like gunfire, from somewhere far away. Then everything was quiet, and someone shouted for the masks. Something fell into the trench. Just a metal canister, but we knew what it was. The masks would last us two hours. Maybe less. But it was the front. We were supposed to defend it. We were supposed to stay there.'

'You were fifteen, Em. Only fifteen.'

'I didn't even think, I just ran. I left them there.' He looked up and stared at Francesco. His eyes were blurred with tears. 'I'm not what you thought. I'm what they always said we were. Weak. I run. I betray my friends. I hide in the dark.'

'It was a long time ago, Em.'

'It doesn't matter. They kill men like me. There's no island for deserters.'

'That's why you were working for Rapetti. He knew.'

'It's my fault that you are all here. I got you into this.'

'You had no choice! Just like me. They didn't give us a choice, Em. Leave it here.'

'They'll shoot me if I ever get back home. If Marcello doesn't do it first.'

'They might not know now!' For a desperate moment, Francesco wondered if what he had done to Rapetti might have saved Emilio after all.

Emilio shook his head. 'Molina has everything. It was him that passed me on to Rapetti, when he realised what I was. But for him, I would have been shot years ago.'

'So, we could run. Why not? Emilio, let's run.'

Emilio laughed. 'So now you agree?'

'I would do it, for you.'

'I'm not like you, Francesco. I can't hide myself away like you can. I can't pretend I'm not what I am.' He shut his eyes. 'I can't watch you get married.'

'I won't! She won't want me now anyway. No one will.'

Emilio squeezed his hand tighter, his voice suddenly urgent. 'You have to. All those things I said. That you are a coward. I wasn't fair. You have to – it will keep you safe.'

'I don't care.'

'I should go back and face it. I'm the one who is a coward, not you.' He turned to Francesco and gave a quick, forced smile. 'You never knew that about me. I managed to hide that much, anyway.'

He slumped forward suddenly, leaning his head on

Francesco's shoulder. Francesco took him in his arms, feeling Emilio shake against him as the tears fell. He held him for a long time. The sun was low in the sky when he was finally still.

'We'll miss the count,' Francesco said, stroking Emilio's hair as though he were a child. 'We should go.' He smiled. 'It's the last one.' Emilio didn't reply. Neither of them got up.

'You'll be all right now,' Emilio said, holding him tighter. He gestured to the pile of ashes, the remains of Francesco's past. 'I'm so sorry I got you into this. I didn't have a choice.'

'I know.'

'Promise me. Promise me, if you ever get home, you will still get married.' He drew back and took Francesco's hands in his. 'You should be careful. They'll watch you.'

'I don't want to. I can't.'

'I know. But you will. I was wrong. You have to.'

In the dark, he felt Emilio pull him close again, his chin resting on his hair. 'I love you,' Emilio whispered, and for the first time, Francesco knew it was the truth. He hadn't known, until then, how much he had needed to know. He felt all the tension of the past two years begin to drain away. He leaned his head up and put a hand to Emilio's lips. They were soft beneath his fingers. He could feel Emilio shaking in his arms as he leaned forward and kissed him.

'It was worth it, then,' he whispered, and felt Emilio's smile against his cheek.

'Little idiot.'

He let Francesco go in a quick, sudden movement. Standing up, Emilio looked tall and suddenly more like himself again, stronger. The wind rose, screaming above the sound of waves beating against the rocks below. There was hardly time to register anything else. Francesco heard himself scream, a high, wailing sound he had never made before, a sound like the birds that cried out in the night. In the half-darkness, he saw Emilio's shadow at the edge of the cliff, his arms stretched out on either side, and then he wasn't there. There was no one there.

He stood alone at the cliff edge, staring down at the rocks, slick and dark with waves. The cry continued, but he couldn't tell if he was making it any more, or if it came from the birds circling the sky. Beyond them the sea swelled grey and hungry against the horizon, breaking onto reefs in great explosions of foam, big and white as wedding dresses.

Forty-Six

Catania, February 1939

May Italy's males be more masculine and its females more feminine. From their union the new Italian will be born; instinct-form, sentiment-will, faith-reason.

A. Signorelli, *Sesso, intersesso, supersesso*, 1928

A few days before they take Francesco from the city, on what will become the long journey to another island, they let his mother come to visit him. They are only given a few minutes, in the tiny cell they have been holding him in. As he waits for her, he wishes he had a mirror, some way to check how much he has changed since he saw her last. It has been weeks. He can feel the change in the way his cheekbones are hard against his skin, the bones in his chest visible beneath his shirt. He spits on his palms and runs his fingers through his hair, finding it unexpectedly long.

When they bring her in, it is Francesco who hardly recognises her. Her hair is tied in neat curls beneath a hat pinned carefully at an angle. Her coat is not new, but she has sewn a lining of red felt into it, and a new collar of fur. He thinks of how it must have been for her, walking through the streets with the eyes of the city on her. The nights she must have sat up with her sewing, fashioning her armour, her disguise.

Beneath the hat, and the powder that clings uncomfortably to her skin, her eyes are red and ringed with shadows. He stands up and holds his hands out to her, and she shrinks away, looking nervously back at the guard who still stands in the doorway.

'It's all right,' the guard says, the keys on his belt ringing out musically against his waist. 'He's quiet.'

She sits opposite him in a chair. Francesco perches on the edge of his bunk, his hands pressed tightly together. He can feel them shaking, and tries to keep them still. The door shuts behind the guard.

'Is it true?' she says in a dull voice, without looking at him. 'Are you . . . what they say?'

Later, much later, Francesco will remember this moment. He will wonder what the right thing to say would have been, what would have been fair, what he could have given her to take away with her, to console her. What his father would have wanted him to do. Later, he will write her a letter explaining everything as she would want it to be explained. But in those five minutes, after weeks of prison and medical tests, he is weakened. He doesn't have time to think before he answers.

'Yes. It's true.'

She bows her head, the weight of what he has said settling on her shoulders.

'Your friend. The boy that used to come to the house.'

'Yes.'

The silence is unbearable. He wants her to cry, to shout at him, to laugh. Anything. He thinks of her in the library, pearls around her neck, smiling at him and his father sitting at the table. Kissing the top of his head as she puts a plate of food in front of him. Laughing at his deliberately clumsy attempts to spell out words. Folding the pamphlets at the polished table: *Non mollare*. Perched on the chaise with a drink in her hand, holding his father's hand in the tiny lodgings they fled to after the fire. She is his reason for everything. They both are. But in Francesco's darkest moments, lying in his cell, listening to the crowds outside, the thought has returned to him unbidden. Did he do it for his family, to keep them safe? Or was it always because he loves Emilio?

When she still says nothing, he stands up and tries to put an arm around her shoulder. She pushes him away. From the corner of his eye, he sees the guard outside the door turn towards them, a hand to his waist.

'You have broken Lucia's heart.'

'I know.'

'Your father. What would he think of you?'

Francesco flinches at the thought. What would he think? What would he say if he were here? 'I don't know.'

'He fought so hard for you, Francesco. For your future.'

'I did this for him.'

'How can you say that?'

'I know that doesn't make sense. I can't explain, but it's true.'

'You did it for yourself. You have thought of no one but yourself.'

'Where is he now?' Francesco has not dared to ask the question in all the years they have been running, but he asks it now. What does it matter if she tells him? He can't follow his father, wherever he has gone.

She looks over at the guard, still standing in the doorway. They have both been speaking in low voices, but still they are wary. They have spent most of Francesco's life being wary.

'He is not here to see this. What you have become. Isn't that enough for you?'

Francesco nods, feeling tears slide across his cheeks. 'He used to talk about freedom, didn't he? Wouldn't he have understood?' His voice shakes as he asks the question.

His mother looks up at him, her tear-filled eyes blinking at the harsh strip lighting above them. Slowly, she shakes her head. 'God help you, Francesco. Wherever you are going.'

She stands up. He cannot bear to watch her leave, but as the guard opens the door for her, she crosses the room quickly, leans down to him and puts her arms around his shoulders, kissing the top of his head.

She doesn't look back at him as the guard leads her out.

*

A few days later, they drive him out of the city. He sees some of the other *arrusi* in the corridors as he is marched away. Luca, hollow-eyed. Dante, slumped between two guards, who hold him up by the elbows. They smile at each other, their faces, in the harsh, artificial light of the prison, almost unrecognisable. *Good luck*, he thinks, watching them marched away along different corridors, wondering if he will see any of them again. *Good luck, arrusi.*

He keeps his eyes open in the car. A few people are out on the streets. They stand watching him go by, and he looks back at them through the dirt-smeared window. Hot shame runs through him like a knife.

They drive through the Piazza Stesicoro, the trees now leafless. The excavations have paused; there is no evidence now of workmen or debris from the pit. Just a dark, hollow space at the centre of the square, as though it has given up all its secrets.

He thinks of Emilio. Wonders where he has been taken, if they will ever see each other again. Their first dance was beneath those trees. There was no music, other than the distant sounds of the cinema, their own laughter. They did not know, of course, that it would be their last, or else they might have lingered longer, made more of the silence, the emptiness of the streets, the safety of darkness.

Forty-Seven

San Domino, June 1940

> I dreamt a lot about the qualities of the Italian people, and I thought during these past 20 years that I had tempered them for sacrifice and given them back a sense of national unity that they had lost centuries ago. It was nothing more than a great dream.
>
> Benito Mussolini, January 1944

The sun was bright the morning the *arrusi* were taken from San Domino. After months of hiding behind a sky thick with rain and mist, it shone fully on the corn-flecked fields. Francesco had lain awake all night watching the light work its way through the cracks in the walls, remembering his first night, the heavy darkness, when he had thought he was alone, not knowing Emilio was nearby. Emilio had been there all the time. Lying so close to him in the dark.

The guards had conducted a thorough search of the island. They had scoured it, bringing in extra men from San Nicola to pace the length of San Domino in lines, holding hands, shouting his name. The *arrusi* could hear them long after they had been locked in, their voices high on the air, shouting enticements, bribes, threats. Francesco didn't bother to tell them it was useless. He had stood at the cliff edge for a long time afterwards, staring down at the water, terrified of what he might see. But he had seen nothing but the rocks rising from crests of sea foam like teeth, the waves rising higher around them as the sun fell.

He didn't tell the *arrusi*, either. When Emilio didn't appear for the count that night he saw it in their faces, the suspicion.

After the guards had left to organise their search there was a frenzy of speculation. Emilio had escaped, after all. He was already on his way to the mainland. He knew what was planned for the *arrusi*, and he had left them behind to face it. In their excitement, they seemed to forget Francesco. Only Arturo looked at him as the *arrusi* shared their theories, his head tilted to one side, a questioning look in his eyes.

As the sun spilled across the floor, Francesco watched it touch the metal feet of Emilio's bed, climb across the undisturbed blankets, trace its way along the empty pillow. He closed his eyes and tried to bring back the memory of the night Emilio had come back to him. A voice in his ear, soft, a warm hand on his cheek, pressed against his lips. *Shh. You are safe now.*

When he opened his eyes, Favero and Santoro were standing in the doorway.

They were marched across the island in chains. Francesco felt he was seeing everything for the first time: the pines, the sun breaking through gaps between the trees, the beach. The cliffs, the waves beneath them quiet and still. He felt suddenly afraid to leave all this strange, unexpected freedom. To leave Emilio here alone.

He was chained to Arturo, the two of them walking in silence.

'Where do you think we're going?' Arturo said as they reached the turning from the Cameroni district, looking over his shoulder at the guards. Francesco said nothing. All he knew was that they were going without Emilio.

'I think I might even miss this place,' Arturo went on.

'Really?'

Arturo smiled. A bruise was already rising on his forehead, where Santoro had struck him. 'No. But I think it could have been worse. I think it could have been much, much worse,

Francesco.' Between the chains, he felt Arturo's hand reach around his.

They reached the pines above the beach. Looking down, Francesco saw three figures racing each other through the surf. They were too far away to recognise. Though they ran at different speeds, had differing heights; though one of them ran in fast, straight lines across the sand, the other two winding their way in patterns, dodging waves and skipping over rocks, there was no way to tell which of the three was a girl, which were boys.

'So,' Arturo said as they began the steep descent to the beach. 'Did you do it?'

Francesco looked at him, surprised.

'Did you give them our names?'

'You still think I did?'

'I just . . . Now Emilio is gone, we'll never know, will we?'

'Does it matter?'

Arturo thought for a moment, as the guards urged them on with shouts from behind them. 'No,' he said at last. 'We all did things to survive. Back home, and here. They're diff places, aren't they? No point taking one to the othe they brought us here. To keep our world separa alt-

Francesco looked at him, remembering few months on the island, his face red clenched, living out a version of hims was, whatever Catania for so long. He had finally e it behind you.' ing for him, Francesco wondered

'To keep our world separat

'Leave it here then, Fra they reached it, still cuffed you did. Wherever we're ked to the water's edge, peering at the

The beach was e together. The g

horizon for the boats, while the *arrusi* massed silently on the sand, avoiding each other's eyes. Francesco looked to the horizon, beyond the flat plane of water, sunlight dancing from it in droplets like rain. He thought of the mainland, somewhere ahead of them. Wondered what was waiting for them there. If he would ever be allowed to go back, and if he did, how he would be able to walk those same streets without Emilio beside him.

He felt the cuff being taken from his wrist. Favero turned the key, then put a hand on his shoulder, smiling grimly. As the others were unshackled, Francesco walked away from them, sitting alone on a dune at the edge of the beach.

He watched the *arrusi* walking in dazed circles through the sand. Gio was alone at the edge of the water, staring across at the dark shadow of the mainland. Father Eugenio, too, stood a little apart, gazing at the horizon, his arms folded across his chest. Arturo stood beside Elio, their heads bent together, talking in low voices. As Francesco watched, they moved away ... the rest of the group and stood close to where he was

... he heard Elio say. His hand was gripping
hardly b...
then wrapp...
with the force o... right,' he said quietly. 'I understand.
toro was separ...
... in Elio's eyes. Francesco stared,
'Poor Salvatore.' ... aned forward and kissed him,
guard. 'He is so afraid to ... him, both of them shaking
Francesco looked up at him ... he heard a shout, and San-
the year they had spent on San Do... oint of his gun.
somehow. He looked less like a child ... de him, watching the
'You are being sent out?' ... ce had changed in
... d grown harder,

'We expect it.' His hands were in his pockets, a cigarette dangling from his lips. He pushed at the sand with a boot. 'Funny, isn't it?' He smiled, passing the cigarette to Francesco. 'I doubt they'll ever send you out there. Chances are I'll be gunned down while you're still wiping tables in Catania.'

As he sat alone in the dunes, Francesco saw a dark point on the horizon, growing stronger and more distinct against the sky until it resolved itself into the shape of a small boat. A few minutes later, another appeared behind it. He watched them fight their way through the waves, and stood up. Gio had turned around, beckoning him towards the shore with wide, uncertain eyes.

'Wait!'

The voice came from behind him. Francesco turned around. A woman was standing in the dunes. She was dressed in a shapeless cardigan over a long white cotton dress. She was pulling at her hair, which had begun to spring loose from a carefully pinned arrangement at the nape of her neck. Aside from the cardigan, the unkempt hair, she looked dressed for an elegant party on the mainland rather than a stifling day of heat and silence on San Domino. Francesco hardly recognised Elena at first, until she took a step towards him. There was a silence while they stared at each other.

'I can't stay long.' She looked over her shoulder. 'I have to . . . There's somewhere I have to be. But I wanted to tell you. I wanted you to know. They are sending you back home. Not to another prison – they are sending you back to Catania.'

'Home? Why would they let us go home now?'

She shrugged. 'I don't know. They have run out of uses for you, perhaps.'

Francesco looked towards the shore, where the men were massing around the boats. Father Eugenio was stepping gingerly into the first without looking back. Francesco wondered what would happen to him back in Palermo. There would surely be no more work for him in his old profession. How would he live – how would any of them?

'They are taking my brother Marco,' she said, staring at her feet. 'And my father. They are going to be soldiers.'

Francesco thought of the boys he had seen running on the beach, jousting with sticks. Children, playing at war.

'I'm sorry.'

'It's what they wanted. Or what they expected. There is no other way, for them.'

Francesco nodded. He thought of Lucia, the wedding, all his mother's plans. Wondered if any of it would be possible now. If there was any other way to survive.

'What about you?' he said, looking at her dress, the way it hung too large around her thin frame. She blushed, and glanced away from him for a moment, then shrugged her thin shoulders.

'I can't take you with me.'

'I know. I will find a way out. I don't know how. But there must be one.'

He took a deep breath. It was the last time, the last chance he would have.

'Elena, the notes you left for me.'

She turned away from him.

'It was you, wasn't it?'

She said nothing, looking back at the cliffs of San Domino, a hand over her eyes. When she turned back, he recognised that same expression of revulsion, of fear, that she had worn the day she ran from him into the trees.

'Was there anything else? Were you given anything else for me?'

She shook her head. 'Why would I tell you if there was? Why would I try to help you any more?'

'Ready?' Arturo said, looking curiously at the woman behind him. Francesco nodded. Gio was still watching them from the shore. Francesco felt Arturo's hand on his shoulder.

The bruise around Arturo's eye had swollen up purple, like a fruit ripening in the summer. Fat and bright. Together they walked towards the boats, towards Gio.

'Wait!'

They turned together. Elena was running along the beach after them, holding the dress above her ankles.

'Wait – it wasn't true. What I said.'

'What wasn't true?' Francesco felt his heart beating faster.

She looked up at the cliffs of San Nicola, rising like a fortress from the sea. From the beach, they could see figures moving languidly against the pale rock, prisoners indistinguishable from islanders at such a distance. 'He did give me something else for you.' She shook her head. 'I think he must have liked the look of you.'

'What is it?' Francesco held out a hand, feeling it shake. He heard a shout from the boat, the guards loading them in. Arturo called out to him again.

Elena pulled something out of the pocket of her cardigan and handed it to him. 'They are keeping them there,' she said. 'The prisoners on San Nicola. He is one of them. They are not being sent home like you. They must have done something worse.'

He looked down at the square of stiff card in his hand. There was nothing written on it. 'What did he say? He must have said something!'

She shook her head, looking away from him. Francesco turned the card over. It wasn't blank. It was a photograph. He hardly heard Elena's next words as he stared at the image, blood pulsing in his head.

His mother must have taken the picture, balancing the camera against a rock, halfway up the volcano. He thought he remembered the moment. His father, holding him steady by the ankles. Francesco gripping tight to his father's hair, his arms reaching around his neck. In the photograph, Filippo Amello was staring at the camera, a smile on his face.

Francesco was dressed in a dark jumper. He couldn't have been more than five years old. His head was tipped back towards the sky. He remembered the feel of the cold water from his father's water bottle running across his hand, burning from the heat of the volcano. The rhythm of his father's footsteps beneath him, carrying him higher, on towards the summit.

'*Recchione*,' Elena said. 'You will never be cured, will you?' She sighed. 'He said to tell you that he loves you.'

He looked up at the pale cliffs of San Nicola. The sun glowed from its sheer white cliffs, reflecting into his eyes until the island looked like a halo of light spilling onto the horizon. He tried to make out individual figures, tried to focus on the yard, the prisoners' dormitories, the road running between them, but he could only see the outline of the fortress walls enclosing them, and above it, the abbey's iron cross cutting into the sky.

There was a shout from the soldiers by the boat. Francesco turned for a third time towards it.

'Wait! What will you do now?'

Francesco shrugged lightly. 'We will go home.'

She nodded. 'Home. And then?'

He looked at Arturo. They stared at each other for a long moment. Then, finally, Arturo smiled, and the bruise changed again, sinking into the soft yellow of a sunset.

Francesco looked at the photograph, meeting his father's eyes, the determination in them, the fire. He raised his face to the sun, felt the warmth of it behind his eyes. *Non mollare.* His eyes met Elena's, and he saw the same light in them. His mouth set in a thin, determined line.

'We will fight.'

Postscript

Very little is known about the forty-five men from Catania who spent a year of their lives imprisoned on the island of San Domino. Most of Catania's *arrusi* were illiterate, from poor families, and left few records behind of what happened to them.

On returning to Catania in June 1940, they spent two years under constant surveillance from the police. Some fled the country. Others went on to marry and have children. Most remained with their families, living quietly, enduring the state's inflated taxes for unmarried men.

No record of the *arrusi*'s imprisonment on San Domino existed on the island until 2013, when a small plaque was laid in memory of the exiles.

Founded at the end of June 1921, the Arditi del Popolo (People's Squads) gathered approximately 20,000 members committed to resisting the rise of Benito Mussolini's Fascist Party and the violence of his blackshirt paramilitaries. Comprised of socialists, anarchists and communists, the movement was short lived. After the formation of Mussolini's government following the March on Rome in October 1922, numbers decreased significantly. It was dismantled by 1924, most of its leaders either arrested or assassinated, with the complicity of the fascist state. Their name was taken on by the Italian resistance movement during the Second World War.

Author's Note

Although this is a novel based on true events, all of my characters – with two exceptions – are entirely fictional. I am hugely indebted to Gianfranco Goretti and Tommaso Giartosio for their book *La Città e L'isola*, which tells the true story of Catania's *arrusi* before, during and after their imprisonment on San Domino. To my knowledge, there is no English edition – eternal thanks to my dad for his help with translating the text from the Italian. Any errors or deviations in this book are, of course, mine.

Alfonso Molina and Francesco Coviello are both historical figures. Molina was removed from his position as Catania's chief of police on 5 August 1943, and in January 1946 was acquitted of his role in imposing the Fascist regime and his overzealous assignment of *confino*. Three years later, the Ministry of National Security awarded him the silver medal for civil bravery. Coviello continued to run the internment camps on the Tremiti islands until the fall of the Fascist State in 1943, when he was arrested and imprisoned at Padula. On his release in 1945, the Tremiti islanders wrote a letter demanding his return, claiming he was an honest hard worker with a strong sense of duty. There were just thirteen signatories.

Many of the details of the police force's treatment of homosexuals in Catania, and Molina's role, are taken from Lorenzo Benadusi's *The Enemy of the New Man: Homosexuality in Fascist Italy*. This work also provided the source for many of the historical quotes included in the novel.

On Fascism and its use of *confino*, Michael R. Ebner's *Ordinary Violence in Mussolini's Italy* was invaluable, and on resistance movements, *Fascism, Anti-fascism and the Resistance in Italy*, edited by Stanislao G. Pugliese.

The text of Mussolini's 'Doctrine of Fascism' is freely available on the internet. Although I have followed the convention of attributing all quotes from the Doctrine to Mussolini, it is thought that at least the first half of the text was 'ghostwritten' by the philosopher Giovanni Gentile, who described himself as 'the philosopher of Fascism'.

Acknowledgements

I am enormously grateful to everyone in Catania and the Tremiti Islands who helped me research this story. In particular, heartfelt thanks to Attilio Carducci on San Domino, for tolerating my terrible lack of Italian with such humour and warmth, and sharing his memories of the San Domino prisoners with me (not to mention an excellent ragu). Thank you to Luigi Grifa and Elena Palumbo for their kindness, and for showing me around their home, once one of the prisoners' dormitories. Thanks to Stefania Politi for her assistance as translator, and to all the wonderful people of the Tremiti islands who didn't hesitate when I asked for help. I was there for such a short time, and I came away with friends.

This book would never have been written without the encouragement, enthusiasm and wisdom of my agent, Juliet Mushens. Huge thanks to her, to Sarah Manning, Nathalie Hallam and the team at United Talent.

Many thanks to my editor, Imogen Taylor, for her support, editorial wisdom and for taking a leap of faith. Thank you also to Amy Perkins, Millie Seaward, Laura Hall and everyone at Tinder Press for making me feel so welcome. And to Jane Selley, for such a detailed, thoughtful copyedit.

I am so lucky to have the support of more amazing friends than it's possible to list here. Thank you to everyone who has encouraged, cajoled, consoled and cheered me along the way. Special thanks to Claire McGowan and Angela Clarke for always, always being there – I couldn't do any of it without you. To Kate McNaughton and Jeremy Tiang for many pep talks over marmite chicken, Margaret Pritchard Houston for many pep talks on the Northern Line, Rebecca Fenton for early cheerleading, Helen Wilson, beta reader extraordinaire,

Ruth Houston and Adam Kissack, companions in space exploration, Heather Sills and Clare Hearty, my linguistic consultants, Ciaran Williams for further language help, Jane Mayfield, Mary Clare, Ellie Decamp and Emer Cullen for words of wisdom and Anna Mazzola, my publishing twin.

Thank you to all at the Geological Society for support and friendship, especially Ted Nield and Michael McKimm – the other two corners of the literary triangle.

Thank you to Jess Bryant, Andy Grieve, Francis Booth, Dan Wansell, Caroline Hall, Andrew Hayes and my many other band mates for music, friendship and inspiration.

Thank you to Matteo Aquilina, Renata Palmer, Roberto Mondini and Simone Marzani for their help with my terrible Italian – we've never met, but I owe you all vino. Any lingering errors, of course, are mine.

I am very grateful to City Lit for introducing me to a world of brilliant writers and friends – and to my classmates for sharing their writing and thoughts. Thanks also to Arvon and to Maggie Gee and Jim Crace – I learned so much from you that I've kept with me. And to all the teachers in numerous fields I've been lucky enough to learn from – you make such a difference.

This book, like so many others, began its life at the wonderful Retreats for You. Thank you so much to Deborah Dooley and Bob Cooper, who welcomed me into their home with so much kindness and friendship.

The greatest thanks are to my family. Thanks and love to Jess and Freya, and to my amazing parents, for their boundless love and support – and for being such excellent company on many a research trip. I am so lucky to have you.

Lastly, thank you to Matt, for patience, love, understanding, and for believing I could do it before I did.